JASMINE

JENNIFER BENE
SHANE STARRETT

Text copyright © 2019 Jennifer Bene & Shane Starrett

All Rights Reserved

No part of this book may be reproduced in any form or by any electronic or mechanical means including information storage and retrieval systems, without permission in writing from the author. The only exception is by a reviewer, who may quote short excerpts in a review.

This book is a work of fiction. Names, characters, places, and incidents either are products of the author's imagination or are used fictitiously. Any resemblance to actual persons, living or dead, events, or locales is entirely coincidental.

ISBN (e-book): 978-1-946722-51-5

ISBN (paperback): 978-1-946722-52-2

Cover design by Laura Hidalgo at Spellbinding Design. https://www.spellbindingdesign.com/

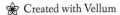 Created with Vellum

ONE

Her

My knees hit the dirt. Hard. I must have tripped over something, or just my own panicked feet, but it doesn't matter. I'm bleeding, knees stinging as I brush them off with dirty hands, but that doesn't matter either because I can't stop.

Not here.

The road stretches out before me in the hazy half-light of evening, and if I give in to the urge to sit down and cry I'll be lost. I have maybe twenty minutes of light left, and at my current pace I'll still be in the middle of nowhere by the time the last rays of the sun wink out on the horizon. It will be a few hours after that before the moon is high enough to be of any real help. I know I'll be out here in the dark, but I don't care. Even when the light fades I'll still be twenty minutes farther from him as long as I keep moving.

I don't even try to catch my breath. It would be pointless with my heart racing and the cold fear-sweat trickling down my spine, so I just run. These shoes are at least a size too small, and my toes pinch at the corners, my heels rubbing raw and there will be blisters when I eventually stop. I know that tomorrow I won't be able to run like this — so I run harder.

The narrow dirt road winds ahead of me. Curving around trees, dipping and rising with the shape of the land, making my thighs burn on a steeper hill where even at the top I can't see anything. No lights from a main road or a town, no fence to mark the edge of his property — just more road. More dirt carved out of the endless sea of grass. I'm soaked in sweat even though the air is cooler, the first bite of evening chill that will only get worse tonight. But, for now, it feels nice. I drag my arm across my forehead to keep the salt sting out of my eyes, but I don't bother with the rest of it. The sweat is matting my hair to my neck and sticking the thin shirt to my skin, and if I think too long about my body, I'll focus on the sharp pain under my ribs where my lungs are demanding I stop.

Using the slope of the hill, I pick up speed, half-stumbling on the way down, but it's more like a controlled fall. As long as I never actually hit the ground, *again*, I can use the momentum to force my burning leg muscles to keep going. Before this I could run a seven-minute mile on a good day, but I haven't had a good day in too long. So it's probably eight minutes, or more likely nine. Maybe ten because the few breaths I'm getting are high-pitched wheezes and my form is closer to shambling zombie than marathon runner.

At least I tried.

I tried... I try to remind myself of that, but as the edge of the horizon finally goes dull and monochromatic — I know I'm done. Every muscle is shaking as I slow on a long flat stretch of the road and finally stop. Still no lights, no fence, nothing but endless grass that I can see less and less of as night descends. If my math is anywhere close, that's only three miles if I'm lucky, and he has a truck, which demonstrates once again just how unlucky I am. Cursed, damned... whatever you want to call it, this moment is just one more in a lifetime of shit.

I stare out into the darkness and force air into my lungs, but it's pointless. My legs wobble, and my shoes squelch as I stagger. Left, right, left, and right off the road. I fall into the grass as my knees give out, and everything hurts so I can't even pick out what might be a new injury. Crawling is just as shaky, but I force every painful movement until I'm deeper into the grass. There's no shelter, just a scrawny tree with spiky bushes at the base, but I nestle into them like there's a chance they can keep me safe. It's an easy lie to tell myself, and what are a few more scratches anyway?

Sleep doesn't come, and I don't expect it. I'm not tired, not mentally. My muscles are jello, my bones feel soft, and my lungs bruised — but I'm wide awake. I couldn't fall asleep even if I wanted to. Instead, I watch the waxing crescent of the moon inch its way across the sky. The crickets and katydids are chirping out their music, and somewhere in the distance I can hear coyotes. A primal part of my brain wants me to seek shelter, but anything the coyotes might do would be so much better than what's waiting for me.

I'm not sure how much time has passed when I hear the dull rumble of an engine growing closer. The bright headlights make the grass seem thinner, shorter, and I'm sure he will see me... but the truck passes without a pause. He's driving slowly though, he's looking, and even though I try to rally the strength to crawl deeper into the grass, my muscles don't answer.

The moon moves, clouds drift across the stars, and my eyes are just starting to droop when I hear the truck again. This time the light is brighter, *so much brighter*. It's angled into the grass, sweeping closer, and I hold my breath and close my eyes against it like I did when I was little and noises in the house made me think of monsters.

As if not looking would have saved me.

It wouldn't have, not if monsters had really lurked under the bed, but the sound of the brakes squeaking and the truck shifting into park are noises that promise a real monster. I'm shivering, but it's not from the autumn chill in the air; it's from the fear that makes me keep my eyes clenched tight. The futile panic that makes my chest hurt and offers me enough of an adrenaline spike to clench my fists and contemplate running.

But then the truck door opens. Shuts.

Once again, I'm nothing but a limp husk. Waiting. Uselessly lying halfway under a tiny bush with sharp, pointy leaves. I open my eyes and the spotlight from his truck lights the trunk of the tree. I know he's found me before his boots scratch over the dirt, before I hear the whisper of the grass against his clothes.

Each step is worse than a death knell, because I know he won't kill me. He's never even threatened to kill me. No, he says so much worse than that.

Sometimes he tells me he loves me.

"Hello, Jasmine." He's standing over me, blocking the

spotlight, backlit by a vibrant white glow, and I wish I had the strength to kick him.

But I don't.

I don't have the strength to do anything but stare at him and breathe. As he crouches down next to me I can see his face again, and I don't bother reminding him that my name isn't Jasmine.

He never listens.

TWO

Her
———

He doesn't have to fight to get me back into the truck.

I think about it, think about all the things I could try, should try, but don't. I just follow. Like he expects. Demands. I hate myself for not struggling, because he doesn't even reach to grip me, as if he knows I'm not going to fight, so why bother? I'll do as he says because — what are my choices? I'm going to be punished, and he knows I know. He knows I'm not going to do anything that would make what's coming even worse, and that makes me hate myself a tiny bit more.

Compliance.

I'm giving him exactly what he demands from me, and it's all swirling around inside me like a hell-broth that has my stomach churning. And not just because of my meekness.

No. It's also for what awaits me when we get back to the ranch.

This is only the second time I've been in the truck. I'm not allowed in it, it's off-limits, and he's only had me inside the one time before. I notice again how clean it is, even though it's a work truck. Clean, maintained, nothing extraneous or out of place. Like everything else about him and the ranch, the prison I'm trapped in. I study the dash, noticing the empty socket where a radio would normally be. It's gone, covered over by a piece of something he's scavenged. And even that is neat, precise. No duct tape slapped on to hold it in place. No, it's evenly cut, fitted, held in place by tiny screws. Trim, almost fastidious, like so much else about him.

When I glance out the front windshield to the road ahead of us, I wonder again — for the thousandth time — where I went wrong tonight. It should have worked. I'd gotten away. And he'd driven past me, hadn't seen me. I was sure of it. So... how? *How?*

The dusty dirt road rolls past slowly, and suddenly I can see them.

My footprints at the edge.

A clear track marking my advance away from the ranch, as if I'd laid breadcrumbs out for him. Sometimes they disappear where the road is hard packed, at others it's as if they're outlined in neon. I'd run, but I had left him everything he needed to find me.

That's when the tears come. Unbidden, hated, pushed by rage behind eyes that blink as

rapidly as I can to try and hold them back, force them back inside me where he can't see them. He does though. He glances over occasionally at me, and I know he sees their tracks. He doesn't say anything. His face, like most times, is a complete fucking blank. Like he isn't even human. An emotionless automaton. I push savagely at myself to stop.

Stop fucking crying. Don't give him this.

But it's so very hard with my failure confronting me in each of those tiny, scuffed footprints leading me back to hell. By the time I stop, there is the faintest hint of light from the horizon, a bluish tinge that pushes back the black of night, and I realize I'd gotten further than I thought, that it has taken him longer than my memory allowed for him to find me. It's cold comfort, but I grasp at it. A tiny sliver of success in the miasma of failure that everything else seems to be.

We pass the fence line, rattling over the cattle guard with a *brrrump* that shakes the cab of the truck as his house comes into view. There are cattle just beyond the road, standing immobile in the last remnants of the night air. Waiting, like me, for whatever he decides to do with us next.

I think of how long I've been up now, how long he has too. In a few more hours it will be twenty-four, and even if he acts like some sort of Terminator-like android, I'm positive he'll be feeling the hours too, like I am, as the adrenaline finally begins to wear off.

Maybe he won't punish me now. Maybe he'll just take me back to the house, put me in that bedroom and lock the door. Or in his bed, pulling me against him as he fades off to sleep, and I can catch a little myself, and then... maybe while he's out I can sneak away again. But do better this time, stay off the edge of the road, cut out into the brush, cross country this time.

Jasmine

The truck swings into the large, circular drive, the headlights washing across the legs of the

windmill, the curving sides of the silos, the barn. He shifts down, angles the truck across the packed dirt, and hope evaporates inside me, raw despair taking its place.

He's headed for the barn.

I'm trembling, I can feel another rush of adrenaline, but it's weak this time, weaker than anything from earlier. Too much has gone on, too much has happened, and my body simply doesn't have it in me to do anything more.

He pulls the truck up in front of the barn and shuts off the engine, not even sparing a glance in my direction. He simply climbs out and heads over to one of the massive sliding doors that close off the front of the barn. He steps inside and lights flicker on, backlighting him and the rectangular opening that is a portal to Hell. Slits of light bleed out between the old boards that make up the structure, and I watch as he disappears inside.

I could run right now, jump out and try again… but it would be futile. I'd fail yet again.

He knows it too. It's why he doesn't even bother watching me, or forcing me to come with him. He knows I won't run again, because even if I could make my feet carry me, it would only add to what's about to happen. He's going to punish me for what I've done, and if I run again? He'll make sure that punishment is a thousand times worse than what I'm about to receive.

Not worth it.

His shadow appears in the doorway of the barn, a monster

made of darkness that I can't overpower even on my best day. I keep my eyes on him because I need to see what he does even though it won't help. I watch as he stops at the edge of the light, looks back inside one more time, then starts toward the truck.

Frozen, I sit rigidly, facing forward, trying to feel stronger than I am. *Don't let him see how scared you are. Don't give him that.*

He opens the door, the overhead light comes on, and he stands there looking at me for a long moment before he says, "Jasmine."

I don't move. I need to, should, because nothing is going to stop what's about to

happen, but I can't. A few more seconds, just a few more so I can try and gather myself, prepare for whatever he's planning to—

"Jasmine." He says the name so blandly. Patiently. He should yell at me. Any sign of emotion — anger, rage, hatred, *anything* — would be better than this. But he never does. He's always like this. Placid, calm, quietly terrifying. Except... except when he's finished. When he tells me he loves me, which is always somehow worse.

He's still standing there, waiting, not even reaching for me. He knows I'll come to him. Because it's what he wants, what he's ordered me to do, and I must obey.

'You cannot escape punishment. What would be the point otherwise?' He'd explained that to me... a month ago? Longer? Whenever he first brought me here. The exhaustion is making me fuzzy now, my thoughts are

muddled, and right now I can't remember how long this hell has gone on.

But I move.

I slide slowly across the seat and he takes a step back so I can slip out of the cab. I stand on the ground, the cold of the hard earth coming up through my soles. It should shock me, should bring the pain I know I should feel, but God... I'm suddenly so tired and I just want this to be over.

He quietly shuts the door and heads back toward the barn. I know I'm supposed to follow, but again, just like in the cab of the truck, I pause, sucking down precious seconds of delay. He doesn't stop, doesn't look back, and as he gets closer to the rectangle of light, I glance around. The sky is showing signs of light, the black above turning to deeper purple, and the horizon now has a dull, pinkish band cut by the silhouette of rolling hills. *Useless, it's all so useless.* I move, forcing my legs to follow after him, because I can't afford to make this any worse.

He disappears inside the barn, and too soon after I cross the threshold myself. My eyes take time to adjust to the lights. The barn floor is concrete, and like everything else it's pristine. Swept clean, and except for the slightest trace of dust from the soil outside, you could eat off of it. He's by one wall, near the long workbench which runs down one side. The large center posts separate the barn into two halves, and he stands on the side not taken up by the two tractors. There is the bench, a toolbox, a row of leather harnesses and straps and things I think are for the cattle or the horses — I don't really know — all laid out neatly on the bench. Dark leather standing out against the worn gray wood.

He turns, looks at me. "Come here, Jasmine."

I obey, my head muddy. He's standing next to the wall, and I notice there's a long, vertical board nailed to it. It has a column of big holes, neatly spaced, and in two of them dowels have been inserted — one up high, the other a little lower. I stop in front of him, a few steps away, and wait for his next command. Exhaustion is settling in, making me feel empty, numb... maybe it will help ease the pain of whatever he's going to do.

"Take off your clothes."

Goddamn him. Could he not put *something* into that voice? Does he have to make it sound so... normal? So ordinary, as if he'd just asked me to tie my shoe rather than to strip naked in front of him?

"Please..." I whisper, but it's stupid. It won't help sway him or prevent what he has planned.

He stands for a beat, staring at me stoically before he repeats, "Take off your clothes."

"I..."

He doesn't even look at me as he turns and picks up a tin from the bench. I can't read the label as he pries off the top, but I see whatever is inside glistening in the overhead lights. He dabs two fingers into it, and then he swabs it over one of the dowels, the one that is about waist height, lathering the rounded wood with a coating of the material.

What the fuck?

Dully, almost without thinking, I reach down and lift my shirt over the top of my head. He doesn't turn to watch me, devoted only to the task he's performing. I toe off my shoes and kick them away in a small act of defiance. He makes no reaction. Not even a twitch. My feet sting as the grit on the concrete shifts under me, and I know it's pointless to drag this out. The bra comes off next, then the shorts, then my underwear until I stand there naked, my clothes a jumble at my feet.

This isn't the first time I've been naked before him. No, not hardly. But his response is the same as it was the first; he turns and inspects me as if I am a thing, like the toolbox or one of those pieces of leather lying on the bench. To him I could be one of the cattle in the pasture outside, except for this: I am a woman, and he's used me like one... but he doesn't look at me like any man has before. I'm not something cherished, something wanted. I'm just another thing he owns. One that has a specific place in his world. Fills a slot. Serves a purpose. Nothing more.

He moves to the bench, selects an object, and then comes up close to me. "Give me your hands."

It's a long, leather belt. One he's used before, when I haven't 'behaved.' I slowly raise my hands in front of me, my body shaking. The air in the barn is cold in the way it is right before dawn. He snakes a loop around my wrists and cinches it tight. The leather bites into my skin, and it hurts, but everything seems to be happening in a dull fog, movements and actions coming as if I'm three beats out of sync with the world. He tests it one more time and gives a slight huff of satisfaction.

"Turn around."

I do as he says. I have a good idea what's coming. He'll

secure my arms above me, and then whip me with his belt until I scream from the unbelievable agony of it. He'll punish me. Teach me the error of my ways. This isn't the first time... nor will it be the last. The barn is for punishment. I'm never punished in the house, because the house is for cooking, cleaning, sleeping. Fucking me.

"Raise your hands."

Just do it. For fuck's sake just get it over with.

I raise them above my head, muscles quivering with strain not because I'm terrified, but because I can feel my body preparing, shutting down to avoid as much of the pain as I can. Because I know it's coming.

He loops the strap over the dowel up high, and I hang there with my arms stretched above me as I listen to the shuffling of one of the horses. He picks up a length of rope from the bench, neatly coiled, and within a few minutes the strap that I'm bound with is secured to the board by the rope. I can yank and twist all I wish — and I will, I know I will — but my arms won't be able to jerk free. My feet are firmly planted to the concrete, the cold seeping up through my bones to blunt muscles that still ache from my run. My arms don't carry the weight of anything other than themselves, and they'll burn with fire before he's done — but I'll survive it.

I have before.

I wait to hear it. The sound of his belt coming free. *That* will be my signal that he's ready to begin, ready to punish me for what I've done. This one will probably be the worst I've ever received, but... what did I expect? I ran, and while this is only the second time I've tried, that only makes it

Jasmine

worse. I feel him behind me, and I wait for the first lash to fall, but that's not what happens. Instead, his hands land on my hips as he presses his body against my back.

This isn't right.

He doesn't do this, hasn't done this before. Is he going to fuck me here? Wait... is he really going to fuck me here like this? Before he punishes me? He leans over the top of my shoulder, glancing down as his fingers dig deep into the backs of my thighs. As he does this a thought startles me; this isn't where he's punished me before. Before it's always been tied to the center post of the barn, arms up and laced around the pole. I've never been strapped to this board on the wall. In my exhausted state it never occurred to me, and I didn't even notice... until now.

The shifting of his hands causes a surge of adrenaline to flood me. Why is he lifting me, moving my hips? Why is he pressing me so that the lower dowel is touching me, coming close to my...

He adjusts, aiming me, staring around my side as the dowel presses into one inner thigh, then closer, then directly against my labia and I scream as realization hits me. I try to force my body back, but he's strong, so goddamn fucking strong.

"No, no, NO!" I kick against the wall of the barn, my already damaged feet pulsing with new pain, but I keep pushing back as one of the horses whinnies like they agree this is too far. "Goddammit, PLEASE! NO!"

He ignores me as I fight, like he always does, but this? He shouldn't be able to do this. It shouldn't work. That dowel shouldn't be able to find its mark, the dull round tip coated in whatever the fuck he pulled out of that container now smearing against me, pushing past my clenching muscles as he forces me down. Shoving it up inside me. It's too rigid, unyielding, and it shouldn't fit inside me at the angle it is, but it does. It stretches me as he forces it in silently, his hands manipulating me like the thing I am. A tight nut to an old bolt, a recalcitrant calf into a chute.

"Stop, stop, stop... *fuuuuck*! Please, please no, no..." I choke on my next breath as the hard wood fills me. Why am I still pleading? It's already inside me and it hurts unlike anything I've ever felt. The dowel jams against my pubic bone, and I swear it's cracking, I can hear it cracking, and he is going to break me... but he doesn't stop as he presses hard, holding me in place until I stop fighting back.

As I sob, he releases the pressure slightly, and I want to push back, push myself off this thing he's crammed inside me, but instead I grit my teeth and keen out a wail of frustration. Because if I do manage to climb off, he'll only force me back on. There will be no understanding of what he's doing to me, the damage, possibly permanent, he's causing. It won't matter. This is punishment, and punishment must be administered. I must take it, accept it, or be given worse — and I can't handle worse than this.

I may not even be able to handle this.

When he shifts, I let him ease back without fighting, and I hold myself in place even as the discomfort amplifies with every involuntary squeeze of internal muscles. I try to dig into the concrete with my toes, my arms burning with the effort to ease the pressure inside, bringing everything, every part of me, into razor sharp focus. I groan, sucking in lungfuls of air as I talk to the wall. "No, no, no..."

Jasmine

He finally steps away, surveying his handiwork. This is his punishment for my disobedience, and this is worse than the lash I've been given before. Without a word, he simply stands and listens to my groans and whimpers. I've stopped begging, making coherent words, because it's wasted. Fruitless effort expended for nothing, and I need my energy to last for however long he plans on keeping me impaled here. He releases a placid sigh of satisfaction as he stands out of view behind me. *A job well done.* I want to scream at him, but I don't, because it would mean nothing. I've tried before to get a rise from him, to show any sign of empathy, compassion, humanity.

There is none.

I stand on tiptoe and my body slowly adjusts, conforming somehow to this invasion. My breathing slows a little, my chest ceases the vicious heaving of a minute ago, and that's when I hear it. The sound of his belt.

No.

No, God, no... Not that. Not now. This... this thing he's shoved inside me is enough.

I hear him pull the belt free, followed by the ever-so-quiet sound of him folding it back upon itself. I scream at him now, pushing up on my toes, trying to force this thing out of me. "Fuck you!" I shout. "Fuck you! Fuck no. No. NO! YOU CAN'T DO THIS!"

I'm leveraging myself up to the tips of my toes, pulling with all the strength left in my arms, and the wooden rod *almost* slips out. I'm nearly free of it before he's back on me, and the shove is sharp, savage, brutal as he forces me back down. Pain is a searing white curtain that blots out my vision as the dowel splits me like a knife rather than the dull, rounded wood it is.

He never says a word. There is barely a grunt. I keep shrieking obscenities, mindless ones that finally fade into whimpering, and only when I'm crying do I feel him positioning himself. At some base animal level I comprehend what he's doing; keeping me trapped so I can't free myself while he applies the other portion of my punishment. Because, of course, fucking me with a dowel isn't enough. What kind of punishment would that be? Not enough for him. No. Punishment is whipping, and any punishment without beating me with his belt isn't truly a punishment, now is it?

I feel insane as he lets go, steps back, and I hear the dull clatter of the metal buckle in his hand.

I'm lost, so lost.

The first crack of the belt across my ass is liquid fire, pulling a scream from my lungs at the same time that my hips buck and my legs buckle, forcing me even further down onto the dowel. My body recoils instinctively, and then the next blow lands, and then the next and the next and soon there is nothing I can do but let the scorching fire consume me.

The sounds coming from me aren't real. No human can make them, and yet I know they are. I can feel each one torn from my throat until it's surely raw, my voice cracking. The lashes don't stop, I don't count them but there are easily a hundred, a thousand, and he's going to kill me this time. Beat me to death on this fucking wooden rod.

But I don't die, *unfortunately*.

Jasmine

I continue to breathe. I survive, even as the belt continues to land, and then, suddenly, there's nothing more. I'm panting, making half-formed cries while he stands unmoving behind me. He should be winded. I should hear something from him, a gasping of ragged breath from the effort, but there's nothing. He simply steps back as I hang limp, my ass and thighs a wall of fire, and his breathing is normal, unhindered, while I'm at the point of passing out. The agony between my thighs and across my backside are the only things keeping me tethered to this world, and I want desperately to push it all away, to give into the darkness and fade.

But that wish goes unfulfilled, and instead one thought takes root: *at least it's over*. My punishment is complete, and I survived. I feel as if I'll never be okay again, not after everything he's done since he took me, but this... at least this is behind me now. These thoughts keep swirling inside me, consuming every ounce of energy I have — until his fingers land on me again.

Touching the tight opening of my ass.

I can't cry anymore. Desolation is all that's left inside me now, and I simply become what he's always seen me as. A thing. An empty vessel that has nothing living inside it. *This* is what he wants, and so I simply give up. I don't move, I don't cry — I let go. Cease to be anything human.

He smears more of that substance onto me. The same as he put on the dowel earlier. It is cool, greasy, and he lathers it around my ass in a thick gob. He pushes one finger against the tight opening, pressing hard until it passes inside. I feel disembodied, but my body reacts without me, clenching and then pushing back against him. He withdraws, gathers more of the gooey substance, returns to where he's just been. He spreads me, enters a place inside me that no man has before. My mouth opens and closes with his movements, and sound escapes me, but it's nothing human. None of what is happening now is me. These are the reactions of a thing, the responses of a single-celled creature with no thoughts of its own. Two fingers, and he is prying me wide. I'm sure there is pain somewhere, but I can't find it in the haze. Then he pulls away, only to reappear a moment later with another coating of something that is meant to ease what he's doing, but he needn't bother because it doesn't matter.

As a thing that doesn't feel there's no point to his efforts.

The fingers leave me and I know what's coming next. No emotions bubble under the surface of my skin, just an empty void, and I'm divorced completely from what's happening. It's funny how quiet it suddenly becomes. I can hear him slipping out of his jeans. I don't look, but it's so easy to discern. He takes them off, folds them, places them on the bench. He'll be doing his underwear too.

A place for everything and everything in its place.

Then he moves behind me and a slick sound comes from him. He's lubing his cock. Of course. He doesn't want this to hurt *him*. That was dumb of me; it was never about what I might feel.

He positions himself, and finally — finally! — makes a noise. Pushing past the ring of virginal muscles in my ass is probably harder than he thought. *Stupid motherfucker.* I hope it fucking hurts, because it hurts me as he forces his way inside. I can't bite back the groan of pain as a lightning strike makes it through the emptiness inside me. He grunts in a strained way, and I take it as a victory. It's cold comfort, though. He's inside me now, fucking my ass in long, slow strokes, fucking this *thing* he owns, and there is nothing I can or will do to stop him.

For a moment I think that maybe this is part of my punishment, but then I dismiss that entirely. *No.* No, the dowel that he now grinds me against, the painting of pain he created on my skin with his belt; those were the punishment. This? This is his love. This is his love for me played out with my ass splayed over his cock, his fingers digging into my hips so I will know how much he *cares* for me. This is how it's always been, from the first time he took me.

Be good. Follow my orders. Do as I say and you won't be punished.

I think this might be the first time for him too. First time fucking a woman in the ass. What is the taking of one new hole against all the others? But it's different this time. He's moving faster, reaching his peak more quickly than he has since that first time he took me. I can hear myself grunting in time with his thrusts, the haze of disembodied pain buzzing somewhere that can't reach me, and then I hear him making noise too. Groans that are asynchronous with my own, and with his own thrusting. He's going to come soon. His breath huffs out as he swells, and his rhythm becomes rapid, disjointed, nothing like the control he normally displays.

"Jasmine," he groans, his fingers digging into my hips, and I can feel there will be marks there tomorrow. His hips slam into my welted ass, holding still where he presses tight to my back, his voice an elongated groan as he releases his seed deep inside. I feel it, every heated pulse that hits me where I've never felt this sensation before — and then he's done.

He doesn't move. No, he holds me, impaled on one side by the wood of the barn, on the other his own flesh. Flesh that still twitches within me. His breathing slows, becomes even, and control is established once again as his fingers loosen but don't let go. No, now he holds his precious object, his treasure, in his hands. I feel him lean down, and I crush my eyes shut.

I know what's coming.

"I love you, Jasmine." The whisper is a razor, and I wish he would drag it across my throat and end it all. But he won't kill me. He just holds himself there, his lips soft against my ear, and I feel his breath. Calm. Smooth. Easy.

My punishment is over.

For now.

Lucky me.

THREE

Her
───────

I thought everything hurt before, but when he lifts me off the wooden shaft it slides out of me like slick sandpaper. Grating, painful, a throbbing ache to match my newly violated ass. I hate him, but I'm so exhausted I can barely summon the anger I know I should feel. It's a weak buzz in my blood, hazy as his fingers slip from my hips. My rage may be dull, but my feet burn on the thin layer of dust on the floor — more fresh wounds to focus on as he dresses. The rustle of clothing, the metallic clatter of his belt returning to his pants... I try to tune it out. It won't take him long, and I resist the urge to look, to acknowledge him in any way. He's not real, and he doesn't want me to be either.

For one glorious moment I'd felt as dead inside as I should be after all of this, but as my eyes wander up to the rope keeping me tethered to the wall, I can feel the sting of tears.

You will not cry anymore. Stop it. Fucking stop it.

Clenching my teeth, I squeeze my eyes shut and pull on the leather and rope keeping me bound. Letting my body weight do the work until my fingers start to tingle, going numb, and I wish it would spread. Take me over. Break the rope and knock me out cold on the chilled concrete. Maybe crack my skull hard enough that I'd never wake again.

But then he's there. One large hand on my back, forcing me toward the wall as if it's so easy to move another person. It's all so useless. Wasted effort, wasted energy that I don't have to spare. When he releases the rope, my arms fall limp against my front, blood rushing back to my fingertips with icy sparks. A few months ago I probably would have hissed, tried to shake them out, laughed and whined about the weird sensation — but now it barely registers.

A second later, the leather strap is removed, and he hangs it back up where it belongs. Carefully, as if it really matters whether the long strip is flat or not. He's not talking now. Exhaustion is probably eating at him too, and my brain stumbles as I stare at the soft morning light leaking through the top edge of the barn.

Did I really lie under that tree all night?

I could have crawled deeper into the grass. I should have forced my body to move as the moon carved its path across the night sky. I should have crawled directly toward the coyotes and begged them to end me, because he never will.

"Carry your clothes, Jasmine," he commands robotically. He has my clothes neatly folded, stacked in a small pile in his massive hands, and I take them because I don't have the energy to throw them only to have to pick up each item again.

He doesn't wait for me to speak, I don't think he even expects me to as he moves toward the door, grabbing my shoes from the floor on his way — but then he stops short. Tilting one of the sneakers, he stares at it for a long moment before he turns those flat brown eyes on me.

"You hurt yourself," he accuses with that ridiculous deadpan delivery that makes everything he says some kind of joke — but this might be one of the funniest things he's said. A bitter laugh bubbles up in my throat, and it cracks out in a dry, choking huff.

"Really?" I tuck the bundle of clothes against my chest just so I can point at the shoe that looks so damn small in his grip. "You're worried about the fucking shoes hurting me?" My brain is too tired for this bullshit. Another weak laugh croaks free as I watch his placid expression twitch, a tiny movement as he slowly turns over the comment, but I'm too impatient to wait him out. "*You* hurt me. *You!* With the fucking wooden stick, and the goddamn belt, and— and you fucked me in the ass! YOU HURT ME; NOT THE FUCKING SHOES!"

It feels good to yell at him, but there's no real satisfaction in it. He never rises to it, never shouts back, and that was the last of my energy anyway. When he comes closer, those heavy boots thudding on the concrete, I'm ready for whatever he wants to do — but he only grabs my chin, which is more like grabbing the bottom half of my face because he's completely out of proportion with normal people.

"Do not take the Lord's name in vain, Jasmine. It's wrong."

'Wrong? You want to talk to me and God about 'wrong' right now, motherfucker?' The thought flashes through my mind, the urge to say it aloud even singes the tip of my tongue, but

with him tilting my head back I can't open my mouth even if I want to be that stupid.

"There is blood in the shoes. I'll clean you up." He releases my face and turns his gaze to my feet like he's sizing up one of the cows outside. "You'll clean up the mess you made tomorrow."

Rolling his shoulder is the only warning I get before he bends and tosses me over it like a fucking caveman. He turns toward the door and I see it. On the floor where I stood while he hurt me, violated me, there are dark smears on the pristine concrete. My blood in smudged footprints. He wants it cleaned, but now I'm almost upside-down, scrambling to hold onto the clothes, and as soon as I secure them I wonder why I did it in the first place. I don't care about the clothes, but I maintain my death grip on them as he carries me outside, balancing my weight like he can't even feel it. He tilts me, wrapping one arm over my hips as he opens the door, and then I'm fully in his arms. Cradled by the monster that won't end this game once and for all.

It's somehow worse to be held gently by the man who has done everything he can to destroy me with violence and false kindness. Yeah, he's held me like this before. Carried me when I was too weak to stand after he was done teaching me another lesson.

Just one more thing he calls 'love.'

At least he doesn't kiss me this time. The spell breaks and he leans into the cab of the truck, dropping me into the seat, and I yelp. My whole body goes rigid as pain flares violently between my thighs. Breathless, I stare at the ceiling of the cab and wonder if I actually did break something on the damn wooden rod. It would be a kind of glorious irony if one of his punishments ruined the only reason he was keeping me alive. *What's the use of a sex doll you can't fuck?*

Although, why I think a broken pelvis would stop him... I don't know.

As I pull in slow, shuddering breaths, the shock wears away, the pain fades, and I know I'm not broken. Or, at least, my bones are still intact. After a few moments, the exhaustion starts to win, and my tense muscles shake with effort to keep my sticky ass off the seat. Shifting my weight, I lean into the center console and carefully lower myself. Even as cautious as I am, I become keenly aware of the fierce welts, the deep bruising I'm certain I'll see in the morning, and the throbbing ache that seems to own every inch of space between my legs.

This time was definitely worse.

He shuts the door without comment, and I watch him walk around the front of the truck. Slowly, not a care in the world, no rush because I can barely sit. He knows I won't be fighting back anytime soon, won't be running again — maybe ever.

No, you can run again. You just have to plan better. Find your shoes, not whatever unfortunate girl wore the ones you just bled all over. Don't give in.

'Don't give in.'

I've said those words in my head almost every day of this hellscape. I screamed it at first, promising myself I'd fight. Filled with so much fucking hope the day he found me, took me, hurt me that first time. But with each day, each new failure, that voice gets quieter. Softer. Weaker. And I know there will come a day when I don't think it at all.

Then a whole week. A month. A year.

I'll be as empty and dead as I need to be so I don't have to be here anymore. Maybe that's what Stockholm Syndrome is... finally escaping and leaving the version of you in place that doesn't get tied to the wall of a barn and brutalized by some fucked-up double penetration designed by a monster. As I try to shift in the seat, another stab of pain steals my breath on a gasp, and I'm having trouble finding a downside to that possibility. If I'm honest, it sounds like a pretty good plan. I wanted to be an actress before this hell, I wanted a lot of things in life, but now playing the part of his 'good wife' might be the only thing that makes this nightmare bearable. Just give in and commit to the only role anyone ever chose me for.

How fucking sad is that?

The truck rocks as he climbs in and shuts the door, the internal light glowing on his forehead where twin, fading lines trail from hairline to eyebrow.

I did that to him. Early on. During the first week when he climbed on top of me, trying to fuck me again in the middle of the night. I'd aimed for his eye, but just ended up making him bleed. It had felt like a victory until he realized how much safer it was to take me from behind. Before I'd spent enough time in the barn to know better than to try to hurt him.

Now I know the truth.

There is no defeating him. There are only two options — escape, or die here.

Him

Jasmine isn't talking. I know this is just her thinking about her punishment. When she gets angry, when she yells, it means she doesn't understand... and that's when I have to remind her of her place.

Here. With me.

But when she's quiet, meek, I know that the punishment has made a difference. Thinking about it, about why she earned it, will help. It's only through pain that we learn the harshest lessons life has to give, and she has to learn. I'd be failing her as a husband if I didn't teach her.

Still, even making soft sounds of pain in the passenger seat, Jasmine is perfect. Her dark hair is tangled around her shoulders, and I reach to pluck a leaf from it — but she winces, so I leave it. For now.

She's dirty, filthy from lying on the ground after she realized her mistake. There's nowhere for her to go, nowhere she's supposed to be except here, and I know that is what made her stop running. It's why she lay down by the driveway and waited for me to find her. If she'd made it out to the county road, someone else might have tried to take her from me.

That idea makes me grip the steering wheel hard, my heart pounding in my chest. Vision tunneling on the dimming light that coats the dash, and I force myself to turn the key in the ignition before I lose myself. Dad's truck turns over, rumbling under us, keeping us safe — *Jasmine is safe* — and I know they'd be proud of me. For finding a wife that will meet their expectations as soon as she understands. Jasmine has always been so close to perfect, and Dad taught me how to correct mistakes. He taught me how to fix the small imperfections that would keep her from realizing her true potential — and I won't fail her. Not again.

I'll do whatever it takes to make her *right*.

Shifting the truck into gear, I turn toward the house and let the truck roll slowly over the uneven ground. Out of the corner of my eye, I can see her flinching, wincing. Her breath catches on the bigger dips, her body shifting as she lets out the smallest sounds of pain.

This is the way I should have always done it. Pain is educational. Suffering brings us closer to glory when we fall short of the state God has meant for us. Jasmine is still learning, and I love her for her strength. It's just one more piece of proof that she was always meant to be mine.

"Wait here. I will carry you," I say as I turn the truck off in front of the house. Most of the lights are still on from when I searched for her, before I'd realized she'd left, and so the windows still glow in the weak light of morning.

I'm tired, but when you love someone you take care of them. Punish their mistakes, lead them to the true path, and tend them when they need you.

Jasmine needs me now.

I take each step carefully around the truck, keeping my eyes on the dirt instead of on her naked body. If Momma was alive she'd be angry that Jasmine isn't dressed, but the clothes are so dirty, and so is she. She needs to be clean more than she needs to be hidden. No one will see her nakedness except me, and I can see her. Husbands are allowed to see their wives as God intended.

That is the thought I pull front and center as I open the door, and her soft curves are revealed again. Part of me just wants to take her to the bedroom, to hold her against me and tell her how much I love her — but we both need to be clean. You don't get into bed when you're dirty. I know that, and so does she.

"Leave the clothes, Jasmine," I command, and I'm comforted by how she tries to tuck the shirt and shorts into a neat stack as she sets them on the center console. She understands. She knows that what she did was wrong. She took her punishment, and now I can remind her of what a good husband does when his wife is penitent.

I pick her up as carefully as I can, mindful of the marks on her backside as I lift her against my chest. Her weight is a comfort, a reminder of my responsibility, and I kick the door shut so that I can carry her home.

The stairs up to our bedroom call to me, but I avoid their temptation and march straight to the downstairs bath once we're inside. As soon as I set her on the small counter beside the sink, she flinches, hissing air between her teeth as her delicate fingers clench at the edge. White-knuckled and taut. Yet, for once, her knees stay apart, like she is welcoming me as a wife would a husband.

If only I hadn't spilled my seed in the barn.

Brazen, I stroke my hands over her smooth thighs, the

golden hue a reminder of just how much of herself she's allowed to be seen by others. I feel the jealousy, the urge to protect what is mine, but I push it back down as I turn away from her to gather the antiseptic and a cloth. Forcing my eyes to look only at her feet, I shake my head and dig out the gauze from its small case near the back of the cabinet. Dad built this furniture with his own hands, and he'd be proud of how it supports my wife — of how *I* am supporting my wife. I won't be tending to the marks from the belt, because punishments don't deserve first aid, but she'd hurt herself before I'd ever found her. I'd gone out to the edge of the property, worried for one fleeting moment that I'd lost her to the dangerous, corrupting world outside.

But, no. She knew better than to go so far. I found the end of her tracks. Found where she waited for me, and for that she has earned the care I can provide.

I don't rise from the floor as I shut the cabinet. Instead, I move to kneel in front of her, delicately lifting one foot, and then the other, to see the damage she's done. Blisters, already broken and weeping, several spots on her heel and the balls of her feet are raw. Bleeding. *That* is what ruined the shoes, marred the floor in the barn. I know I shouldn't have left the barn in such a state. The longer the stains sit, the deeper they'll embed themselves, but we both need sleep.

To be clean, and to sleep.

The bottle of antiseptic is heavy, barely touched, and I'm careful as I tilt it onto the rag. Just enough to wet it, and I feel it bubbling against my fingers before I even drag it over the bottom of her foot. Jasmine jerks, whining, but I catch her ankle to keep her still.

Jasmine

"Please..." she whimpers, softly, and I am sure this hurts. I remember the sting of the antiseptic too, and I steel myself against her quiet sounds of discomfort as I disinfect her injuries. The cloth is a mixed set of dark smudges of dirt and the pale pink of her blood before I'm done. Cleanliness is important, more important than her comfort for now, but I will welcome her into our bed soon. I will remind her that she has not strayed so far that she cannot be saved.

In a matter of minutes, I'm finished. Twisting the cap back onto the little bottle, I raise my eyes to the place between her legs. I shouldn't look, shouldn't stare, but her flesh is flushed pink and swollen. Through the thin smattering of hair, she is still shining from the lubricant I provided. It had been a gift, but she hadn't understood it as such. She'd screamed, fought, and I had done what any good husband would as I'd held her firmly until she'd accepted her mistake, and her punishment.

She cleansed herself through the pain, while I became weak. Unable to hold my needs as I watched her naked body jolt and twist.

I will punish myself later. For spilling my seed in a forbidden place... but even the memory of her body accepting me in all ways has my manhood twitching. Tempted by the gift of Eve that is inherent in all women.

Stop.

Tearing my gaze from her, I stand and turn the tap on in the bath. Waiting for it to warm, I begin to disrobe again. This time, I keep my back to her, folding each item and setting it in the wire-frame hamper until I am naked, and steam balloons out of the basin of the tub. A sharp tug pulls the curtain around the curve of the bath, and I switch the flow to the shower head, testing it with my hand and adjusting the temperature until it's only warm, not so hot it would burn her perfect skin.

"Come here, Jasmine," I beckon, holding out my hand.

Pain flashes in her expression as she slides off the counter, ignoring my hand as she approaches, but she comes to me. As much as she wants to be chaste, she knows where she belongs. I take her hand anyway, helping her into the stream of the shower before I join behind her. Jasmine relaxes in the warmth, breathing deeply, her eyes closed as she steps forward and lets the water sluice over her head and shoulders. I can't resist the urge to touch one of the trails flowing down her side. She twitches, tenses, and I brace my other hand on her opposite hip.

"I want to shower alone," she whispers.

"No." I shake my head, but she can't see it as she stares straight ahead. "I will help you."

Jasmine moves slightly, a little further into the stream, and I appreciate it because it means some of the warm water hits me. I take advantage of the chance to grab the soap, lathering it up on my own skin before I start to wash her.

This... this I'm certain she understands. The washing of feet, the cleansing of another to show care, reverence, love. I'm positive Jasmine feels it with every swipe of the soap, just as I am positive I should not enjoy this. My manhood should not react to the supple feel of her breast. Not now. Not when I am caring for her like this.

Still, some things are simply beyond the capacity of man.

We are flawed, fallen, and therefore driven by the traits Satan drew out of us in the garden. But I refuse to be ashamed of my nakedness, of the steadily hardening length at my hips, because Jasmine is my wife. Each of our unions is blessed.

"Don't. Please don't?" she pleads as my fingers slide over her backside, gliding down the crack to clean her. Her small fingers wrap around my wrist, but she doesn't try to move my hand away. She just twists, and the swell of her breasts shines in the pale light.

"You have to be clean," I explain, using the slickness of the soap to move one finger inside just a little. Remembering the way her body gripped me, pulled, urged me deeper with every squeeze until I was lost. She whines, releases me to obey like the good wife I know she can be, and perhaps I linger too long as I glide my finger back and forth. *This is where I spent myself.* Not in her womb, not where it may be fruitful, but, still... my seed is not a sin inside her. I try to remind myself that I only entered her other hole because she was being punished, and it would have been wrong to end her punishment for my own satisfaction. Part of her redemption was the dowel, the belt, but the other was in redeeming herself to me. In serving my needs. "Clean yourself, Jasmine."

I direct her hand between her legs, and she only fights for a second as I press closer to her back. Pushing her hand to the valley at the top of her thighs as I work my finger back and forth, preserving the memory of the tight, forbidden place I've allowed myself to explore. She used such vulgar words, still so angry, embarrassed at being punished for her transgressions, but it is my job to show her that there is nothing hidden between man and wife. Nothing is truly forbidden in the eyes of God when two people are bound together as Jasmine and I are.

The first stroke between her thighs is stiff, tentative, and I push harder, forcing her hand flat against her skin as I guide her fingers through the process of cleaning away the lubricant. "Like this, Jasmine," I whisper.

"Please stop..." There is something else in her tone, perhaps tears, more contrition for her failings, but all of that has been cleaned away. Just as all of the dirt and grime is being carried away by the water.

When her touch is still tentative, I abandon her back entrance to hold her hip in place and push her fingers inside. She trembles, a keening sound leaving her lips as she presses back against my chest. Seeking shelter, my guidance, my hand — and it would be wrong to abandon her now. Wrapping my arm over her waist, I hold her still so that I can trace her folds. Erasing the lingering mess, dipping my fingers inside her to ensure she is clean. I feel her shudder, her back arching, which brings her backside in contact with my manhood and my response is instantaneous. Completely hard, pulsing, all I want is to be inside her again. The right way. Where my seed is meant to lie.

Pulling my hand away, her body relaxes, and I know she wants it too. She needs my direction, my leadership, my strength — and I will always give her what she needs.

Whether it is the gift of intercourse, or the punishment she needs to stay on the true path, I will always provide.

Because good husbands provide.

FOUR

Her
———

I don't fight when he dries me off with the coarse towel. I don't fight when he puts me back on the counter to wrap my feet in gauze, nor when he takes me to his bedroom and tells me to get into bed... because I'm so tired. The kind of bone-deep tired that means I'll be asleep fast.

But then he slides into the bed beside me, beneath the covers, and his large hand moves across my stomach. The second I feel it moving south, I grab onto his wrist, clenching my eyes tight because I can't handle more of this. Not tonight, today, whatever time it is.

"Jasmine." He says that name like a warning, a patient one, with no anger in it but a threat all the same. He'll make me if I try to fight... and so I let go. I let his hand slide between my thighs without so much as a *'no.'* His leg moves over mine to pull it wider, and then he pushes two of his big fingers in and my body locks up. Tense, a whine escaping through clenched teeth as I try to take the pain, but I can't.

"I need to heal," I whisper. "Please."

"This will help," he replies, like he knows anything at all about what it feels like to be violated. To have a wooden shaft forced inside you until you can feel your bones straining to hold their position. I've never felt this bruised, never felt this kind of sharp ache as he thrusts his fingers slowly, just like he did in the shower. His cock is hard against my hip, and my body knows what's coming, knows what to do — I don't even hate myself anymore for getting wet. It's self-defense, my body trying to protect me, because there's nothing else I can do. Even if I had the energy to fight him, it wouldn't work. It never works.

"Please," I whine as he pushes his fingers all the way in, stretching torn and tender skin until I have to clench the sheet in my fist to stop myself from shoving him away. "Please don't? It hurts."

I'm begging, but it doesn't matter. He draws himself to my side, his cock rubbing against me as he presses a kiss to my shoulder.

"It's just the reminder of your punishment, but that's over now," he says softly, like it should be comforting.

It's not.

I gasp when he pulls his fingers out, a grating kind of pain from the sudden removal, and I wait for him to roll me to my stomach — but instead he moves over me. Knees between mine as he spreads me, and the urge to cry moves like a ball up my throat. My fingers are clenched in the sheet on either side of me, trying so hard not to shove him, go for his eyes, any of the myriad thoughts flickering through my head. I can't take another punishment right now, and it won't stop him anyway.

Jasmine

It won't stop him.

I try to disappear behind my eyes, to leave my body and let him have it again but, as he settles between my hips, he kisses across my breast. Sucks my nipple into his mouth until those unavoidable tingles race through my nerves like little traitors. I make some kind of noise, weak and desperate, and a quiet groan leaves him. His hips move, rubbing his hard shaft against me, and I can't do a thing about it because he's too big. My legs are spread obscenely wide just for him to lie between them. He's overly tall, overly broad, heavy with dense muscle, and as he leans over me, I know what he's going to do before he does it. I press my lips together as he tries to kiss me, and he sighs.

"You don't need to cry, Jasmine. I forgive you." He gently brushes my cheek, thumb passing over my lips, and I open my eyes because I can't believe that *he* believes what he's saying.

Forgive me? Is he insane? Yes, he is, and I knew that already, but I still can't believe it sometimes when he says this shit. Another tear rolls out, and I'm barely even aware that I'm crying, but he sees it. Brushes it away. Brows pulled together like he's concerned for me — but it's a lie. This is just more of his insanity at work.

"God forgives you, Jasmine. He sees your contrition, and so do I." Just as he finishes speaking he kisses me, and I don't bite his lip. I don't do anything but hold onto the sheet until my fingers ache as his tongue teases at the seam of my lips, parts them just enough to kiss me in the mechanical way he always does. Half-exploring, half-tentative. Like he hasn't ever been kissed by someone who wanted him... which isn't hard to believe. He's psychotic, and I'm just his latest victim.

Him

I feel such joy as Jasmine submits under me. She lets me kiss her lips, her neck, her breasts, and I know it is because I have been a good husband. She is finally understanding, and I want to make her feel better. I want her to see that I still love her, that God still loves her through me. She doesn't need to cry anymore; she doesn't need to feel her guilt for running away. Her punishment has absolved her of it. In God's eyes, it's like it never happened now.

The throbbing at my hips is growing urgent, and I release her nipple from my lips so that I can position myself above her. She is so much smaller than I am, so delicate, and I take care as I gently bend her knee up so that I can be close to her. Like man and wife, like it should always be, and I am glad she has finally accepted that so I can be with her like this, able to see her beautiful face as I enter her.

Her folds are slick and soft as I seek her entrance, pushing gently until I feel her body give way to mine. Letting me in, even as she gasps and arches. I know there is still pain from her punishment, but God will take it away as we come back together. The right way.

The first inch of my body enters hers, and she tenses, whines, and I shush her softly. "It's okay, Jasmine, it's okay."

I try to be patient with her body, to let her accept me slowly, but the warmth of her wraps around my shaft, and I cannot help the twitch of my hips. She cries out, more tears on her cheeks as her small hands grab onto my biceps, seeking my strength, and it makes me feel strong. Strong enough to ease inside her as I bend my head and kiss her. Jasmine is perfect. Her body stretches to accept mine, made by God just for me, and I know she can feel it too as I push one last time and our skin meets.

Surrounded by her heat, the gentle squeezes of her tightness around my shaft, I thank God for bringing her to me. I promise that I will always care for her, show her the right path, be strong for her so that she may serve Him properly.

"I love you, Jasmine." Just as I say the words I pull back and thrust forward, and she yelps, her fingers tight on my arms, her breathing already faster than mine.

"Please, don't," she whispers, and I kiss her to give her strength as I start to move. That holy feeling of her body makes it hard to be gentle the way I know she needs, but I do my best as I bring our bodies together again and again. She makes soft, high sounds as I make love to her, and I try to hold back my completion, so that I can appreciate everything she gives me.

This is so much better than having her on her stomach, or her hands and knees, but those times it was necessary. Jasmine tries so hard to be chaste, but I think that now she's finally understanding that our unions can never be tainted by sin. God has blessed us, together, to be fruitful and multiply. It is the image of her swollen with child, my child, that takes control of my body. I surge inside her, hearing her cries against my ear as I lean over her. It is always harder for the woman, but I know she is slick between her thighs because she wants to accept me, my seed. Our skin meets again and again, and I feel as she tenses around me, pushing me to fill her, and I give in to my needs.

Pleasure, a gift of God, ignites like a fire inside me. I bring our bodies together hard, burying myself in her slick heat as fire jolts down my spine, through my shaft and into her. I shout in bliss, feeling her soft body mold against mine as I press her into the bed and spill my seed inside her in rapid pulses that erase everything in the world except for her for one glorious moment.

"Jasmine," I say, breathing hard, so grateful for her that I feel filled with light as I keep us together. Her nails are pressed to the backs of my arms, holding me to her, and I cannot deny her need to be close to me. I pepper her skin with kisses, seeking her mouth, and she lets me in. Lets my tongue taste her lips, her mouth, as she breathes quickly. Little whimpers buzz against my lips as she shifts her hips against mine, and I push myself deep again as I feel my flesh growing softer. "I love you."

I am sad to leave her, to leave this moment when she finally understands the way a man and wife should be together, but I can feel my seed inside her. The slickness of it around my shaft, and I know that even as my body leaves hers, I am still with her. Still inside this sacred space where she may create a child.

Reluctantly, I push myself up, listening to her gasp as I slide from her, and as I sit back, I simply look at her. There is no shame in it, she is mine and I am hers in the eyes of God. I can look at her body, at the swell of her breasts, and the place between her thighs where I can see my seed shining. She does not look at me, her eyes are on the ceiling, and I know that is because she is still coming to terms with this act.

Exhaustion suddenly hits me, a yawn taking me as I shift and lie beside her. Immediately, I tug the covers up and pull her against me, wrap my arm around her waist so that she knows I am with her. But, just before sleep, I move my hand down the softness of her stomach, resting it above her womb as I pray for a child. A child to give her joy, to give us a family.

Jasmine whimpers, sniffles, and I know she is still thinking of her guilt, so I hug her against me again. Comforting her, giving her my strength so that we can sleep.

Together.

FIVE

Mason

I really hate this job some days.

Today is one of them.

LAPD Central is a shithole. I think this every time I come here, and today is no different. Over the years they've tried to make this place... bearable? Livable? A decent 'working environment', or whatever ergonomic, collaborative workspace, feng shui bullshit is being spewed at any given moment in time. It's all failure, and only ends up making the place look like a cross between the set of *Sanford and Son* and a Herman-Miller warehouse hit by a bomb. The FBI building is better; not by a huge stretch, but better, and one of the reasons I hate coming here is because it makes me feel bad for the people who have to work in this place. But I know the drill; when a missing person case goes beyond the jurisdiction of the LAPD, it gets handed over to the FBI. To a guy like me. Hopefully to someone *other* than me, but that isn't the case today, and so now I'm in this armpit when all I want to be is gone.

"Where can I find Detective Ressner?" I ask the first person to make eye contact with me.

"Should be in that office over there."

Office over there. Huh. That means he's a senior detective and not some grunt, which could either bode well for me or not so much. I knock on the office door and a painfully slim-looking man gets up and comes over, pulling it open.

"Oh, you must be Agent Jones."

I stick out my hand. "And you're Detective Ressner."

He grips my hand, and despite his Lurch-like skeletal demeanor, the shake is surprisingly firm. "Come on in."

His office is one of the ones they tried to upgrade at some point. I feel sympathy for him, because at least the older offices have some degree of character. This one is so devoid of anything that would make it personable that it is almost painful to be in—an office decorated by committee, and gutted of humanity by all. I sit in a chair that is mismatched to everything else in the room, and also three inches too short for the height of his desk. I reach underneath, pull the lever up to let the piston rise—

"Umm... it doesn't..."

The chair immediately sinks back down.

"...work."

I smile at him with faux sincerity. "No problem."

"Sorry 'bout that."

"It's fine," I lie, attempting to get comfortable in the miserable seat.

He looks apologetically about the office. "Umm, can I get you anything to drink? Coffee? Bottled water?"

"Really, I'm fine, Detective." *I just want to leave.*

"Okay. All right." He sits at his desk and looks down at me. "So. Did you have a chance to look at the files we sent over?"

"I did."

"Good. Is there anything you want to ask me?"

"Yes." I pause for a moment, staring at him. "Why are we pursuing this?"

His brow beetles in confusion. "I beg your pardon?"

I reach down, open my briefcase, and pull out the file folder. For a case — any case — it's surprisingly thin.

"Sloane Finley. Age twenty-three." I withdraw the most recent picture of her, the *Headshots LA* one she had taken four months ago. I look at it, look at him. "Pretty girl." I set the picture down on the edge of his desk. "Dead girl."

He looks back at me, his face going stony. "You don't know that."

"Detective Ressner"—I tap the picture with my finger—"you and I both know this girl is dead. Let me paint you the picture we both know is true. Sloane Finley comes to LA from Shitstick, Indiana…"

"Indianapolis."

Jasmine

I smile indulgently at the interruption. "...to become a movie star. She fails. Waitress..."

"She worked at Barnes and Noble."

Again I ignore him. "...shitty apartment, few friends, not one single role, even as an extra. No SAG card, no fucking anything card. Hell, she didn't even try to go flat on her back in the Valley to break into the business."

Lurch gives me a long sigh, rolling his eyes.

"So, she leaves town to head back home and a week later disappears off the map."

"What's your fucking point here, Agent?" His voice has lost the apologetic tone from earlier and I know I've hit close to the bone of his own thoughts.

"My point is this. This girl is dead. You know it, and I know it. Now, not to put too fine a point on it, but this shit happens all of the time, Detective. In, oh, let's give it ten years max, some hunter or rancher out there in Texas is gonna stumble across a pile of bones that got washed out of a gully during the last storm, and that'll be our girl. But I'll be long since retired, and so will you, and we'll both just read about it in section C, fourth column, five lines total."

He just stares at me.

"So, I ask again; why are you guys asking the Agency to take on this case?"

"She's a missing person."

"So's Amelia Earhart."

"You know what, my day is super fucking busy. So, if you

have any questions that you want to ask me, Agent Jones, then please ask them. Otherwise, kindly get your ass out of my office."

"You know I'm right."

"I don't give a shit if you're right or wrong. This is your problem now, not mine."

I sigh. "I just want to know why?"

Lurch leans across his desk. "You want to play tough-as-nails-I-seen-it-all? Fine, I can play that role too. So, here's the deal; Miss Finley's daddy works for a big military facility out there in Indiana that handles chemical weapons. Now, as you might imagine, with everything going on overseas at the moment that makes him a pretty big fucking deal. Well, I guess when daddy is worrying about his little girl who hasn't called home in four weeks, he might be having a hard time concentrating on WMDs or whatever the fuck it is he concentrates on. But the thing is daddy has some connections with a senator or two, and those senators are giving hand jobs to other senators including — wouldn't you know it! — Senator Harris from the great state of California. Who then asks some people to ask us to take a look into this. Which we do, until it turns out that the trip little Miss Finley there"—he stabs his finger at the photo—"decided to take comes to an abrupt end somewhere out in Texas. Now, since she is no longer in California, that puts her outside of our jurisdiction. Enter our good friends at the F, B, fucking I."

He flicks the photo with his finger, and it teeters at the edge of the desk.

"You don't want to take this case, I don't fucking care. You take it up with your boss or Senator Harris's office, not me. We did what we have to do in cases like this. Contacted *you*." He leans back in his chair, looking supremely smug. "There. How'd I do? Do I get the role?"

I laugh. *What else am I going to do?* "Okay. Now I understand."

"I'm sure you do." He blows out a gust of air, hitching his shoulders to release the tension that has built up between us. "Listen, Agent, I feel for you. Really, I do. But these are the cards that have been dealt, and you're just going to have to roll with it."

"Yep. I can see that now. Pretty much out of my hands, isn't it?"

"Pretty much." He swivels his chair a bit, studying me. "So... what are you going to do?"

He seems genuinely interested, which makes one of us. "Only thing I can do. Waste time, pretend I'm 'looking into it,' wait for it to fade, or until they assign me to something actually worth working on."

"How long you think they'll keep you on this?"

"I dunno." I shrug. "A month? Maybe two?"

He looks down at the hovering picture. "You really think she's dead?"

"I know she's dead. They always are." I glance at the picture of the smiling, brown-haired young woman staring back at me. All American girl next door, everybody's sweetheart.

Worm food.

"She shoulda got down on her knees in the Valley. Sucked a few dicks, took a load or two to the face."

Lurch looks at me, eyes bulging, disconcerted by my crassness. I give him a bland smile.

"She'd probably still be alive."

I don't head back to my office. Instead, I head out to Naja's on the boardwalk in Redondo. It's a nice day, and I've got time to kill.

It had been a long shot to think that something would turn up, and I could walk away from this assignment. The file told the story with a few more details than I'd gone over in Detective Ressner's office, but not much. Miss Sloane Finley had come to California to make her way into movies, like every other stupid young woman that somehow thinks it'll be different for them than it was for the umpteen-million girls before her. She'd failed, because that's how this story plays out. Her options boiled down to three: get discovered, do porn, or fail and go home. Option one was a non-starter from the get-go, all-American girl or not. Nobody skips into LA and gets discovered. She could have gone with option number two, but even that was a long shot. In the day and age of Pornhub and celebrity sex tapes, even the number of jobs available to pretty young women who don't mind 'sucking a few dicks, and taking a load or two to the face' are fewer and farther between than they used to be. So, Sloane Finley chose the only real option she'd ever had, sans staying a sales associate at Barnes and Noble forever — she headed home.

Jasmine

I grab a stool at the long 'U' shaped bar at Naja's, order an Artifex, and turn, staring out over the white crescents of light dancing on the wave edges beyond the surf.

This is nice. A month or two of this I can deal with.

The bitter taste of hops hits the back of my throat, and I'm aware it's a pretty little lie I'm telling myself. A US Senator is involved in this now, and even though I know Sloane Finley is as dead as my soul, I will not be able to wait this one out here on this stool or sitting in my office watching Netflix.

No, instead I will have to pretend to do a job that I know is both futile and pointless. I know the statistics by heart. They drum at the back of my head like a dull rumble of thunder: 68,000 women twenty-one years of age or older disappeared just last year in America. From year to year the figures are a rollercoaster of bleak numbers that has long since eroded my spirit like acid to metal. 20,000 unidentified bodies. That's the number — both male and female — that are found every year. Bodies like the one that might wash out of a gully in some rural backwater in West Texas someday. Bodies that will never bring closure to the families of those people who simply disappear off the face of the Earth.

I drain back the last of my first beer, order another, and I try. I *try* like I've been trying for ten years now. Empathy. Care. Concern. Hope. *Anything.* I look for the tiniest spark, an ember on which to blow to summon even the slightest interest in what I'm being paid to do — find Sloane Finley.

I take another sip. *Come on, Mason. You can do this. Care. Care about Sloane Finley.*

I wait. The ocean watches and waits with me.

Nope.

She's dead. A stupid fucking girl who did something dumb, and as I sip my beer, feeling the sun beat down... I just couldn't care less.

SIX

Her
———

Thursday is sweeping, dusting, and mopping.

I don't fight chores anymore. Defiance doesn't even occur to me, especially after this morning. I fought him once early on, told him to go fuck himself, and my reward for that moment had ended with being lashed to the post, his belt flailing me until I thought my skin peeled.

'Those whom I love I rebuke and discipline. So be earnest and repent. Revelations 3:19, Jasmine.' I remember those words too, one of my first memories of him quoting scripture to me.

When I finally woke up this afternoon, sore and aching, I'd wondered if maybe he was going to leave me alone the rest of the day and let me skip the chores after what he'd done to me. Of course, I was wrong. Daniel had come back into the bedroom just to tell me to get dressed and start on my tasks for the day.

All of my clothes are in the drawers, and I should probably

feel lucky that I have the three I do for myself. Except that half the clothes — or maybe more because I'm starting to lose track — aren't mine at all. No, the clothes he took from my car when he brought me here were tossed in with the other things that were already in the drawers. The other girl's. The real Jasmine. Hers and mine all mixed together. The combination is the sum total of everything that I own in this prison.

Except I own nothing. Not anymore. Everything here is his, including my body.

No, that's not true.

There's one thing I still have control over. Under the counter, there's two small pink disks in my bag and this morning I'd dialed one open to the next pill in sequence, popped one out, and swallowed it dry. When he first dragged me here, I'd managed to convince him they were medicine I needed. It was clear he didn't have a fucking clue what birth control looked like, and those little white pills have become the only evidence of his 'God' I've seen here. I watch them like a hawk, keep count of them with the fervor of a zealot, because each pill spells out another day to live. To plan.

When they end, so do I. One way or another.

I can't let those dark thoughts intrude right now, I can't think of my failed escape attempt, because I have *tasks* to do. Of the three chores I have today, dusting is first, and this old ass house has nothing in the way of seals. There are cracks under the doors, in the windowsills, and the dust blowing in from the dry Texas landscape outside is a constant battle.

Jasmine

Even though I'm sore, and my feet remind me with every step of just how badly I fucked up, I finally finish dusting the sitting room downstairs and move into the family room.

'Family room' — what a fucking joke.

These people had no entertainment. There is no phone, no television, no computers, nothing. There's not a single thing here that has any access to the outside world, which means *I* don't, because I have no idea what he did with my cellphone after he took me.

For all I know it's still sitting in the dirt beside my car, battery long since dead.

I have to stop myself from thinking about the missed calls I probably have waiting for me. The voicemails from my mom, my dad, Trish. If I think about them, about anything but escaping from here, I know I'm going to lose it.

Chores, focus on the damn chores.

I'm dusting his creepy family photos, the ones where no one is smiling, when I notice that I accidentally put on one of *her* shirts this afternoon. It's a dull, faded red, the white lettering and cloverleaf emblem cracked. *Stockdale High 4H Club. 'Born to Lead'*. A part of me wants to go back upstairs, yank it off, exchange it with one of my own... but I don't. I have to be numb right now, it's the only way I can handle this shit, and any energy I'd spend on exchanging a perfectly good t-shirt for another — to make a point only *I* would acknowledge — is energy I just don't have.

The massive bookcases covering one wall of the family room exist purely to collect dust because they have absolutely nothing of interest in them. Just books on ranching and the

Bible and *Concordance*, whatever the fuck that is. I used to wonder how he was able to quote so much of that Bible scripture crap to me, but it didn't take me long to understand. These people had no need for entertainment beyond reading about how to raise and kill cattle, and what their fucking God directed them to do with their lives. He's probably done nothing but read the Bible from the day he could recognize the words.

And he's fucking crazy because of it.

I'm on the last bookcase when the duster catches on something. My mind is on autopilot so when the feather snags it yanks the tool out of my hand before I can think to seize it, and it falls to the floor with a clatter. Shaking myself out of my haze, I kneel down to grab it, but as I lean down I notice something I haven't before. On the lowest shelf there is a thin white volume with a tall narrow spine, black block lettering running up the length. It's the first word that catches my eye — STOCKDALE. Even as thick as my brain is running today, that word reminds me of the shirt I'm wearing. I skim the remaining lettering and my breath freezes.

STOCKDALE HIGH SCHOOL YEARBOOK.

Without thinking, I pull it free from the surrounding books. I don't know why I'm doing this, but at the same time I know exactly why I am.

Find her.

I crack it open, and it's like a million other yearbooks that came before it, just like the ones sitting in my old bedroom back at my parents' house. I quickly flip the pages, finding photos of him towering over the other players on the football team, a monster even in high school, and then I come to the class photos. They start with the freshmen, but I have this gut feeling, and I skip ahead, past the freshmen and sophomores. *Juniors*. I pause for a second, staring at the new title page, then begin scanning names. Like most yearbooks, it goes by last names first, which makes my search a little more difficult because he's never mentioned her last name. Only her first. The name he calls me.

Jasmine.

I search carefully, but there's nothing in the juniors, so I start in on the seniors. His photo stands out to me, but I flip past it, knowing that she must be in here somewhere. Halfway through doubt creeps in. *Maybe I'm wrong*. Fuck, maybe there never was a real Jasmine. Maybe all of this is just some distorted fever dream of his fucked-up mind. A creation he made of his perfect wife, and I'm the latest one he chose to make the idea a reality. Even as I'm thinking this I continue turning pages and at the three-quarter mark my heart stops.

I see the name and the picture at the same time. My ears ring with blood. It's nothing so dramatic as if saying I felt like I was looking in a mirror. That would be the stuff of horror movies, or some Stephen King novel. No, Jasmine, the *real* Jasmine, is not me. And yet it's all too easy to see the twisted alterations his mind has made. Her hair is a lighter brown. Higher cheekbones, a sharper nose. Her eyes are deep green, not my hazel, and so serious looking.

Jasmine Turner.

She stares out at me from the glossy page. A young woman who is not me, and yet in his twisted mind *is* me. He wanted her, obviously couldn't have her willingly, so he took her. Killed her. And then waited for the opportunity to take someone as close as he could find to fill the gap. That's the story I build in my head as I study her face, one that's a repeat of thoughts I've had so many times before. All of the *why me's*. Why I'm here. Why he took me that day on the side of that road when all I was doing was taking...

"Jasmine."

I scream, dropping the yearbook as I whirl on my heels, back pressing into the bookcase. The shelves embed themselves into my skin, filled with all those books on cattle and God and now an empty slot where one had been that contains a picture of a girl who should be here instead of me.

I was so wrapped up in what I'd discovered I never heard the footfalls of his boots. I don't know how that could be, because he's so big, and I almost always hear him when he's moving about the house. But I didn't. I watch him closely, waiting for it. Waiting for the disapproval, the commands, the walk to the barn.

"What are you doing?"

"I..." I drag in a desperate lungful of air. "I found... I was just looking..." I can't make the words come together to finish the sentence as I stare up at him, and then he lowers himself. I cower backward, trying to bury myself further into the bookcase, away from him. He makes no sudden movements toward me as he picks up the yearbook, glances at it, and then at me. Tears well in my eyes for what I know

Jasmine

is coming. I tell myself I won't plead with him, but in the same breath I realize I will, when the time comes, when those leather straps wrap around me, pulling me tight against the barn post.

He looks down at the yearbook, flipping through it in silence, but there is one page that folded over when I dropped it, and he flips to it. It's the page with her picture, Jasmine's photo.

"You were so beautiful. Even then."

I swallow. His voice is gentle, tender, as he stares down at the page. Staring at *her*. I want him to look up at me. I want him to look at me and realize I'm not her, not the girl in that book. I want him to recognize it, to ask me who I am. I want to tell him my name is *not* Jasmine for the millionth time, and have him fucking listen. I am Sloane, Sloane Finley, and I do not belong here. I should be in California with Trish, going to another audition that they won't pick me for, or back home in Indiana listening to my dad complain about work. I should be home, anywhere but here, and I want to stab my finger at that picture and scream '*I am not her!*'

"Do you remember the first time you came over?"

Fuck. He's looking at me and smiling. Like an actual human being. A real expression, and I can't speak, but I manage to shake my head.

"I do." He gives a quiet, almost playful chuckle, and my head spins, going light. No. No, he can't do this. He can't show emotion, act human. Not now.

Not after this morning. Not after everything.

"I remember the day because your momma brought you

with her, and then she and Momma got to talking in the kitchen. And then Momma told us to go outside and play, but you asked if we could go play in the room with all the books, and she said okay, but not to make a mess or touch the pictures."

He looks at me, and his grin is genuine, real, and this is surreal, and I want him to stop.

Daniel glances back at the yearbook, still smiling. "You were always reading those books of Daddy's. Anything you could find about cattle, livestock, animals, any of it. Daddy sure did think the world of that. *'That there is a good girl, Daniel. You'd be wise to take note of it.'* That's what he said. No lie."

I need him to stop. I need him to shut up. I don't want to hear this, any of it.

"I remember this," he says, turning the yearbook toward me so I can see.

It's Jasmine. A blue 4H jacket draped over her shoulders, open to a pale red shirt underneath that I think I'm wearing right now. My stomach twists as I see how happy she looks with her arms around the neck of a calf, chin resting on it. She's smiling, and holding a ribbon with a big number one in the center.

"I swear to you I think Daddy was more proud of you winning that than he was of any game of mine," he says softly, and it's as if the air is being sucked out of the room. "I've always loved you, Jasmine."

There's some kind of emotion in his voice, and if he weren't so fucking evil the words might even be sweet. But they aren't. They're words meant for a woman who isn't me. The woman whose shirt I'm definitely wearing. They're meant for the girl on that page who isn't here anymore, who's probably dead, whom he's trying to make me become. But I won't. He will *not* do this to me, he can't make me think of him as anything other than the monster he is.

I close my eyes, shake my head, and whisper, "I'm not Jasmine."

He ignores me. He's always done that. Back in the beginning I would scream it at him, beat at his chest while I shouted my name, my real name, even as he would gather me in his arms and crush me to him to silence me.

"I knew even back then you'd be my wife. That we would live together with God's blessing, that we would become one flesh as He tells us in Genesis." He closes the yearbook and gently places it back where I pulled it from. "Together, Jasmine. We will build our family here together."

Standing, he moves toward me, and I scoot back, flinching as his hand closes on my arm. He takes no notice of it, pulling me toward him even as I stiffen at his touch.

"Ours will be a fruitful union, Jasmine. We will be as the Lord teaches us in Psalm 127, verse three. *'Behold, children are a heritage from the Lord, the fruit of the womb a reward.'*" He holds me tight to his chest, his arms encasing me like a cage.

I feel his fingers on my skin, but they don't chill me nearly as much as his next whispered words.

"I cannot wait for you to grow round with our child."

I grit my teeth. *No.* No, that will never happen. Those two little pink disks of white pills in the bathroom will make sure of that. And before those run out, I will find a way out of here. I will make goddamn sure of it. Because I will not allow his fucked-up little plan to come to fruition. I will not let him use my body, my womb, to create his perfect fucking family.

I'll kill myself first.

SEVEN

Him

Jasmine has been so meek and obedient today. She did her chores without complaint, scrubbed her blood from the floor of the barn without argument, and I am filled with pride in her. She is a good wife, and I know there is no sin in feeling proud of her. God guided my hand rightly to administer the punishment I did this morning, just as he guided her to stop and wait for me. To not be tempted by the outside world and the Devil's whispers.

Thank you, Lord, for thy guidance in all things.

I want her to know I am proud of her, and as I lead her upstairs I decide just how I will show her my gratitude for her obedience — I will cook her dinner tonight and allow her to rest her feet.

Jasmine hesitates at the door to our bedroom, her lip caught in her teeth as she stares at her hands, and the sight makes me smile. I'm sure she expects us to return to bed together, but my plan will also bring her joy.

"Put this on," I tell her, pulling a dress from the closet to drape it over the chair.

"Why?" she asks softly, and I pause, uncertain why she's asking. Is it because I did not take her as I am sure we both want? Or is it because I have dictated that dresses and skirts are necessary only for the Sabbath? Whichever it is does not matter, for hers is the duty to obey.

"Because I said," I answer, and it is enough.

She approaches, looking down at the dress. I watch as her fingers close on it, wrinkling the fabric, and then she turns silently, heading into the bathroom. She starts to close the door, but I put my hand out, stopping her.

"Go on," I say, motioning toward the dress. Jasmine looks into the mirror, into my eyes as I stare back, and then she carefully begins to undress.

So dutiful today. I've done well.

Gazing at the slim, smooth lines of her body while she changes, my blood burns with desire as the Devil does everything he can to have me break my covenant with God. I do not give in to his temptation. I will show her, show God, that not even the Devil himself can influence me to sin.

She dresses, and when she turns to me, her beauty stuns me. *'You are altogether beautiful, my darling; there is no flaw in you.'* Solomon chapter four, verse seven. Jasmine is the living embodiment of scripture standing before me. As I stare, I see her injured feet are still swathed in the same bandages from yesterday. Seeing them now, God inspires me.

"Sit, Jasmine." I point to the toilet seat, and though she gives me a curious glance, she does as I say. When I kneel, both the story of Mary anointing Jesus at the home of Simon in Bethany, and that of Jesus anointing the feet of his disciplines as told in John 13, comes to my mind. I reach for Jasmine's foot, and gently remove the swaddling.

The room grows still, but for her gentle breathing. The bottom portion of the bandage is a dull ochre color, but it does not stick to her skin as I pull it away. While the marks are still there, and raw, the bleeding has stopped, and the wounds have begun to close. I run my thumb with tenderness along the length of her foot, and she draws a sharp breath, foot jittering in my hand.

"Does it hurt?"

She shakes her head, biting her lower lip. "No. It..."

I watch as her eyes close when the pad of my thumb grazes lightly toward her toes, feeling her foot jerk as I do.

"It tickles," she says, gasping in a quick breath.

"Oh." I try not to smile at her reaction, though it is hard not to. She seems embarrassed by it and continues to bite her lip as I stroke the bottom of her foot. Her breathing hitches, and I know she is trying hard not to laugh. I revel in the joy of such a simple thing and continue to massage her foot while she quivers to my touch.

I finish one foot, and then with gentle insistence do the same to the other. I do not linger, though there is a part of me that wishes to. It fills my heart with joy to find I can make her laugh, even if she tries to hide it from me. Dinner, however, is what I have set out as my goal, and that will not happen if I remain here indulging myself. So, I rebandage both of her feet, and put the supplies away before I stand.

"Put your socks back on, and put your dirty clothes away. I will be finished in a moment."

She looks up at me in silence, nods, and I go out to the closet. I change from my work clothes into a white dress shirt and a pair of dark blue pants. Though these are normally for the Sabbath, there is no sin in wearing them today. In that I am certain of the Lord's approval.

As I finish, I check to see if Jasmine has done what I ask, and she has. She is waiting for me, obedient and meek, and so I beckon her with a smile. "Come, Jasmine."

She hesitates, before finally moving to step past me and out into the hallway. I follow her into the kitchen where she moves to the icebox expectantly. "What do you want me to make for supper?"

"I will take care of it tonight," I answer, gesturing with my hand toward the stool near the counter. "Sit."

She looks at me, confusion painted across her features. "You will?"

"Yes." I nod, pointing again to the stool. "Sit."

Her eyebrows pull together as she takes her seat, and I almost smile. She's confused because I have taught her that fixing the meals is her task, but Jasmine is an obedient wife and she does not argue. As she watches, I pull things together to make our evening meal. Steak. Potatoes. Fried onions. Okra. These I can make well enough. Just as I start to chop the onion, Jasmine's voice interrupts my focus.

"I can peel the potatoes if you want."

I look over my shoulder at her, and pride swells within me. Even though she has sinned, she is a good wife, faithful and submissive, just as Peter said in 1 Peter 3, verse 1.

"Yes, that will be helpful." I nod, and she slips off the stool, taking the potatoes to the sink to start on them.

I return to fixing the meal, and as she works, a memory hits me. A day when I was young, sitting on the stool shelling peas while Momma prepared dinner. We were exchanging scripture, trying to catch each other up identifying them, when Daddy walked in. I remember Daddy coming up behind Momma, taking her shoulders in his big hands and kneading them. Momma sighed, forgetting scripture, her motions slowing as she leaned back into Daddy's chest.

Thank you, Lord, for your divine wisdom.

I move behind Jasmine, and she stiffens, her motions faltering as I reach for her shoulders just as Daddy had. Her body shudders when my fingers brush against the fabric of her dress, and she's tense as I begin to massage, the peeler frozen halfway along the potato. The only sound is that of us breathing, and the rustle of fabric against flesh as I mimic the motions Daddy made. Jasmine stays silent, rigid, and I try to be gentle, because this isn't punishment. It shouldn't hurt, because Momma hadn't hurt, not with this. I move my fingers in and out, kneading either side of her neck.

Eventually, the muscles butter up, releasing as the stiffness she'd held seems to flow away. She softens, and her breath comes back out as a sigh, a sound of pleasure I cannot remember hearing from Jasmine before. What I've done must have been good, so I do it again. The reaction isn't exactly the same, but neither does she tense. Her hands rest against the edge of the sink, still holding the potato and peeler, but they are forgotten. She is lost in what I'm doing. Lost in the pleasure that I, her husband, am giving her.

God gifts His chosen in his own time and way.

I continue to massage my wife, and I cannot stop the swelling of my manhood in response to her appreciative sighs. She leans back, and I have no need to pull her to my chest, for she comes freely.

I don't want to break what I have created, so I keep my thumbs moving in patient circles. My cock strains against my pants, and if I were to pull her even tighter, she would know it, but I don't. I work at her shoulders to keep her in bliss, wanting nothing more, for the Lord has blessed me with this and I must honor it as I should.

And then she gasps.

Jasmine jerks in my hands, yanking herself forward, head snapping to one side. "What..." she whispers, voice hoarse, quivering. "What are you doing?" Jasmine tries to pull further forward, but my fingers hold her frozen in place.

"I'm taking care of you, Jasmine." With gentle pressure I try to pull her back where she was a moment ago, but she resists. "I will always take care of you."

"No." She shakes her head, at first a slight twisting back and forth, and then she does it savagely. "No! You can't do this. You can't treat me like this!"

The potato falls with a thump into the sink.

"You can't make me feel like this!"

I grip her, fingers digging in. *Why? Why is she doing this again? Why can't she fight the darkness as she should and not give into Satan's temptation?*

"But you enjoyed it, Jasmine. I felt it. You've enjoyed the pleasure I gave you. This is what a good husband does." As each word comes out, I feel the tension in her grow until she is coiled like a trap spring.

"You are *not* my husband!" Jasmine's voice rises to a shriek, and she whirls.

It feels as if she's punched me hard in the arm, but it barely registers at first. Then her eyes go wide, and when she wrenches her hand away, there is a pulse of pain followed by warmth on my bicep. I look down to see the peeler jutting outwards, quivering where she stabbed me. The sting of it makes my jaw clench.

Whore.

Red begins to close in at the edge of my vision, and it is only the sound of her crying that brings me back from the brink. My fingers are digging sharply into her flesh, and she starts to slip toward the floor, screaming, pleading with me to let her go. I want to hit her, punish her for what she has done, but Daddy's in my mind again. Admonishing me, guiding me.

Never give into your wrath, Daniel. Lucifer tempts us down that path to lead us astray. Accept the anger pain brings, draw it into you, embrace it. But do not give into it.

Control it.

Control it. I ease my grip but do not let go of her entirely. Holding her limp body in place, I reach across with slow deliberation, extracting the peeler. She is weak, as women are, and it did not go in far. As I pull it free, the red of my blood soaks through the white fabric.

You will pay for that, harlot. You will clean that with your tongue.

I hold the peeler toward her, and she shrinks back as if it's a cattle prod.

"The devil is in you, Jasmine." I lean forward until my face is in hers, bringing the peeler up, blood dripping a slow patter onto the floor. "But I will drive him out of you. I swear it."

And I will.

EIGHT

Her
———

His fingers are pinched onto my shoulder so painfully hard that I buckle under the agony as he talks about the Devil... but then I see it. The potato peeler, still dripping with his blood, and all I can think of is him using that on my skin.

The horrible image gives me the strength to twist, and I kick away from the cabinets, breaking his hold as I scrabble backward on the floor. He drops the peeler to grab my leg, that same hard grip digging into my calf as he yanks me back toward him across the slick linoleum floor, but I kick again. Catch his chest, and then his arm, and I manage to break his hold again.

It's the first fucking miracle I've witnessed in this house, and I don't spit at it. I flip over and run out of the kitchen, into the never-used dining room and then out into the front entry space. I reach for the front door, but I hesitate as memories of the barn slam into me — and then Daniel *actually* slams into me.

The world rolls, flashes as my head hits the hardwood, and

then he tries to move over me and... I lose it. I'm screaming, shouting as I twist and hit and kick and punch while he tries to pin me. I've never fought this hard. Not even that first time when he dragged me into the grass saying crazy shit about how happy he was that I came back. Of course, back then I didn't know what he was capable of. I still thought I could reason with him because I didn't know just how terrible things could be.

And for one fucked-up moment I'd actually enjoyed his hands on me.

Unforgivable.

The thought brings another scream from my throat, and I manage to plant one foot in his stomach and kick hard. He doesn't move, but I do. I slide backward, leveraged away from him, and I'm not even able to think about where I want to go or what I want to do — I just want away. Away from him, from his touch, from his fucking massaging hands that almost made me drop my guard.

"God will give me the strength to help you, Jasmine," he says as he catches my wrist, my latest attempt to hit him foiled by his huge hands, and then I'm sobbing as I try to land another hit and he swats it away.

"No, no, no..." I hiccup as I try to pull in a deep breath, worn out from the fight as he holds my wrists and shifts until he's straddling my thighs. When he drops his weight over me, there's no fucking hope left. I don't even know what I expected to come from this, other than to make it clear that I'm not going to play the part of his obedient little wife. I'm not going to wear a dress for him while I dutifully peel potatoes just because he decided not to brutally punish me when we were in the barn this afternoon. Just because he didn't fuck me in his bedroom after. The barest hints of humanity in him won't erase every other monstrous thing he's done to me, and *that* is what I fought to remember. I had to remember it, have to always remember it. I can't let a kind touch erase any of it.

"I hate you," I whisper, and his eyes narrow.

"This is the Devil testing us, Jasmine, but he will not win. Not today when God has shown you what is meant to be." He shakes me, his arms bulging as he tightens his grip on my wrists until I can feel the bones grinding together. "I will not break my covenant, but I will get the Devil out of you tonight."

"There is no Devil!" I shout, and only realize as my voice breaks that I'm crying. Hard. "Jesus Christ, you're insane! YOU'RE CRAZY!"

He lets go of one of my wrists to cover my mouth, holding onto the lower half of my face in a harsh grip as his wild gaze drills into mine. "That's enough. You will not take Christ's name in vain in this house, and I will teach you just how I was taught."

I shout against his hand, but then he flips me to my stomach, and I hear his belt rattle. If it weren't for his iron grip on my wrist, I would run again. I don't know where, I don't know what I'd run to, but I'd run away. Just away. But the fear is taking over now as I go limp against the floorboards in front of the door, waiting for the belt to lay into me.

"I am in control," he whispers as he takes deep breaths above me. "I will not give in to temptation."

Crazy. Completely fucking crazy. It's all I can think as I feel him loop the belt around my wrist, and I immediately lunge my free arm forward, but it's a fleeting grasp of freedom, because in another second he has it pulled back with the first. I buck against the floor, barely able to move at all with his weight on my ass, and then I can't move my arms either.

"Normally I would take you to the barn for punishment, but you have tried so hard today, Jasmine... so hard," he mumbles as he climbs from my back and pulls me off the floor with so little effort. I stumble upright, only to come face to face with him as he leans down close. "So, we're going to drive out the Devil together. Do you understand?"

"I don't understand any of this shit!" I growl at him, jerking at his grip on my arm, and he just stares at me as his grip turns to iron once more, probably leaving bruises because he's so damn strong and it hurts.

"It's okay, Jasmine. I'll teach you." He nods as he drags me into the living room, the room where he actually sits on the sofa, the place where I've seen him reading those books on the rare nights he isn't watching me cook dinner.

He was going to cook you dinner tonight.

I scream and kick at the door frame, but it only makes my foot hurt as it bounces me back into him, and he doesn't move at all. Fucking mountain of a monster. I don't know why I keep fighting. I'm only making this worse for myself, but every time he says something in his incessantly calm voice, I remember how I'd almost fallen for it in the kitchen. How I'd almost been exactly what he wants me to be and for that... I hate myself even more than I hate him. I want him to hurt me, because that will remind me of who he really is, I want him to hurt me because I deserve it for leaning against him like some kind of lover.

He wraps his arms around me, pressing his lips to the side of my head as he forces me forward into the living room. "*But the way of the wicked leads them astray.* That is Proverbs 12. I'll teach you everything you need to know, Jasmine, because that's what a good husband does. He does not let his wife go astray from the word of God."

I almost manage a retort before he pushes me onto the couch. I land in a graceless huff, face first into the cushions, because my arms are bound behind my back. Then I hear him walk away, and I roll sideways to land hard between the coffee table and the couch. Leveraging my elbow on the cushion, I pull myself to my knees, almost standing before I see him return to the room with rope in his hands.

"Jasmine..." He sighs and grabs me, hauling me back onto the couch, face down, and I feel the rope go around my ankles in quick loops before he's hauling the rope between the leather on my wrists. It doesn't take ten seconds before he's standing next to the couch again, and I'm stuck. Hogtied. Literally tied in place. "I cannot allow you to defame this day with the Devil's sin. You atoned so well this morning; you were dutiful today. We will make this right, and then I will make good on my promises."

"NO!" I shout, but he's already leaving the room. Twisting, I try to get my fingers around the rope, looking over my shoulder as much as I can to figure out what the fuck he did with the rope so quickly, but I can't even find the knot before he's back.

"This is for using our savior's name in vain." He holds up a well-used bar of soap, the one from the kitchen sink, and I immediately clench my teeth.

Hell no.

But, like everything else he's wanted to do to me, my fight is for nothing. He pries open my mouth, shoves in the soap, and I instantly retch. It's dry and it's as if it sucks up all the moisture on my tongue as he yanks a handkerchief out of his back pocket, catching the soap when I try to spit it out. When it's pushed back between my teeth, they scratch over the soap and I gag again when it slides even further back as he ties the handkerchief at the back of my head.

"Now... the Devil is not gonna get his claws into you tonight," he declares in that deadpan way, but it doesn't sound like a joke right now. With a tug, the rope releases from where it connects to the belt on my wrists, but my ankles are still trapped, tied together. As he leans over me, I feel them tighten with another quick movement. I'm sure it's some kind of cowboy thing, because he does it without a thought and with such confidence... but I'd bet another trip out to the barn that he's never done it with a woman. Except maybe Jasmine.

Poor fucking Jasmine.

Her face flashes behind my clenched eyes as I feel the couch cushion dip in front of my face. I wonder if he ever tied her up like this on this couch, if she was choking on soap when he did it. I wonder what line she finally crossed that made him kill her, because I know she's not walking free somewhere.

Suddenly, he's lifting me, and it's always eerie how it seems to never strain him. Like I don't weigh a thing. Even as he moves me, lays me across his lap, he doesn't struggle, and all I can think is how grateful I am that he can't spread my legs without undoing the rope.

At least that will be some kind of warning before he fucks me.

I'm so distracted by that small comfort that it takes a second for me to realize how I'm positioned. Ass up, his erection pressed into my stomach, and I know what he's going to do. I kick my feet, twist my hips, not even caring if it sends me tumbling into the coffee table, but his massive hand lands on my hip and yanks me into his body. Securing me.

"Be still, Jasmine. We're going to face this together, as husband and wife, and you're going to push the Devil away so we can enjoy this evening that God has given us." His voice is that same infuriating monotone as I scream, only stopping when I gag on the soap as saliva pools in my mouth and drips suds down my throat. When I kick again, he just swings one of his legs over mine and pins me down.

Useless.

With his elbow against my spine, and my legs trapped, all I can do is whine when he lifts the back of my dress and runs his hand over my ass. It's not even sexual, and despite the hard-on I can feel. It's almost like he means it to be soothing as he shushes me.

"It's okay, Jasmine. God has shown me what you need tonight to stay strong against the Devil." He tugs down my underwear with a few quick jerks, and I feel them trapped between my thighs, wedged under his leg. My ass is bared to him as he lays his large, warm hand on me. "Think about your actions tonight compared to your obedience earlier today. How did you feel after you let the Devil tempt you into sin against your husband, and how did you feel before that when I was showing you my gratitude?"

You're not my husband! I want to scream it, but before I get the chance to even garble the words through the soap, his palm lands in a fiery spank across my ass. This isn't like the random swats I'd earned as a kid. This is bone-jarring, and it hurts before he even lands another. Two and three burn, and my back arches as much as it can before his elbow digs in and forces me back down.

"Don't fight this, Jasmine. It will help you." Another brutal series of spanks sets my ass on fire, and I go limp over his lap, soap-tainted drool soaking the handkerchief that pinches the corners of my mouth.

The pain spreads as he continues, and I lose count of how many times his palm has crashed down as the blistering heat spreads.

"I know you didn't want to hurt me. That was the Devil in you. The outside world tainting you, tempting you into violent acts to disrupt the sanctity of our home."

I shake my head, arguing even though it's pointless. The tears are making my nose run, stopping it up, and I have to hiss air in past the soap, which drags more of the taste down my throat. I retch, stomach heaving as he lands another harsh set of swats, jolting my entire body on his lap with each one. Somehow, it's worse than the belt. Being this close to him, feeling his body against me as he hurts me over and over and over.

"It's okay to cry, Jasmine. That's God helping you be penitent, helping you push the Devil out." He spanks me hard again before running his hand over my hot skin. "I will not let the Devil come between us because I love you."

I don't respond at all, so focused on trying to keep from throwing up that I just lie there and cry pathetically. He's not done. His hand circles across my ass a few times before he's back to it. Pain turns into a pulse across my backside, the skin throbbing as he layers swat after swat over skin already raw and aching.

"You did so well today, Jasmine. That's why you're not in the barn right now, that's why I'm giving you a loving punishment even though you injured me." He spanks the sensitive spot at the base of my ass, targeting it with a few brutally hard crashes of his hand, and I wail into the gag. He doesn't sound angry, but every strike tells me how angry he really is, and even though I hate to admit it... I know I'm lucky he's only using his hand. If this were leather, I'd probably be bleeding by now.

What's worse is that he's right. He didn't touch me all day. I did my chores, I scrubbed my blood from the floor of the barn, and all he ever did was hug me when I was caught with the yearbook. Of all of the nightmare days I've spent in this hell... this was the best one. He was even going to make me dinner, let me rest while he worked, and I ruined it by stabbing him with a potato peeler because he gave me a fucking massage.

And now? Now I don't know what he's going to do. I don't know if this milder punishment is just an appetizer, or if this is honestly all he plans to do to me for fucking stabbing him.

If it is, I don't know what to think.

He once whipped me with the belt for not cleaning the dishes well enough. Told me his momma would be disappointed. And after that whipping I hadn't even been able to walk... but jabbing a potato peeler into his goddamn arm means a spanking?

Crazy doesn't begin to wrap around the insanity of *Daniel*. But if the voice in his head that he calls God is telling him not to brutalize me again, not to stick me on a wooden rod and see if he can break me, then why should I complain?

Why did you complain when he was nice to you?

I hiccup as I start sobbing, not even gagging anymore as my tongue goes blind to the taste of soap. I don't want to be this person. I don't want to be Jasmine. I don't want to give in, to accept his affection as easily as I accept *this*, the vibrant shock of pain on already aching skin with each vicious spank. His heavy hand landing again and again until even that starts to fade and I go numb, my cries slowly fading until the room is silent except for the steady sound of his hand colliding with my flesh.

And then that stops too.

I'm sniffling, completely still on his lap as he begins to stroke my thighs below where the skin burns and aches.

"Meek and gentle, that is what God asks of you, Jasmine. Remember Isaiah sixty-six: *'But to this one I will look, who is humble and contrite of spirit.'* When the Devil seeks to tempt you into sin, into disobedience or violence or disrespect... you must fight him. You must control yourself so that you may always walk in the light of the Lord. With me." He squeezes gently behind my knee. "Do you understand?"

I hate myself even more for it, but I nod.

"That's good, Jasmine." A sharp tug frees the rope from my ankles, and I'm certain he's learned that from handling the cows outside. I'm just livestock to him. Breeding stock. Nothing more, nothing less. Then, with an arm under me, he removes his leg from mine and lifts me upright, holding onto me until my shaking legs are somewhat steady. He pushes the coffee table back further with his foot, and then nods toward the floor. I kneel because I can't do anything else, and my quaking thighs aren't dependable right now anyway. "You are so beautiful when you are penitent."

I just stare up at his flat brown eyes, still somewhat surprised he can be this zealous. This insane. This is his parents doing. The way he talks about his father and mother, the books in the house, the way he was raised... it's all led to this. He made his own choices, but he's a product of his environment as well, and I know that he spent a lot of time in the barn himself. He's said it before, casually, like it's no big deal to have been tied to a whipping post as a child. His back has shiny scars from the things his father did to him.

It's why he thinks this is normal. It's why he thinks it's okay.

It's why he'll never let me go.

"Are you sorry for hurting me?" he asks, and I nod, hating myself a little more that I feel sorry at all — it's just not for the reason he hopes.

I'm sorry because it was stupid, because there was nothing I could have done to get away from him, and I'm even more sorry that I didn't jab it into his throat when I had the chance, because I'm certain it's the last time I'll get my hands on anything sharp anytime soon.

He coos at me, making a soft noise in his chest as he smooths his massive hand across my cheek to brush away the tears. "And do you swear not to take the Lord's name in vain anymore? Either God or our savior?"

I nod because I want the goddamn soap out of my mouth, but I do make a mental note to try and curb the language. At least out loud. That's easy enough to avoid a punishment.

"I'm just helping you to be a good wife, to walk the right path. You'll see." Reaching behind my head he unties the handkerchief and eases the soap out of my mouth. I work my jaw, flinching as my teeth come together and I can feel the soap embedded in them, tasting the bitter waxy flavor again. He reaches down to wipe the corner of my mouth, and I only flinch a little, but he doesn't seem to notice anyway. "You did well today, Jasmine. I am not forgetting that just because the Devil led you astray."

I should probably say thank you, or... something, but nothing comes to my lips as I watch his eyes trail lower. With a gentle touch to my arm, he helps me stand and I try not to jerk away as he straightens out my twisted underwear and slides them up, under my dress and over my blistered skin until they're in place again. His touch brings back the nausea in an instant, but I force it down.

"Come."

I stare at him in silence as he stands and guides me forward, back to the kitchen. I know better than to ask him to free my arms, even though my shoulders ache and my hands are tingling a little — he won't do it. But when he walks me to the corner beside the small kitchen table and turns me to face it, I can feel my anger flickering underneath the numbness brought on by his punishment.

"You'll stay here to think about your actions and contemplate how you can keep yourself closer to God so that the Devil cannot reach you so easily." He's close to me, his shirt touching my hands as his palms slide down to rest on my hips. "If you behave, I'll feed you dinner."

I turn to look at him, almost in shock, but he just stares at me until I face the corner again. Dull, off-white paint that shows cracks in the depth of the corner where the two walls meet. As soon as I'm obediently in position again, I hear him leave the room, his boots making the floor creak as he goes into the downstairs bathroom.

It's miserable staring at the wall, listening to him clean up the wound I gave him before he finally starts dinner. The scents immediately rouse my hunger, but I refuse to turn and look at him. I'm not going to give him another excuse to hurt me, not going to tempt him to drag me out to the barn and give me what I'd expected the moment I realized I'd stabbed him.

In the scheme of things, I'm damn lucky, and I hate that it's true.

He wants me to think about God and the Devil and being penitent, but all I'm thinking about is how I'm going to survive this — if I even *want* to survive this. Eventually my birth control pills will run out, even though I'm only taking one every three days, and that's already risky. I've read the little paper insert a hundred times, and I know that even skipping one pill statistically increases the likelihood of pregnancy, but I need them to last. I only have one pack left, and one pill left in this pack. That's... what? Two more months of shaky safety?

Do I even want to survive this hell that long?

The idea of it weighs me down, leaves my chest aching and cold as I stare at the blank wall and torture myself with thoughts of getting pregnant, carrying his child. My stomach turns at the idea, but I don't even know if I'll survive to next week, much less two months.

Worry about one thing at a time, Sloane.

The bang of the oven door and the smell of smoke makes me turn my head, but I correct myself instantly as I realize it was just him taking the steaks out of the oven. The smell makes my mouth water, which is a misery all on its own because it refreshes the taste of soap.

A few minutes later, I can hear dishes laid on the table behind me, the clatter of silverware, and running water in the sink. But, I stay where I'm supposed to be. Staring at the wall, pointedly *not* thinking about what his God wants of me.

"Jasmine, you may take your seat."

I turn to find him holding out my chair, and I approach it, hesitating beside it before I realize he doesn't have any plans to unbind my hands. *Shit.* Biting my lip to avoid saying something stupid, I gingerly sit down, feeling my eyes sting as my burning ass makes contact with the chair. He nudges my chair in, and I try to find a comfortable position to sit with my arms still tied by his belt. Clearing my throat, I

Jasmine

keep my eyes on the plate of food in front of me. "May I have some water? Please?"

He immediately lifts it to my lips, and only a little spills past my mouth as I pull in a large sip and swish my mouth, feeling the soap bubble into suds. I start to stand to spit it out in the sink, but he catches my arm and nudges me back into the seat. "Swallow it, Jasmine. No avoiding your punishment by washing it away."

For one delightful moment I imagine spitting the water in his face, but then I think about what would come after... and I swallow. It turns my stomach, and suddenly the meal doesn't look good anymore.

"Bow your head so we can pray." Clasping his massive hands, he sets them on the edge of the table and begins to speak. "Lord, bless this day and the food we are about to eat. Bless our home, and know that we are grateful for Your guidance in all things and praise You for the lessons You have given us this day to keep the Devil at bay. May we be fruitful and honor Your name in all ways. Amen."

His eyes lift to mine, and I can tell he knows I didn't bow my head, but I whisper "Amen" to keep him from doing something.

He cuts himself a bite of steak first, putting it in his mouth to chew while he reaches over to cut me a small piece. I hate being dependent on him, it's terrible, but I can't do anything except open my mouth for him to feed me.

It tastes like soap-glazed steak. Disgusting.

Long before I'm full, I lie and tell him I can't eat anymore. Mostly because I can't stomach another soapy bite of steak or potatoes or the slimy okra, but also because the way he feeds me is so gentle that if my hands were free, I'd probably have stabbed him with a fork by now.

His violence terrifies me, but his gentleness gets under my skin in a way that makes *me* want to hurt him. It's because it's a lie. Everything is a lie. His fictional justifications for doing this shit to me, the name he uses for me, the girl he thinks I am... all a lie.

The only thing that's real is the hard-on deforming his slacks and the blood staining his white shirt. That's it.

I watch him finish dinner, biting my tongue to avoid any further punishment, and eventually he stands to clean the kitchen. I'd half-expected him to undo my hands to clean, but he probably doesn't trust me around silverware yet.

Smart.

Clean and showered with my teeth finally brushed to get rid of the soap — even though I still feel like I can taste it — he lets me get into bed.

But this time he doesn't pull the sheets up to cover our nakedness.

Instead he looks at me, trails his fingers over my breasts, squeezes one lightly, and then glides his calloused palm down my stomach. I clench my eyes closed, but he stops short of pushing his hand between my thighs.

"I know that you are a good woman, Jasmine. You always have been," he says quietly, and I open my eyes to see he's

Jasmine

looking at me. He strokes my cheek and then slips his hand to the back of my neck to pull me toward him… and down.

God no. Not tonight.

"Show me you are penitent."

It's his fancy way of demanding a blow-job, and all I want to do is refuse. I even stiffen, my muscles tightening, fighting as he continues to pull me forward with his impossible strength.

This is my fault.

I showed him this early on, when I hurt so bad between my thighs because he was fucking me four or five times a day. I felt raw and I went to my knees out of desperation, hoping to stop him from using me again — but it had been a mistake. He'd come quickly, but by that night he'd been ready to be inside me again.

And now he wants this and my pussy… and probably my ass too. Just a set of holes for him to play with, and if I refuse now he'll just hurt me and make me do it anyway.

I twitch out from under his hand and shift down the bed, staying at his side even though he spreads his legs a little so I could move between them — but this is easier. Not better, but at least with the edge of the bed under my leg I can trick myself into thinking I can stop this at any point.

Another stupid lie.

He's big, like he is everywhere, and all I can really do is work the first few inches of his thick cock between my lips, my hand wrapped around the rest, but that's more than enough for him. He grunts, lifts his hips, touches my hair to urge me down, and I move because it means he'll finish sooner. Still, I'm not doing a great job. This is bare minimum effort for having a dick in my mouth, but I don't think he knows the difference.

Maybe Jasmine never tried to get out of fucking with a blowjob.

Maybe Jasmine was smarter than I am.

I can tell he's getting close, but he stops me and drags me up the bed like a caveman. A sudden yank and I'm under him, my legs spread, and he thrusts in hard. It hurts. It hasn't even been a full day since he forced that fucking wooden dowel inside me, but I know he doesn't care.

As he fills me again and again I feel the stinging ache each time his body slaps against mine, driving deep, summoning those traitorous little buzzes of biological reaction. Not pleasure. Nothing about this is good, but when I make a noise, he slows down, rocks his hips between my thighs, and I hate him for it.

I hate him for massaging me earlier, I hate him for giving me a relatively gentle punishment, and I hate him for this. For fucking me like anything other than the monster he is. For making me enjoy it for even a second.

No matter what he does, I have to remember I hate him.

I have to remember that I still need to escape.

NINE

Him

It's mornings like these that God reveals the glory of his divine perfection

Because having Jasmine underneath me *is* perfection. Her body was made for mine, made to come together like this, and although I want it to last I feel the electric tension in my spine as pleasure suddenly surges, and I groan as I spill my seed inside her in a rush.

"Jasmine..." I whisper, our heavy breaths mixing together as I kiss her in the pale light, tasting her lips. I would like to just stay in bed with her, to pull her against me and let her rest a little longer... but it's Friday and that means I need to move the cows to the next pasture. I've put it off already once, and I promised myself and God that it would be done today. That means I'll have to keep Jasmine in the basement so the Devil doesn't tempt her to sin again.

I know this day of separation will seem long, but with my seed inside her she'll have something to remember our time together.

I reach up to brush her cheek and notice tears in her eyes before she closes them. Jasmine must remember what day it is. She doesn't like the basement, and the day will come when it won't be necessary. In time she may even ride out with me and help. The thought makes me smile as I kiss her again. She's always loved animals, and one of her favorite things was to ride the horses when she came to visit. Soon we'll be able to do that again, and my chest fills with joy as I imagine the wind whipping her hair as she smiles and laughs.

I look forward to the day I see her beautiful smile again.

"I love you, Jasmine," I whisper against her lips, and then I pull away, climbing off the bed. If I let myself lie in bed I'll give into temptation, fall back asleep beside her, and the day will be wasted.

I'm about to go shower when I look down at her and notice a haze of dull red between her thighs just before she closes them. Looking down, I see the same reddish haze around my manhood, another swipe of it on my thigh, and my heart starts to race. "Jasmine... did I— did I hurt you?"

"Yes," she whispers, and I feel sick.

"I didn't mean to... I didn't—" The words stick in my throat, choking me as I look down at the blood. Because it is blood, I know the sight of it, and I feel nauseous.

She opens her eyes again, barely lifting her head to look at me and I watch as her eyes drop to my hips before she parts her knees to look between them. For a moment I see something like surprise pass over her face, and then she swings her legs over the edge of the bed to stand. When she starts to walk past me, I catch her arm as gently as possible, but she yanks it free, and I don't blame her. I've hurt her, and I don't know how.

"Jasmine, please, I don't... what did I do?" I ask, unable to suppress the panic creeping in.

"You hurt me," she snaps, stepping back from me. "Did you really think that fucking wooden rod wouldn't hurt me? It did! And then you kept fucking me! You *keep* fucking me!"

"You're bleeding," I mumble, unable to even correct her language. I look down at my body, still in disbelief. God will be angry for this. I will have to punish myself in the barn, but only after Jasmine is safe. After I move the cattle. *Tonight.* Tonight I will punish myself.

Jasmine huffs out a small laugh and walks past me, saying, "Yeah, I am."

I turn and follow her, concern burning through me because I am supposed to keep her safe. As her husband I must always keep her safe, but somehow I hurt her... even though I don't think I did anything different when we lay together. "Please tell me what I did wrong, I'll never do it again."

She gives another quiet laugh, ripping back the curtain on the bathtub and starting the water. She doesn't answer me, and I don't know what to do. Normally I would demand she answer, but I keep seeing the haze of her blood on my skin and I can't do anything.

Turning, I return to the bed and see a spot where she was. It's a shadow of red, a few smears across the fabric. If I had hurt her badly there would be more blood. Even though it's not much, it's more than enough to have my heart pounding and my vision tunneling as I go back to the bathroom, where she is already in the shower. "Jasmine, I'm sorry."

"You're sorry?" she asks through the curtain. "Oh my G— I can't do this."

"Are you still bleeding?" I ask, and she makes that sound that is like a laugh but isn't.

"Of course I am."

"Perhaps you should lay down? Let God take his time to heal you, and I will—"

"Just stop!" Jasmine makes a sound of frustration as I hear water pouring off of her. "Yes, you hurt me. You *always* hurt me, but this is... it's— it's my period."

"You're... menstruating?" The realization settles slowly over me, and I touch a hand to my chest where my heart is still beating wildly. "I didn't hurt you?"

"No, you *did* hurt me. You have to know that, you *have* to realize that you hurt me," she says and I walk forward to pull the edge of the shower curtain back. She has a washcloth in her hands, but she freezes as her eyes meet mine.

"I did not make you bleed."

Her jaw is tense as she stares at me, refusing to answer, but all I feel is relief. I didn't hurt her. The punishment was painful, but it was supposed to be, and she's healed from it. This morning I did nothing wrong, it's just her body doing what women's bodies do. It's natural.

But sadness follows quickly on the heels of relief as I realize what this means.

She isn't pregnant. God has not blessed us with a child this month.

Letting go of the curtain, I turn away and return to the bedroom to sit on the edge of the bed. Her blood is on my skin, and the bedding. I will have to shower it off me and she will need to clean the sheets, as well as my shirt, so that the blood doesn't stain. Technically, laundry day is tomorrow, but if she works on it today it will keep her busy while I move the cattle.

And as I work, I will contemplate why God did not find me fit to become a father.

Her

As he leads me down the steps into the dim, dusty basement, I cringe at the smell of damp that permeates every breath of air in this fucking room.

I hate it when he locks me in here, and he knows it. However, his 'love' doesn't extend to letting me roam the house when he's far away. I only got the chance to run the other day because I knew he was inside the barn, occupied. I saw the opportunity, knew that if I could just get on the other side of the rise leading up to the house he wouldn't be able to see me anymore. He'd think I was still inside, waiting for him, and he had... but it hadn't mattered. I'd failed.

Defeat washes through me as we stop near the old washer and dryer. I drag the bag of dirty clothes and sheets over to it, clutching the box of tampons at my side. Daniel sets his bloody shirt on the washer and then turns, facing me.

"There is a scrub brush and a basin on that shelf, you'll need to work on the blood to—"

"I know how to get blood out of clothes," I interrupt, my irritation showing through, but he just nods.

"Good. I will not be back until late this evening, but don't worry, Jasmine." He steps closer, and I have to fight the physical urge to shove him away as he brushes my cheek with his huge hand. "Time will pass quickly with good works."

I don't speak, standing stiffly as he presses a kiss to my lips and another to my forehead before he moves back. I may hate this fucking basement, but any moment away from him is good.

Just as he starts up the stairs, I realize there's a problem. "Wait!"

He turns and almost smiles. "Jasmine, I promise it will not feel so long, and—"

"No." I shake my head, sighing with ill-concealed irritation. "I'm on my period and there's no toilet down here. You can't expect me to use the bucket right now."

With a sigh of his own, he rubs the back of his neck and looks up at the basement door, thinking slowly. Eventually he shakes his head. "You must earn the right to be in the house while I'm gone, Jasmine."

"You can't be serious." The words come out on reflex, but one look at his placid expression let's me know he is.

Jasmine

Gritting my teeth, I open the box of tampons and count them quickly. "There's only five in here, you'll have to get me more. Today."

He is silent for a moment, his brows pulled together as he studies the floor at our feet. Eventually he shakes his head. "No, I cannot go into town today. Moving the cattle will take all day. I will go tomorrow to get you your things."

"But... please don't leave me down here," I beg.

His flat brown eyes meet mine.

"You will have to earn the right to be upstairs, Jasmine." He points to the napkin-wrapped sandwich beside his bloody shirt. "You have lunch, and that is all you need. Good works will bring us both closer to God today, and I know He will bless us with a child soon."

Before I can even come up with a response to that insanity, he's trudging up the stairs with heavy footfalls, and I have to clench my teeth so I won't scream. The damn bucket in the corner, with the roll of cheap toilet paper on the shelf beside it, is the worst part of the basement. Usually I'm not down here long enough for it to matter, but today it will. I won't be able to hold it for an entire day, and I'll have to change my tampon no matter what.

Motherfucker!

The rage I feel burns bright for a second before I turn to look at the washer and dryer and my fury fizzles, drowned by the futility of it all. I can't do anything with my hate. There's no solution here. The short windows at the top of the wall are too small for me to squeeze through, and the door has a latch and a padlock on the outside, not a simple door lock that I might be able to teach myself to pick.

It's hopeless. *I'm hopeless.*

And the only way I'll get another chance to run, to escape, is if I play his dutiful wife for long enough to get him to fucking trust me again. To *earn the right* to be upstairs.

All I can do is cross my fingers that the blood will keep him away from me for a few days. If I don't have to deal with him touching me, I can fake it. I can be Jasmine for him… and then I'll get out.

I have to.

TEN

Mason

Over an hour in traffic and I'm ten minutes late to this girl's apartment where the definitely-dead Sloane Finley used to live.

Three o'clock on a Friday afternoon in LA is a shitty fucking time to schedule an interview. *What was I even thinking?* I should've never agreed to work around her schedule. I should've just told her to skip classes since *she's* the one who started this shitshow in the first place. It takes me another ten minutes to find her crappy little apartment in this crackerbox complex, and I'm pissed before Trish Tucker even opens the door with a slim smile.

"Hello, you must be Agent Jones."

"That's correct, Ms. Tucker." Somehow I manage to sound slightly less irritable than I actually feel as she waves me inside.

"We can sit at the table to talk, if that's okay. Do you want some coffee?"

"Yes, thank you." Setting my briefcase down, I stretch my back out for a moment before I take a chair. Ms. Tucker returns with a cup of coffee, setting it on the table as I take my seat. The first sip takes the edge off, and I manage another "Thank you" as she sits across from me.

I flip open my file, catching the pain that washes over her face the second Sloane Finley's pictures come into view. That alone makes it clear Trish Tucker isn't the normal LA trash I deal with. Based on the LAPD's notes, I know she's a journalism student, which tells me she's idealistic, probably passionate, because everyone knows that journalism is a dying field, and only someone with those qualities would voluntarily go into it. And the look she gave a moment ago tells me, at least on the surface, she's a decent young woman who has the critical character flaw of caring about people — including her ex-roommate.

I start with the boring shit. Reviewing the same questions from her previous interview with the LAPD about her connection to Sloane. *How they met, job, roommates, blahblahblah.* She gives the same basic answers she did before. No mistakes, no slip-ups, nothing that's even remotely interesting. Trish Tucker is surprisingly straight forward, not hysterical or dramatic, and as I finish the cup of coffee, I have to admit I don't dislike the girl as much as I expected.

Time to ask a few of my own questions.

"So Ms. Finley's plan was to make this road trip as a way to generate publicity for herself?"

"That's what she hoped." Trish pushes a strand of long

black hair behind her ear, the tone of her voice wavering a little.

"And you said you were following her progress on social media."

"Yeah. Facebook, Twitter, Insta. She was posting pictures from every place she stopped. You know, in front of weird things, funny signs, or scenic spots. Just like Lexie Strassen had done."

"Right. The road trip she took right before the release of *Homecoming*."

"Yeah."

"What did you think of her plan, if I may ask?"

"I thought it was..." Trish looks down at the tabletop, chewing a fingernail before looking back up. "I told her I thought it was dumb. That Lexie Strassen had a bunch of publicists that had set it up, primed the media, and that she probably hadn't made an actual road trip at all, but had just had herself photoshopped into a bunch of pictures to make it look like she had." She stares at me as if I might think her assessment criminal, which is comical because I have no doubt she is one hundred percent correct.

"Ms. Finley obviously thought differently."

"Yeah." She presses her lips together in a thin, tight line before continuing. "She said I just didn't understand how to engage. That this sort of thing was necessary to generate buzz about herself, and that once she'd completed it she'd be able to leverage it with agents based on all the followers she'd be getting. So they'd have to fast-track her into decent opportunities to ride the wave she'd created."

I want to laugh, but I keep my face straight. "It would seem Ms. Finley knew quite a lot of buzzwords."

Ms. Tucker's laugh is sharp and mirthless. "Yeah, and she didn't understand a single thing about the reality behind any of them. That was Sloane's problem. She'd learned the lingo, and she thought it was like grandma's pie recipe at the county fair. You just follow the instructions, use the right ingredients, and — boom! — guaranteed ribbon."

"That's not the way it works?"

"No, Mr. Jones. That's not the way it works." Her tone is thick with disapproval, making it clear she knows I know better. I can't help but smile.

"You're from LA?" I ask, not wanting to dig through the file again to verify my instincts.

"Born and raised."

"Parents in the business?"

"Dear God, no!" She rolls her eyes, not even trying to mask the disdain that laces her chuckle. "My dad's an engineer at Northrop. My mom works for US Bank."

"You seem to know a lot about the business."

She gives me an assessing stare. "Are *you* from LA?"

I match her gaze. "I've lived here for over 20 years."

"Touché." She tilts her head to the side, lips pulling taut. "Then you know exactly why I know this stuff."

"Hard to escape it, isn't it?"

"Everyone has a script, Mr. Jones." Crisp, direct, and

straight to the point. She's not what I expected from the outset, the overly concerned roommate, and it's refreshing. Maybe I can be blunt with Ms. Tucker.

"Ms. Finley was naïve," I say, leaning back from the table.

"That wouldn't be putting too fine a point on it." Trish blows out a breath. "Look, Sloane wasn't stupid, Mr. Jones. I want to be clear about that."

I nod, letting her continue what she obviously wants to share.

"But..." There's another huff of air. "Yeah, as far as LA goes, she was your typical Midwest girl come to town to make it big. The thing was... she was *just* smart enough to be dangerous, but too sweet to be the kinda smart you need to be to survive here."

I can't help but chuckle.

"Yeah, exactly." Trish shakes her head a little. "She would make friends with anyone that was even remotely nice to her and never recognize until it was too late that they only had one intention — to get whatever they could out of her."

"Boyfriends?"

Trish holds up two fingers. "Two, at least in the time I knew her. Both jerks. One more so than the other."

"Slept with them?"

"Yeah. Like I said, she had trouble recognizing people's motivations. I talked to her about it, but it was always the same thing." Trish pinches the bridge of her nose between two fingers. "I was jaded, I had 'trust issues,' I wore my cynicism like a suit of armor."

"Nice imagery."

"Like I said, she wasn't stupid. Everything to her could be figured out by following a formula. You just needed the *right* formula. And Sloane was always looking for the right one, always willing to try something different if she thought it'd get her the results she wanted."

"Like going on a social media-curated road trip."

"Yep." Trish draws the word out on a tongue dripping with irony.

"She never tried the path through The Valley?"

Trish's left eyebrow goes up a tic. "Porn?"

I let the silence answer for me and she sighs.

"No, Mr. Jones. That is one thing I can assure you she never even contemplated. She liked guys, wasn't above the vanity of having a good-looking dude hanging off her arm, and — hey, what do I know? — maybe she even enjoyed whatever she gave up in the bedroom. Her boyfriends never came out in the morning looking like they'd had anything but a bang-up time. But they both left her after they got what they wanted. Getting laid here is like eating sushi. No sense in grabbing a piece in the same place twice when there's a new bar that just popped up a block away, you know?"

"The Age of Friends With Benefits."

"Wow." She gives me a look, and then shakes her head, biting back a smile. "You *are* an old dude. That is so 1995."

I laugh. An actual laugh. Not fake, not forced, but a completely right from the gut real laugh.

Jasmine

I like this woman.

"You have no idea, Ms. Tucker."

"I kinda do. You wear your cynicism like a suit of armor."

I shrug, admiring her for the quick turn of phrase. "Guilty as charged, I suppose."

"Journalism major." She raises a hand, finger pointing to the top of her head, and I smile.

"So, no porn."

"No, Mr. Jones. No porn. She had plenty of formulas she was certain would pay off. And I don't think becoming the next Riley Reid was one of them."

What does it say about me that I know exactly who she's talking about?

Clearing my throat, I sit up in my chair again. "Okay, so she takes off on this promo road trip, and it's going gangbusters, right?"

"Oh, yeahhh." She doesn't even try to mask the sarcasm. "It was a *huge* hit. Gimme a sec, lemme see if I can remember the numbers..." Trish makes an elaborate pantomime of contemplation, and I'm grinning again. "Hmm. Yes, yes, I remember now. It was... twenty. A whopping grand total of twenty people followed her. And ten of those were our co-workers."

"Those are not good numbers."

"Really? You think?"

"You were in contact with her. How was she taking it?"

Trish holds up her hand. "I know where you're going to go with this. Same as that other detective did." She shakes her head with vehemence. "Sloane was *not* depressed. She didn't go all emo or suicidal. Just the opposite. She kept telling me that it was going to take time. That you had to let these things build until they gathered traction. That it would be a mistake to panic and abort it too soon. I almost *wanted* her to go into a funk. If I could've just made her recognize how futile this whole thing was... maybe I could have convinced her to turn around and come back here, or just pull the plug on the whole thing and head straight home."

She looks at me as if I'm yet another in a string of people who won't believe what she's saying. But I'm not. I *do* believe what Ms. Tucker is telling me about Sloane Finley. The problem is that I just don't care. Caring about a dead body isn't something I do, and there are too many of those littering my past to make it happen now. But Ms. Tucker seems to be a good person, so I slap on my best 'serious agent' face because she deserves better than my normal go-fuck-yourself disdain.

Nodding, I tap the file folder in front of me. "You told her to go home, to Indiana."

"That was where it was supposed to end anyways. At her parents' modest suburban home. The humble place where it all began for up and coming rising star Sloane Finley."

"That didn't happen, did it?"

"No, it didn't! And you know that, Mr. Jones, if you've read the reports from the other detectives, which I'm pretty sure you have. Sloane didn't give up. She didn't come back here or go home. She got to..."—she stumbles on the name of the place in the rush of words that spill out of her in an angry torrent—"...that place, wherever the hell it is in Texas. The last place I got anything from her. It stopped there. It stopped there and she disappeared."

"Stockdale."

"Yes, Stockdale! Whatever!" She waves her hands at me as she says it, her voice rising, and then she holds both fists clenched in front of her face, doing her best to calm herself. "Sorry."

"No need to be." I shrug. I suppose I should be consoling in some manner, but I respect her too much now to fake that. Instead, I manage to simply smile with understanding and wait in silence as she composes herself.

"Stockdale. That's where I got her last message, along with a copy of the picture she'd just posted. The one where she tried to mimic that girl from the famous painting."

"I'll be honest, I didn't know what that was about until I read the report."

The laugh she gives is sharp with both derision and pain. "Yeah. Andrew Wyeth. *Christina's World*. Laying there in the grass looking back toward that old house and barn in the background. You want to hear something really rich?"

I give her a silent look of encouragement.

"She didn't even have the picture she was mimicking right. She put it in her post that it was a famous image from a poster for the movie *Giant*. But she was wrong. Not even fucking close."

It's the first time I've heard her curse. It's stark, the word far more brutal than it should be. The pain in her voice is a scalpel, and I wish for a second it affected me at all.

Sloane Finley isn't the only one dead inside, Mason.

"She wanted to be a star, and she didn't even know the difference between Elizabeth Taylor and Andrew Wyeth." Her voice is low, and even though I'd been honest and admitted I didn't know the difference myself, the way she says it makes it obvious just how out-of-her-element she believes Sloane Finley was.

We sit for a moment in silence. She isn't looking at me, or at anything in particular, but wherever her mind is I can see it is a place filled with pain. Her pulse beats a rapid tattoo in the hollow of her neck, and the muscles of her throat ripple as she swallows. When she comes back to the room, to the here and now, her eyes find mine.

"Are you going to find her, Mr. Jones?"

The question is both plea and resignation, a query and answer all in one. I try to keep my face neutral, to hide my natural inclination to say without words what I already know. Her eyes scan me, flicking from left to right to read what I try to disguise, and the plea fades into a look that hardens, resignation winning out.

"You aren't, are you? No one is."

"I'm going to do my job, Ms. Tucker. I can't say if I'll be able to find her, but I am going to do what I can."

She huffs out a grunt that is less recognition of my non-answer than it is confirmation of her own assumptions.

Turning away from me, she stares out across the room. "Of course."

Trish shakes her head, pushing something away inside her. If we both wear our cynicism like armor, she's fully girded herself by the time her gaze returns to me.

"Of course you are." She scrutinizes me for a moment, head cocked. "You think she's dead, don't you?"

"It is one possibility in a field of many."

"She did *not* kill herself, Mr. Jones. Okay? So, if she's dead out there"—Trish waves a hand toward the window—"then it was either an accident, or you have a murder case on your hands."

It's a dramatic statement, but understandable given the situation.

"All possibilities, as I said." I look down at the tabletop and muster every bit of sincerity I can dredge up before I turn my face back to hers. "But, in my experience, it's unnerving how often we find out after the fact what someone is capable of doing given certain circumstances. And we do ourselves a disservice if we try and hide from that fact, pretend it doesn't exist, and blind ourselves to it."

Her face turns to stone, eyes opening wider to let the hatred for what I've said slip free. *Well, it was nice while it lasted.* When she finally speaks it's with a calm voice, but one barely concealing the bitterness she obviously feels. Faux politeness wrapping a core of rage that is clearly directed at me.

"Of course I'll have to defer to your learned expertise, Agent

Jones. Far be it from me to say otherwise, given the vast years of experience you have in judging people, and me only having lived with Sloane for the short time I did. But you'll pardon me if I say I hope to God you're wrong. I really do. She may be just some dumb kid to you and everyone else, but she was a good, kind, decent human being. And she sure as fuck deserves more than just being forgotten."

"As I said, I will do my job, Ms. Tucker," I say, staring back at this good, decent person trying desperately to shield herself from pain, and failing.

"And that's it? You're going to *do your job*? Does that mean you're going to go and look for her?"

For a moment I don't understand what she means. And then it dawns on me. "To Texas?"

"Yes, Mr. Jones. To Texas. The last place anyone ever saw her alive. All twenty of us."

Nice cut. Have to admire it.

"I suppose that will ultimately be up to my supervisor, but I suspect I will. Or another agent."

She stares at me. Through me. If I had a soul I might find it unnerving. But, why would I? Whatever she might see inside me is nothing compared to what I have in all these years.

"You really don't want to be doing this, do you?"

"I do my job, Ms. Tucker." I don't have to force the stoicism into my voice.

"No, you don't. You mimic it. Walk through the paces, put up a nice façade. But you're just marking time."

Jasmine

It's another cut. One that might have gone deep if it had been slashed into anyone but me. I give her a bland smile. "May I assume you have nothing further to offer beyond what's already in those reports I've read?"

Her eyes are tempered iron, and yet I can't help but see the glossy sheen of her tears. "I'm not gonna beg you, Mr. Jones. But I like sleeping at night, so I will ask. Please. Look for her. Just go and look for her. She's out there. I know it." She closes her eyes for a second longer than normal, and when she opens them to pick up where she left off, her voice doesn't even crack. "And you may be right. Maybe she's dead. Doesn't matter. One way or another, she's out there. Someone just needs to look, and they'll find her. She deserves at least that."

I rise, gathering my things. "We'll do all that we can."

It isn't a lie. And yet it is. It's a lie of omission. We're already doing all that we can, which is almost nothing. But there is no reason she needs to hear that. If I do end up in Texas it'll be a waste of everyone's time, resources, and effort. I could bring a hundred cadaver dogs to those West Texas plains and never find her corpse in all the miles of empty land.

I leave with as much sincerity as I can manage and get back into my shitty car outside. Shoving my phone into the dash holder, I look out at the burnt orange of the evening LA sun, waiting for my GPS to tell me how the hell to get home from here. *Calculating... calculating... one hour, thirty-six minutes.* Fuck. That's a long time to sit in bumper to bumper traffic, thinking about Trish Tucker's goddamn face about to cry because Sloane Finley was too stupid to just go home and give up on her dreams like everyone else.

Ms. Tucker wants me to try to find her friend so she can sleep better at night. Would I sleep any better than I do right now if I went out there and at least *tried?* Statistics say the likelihood of even finding a body is slim, and all my instincts tell me she's buried in a hole somewhere. And even though I sleep decently as it is... I suppose it's possible.

It's also possible aliens abducted Elvis and he's partying it up with the real JFK somewhere amid the stars.

Fuck it. I'm going to have to go to Texas no matter what, so I might as well get it scheduled. After that... we can see who gets to sleep better at night.

ELEVEN

Her
___

The light outside the basement windows is a thin, darkening orange and I wonder how late it is, how long he's been gone. No clocks down here, because of course not. Why would a woman doing laundry need a clock? I sneer as I fold another pair of his boxers and thump it down on the stack I've created. *Women's work.* That's what laundry is to him. Just another task a good wife is supposed to perform. Did he ever feel like less of a man when he was down here doing laundry before he took me? How long did he have to do it for himself?

How long since the real Jasmine was down here folding his clothes for him?

I grimace as I stare at the bare floor, imagining the girl in the yearbook picture pacing it as I have all day. Counting the boards in the ceiling, angling on tiptoe to see the sky and the grass outside. It's a depressing thought, and I try to distract myself from it by folding the last few items from the fresh laundry. It's not a complicated task, it's mindless — which doesn't help the constant boredom — but it's easier than cleaning.

I would have been done long before now if I hadn't delayed so long this morning fuming, jamming an errant piece of metal into the frame of the door at the top of the stairs to see if today I could figure out a way to pry the latch free. It didn't work. It never works.

Nothing does.

"Shut up," I grumble at my brain as I pick up the cracked, plastic basket and set it at the base of the stairs before I return to the chair. It's another thing he wants me to be grateful for, providing a chair that's probably been down here for thirty years. But I'd happily have no chair, no table, a completely empty room if there were just two more inches of height to the windows near the ceiling. I'd only tried to push through those once, but my ribcage wouldn't fit. Too narrow — which he probably knows.

Of course he does. Jasmine probably tried it too.

Just when I think I might lose it and start screaming, I hear his heavy footsteps on the porch. He walks over my head, *thump thump thump,* and I follow his path with my eyes because he walks right past the basement door.

The sound of the water squeaking in the pipes brings back my anger. He's taking a fucking shower instead of letting me out. My rage carries me up the stairs to the door, and I lift my fist to bang on it, prepared to shout and scream at him — but my knuckles freeze inches from the wood.

No.

Jasmine

I back up, down one step and then another. I have to *behave* right now. I have to fake it, to play the part of his dutiful wife, his 'Jasmine.' It's the only way I'll get another chance to escape, because if he locks me down here whenever he's too far from the house… I'm fucked. Literally and figuratively.

As much as it grates me, I grab onto the railing and head back down the stairs. I even scan the basement, with all of its scant furnishings, just to make sure everything looks *right*. I need him happy; I need him to trust me.

Then I'll get the chance to run again.

Even after I've made the decision, it's not easy to sit in the chair and listen to the patter of the downstairs shower. My fists clench as I listen to the pipes squeak as they shut off, forced to listen to him walk out of the bathroom and up the stairs, the sound of his movements fading farther and farther away until I know he's getting dressed.

"Just fake it. You can fake this." Empty reassurances to myself, but I try to imagine they help. I can do it tonight because he won't want to fuck me, or he'll ruin his sheets.

Thump, thump, thump.

The sound of him returning downstairs brings me to my feet, staring at the basement door, and I quickly tuck my hair behind my ears, tugging at my clothes to straighten them.

You wanted to be a fucking actress, well, time to perform, Sloane.

Just as he arrives outside the door, I jump forward and

scoop up the basket of clothes, holding them in front of me like an offering. Like a good wife.

Trust me. Jesus Christ, just trust me for a few days.

I barely hear him removing the lock, but the light spilling down the stairs brings my head up again and then his shadow is blocking most of it. His bulk practically fills the whole doorway, an eclipse of monster, and I have to fight the urge to back away as he starts down.

"Jasmine."

"Yes?" I answer him for the first time, hating myself for responding to a dead girl's name. He pauses for a second, five stairs up, and my palms start to sweat against the cheap plastic. "I finished the laundry."

"Good. That is good." He nods once and scans me, then the basement, his eyes lingering on the dress shirt he'd been wearing when I'd stabbed him. I'm almost tempted to fill the silence, to explain I got the blood out, mostly, but my tongue sticks to the roof of my mouth. Frozen. Eventually his gaze swings back to me. "Take the laundry upstairs and put it away. It's too late to cook dinner, but I will make us sandwiches."

I nod, tongue still stiff, and he steps off the end of the stairs toward the bucket. I breathe a silent sigh of relief that he doesn't expect me to empty it and scramble up the stairs, doing exactly as he said. It doesn't take me long to put away the clothes and use the bathroom, and by the time I meet him in the kitchen, he's already laying meat on the bread.

"I can help you," I offer, hovering near the doorway, and he looks over his shoulder at me before he shakes his head once.

"Not tonight, Jasmine. Sit at the table." His monotone voice seems more weary today, and I can tell by the drooping angle of his broad shoulders that he's tired. Whatever he did outside today seems to have exhausted him, and I feel a little tremor of hope as I sit in 'my' chair.

Will he actually leave me alone tonight?

I fidget in my seat, watching him finish the sandwiches before he returns the various items to the fridge. When he turns to bring the plates to the table I attempt a smile, but I don't think I pull it off. The muscles in my face feel stiff and my skin pulls awkwardly, so I try for politeness. "Thank you for making dinner."

"You're welcome, Jasmine." He grabs a napkin from the center of the table and puts it in his lap before clasping his hands and bowing his head. I follow suit, napkin then folded hands, and he nods at me. "Heavenly Father, we thank you today for the food you provide, and for the grace and love you show us every day. Amen."

"Amen," I echo, surprised by the brevity of his prayer, but when he instantly takes a bite out of the sandwich I understand. He's tired, hungry, and that tiny, nagging edge of hope grows a little.

Please leave me alone tonight. If there is a God listening, please give me that. Please let me get out of here. Let me survive this.

"Eat, Jasmine," he commands and I pick up the sandwich

and take a bite. Mechanical, even though my stomach growls in agreement to his order.

Daniel is quiet for the rest of the meal, and as soon as he's done, I stand first, scooping up his plate before he can comment and walking to the sink to deposit both of them. It barely takes a rinse for them to be clean of the crumbs, but I can feel his gaze on my back as I set them in the drying rack.

He rises behind me, the screech of the wooden chair a warning, and I turn around to face him, backside digging into the counter edge. Right where I stabbed him last night. Fear trickles down my spine as he moves closer, and I tense when he reaches forward and brushes my cheek, cupping the side of my face with his huge hand.

"You've done well today, Jasmine," he says, flat, deadpan... and then he kisses me. Damp lips against mine, the momentary touch of his tongue to the seam of my lips, prodding lightly. Inside my head I'm screaming, my fingers scrabble for purchase on the lip of the counter and hold on tight, but I manage not to push him away.

Good wife, good wife, good wife.

I let my lips part, and his tongue thrusts against mine in an awkward way — and then it's over. He steps back, brown eyes focused on me, and lets out a slow breath. "Let's sit together."

Sit together? What the fuck does that mean?

Without another word, he walks into the family room and I have no choice but to follow. I'm playing the most important role of my life, the one that will hopefully *save* my life. I have to be the good wife tonight, I have to be 'Jasmine,' but I can't help it when my eyes drift toward the couch where he spanked me and shoved soap in my mouth just yesterday. He doesn't even look at it though; he's at the bookcases pulling out one book and then another before he faces me.

"I believe God has been with us today, Jasmine. Though He has not blessed us with a child yet, He has shown you the light of walking in his path." Daniel moves closer, holding out one of the books, which I recognize immediately as a Bible. "Before we take our rest tonight, I want you to read Ephesians, chapter five. The scripture will keep you in the light, Jasmine, and keep the Devil at bay."

Numbly, I take the Bible from him and sit when he gestures at one of the chairs. I don't think I've ever seen him sit in either of these. He's always sat on the couch and made me sit beside him. *Is this good?* My mind is working overdrive as I flip through the well-worn book, looking for the header 'Ephesians,' but I can't focus. He turns the lamp on and sits down with one of the books on cattle.

Maybe this means he's starting to trust you.

No, that's stupid. It wouldn't take this little. Laundry and thank you's? If this is it then he's simpler than I thought. But... maybe he is. Either way, it's out of my hands, so I simply stare at the words in my hands. I'm tempted to point out the whole part about the 'sexually impure having no inheritance in the kingdom of Christ' but *that* is not what a dutiful wife would do, so I keep it to myself. Then I see what he wants me to read, *'Wives, submit to your own husbands, as to the Lord.'* The whole damned section is about giving my body to him, submitting, letting him do whatever the fuck he wants to me because he decided to call me his wife.

My fingers tremble against the book as I try to wipe my face of any hint of disgust or rage — because I feel both — but *Jasmine* wouldn't. Not the insane image he has in his head of her, and I have a feeling the real Jasmine didn't submit the way he wanted either.

That's why I'm here now.

"Do you see what God asks of us, Jasmine?"

Fuck you.

"Yes," I manage to get the word past my clenching throat, and the ghost of a smile touches his lips before he stands and takes the Bible from me to replace the books on the shelves. I'm glad to be rid of it, sick of staring at his twisted justifications for everything he's done to me.

"See? I know you will be a good wife, Jasmine." He's still talking in that damn monotone, but I can hear a subtle difference in it. *Pride.*

He's proud of me for this shit, and it makes my skin crawl. As he closes the gap between us, it takes effort not to move away.

"No. You *are* a good wife, Jasmine. We were meant to be together in His divine plan. God recognizes our union and knows we are to be of one flesh, and soon we will be fruitful." His hand lands on my stomach so fast that I jump, but he doesn't seem to notice as his thumb brushes back and forth over my shirt. "We just need to stay close to God's word, to His teachings, and we will be blessed."

No, no, no. There's no way in hell I can agree with him, no way I can make *those* words leave my lips.

"Let's go to bed, Jasmine." He gestures ahead of him, and I take a slow breath before I lead the way upstairs.

You can do this, Sloane. You can fake it. It's the most important role you never auditioned for. Be Jasmine a little longer, and he'll believe you.

Then you'll be free.

Then you'll go home.

TWELVE

Him

The sun wakes me and it's like God's light is reaching down from Heaven to fill me up. There is a lightness to my spirit that I cannot remember feeling before now, and I know it is His glory. His joy that I showed mercy to my wife when the Devil tempted her, that I brought her back to His path.

She is a good wife. My wife.

Mine to protect, to lead, to cherish.

I lean up on my elbow to look down at Jasmine, and I'm still caught by the beauty of her features. The absolute perfection of God's creation in her form. Her hair looks darker against the sheets where she's curled into a ball, one hand tucked under her chin, and as much as I want to kiss her lips, to touch the softness of her skin — I wait.

Yesterday was a gift from God. I know without a doubt that He reached out to Jasmine in the basement while I toiled outside. He calmed her wildness, and His strength and mine have barricaded her against the temptations of Satan's silver tongue. Like Daddy always said, punishments are

Jasmine

penance that bring us closer to God, and though she strayed for a while... I have brought her back. The Devil will not stop trying to tempt her to sin, just like he will never stop trying to make me falter in my path, but together Jasmine and I will be stronger than him.

She proved that to me yesterday.

Dutiful, kind, obedient. If only Momma and Daddy could see her, could have known her as my wife and not just my friend... I know they would be proud. *Are* proud, up in Heaven, watching over us, but I wish they were here to know her now. To see her grow round with their first grandchild.

God, please help me to be a shepherd for Jasmine. Guide my hand, help me to stay strong for her and keep the Devil at bay so that we may be fruitful and raise our family in your light. Amen.

As I finish my prayer, I rest my hand over her stomach, picturing her round with child, and the lightness inside me grows. It is God's promise that He will bless us if I keep her on the path of righteousness.

Jasmine grumbles, her nose wrinkling as she twists in sleep, and I lift my hand to let her rest a little longer. I will get ready first, and then let her catch up on her chores from yesterday before I go into town. I know she needs feminine things, and I will provide for her as a good husband should.

It will make her unhappy to be away from me, but she will only be in the basement a few hours today while I drive to town, and I know that will bring her comfort.

Leaning down, I press a gentle kiss to her temple. "I love you, Jasmine."

She shifts again, making the soft, sleepy sounds I've come to cherish so much, but I make myself rise from bed. Keeping my promises to myself, to Jasmine, and to God, must always come before my own desires.

Her

The basement is worse today, because there's nothing to do. No more laundry to wash, nothing to do but read the fucking Bible he sent me down here with.

Dammit.

I thought I was close this morning. When he had me start cleaning the house, completing my 'Friday' chores that I would have done yesterday if not for him being out with the cows, I'd foolishly hoped he would just leave me to it. Drive away toward town and leave me, 'Jasmine,' his dutiful wife, to clean his house alone.

But, *no*.

He doesn't trust me enough yet. Not even after I gave him a fucking blowjob this morning. Not even after I was nice and polite during breakfast and during my goddamn chores.

No. When he was ready to go, he put me down here and locked the door.

God, what I wouldn't give for my iPhone and a set of earbuds right now. Shit, I'd even settle for a fucking AM radio. Something, *anything* to break the monotony of the silence ringing in my ears altered only by the soft sounds of birds outside in the sunlight. But all of that — radio, iPhone, any of it — is a form of 'false idolatry' to him. A blasphemy in God's eyes. So, I sit here, ignoring the Bible on the table, and I hum songs that I can remember the lyrics to, singing as much of them as I can until I switch to a new song when the words run out. Because if I give in to the silence, *that* might drive me mad before he gets the chance.

Movement catches my eye, and I look up to see a quick shadow cross in front of one of the basement windows, like a bird swishing past. The sunlight returns for a moment, and then it's back again. Larger. The shadow turns into legs wrapped in jeans, and I realize he's home. Sighing, I walk to the table to get the Bible so I can pretend I was reading like a good wife, but as the feet and legs move past the second window something clicks and it feels like electricity screams through my body.

That's not him.

The legs are too thin, too narrow. His legs are like tree trunks and these are slender, tapering down into normal-sized hiking boots that are nothing like the massive leather work boots he wears.

That isn't him. That's *someone else*.

Another human being.

Still clutching the Bible, I scramble onto the table and leverage the window open. "Hello? I— I'm down here! In the basement!"

Knees bend and now I can see more than just feet and legs.

There is a torso and arms and a hand that moves to the wall of the house just outside the window.

"Oh, hey, ma'am! Sorry, I didn't see you!" It's a real voice, a man's voice, a human voice with a soft, slightly Hispanic lilt, and I feel tears in my eyes. "I'm sorry to disturb you. I'm with Torros Energy, and I was out checking one of our lines, and I found a break in your fence that some of your cattle could get through. Is your husband around, ma'am?"

He says the word 'husband' and I cringe.

"No! No, you don't understand! He's not my husband. I don't belong here. He took me, and he's keeping me here, but I'm not his wife, and he won't let me go. You have to help me, get me out of here, please!" The words tumble out of me, and I know I should slow down, but I just keep going, begging him to help me, releasing every word I never thought I'd have a chance to say until finally I hear his voice cut in.

"Whoa! Whoa, ma'am! What did you say? I don't understand what you're saying!"

"I'm sorry." I start again, keeping my voice steady, trying to make it sound rational. "My name is Sloane Finley, and I've been kidnapped. There's a man here, and he took me, and he's holding me prisoner. I'm locked in the basement right now, just *please*, please go! Go and tell the police to come as fast as they can."

"¿Qué diablos es?" He sounds shocked, unsteady, and I can't blame him because I know it sounds crazy, but I need him to go. I need him to get help.

"Please just hurry!"

Jasmine

"Okay, okay, I'll go get them. Shit, I—"

I hear the noise and register the sound of it more than I do the sight at first. It's the sound of water splashing against a windshield, like driving through a puddle. Except it's not. A spray of crimson fans across the glass of the window, and tiny droplets spatter against my face. My brain refuses to believe what I'm seeing until I glance down. Pinpoints of red freckle the cloth of my shirt, my chest, and I scream.

Oh God. No, no, no.

I'm screaming and I don't stop even as I drop the Bible to the table, watching as the legs are drug away, one foot twisted unnaturally as the shadow passes out of sight and sunlight floods back into the basement. Something breaks inside me, and I start sobbing, and then scream again when I try to wipe at my shirt where the spots won't go away because the blood — his blood — is soaking in. All I do is smear the specks into tiny arcs and release another pathetic wail.

He killed that man. He just... killed him.

Climbing off the table, I stumble back from the horror show on the windows. I can hear the panic and fear in my voice echoing off the ceiling and walls even as a part of my brain tells me screaming is a foolish thing to do. What's the point? Do I expect anyone to hear me? Someone to come save me? There's no one else, only him, and he just killed a man, the man who could have been my savior. I know I should stop, because it's pointless, everything is pointless, but I don't. Can't. I scream and I sob and then he's there.

Daniel grabs me, and I scream again, but the end of it gets

muffled as he presses me to his chest, his arms holding me tightly. "It's okay, Jasmine. It's okay."

My arms are trapped at my sides and I want to raise them and beat on him because he killed that man. That man who might have gone back into town and told the police about the crazy lady on the ranch out in the middle of nowhere, and they would have come and investigated because there shouldn't be a crazy woman here. I shouldn't be out here, but I am, and he has me trapped not just in his arms but in this place where I don't belong *because I am not Jasmine!*

"No, no, no, no." I hear myself whimper and he must hear me too, because he pulls me tighter to his chest. My ribs creak, and it's hard to breathe, and I wonder if now he'll kill me too.

"It's okay, Jasmine. It's okay. He won't hurt you. I took care of it. He won't take you from me."

"Wh-what?" I choke.

"He won't bother you again. I took care of it. I will always take care of you. I will always protect you." His iron hold relaxes a bit and my breath shudders.

"Protect me? He... he wasn't going to hurt me..."

"I know. He won't hurt you now, Jasmine."

I feel his hand on my back, stroking me gently. He hears me, I know he can hear me, but he's not listening to my words. He's hearing what he wants to hear, shushing me like he would a small child. Saying what he thinks I want to hear. But, what *is* the right to say right now? In this fucked-up situation where he just murdered a man because he was talking to me? Some stupid, innocent guy who just wanted to tell some dumb fucking rancher he had a broken fence.

I let another wail escape, sob, but I don't try to fight him as he lifts me into his arms and carries me up the stairs into the house. I can't do anything about him, about this. This is never going to end until I can make it out of here... or I die.

Die like an innocent man did minutes ago because I spoke to him. Because of me.

I'm sorry. I'm so sorry.

He carries me up the stairs to the second floor, into our room. I don't fight him when he undresses me. His hands are still covered in blood, and it smears across me in red slashes that I wish were cuts that would bleed me out. End me. But they don't.

Carrying me into the shower, he just stands there, holding me while the warm water sluices over my skin. I watch as pink streams carry the horror away down the drain, and the last tiny piece of hope in my chest for a rescue gets swallowed by the drain, along with the blood. No one can save me. I'm not a princess in a tower, no one is coming for me, no God is going to help me or hear my prayers — if I don't get out of here, my only choice will be death.

I don't want to die.

As I watch, any trace of what he's done swirls away in a sheen of water that all too soon becomes clear. Washing away the evidence of a murder shouldn't be this easy, this quick, this simple to do. But for him it probably is.

Will I be so easy to wash away?

I know the answer is yes, and while I continue to shudder, his hands stroke me.

"It's okay, Jasmine. It's okay." He's offering comfort, and I want to lean away from him, lean with my head against the cool tile that might let me feel somewhat normal. Give me back some sense of life. But I can't. He's holding me too tightly, too far from the wall, and like everything else he denies me even this one small comfort.

My thoughts slow, gears in my head grinding to a halt as I remember a kind, Hispanic voice, a fleeting flash of hope, and then it all goes away.

There are lingering traces of soap on my skin where he's bathed me. He cups my breasts, fingers like claws either pressing into my flesh or brushing over my nipples. They've stiffened, a response I can no more control right now than I can the wetness he coaxes out of me when he fucks me. I can feel his cock pressing into my back, and his fingers dip between my legs to clear a path for what I know he wants. In other circumstances I would tense up as he touches me — would already be stiff — but I'm in shock. It's odd to know it, to realize it with utter clarity, and yet be completely divorced from what's actually going on.

He wants a compliant wife, a submissive slave who only obeys as a good wife should? He has that now. In this moment. I can't fight, can't react, no matter how much a tiny part of me screams to do so. I am as lifeless as I can be without falling limp to the floor of the tub.

I just don't care. I can't. For the moment, he's won, and I give him everything.

Me. His 'Jasmine.'

Jasmine

Him

Jasmine is still now. I feel her heartbeat beneath my hand as I cup her breast, and I know she is soothed by my presence. That man would have attacked her, taken her, and he's been dealt with. She need not fear him any longer.

My actions were just, as God said in Exodus 22: *If a thief is found breaking in and is struck so that he dies, there shall be no bloodguilt for him.* Jasmine knows this, it's why she's stopped crying, screaming, gone tranquil in my arms, calm as I run my hands along her curves. I want her so badly as I move one hand to her face, cupping her cheek, tracing my finger along the edge of her jaw. This time I can feel her love for me. Feel it in the way she doesn't go rigid to my touch. How she stands so quiet, placid, unmoving.

I reach down and grasp her under her thighs, lifting to position myself between legs that spread this time with no resistance. She is so at peace right now. So willing to share our love together. Maybe what I did today has finally driven the vestiges of the Devil out of her. By protecting her, perhaps she's realized that I will never let anything take her from me. That she will forever be protected and loved as long as she remains within my arms.

As I push inside her, she does not push back as she's done in the past. She is wet, eager for this union of our bodies, and she welcomes me with the quiet love of a good wife accepting her husband. Usually there is some resistance from Jasmine, an almost unwillingness to consummate our union as man and wife. But not this afternoon. Now she moves with me, rocks to each drive of my hips, and it is all a testament to God filling her with the righteousness of this as it filled me in the hours of the morning.

"Yes, Jasmine. Yes," I murmur as I thrust into her, her womanhood slick with her own desire, and I wish it could be today. Could be here and now to create life within her, but I know that cannot be the case. God's ways are infinite and not to be questioned. But soon. Soon the time will be upon us and the idea of that makes me surge harder, claiming her as mine.

"Jasmine!"

She doesn't call out my name as I have imagined, but it is still too much, too perfect. I feel that sensation again, the one I feel every time. A coming loss of control, and I drive forward with an intensity that makes my thrusts almost violent. She doesn't cry out, nor do I feel her body tense, and knowing her acceptance allows me to continue on in a way I haven't before. Holding her against the tile, I let go, forget restraint for this one perfect moment as the tension peaks inside me in a bright cascade of bliss.

And I fill her with my seed.

My body shudders and, other than the jerking of my shaft inside her, I go still. I hold her encased in my arms, pulled tight to my chest. I'm still inside her, stretching her tight as she surrounds me, and I feel no part of my seed slipping from her. Once I leave her, some will, and it has always fascinated me to know the milky liquid that both fills and flows from her is God's gift from my body to hers. The sight of it always makes pride abound within me, and I must be watchful of that sin, but I know it will happen again.

We are all sinners in some manner in God's eyes.

I reluctantly lift Jasmine from me, making sure she can stand on her own before I release her. She doesn't move, does not pull away to another part of the tub as she has in the past and I run my hands over her, touching my wife. The future mother of my children.

After a final rinse, I shut the water off and wrap her in a towel. When she is tightly curled within it, I carry her to our bed. A voice whispers to me I should make her dress, at least put on underwear and one of those feminine things she asked for to protect the bed during her time. But I don't. For now I let her burrow under the covers still ensconced in the towel, and I crawl in after her. She is tired, needs rest, and for now I am happy to lie with her. I don't feel drowsy, but rather strong, powerful. I pull her to me as she closes her eyes, cradled in my embrace where I can give her the peace and comfort she needs.

Soon, her breathing smooths and she falls asleep. Pressing a kiss to her hair, I whisper, "I love you, Jasmine."

Today was a good day, a blessed day. God looks out for and blesses the pious and righteous among His servants. Today I have proven to Him to be worthy. And I know that soon He will reward me for that.

Reward us both.

THIRTEEN

Her

He wakes me before sunrise. I'm asleep, but I feel his body move and I stiffen because I never know anymore when he's going to exercise his rights as a 'husband.' I flinch as he drags his hand over the bare flesh of my shoulder, his fingers lingering at the hollow where my neck flares out. He lifts my hair letting it run through his fingers and then tumble back to my shoulder before he slips from the bed and moves into the bathroom. The light there blinds me for a second when he turns it on, and I bury my head into the pillow to let the starburst at the back of my eyes fade.

It's Sunday, and he's up early. He doesn't work on Sundays because that is the day of rest and worship, although it's never stopped him from fucking me. He moves around, and the faucet in the sink turns on, then off. I peek quickly from the pillow to see the broad swath of his back facing me. Those pale tracks of his scars stand out where they pass over the hard cords of his muscles in the harsh light from the bulb.

I lie still, slowing my breathing as I listen to him moving

Jasmine

about the room. A moment later I feel the bed on my side dip deeply as he sits on the edge of it. I stay still, and since it's Sunday, I pray. I pray to a God I have never known for him to get up and leave.

Maybe there is a God but if there is... the God of men is not benevolent.

He moves slightly, and once again this morning he strokes my hair. He brushes through it, lifting it and letting it fall back down before he does it again. I don't know if he expects this tenderness to wake me, but I refuse. I just lie here hoping that once he's done pawing at his obedient pet, he'll leave to do whatever it is he's going to do. But God shows me how much concern he has for my prayer.

"Jasmine."

I try and still myself even further, monitoring every breath to make it smooth as I grasp and hold onto hope that he will leave me alone.

"Jasmine." This time it's a little louder and hope slips away because he wants something of me and he will have it — my pleas to his God notwithstanding. He gives me a gentle shake and my eyes snap open. That should tell him something right there, but as I turn my head slightly to look up into his face I see nothing but his blank stare looking down at me.

"You need to get up."

"It's Sunday."

"Yes."

"I... thought Sunday was the Lord's Day. A day of worship and rest."

He nods and smiles a little. Like his pet has learned a trick that he approves of.

"Yes. It is. But today is a special Sunday." He gets up from the edge of the bed, and I do too. He reaches for my hand, interlacing our fingers, and I freeze.

Don't fight. If I fight him, he'll take it as needing to provide discipline, punishment, and he actually smiled a moment ago so I don't want to fuck this up. I can't.

"Come, Jasmine." He tugs at my hand, pulling me toward the shower, and I let him. I follow, because he killed a man yesterday, and I don't want to press my luck.

I finish my shower quickly, and aside from the fact that he *doesn't* shove me against the tile and take me like he has before, it could be any other morning in this hell. It's almost worse that he hasn't, because now my brain is going ten thousand miles a minute with nightmare scenarios of what he has planned for his *'special Sunday.'*

"Dry yourself. Then you should dress," he commands, and I move, trailing water as I step out of the tub to grab my towel.

I need to get dressed before he changes his mind. Maybe if I'm in that stupid cotton Sunday dress he'll think twice before yanking it off me and pushing me down on the bed to fuck me. I start to move, but then stop. *My pills.* They're in my bag in the cabinet, and I'm trying to stretch them out, give myself as much time as possible, but every day that I wait, I'm gambling with my life. My period could stop at any time, and if he keeps fucking me, it's too much of a risk.

Jasmine

I glance from the shower to the sink. I could wait one more day, try to eke out another twenty-four hours of safety, but...

Pulling open the cabinet door as quietly as I can, I fumble out the round pink case. A cry catches in my throat as I open it and remember it's the last pill in this one. A cruel reminder of just how little time I have left. I turn the dial, pushing the pill through the foil, and then pop it in my mouth. Dry. I swallow, pooling as much saliva as I can to get it down.

He's still showering, and the faint outline of his bulk moves behind the curtain as I tuck the case back into my bag. Thank God he's too fucking stupid to realize what those pills are for. At first I prayed to God he wouldn't find them in my stuff, and when he did, and I realized he had no clue what they were for, I'd lied my fucking ass off. 'My medicine' I'd called them. And they are. They're one of the few things holding my life together right now, but the number of empty buttons, the dents of popped foil, are stark reminders that my lifeline is finite and getting shorter every day.

I reach under the cabinet, grabbing the box of tampons only to find it empty. Sighing, I put it in the trash basket as quietly as I can and crouch down to look for the new one, but the purple box sitting beside the little toiletry bag from my suitcase isn't filled with tampons. They're pads. Cheap, store brand, *with wings*. I glare at the shower curtain, knowing exactly why he bought these instead of what I asked for — but I can't bring myself to say anything. If I do, I'll just draw attention to myself, give him ideas of what to do with my body now that there's literally nothing in his way.

I hate you. I hate you. I hate you.

The words are easy to say in my head, but I won't let them past my lips. I just rip the top of the box open, grab one, and move to the bedroom. At least, if yesterday is any indication, I won't have to wear these for long.

By the time he comes out of the bathroom, I'm dressed, and his eyes roam over me for a moment before he says, "You may wear the shoes today."

He moves to the chest of drawers, and I go to the closet to grab my sneakers. Mine, not *her* shoes that I'd accidentally taken that night. The ones too small that made my feet bleed while I ran. Sitting on the chair, I think about how different things might have gone if I'd been wearing these shoes.

Maybe I would have made it. If only I hadn't fucked up.

He puts on dark blue dress pants and a crisp white long-sleeve shirt, those giant boots of his pulled on and tied as the last piece. When he stands, he reaches for me again. "Let's go downstairs, Jasmine."

I follow him in silence, still trying to understand what's going on with him today. Sundays are always a day of rest, and typically there's little that he demands of me. Fuck me in the morning, and then make sure breakfast, lunch, and dinner are made on time. The rest he spends reading the Bible, while I pretend to do the same as I make fantasy plans of how I'm eventually going to escape from here.

Right now I should be making breakfast. Instead he's gathering things from the kitchen while I stand at the island, watching as he pulls leftover roast from the refrigerator. He starts to make sandwiches without my help, because apparently I'm still not allowed to touch kitchen utensils.

He makes four of them, and then turns in a circle, looking a little confused, before he murmurs, "Oh. Right. That's where she kept it."

His hand brushes my arm as he passes me, and I hear him move down into the basement. For a second I wonder if I could lock him in, but I have no idea where he keeps the fucking lock. I'm not willing to risk him catching me digging in the kitchen drawers, because if he did I'd definitely end up back in the barn. Or dead.

Neither are good options, so, I simply stand, unmoving, even more confused by his actions than usual.

This is definitely unlike any other Sunday, and coupled with yesterday I feel completely off-kilter. I'm not thinking clearly, and it's reflected in the fact that I haven't moved from my spot when he returns to the kitchen carrying something.

It's a basket. A fucking honest-to-God wicker picnic basket. I have no words. This day just keeps getting weirder and weirder, and that's saying a lot living in this hellscape he's created.

What the fuck is going on?

He packs the picnic basket with the sandwiches and other food, and all I can do is watch. Numb. Yesterday, last night, right now... all of this feels surreal, disjointed, completely out of sync with reality. Except I know this is real. All of it is as real as him murdering that man yesterday. *Fuck.* It was only yesterday. And now... this? A picnic? He's going to take me on a fucking post-murder picnic?

"Let's go, Jasmine." He's gathered the basket, a blanket shoved under the handle that he grips in one meaty palm. With the other he reaches toward me, and I take his hand and follow. We're passing the small washroom before I realize how compliant I'm acting. But after yesterday, am I suddenly going to strike out against him?

He killed that man.

Yeah. He killed a man. And I'm pretty sure that it's only the insane notion that I really *am* Jasmine that keeps him from slitting my throat and putting me wherever he disposed of that man's body.

Fuck, I'm treading a much thinner rope than I've ever admitted to myself.

All my fighting against him during the weeks since he took me have relied on him continuing to believe that I'm Jasmine. That my defiance has been a function of the Devil taking root inside me. And he has believed up till now that with his guidance, and God's will, the evil can and will be driven out of me.

But I know the truth. The Devil is not within me. No, I'm in a dangerous dance with a madman and I need to start watching my moves and not step on his toes... or maybe he'll look for a different partner.

A new Jasmine. A better one than I've been.

We're out of the house and crossing the packed dirt of the drive toward the truck when I come out of my thoughts. It's still cool, not quite warm yet in the crystal sharpness of the morning light. There's no breeze and little sound except for the *cheep-cheep* of some little bird nearby and the sounds of our feet scuffing the ground as we approach the pickup.

"Inside, Jasmine," he commands, and I scurry around the hood to get in. Daniel starts the truck, and with a shifting of gears we're heading past the barn, out of the drive, moving along the dirt road that was my downfall. I zone out, imagining potential escape scenarios, ones where I don't make the same stupid mistakes, and I don't realize how far we've traveled until he turns the pickup down another dirt road.

I never made it this far.

The rolling terrain, the turn in the fence line here, I don't recognize any of it from my run. I swivel my gaze back around and discover there's no sign of another road, another barn, another house, another anything out here. Just a rolling expanse of endless grass stretching across the horizon.

No one could — will — ever find me out here.

Daniel continues to drive, the tracks of the dirt road rattling the dash and the glass in the windows. He says nothing, staring straight ahead, his face impassive. Whatever thoughts, whatever reverie of madness he's lost in, his face gives no outward indication of it. Wherever he's taking me only he knows, and it's clear at this point he has no desire to share it.

I lose myself in the barren landscape until the engine growls down into a lower gear, and the truck jolts over the ruts of the main road, switching onto a track that is barely two thin lines stretching out into the distance. The pickup splashes through a small stream, a sheen of bright reflection mirroring sunlight and sky, and we continue on until we come to a group of trees at the base of a rise. Daniel pulls the truck over and turns it off.

Silence fills my ears for a moment, broken only by the ticks and creaks of cooling metal, and then he looks at me. "Come, Jasmine."

I don't have any choice except to climb out, hoping he wouldn't pack a picnic to kill me out here. He closes the door behind me and leads me toward the grove. There's only a trace of a breeze, and though it has to be getting past morning and near noon, it's still comfortable. The sun warms the soil and grass around us, the smell of baked earth and dried plant life permeating everything.

"This is one of my favorite places," he says as we walk underneath the shade of the trees, but I don't respond as he lets go of my hand so he can spread out the blanket. "Sit, Jasmine."

He smiles at me, gesturing to the spot beside him, and I obey. The mixture of grass, dirt, and leaves from the trees crunches underneath as I sit, and yet it's soft under the blanket. I'm almost comfortable, and that's the fucked-up thing.

This, here — right now — under different circumstances this could be beautiful. Romantic. Instagram-worthy. A picture-perfect picnic with the trees shading us from the sun overhead, the nearby brook providing white noise to the sounds Daniel makes as he unpacks the food. This *could* be relaxing, soothing. Sexy. Except the man sitting next to me is a monster who killed without thought yesterday. Who has fucked me repeatedly, sodomized me, held me against my will and who, if he has his way, will put his child in me to create his fucked-up version of the all-American family.

No. Fuck no. Never.

When he finishes spreading everything out, he turns to me, face solemn. "Before we eat, we must pray."

Of course. It's always this way. Every meal. He bends his head down, and I mindlessly follow suit. Christ, I've already become more compliant than I ever have before. But, what the fuck, after yesterday? Would anyone blame me?

"Heavenly Father, we thank you on this day of worship for the food you provide, and for the grace and love you show us each and every day of the week. Amen."

"Amen," I echo with a whisper.

It's awkward as we sit on the blanket, my legs to my side and his crossed, because I want to enjoy this. The open air, the mockery of freedom, but I can't.

Daniel hands me a sandwich and takes his own, and we eat in relative silence, only a few polite offers of food from him, which I decline. My appetite has dwindled to nothing, because I have no idea what he wants from me.

Is this just his version of a date? Is it a test?

I can't figure it out, and his face gives nothing away as he watches the empty horizon.

A minute later, I catch his lips moving, and then he nods twice, as if he's decided something from whatever conversation he's been having in his twisted head. He turns toward me, a smile turning up the corners of his mouth.

When he pushes with one hand against the ground, I flinch, thinking he's coming for me, but he doesn't. He just stands and brushes off crumbs from the sandwiches he's eaten.

Daniel looks down, smiling softly as he offers his hand. "Come with me, Jasmine."

I shudder as I obey, letting his hand engulf mine as we walk up the small rise that leads away from where we ate. I can see another small group of trees at the top and we're almost to the crest when I first see them.

Gravestones.

Those are headstones ahead of us and I stop abruptly, stumbling as he pulls me along. I dig my heels in and he pauses, turning to look back at me with a slight frown.

"Come, Jasmine," he urges, tugging at me. I resist for a second, but he's already moving. He drags me forward, and it's either fall to the ground or follow, and I choose the latter.

Under the shade of the trees at the top of the hill, all I can do is stare. I wasn't seeing things. There are two headstones here, and slightly to one side a simple, rough-hewn wooden cross. I'm tense as fuck right now, trembling, because if I thought this day was already completely off the weirdness scale, it just ratcheted up another hundred ticks.

A graveyard. He's brought me to a goddamn graveyard.

He stands there silently, looking down at the two markers, and against my better judgment I stare at them too.

Harold S. Christiansen

Maureen R. Christiansen

Jasmine

Oh, fuck. His parents. These are his parents' graves.

There are dates, and then scripture chiseled in tight script at the bottom of each one. The granite shows little signs of weathering, but the earth beneath them is hard packed, a small mound curving gently above the natural plane of the ground, the ubiquitous grass having grown in patches over each. My throat is dry, and though the day is pleasantly warm, I feel cold as I stand in front of the graves.

"Daddy and I buried Momma here after the sickness took her." His voice startles me, and I jump at the sound of it. He hasn't let go of my hand, and my movement causes him to turn slightly and stare at me, face impassive.

"And then when Daddy passed," he continues, turning back to the headstones. "I did just like he said, took him here and buried him next to Momma." He pauses, and the next words are almost a whisper. "Just like you said, sir. Always just as you told me."

Silence returns, and I am rigid with... something. Fear. Uncertainty. Rattled more than I have been at any point today, because *this* is not what I expected. By any stretch. I'm having a hard time processing what's going on, why he's brought me here, and my thoughts are scattered like a million motes of dust on the breeze.

But there's another marker, a wooden cross made in the typical fashion of these things in a thousand movies. Two boards, one upright, the other nailed asymmetrical crosswise to it, and I swallow as thoughts race through me. Who? When? Why? And then a singular thought coalesces, and I can't stop the words that come out of me next, even though a part of my brain screams at me to stay silent.

"Whose grave is that?" I ask, pointing at the small mound in the earth, the grass thicker only where it is bunched up against the base of the unfinished cross.

He doesn't follow my finger, but looks away, his eyes flicking back and forth, fixing on nothing. I see something else too. He's nervous. No, more than nervous. He's unsure. He looks almost lost. Normally his face might as well be carved from the same stone as those two gray markers, but he doesn't look that way now. His eyes aren't focused on any one thing, bouncing across the landscape, avoiding me — avoiding the cross.

"Whose grave is this one?" I ask again, pulling my hand from his. I take a step toward it, finger pointing.

His head snaps towards me, and then just as quickly turns away again. "Hers."

"Hers?" My whisper matches his.

He won't look at me. He's staring off beyond the trees, and he's struggling, and it's all a guess on my part, but I know I'm right and I will not let him run away from this.

"Who?" This time, even though my voice is soft, I put pressure into the word.

"She ran."

That is not his voice. For the first time since I've been trapped in his hell, this is not Daniel. At least not the Daniel I know. The monster who brought me here. This is... someone else. I don't know who, but the voice is quiet, unsure.

Scared.

Jasmine

"She ran, and then she fell. It was so dark, and she shouldn't have run." His voice is cracking, choking on syllables, and I can't move.

I'm frozen in place because I know who he's talking about. Who this is.

"I kept yelling. I couldn't see her… but then I heard her. I heard her running. And then I heard her fall. I ran. I ran fast that way, and I came up on the edge because I knew it was there, and I found her, but she wouldn't move. She wouldn't get up, and I tried to help her, I tried to help, but she wouldn't move."

"Who, Daniel?"

I think this is the first time I've spoken his name. I don't know exactly why I say it now. I don't know what I expect. That asking him to say her name will change something? Anything? I know it won't. He's insane, he's a monster, he's fucking evil, and admitting that Jasmine is dead and that I'm not her is not going to suddenly make him let me go. But something inside needs to hear him say her name and not have it directed at me.

Because I'm not Jasmine. Jasmine is dead.

And he killed her.

"Daniel." His head comes around, staring at me, through me. There's a wounded look in those eyes that should make me feel for him. But I don't. He fucked that out of me.

"Who? Who's buried there?" I keep my voice as gentle as I can make it. I'm not a goddamn psychiatrist, but I think of every movie or show I've ever seen and mimic what I hope will get me the answer I'm looking for.

"*She is.*" It's the answer of a child.

I wait for the word to cross his lips. The name. Just a single name I need to hear him say. The breeze caresses us both, a sigh that can — should, *must* — carry her name from his lips to my ears. I watch his pupils dilate as he watches a movie I can't see, and I can see his lips move, see them form the word I need, hovering on the very edge of my vindication.

And then it's gone.

Clarity returns to his gaze, and I can't suppress the cry that chokes up from my chest. "No!"

I've lost him, whoever he was there for those moments. Daniel — the Daniel *I* know — is back. I shake my head, slowly at first and then faster as I see it all falling away because the monster has returned.

"It's okay, Jasmine." He steps toward me and I match him in retreat, but then I freeze. I stop because I'm walking onto the grave.

My grave.

That thought scythes through my head before I can prevent it, and I snarl, "No!"

He takes another step toward me and I bolt. I dart to the left, away from the graves and down the rise, back in the direction of the blanket on the ground. Away from Jasmine's grave and I'm right at the edge of the first copse of trees when it all collapses.

It's a weird feeling to watch the dying ember of hope flicker away. To watch like an observer as your own body, your own mind give up. I can't move anymore, my feet refuse to lift again even as a caged part of me screams for them to do so. My body shakes as he comes up behind me, wrapping those huge arms around me to pull me tightly against him. I rail at myself, cries of frustration, anger, and despair escaping in sobs that I don't hold back.

"It's okay, Jasmine. It's okay."

He believes those words, but it's not okay. For one brief, fleeting second up on that hill I thought I'd broken through. Made him see the lie behind it all. But I was wrong. He hadn't. He never will. I *am* Jasmine. I will always be Jasmine. Whoever *she* is to him now, I don't know, but it's not the real Jasmine anymore. It's a nameless, formless thing that causes him discomfort... just not enough to break through the walls of insanity he's built in this world, this hell I'm trapped in.

I'm losing myself, bit by bit, and those little white pills are all that's protecting me against his madness, but it's not enough. Every day, every hour that goes by with him, I lose a little more.

"It's okay, Jasmine," he repeats as if it's a mantra that will somehow make me stop crying, accept what is happening to me. He believes that he can help. Believes that what he's doing will comfort me, provide me with reassurance instead of turning my soul gray with misery. We're at the edge of the blanket, and before I register it, he's lowered me down, curling me into him as he spreads his legs out and pulls me tight against his chest.

"I will protect you, Jasmine. Always," he whispers into my hair as my chest shudders, breath trying to catch up with the anguish that has torn it from my lungs.

He killed a man. And he killed her.

I cry for a while, and he holds me patiently, whispering his falsely soothing words, but eventually I run out of steam. I sniffle one last time, calming down, though it has nothing to do with anything he's doing. It's because I'm giving up. Again. There is a voice in the chaos of my mind, a soft, beguiling warning that beckons me to do it. Give in. Accept this as my life... if I want to continue to have one.

"I will never let what happened to her happen to you. I swear it, Jasmine. Never."

He killed them. He killed them.

"Jasmine." He huffs out my name in an exhalation of passion against the skin of my neck, and I feel his hands pulling at the fabric over my hips, tugging the dress upward. Cloth rustles against cloth, the snicking sound of a zipper coming down, and I realize with dull numbness what he's doing.

It was always going to end like this at some point. It always does. There is no 'day of rest' for me. And there never will be.

"Jasmine." The name is a sigh of fervor as he lifts me and surges up, inside. He hasn't even bothered to pull my underwear off. His fingers simply drag them aside, his thickness ensuring that they stay out of the way as he thrusts.

Just let it happen.

I do. I let it happen, because I have nothing left inside me right now. Yesterday, the day before that, and the day before that, and every fucking day since I became trapped in this horror show, have piled up one on the other, and it's too much. It's simply too much and I'm done, done with it all.

So I let Daniel fuck me. Fuck Jasmine. Fuck his dutiful wife who will bear however many children his fucked-up world requires. Because maybe he's right. Maybe this *is* God's plan. God's will. And as he thrusts, I feel my body react, creating wetness to ease his way inside, and it's then that I feel the panic.

Was there any blood at all this morning? Did I wait too long for another pill? My throat constricts, and all I can think of is that final pink container, the number of little white bubbles left to me, and if they will be enough to stop *God's will*.

This is Jasmine's fault.

Why did the stupid bitch have to let herself get killed? She ran. She fell. Where, how, when, why... none of it matters. She fucking died, and now I'm here, when it should be her letting a monster try and fuck a child into her — but it isn't. It's me. And I shouldn't be here, I should be a million miles away.

This should be her hell. Not mine.

"Jasmine!" He finishes with a cry, his seed flooding me in jets, and I go rigid on a wave of anger that grows in strength to the fading twitch of his cock inside me.

When he finally stills, holding fast to me, I've become a coiled spring. A frisson of rage that I hold in check only by a renewed determination to never give him what he wants.

"I love you, Jasmine," he says, voice full of his 'love' for me...

and I almost gave in. Almost gave up, accepted it, became exactly what he wants me to be.

Jasmine. His Jasmine.

Fuck that. She fucked up, but I won't.

His hand moves, cupping over my belly as he murmurs into my ear, "Soon, Jasmine. Soon. Our life, our family, all of it will begin. As God wills it."

Yeah, I don't fucking think so. Too late, asshole. You almost had me. But not now.

Those pills are running out. Those little, white walls that make up my fortress are being chipped away, but I still have time. Time to fight. To plan. To make an escape. I will *not* give up. Not yet. Twisting my head, I look up the rise toward her grave and grit my teeth.

Even if I can't get away before those pills are gone, I will never give him *me*.

No. I've got one final option.

If it comes down to it, I'll make Daniel dig another grave on that hill.

FOURTEEN

Him
———

"Is it done?" I ask, even though I know her answer.

"Yes," she replies quietly, tugging on her shorts with her back to me. She always dresses facing away from me because she is chaste. Jasmine guards her body like a good woman should, and in time she will recognize that God allows her husband to look upon her flesh without sin. I don't tell her to turn around, because it's not something I need to push her on, not yet, especially when there is such good news today. I was correct that her womanly time is over, which means we can once again try to start our family.

The thought brings a smile to my face as I rub the towel over my hair once more before hanging it to dry beside hers. "Good, Jasmine. I know God will bless us this time."

She pulls her shirt on in silence, still facing the wall as I gather my clothes and begin to dress. Jasmine has already shown Him she is worthy these past days. She has been the wife I always knew she would be. I have not had to punish her since the night I put her over my knee on the couch, since the night I showed her love and mercy as Jesus Christ has called on each of us to do. *That* was when I finally stepped between the Devil and Jasmine, when I finally pulled her out of his grasp so she could stand in the light of God's path.

Since then, every day with her has been bliss, and that blessing assures me a child will follow soon. Perhaps it will even happen today.

"Put on your shoes, Jasmine."

The command makes her turn around, and she looks confused as she passes me to get them. I am overjoyed that she did not question me. She has not spoken against me in days, and the few outbursts of feminine emotion she's had have been because of the man that threatened her, and then the stress of visiting my parents' graves. That was my fault, I should not have surprised her with the trip to their place of rest. I have to remember she is delicate, gentle, and her emotions need a careful hand.

As long as I keep these things in mind, I will be a good husband to her. We will both be worthy.

It doesn't take us long to eat breakfast, and I even let her help cook the eggs. She actually smiles when I hand her the spatula, and we work side by side in the kitchen until the meal is ready. Eggs, toast, sliced fruit. Simple, but perfect with my Jasmine beside me at the table, and now she's cleaning up without my direction. She is my blessing, my gift from God for the pious life I've lived, and I will be forever grateful to the Lord for her.

"You are beautiful," I say aloud, a little surprised that my thoughts have escaped so easily, but I'm glad they have when she turns from the sink to look at me over her shoulder.

"Thank you." Two simple words, but my Jasmine doesn't speak often, and each word is cherished. When we were younger, she used to fill my silence with stories from school, about the animals she cared for in 4H, and maybe that is why she is so quiet. She has no stories to tell me, because we are always together now, and the stories are both of ours. The thought brings another smile to my lips. I've always been comfortable with silence, and I know that what we have together is more important than *idle chatter* as Momma used to say.

When she dries her hands on the towel and turns to face me, I hold out my hand to beckon her forward, and she obeys. Jasmine comes to me so easily now, and it brings more lightness to my spirit to watch her walk and take my hand. I still scan the drying rack to ensure both forks are in their place, but soon there will be a day I do not feel the need to do that anymore.

And it's coming, I know that. A day when the punishments of the barn will be a distant memory, and we can care for the ranch together. Perhaps then she will have stories for me again.

Her hand is damp and cool from washing the dishes, and I squeeze gently to give her the warmth of my body as I lead her outside. There are many things I need to do, but since I repaired the damage I found in the fence yesterday, I know that what I have planned is more important than the rest of my to-do list.

Jasmine jerks to a stop, tugging backward, and her hand almost slips from mine before I tighten my grip and turn to look at her.

"I-I didn't do anything," she whispers, shaking her head with wide eyes, and for a moment I'm confused... but I follow her gaze, and I understand.

"It's okay." I offer a smile as I tug her forward. "You have not earned a punishment, Jasmine. I told you, the barn is for more than penance. Come, let me show you."

Her feet scrape on the ground, still tugging against me for a moment, but eventually she starts moving again. I hear her stumble and I tighten my grip to offer her my strength as we reach the smaller door of the barn. I let go of her to open it, and she stares into the dim light inside with a strange look on her face.

"It's okay, Jasmine. Moses wants to see you again," I say, encouraging her as I step inside. I hold out my hand for her, but she turns to look out at the drive and my heartbeat picks up pace. "Jasmine."

The sound of her name brings her head back around, and although she makes a quiet sound, she still takes my hand and lets me lead her inside. Turning the lights on so I can see clearly, I release her and immediately head over to Moses's stall. He starts shuffling around as soon as I approach, eager to be let out, and I almost laugh as he stomps. Patience has never been his to claim, but he is still a good horse.

"Ready to come out?" I ask, and he kicks the door in eager confirmation. From the corner of my eye I can see Jasmine inching closer, so I continue to focus on Moses as I take his bridle off the hook and open the door to his stall. "Come on then."

Moses steps out, shaking his head before he waits for me to slip on the bridle. Turning, I guide him to the center post, attaching the lead to it before I glance at Jasmine. She's halfway to us, and I don't press. I act as if she isn't here and go to the wall to gather the brush and hoof pick. Her love of animals will overcome her fear of the barn soon, and it will lead us one step closer to being true partners.

I work in silence, ignoring the whinnies of Rebekah, who wants out of her stall too. As I finish working on Moses's hooves, I know I can't put off the farrier any longer. Both horses need to be re-shoed and that's one of the few things I am unable to do myself. The thought of bringing anyone near Jasmine makes my heart race again, that strange tunneling of my vision returning, and I can feel the tension rising, but then Jasmine's voice pulls me back.

"What's his name?" she asks softly.

"Moses," I remind her, running my hand over his back as I give her room to approach. "You may not remember him, but he remembers you, Jasmine."

She looks at me for a moment before her gaze swings back to Moses. Another step closer, and then another, and she reaches for his nose, but he shakes his head, jerking against the lead with a loud huff of air from his nostrils. Jasmine jumps back instantly, and I grab Moses's bridle to hold him still.

"It's okay, Jasmine. He just needs to smell you. Hold your hand up, palm flat." I keep one hand on Moses, and reach for her hand with the other, guiding her until she lets Moses shove his muzzle against her palm. His lips tickle her hand and a smile spreads slowly over her face as he searches for a treat. "Stay here."

Letting go of the bridle, I walk back to the wall and dig in the box of sugar cubes, grabbing a handful before I return to her. She's gingerly petting him, whispering something that stops as I approach, but even though she's tense I can tell she's happy to be around the horses again.

"This is what he wants," I say as I flatten her hand again and place the sugar cube on it. Before I can even guide her hand all the way back to him, Moses moves and takes it. A burst of laughter, like sunshine, explodes out of Jasmine, and I go still as I watch a bright smile make her more beautiful than I've ever seen her.

"Such a good boy," she says in a soft voice, petting Moses with her other hand while he nuzzles and licks her hand free of the sugar.

"Here." I hold out another sugar cube, not moving because I don't want to stop her smile with distraction. Jasmine immediately takes it and offers it up under Moses's nose.

"You're such a pretty boy, Moses. Such a good boy," she coos, and I'm frozen, imagining her using that voice with our children. Sweet and warm and kind.

"You are going to be a wonderful mother." The words slip out, and Jasmine's smile disappears as she steps back from Moses. I'm confused, and I reach for her hand to bring it back to Moses's snout, but she tilts her body away from mine and I frown a bit. "Jasmine, what's wrong?"

She swallows, staring at the floor, her hands tight fists

clenched at her sides as she shakes her head a little. "Nothing."

"Do you want to feed Moses another sugar cube?"

"No, thank you," she whispers, still staring at the floor, and I don't know what happened, but I want her smile back.

"Would you like to feed Rebekah?" I ask, knowing she always favored Rebekah on her visits to the ranch.

"No, thank you." Jasmine is stiff, tense, and my frustration builds as she continues to stare at the floor.

"Look at me." The words come out sterner than I mean them to, but her head snaps up, and I try to calm the chaotic feelings in my chest. "If you do not want to feed them treats, then it's time to groom Moses. After that we will take care of Rebekah."

"Okay," she whispers, and although I hate that her smile is gone, pushing her will only keep it away longer. I just have to give her time with the horses, and she will relax.

Maybe I will even hear her laugh again.

Her

Brushing the horses is the nicest 'chore' he's ever taught me. Moses and Rebekah aren't people, and I doubt either of them would help me escape here even if I did know how to put a saddle on, but being around them has definitely been the best part of my time in this hell.

Watching them run around the pasture, it's hard to believe

that they belong to the same place that made Daniel. He told me that Moses is eight years old and Rebekah is fourteen. She's a sweet old mare, with none of Moses's boisterous energy, but they're both good horses. Genuinely kind in the way that only animals can be.

I didn't even know how much I needed a little kindness until the stupid horse kissed my hand, flipping his lips over my palm. It was even better when he snagged the first sugar cube, licking me like a giant dog as he searched for more.

Daniel watched me the whole time, explained how to brush them, what to do, and although the entire experience would have been better without him there... I can only hope he lets me do it again. It's the only time I've felt like a real person here instead of a thing.

"The horses were always your favorite part of coming out here," he says, and I turn my head to look at him on reflex because we've been standing in silence for so long I almost forgot he was there. Running his forearm across his forehead, he leans forward on the fence, his eyes glued to where Moses is still looping in big circles around Rebekah as she grazes. "I used to think you wanted to see them more than you wanted to see me."

I'm sure that was true for the real Jasmine too.

He looks over at me, and I make myself stay still as he curls a strand of hair over my ear, even though the breeze immediately unseats it again. I'm sure he wants me to reply, wants me to tell him that Jasmine — that *I* — always came here to see him. But, while my acting skills have been top notch the past few days, there's a limit to what I can make myself say. This is definitely over that line.

Fortunately, he never seems to care if I participate in his conversations.

"Soon we'll go riding again, Jasmine. Just you and me, like we used to." Daniel grabs my arm gently and pulls me closer, tucking me in front of him so that I'm trapped between him and the fence. When he moves in close, the bulge in his jeans is unavoidable as he presses against my back, hands on my hips to keep me exactly where he wants me while he not-so-subtly grinds against me. "And sometimes we can ride together, my arms around you like this. Daddy never let us ride together, but we can now, and I know Moses can carry us both."

I don't have words for that image. Trapped against him on a horse, it would be worse than this. He snakes his hand across my stomach as he wraps an arm around my middle, pulling me tighter to him while his lips trace kisses down my neck.

"Just like this, Jasmine," he says, his voice a little lower as he continues to rub his hard-on into my back. "You want that too, don't you?"

No. I grit my teeth to keep the word inside, trying to ignore the sensation of him touching me, grinding against me, and I focus on the horses. Moses and Rebekah. Freer than me, but both grazing contentedly in the wide-open grass. Standing, tails flicking back and forth, instead of running. If they wanted to, they could leave here. Run, jump the fences, and escape. Part of me wishes they would, because they're too good for this place. Too good to live in that terrible barn.

"Jasmine?"

He actually wants me to fucking answer? For a brief

moment I imagine what would happen if I told him 'no,' if I told him that I didn't want him touching me, that I never wanted him to touch me again — but the result wouldn't matter. He'd either ignore me or punish me, and neither would get me closer to escape. So, I play the part and say the only answer he wants, "Yes. I do."

A low sound escapes his chest, and it rumbles against my back as he squeezes me tighter to him, making my ribs ache for a moment before he relaxes his grip. "We will do that. Soon. I promise, Jasmine."

"Thank you." My answer is robotic, automatic, but he groans against my ear and grabs my chin, turning my head until his lips are able to capture mine. My short sound of surprise is caught against his mouth, and I can't move back because his massive hand is still holding my face. Then his tongue is seeking mine, and I try to shut down like I have over the past few days. To give him exactly what he wants so that I can keep the tiny fire of rebellion burning inside, deep down where he can't reach it. But when I feel his fingers at the button on my shorts, instinct takes over and I grab his wrist in a fierce grip and he breaks the kiss.

"It's okay, Jasmine. No one will see. There's no one here." He means for that to be comforting, but it's the opposite. It's damning, crushing, devastating.

I just want a minute away from him. Just one more minute to watch the horses and pretend this isn't hell on earth — but he doesn't stop. He pulls me tighter to him, his free hand working at my shorts until they're open and his big hand moves inside. Fumbling, he shoves my shorts further down so he can get between my legs, inside my underwear so his clumsy fingers can stroke where I'm still dry as a bone.

"Kiss me," he commands as he prods me below, and when I don't immediately obey, he grabs my face to bring my lips to his. It's torture being unable to do anything, to defend myself, to stop this. I grab onto the fence post just for something to anchor me to a space outside of him, away from the thrust of his tongue in my mouth and the mauling way his fingers—

Oh fuck.

My hips jerk as his juvenile efforts between my thighs actually manage to rub against my clit, and I know it's accidental... at least at first, but then it happens again. He's trying to work his fingers inside me, but his fucking hand is so big that he's rubbing back and forth over just the right — horribly wrong — spot. I can't stop the twitch of my body with each stunning twinge of pleasure. I've felt so little *good* in everything he's done that it's like my body has been starved for it, craving it, and now it's so desperate that anything at all is registering like a goddamn firework through my nervous system.

And, goddammit, I'm pretty sure I just moaned.

"Jasmine," he mumbles against my mouth, a low growled version of the name that I hate, but even that can't make my body stop seeking the friction of his hand. "Do you like that?"

It sounds so confused, so naïvely hopeful, and I hate myself... but I nod.

"Okay." He starts to move his hand, but it's wrong and I

whine, shifting and twisting my hips until he's back on the right spot where I can feel good for just a moment. *Just one more minute.* It's a lie, but at least it's a good one, and in some act of his cruel God's intervention, he starts to rub my clit. I don't know if it's just because his fingers are so damn big, or if he's a miraculously quick learner, but he's got it.

"Circles," I whisper, my fingernails digging into the wood of the fence as I curse myself for allowing this.

"What, Jasmine?" He leans down, closer, and I clench my eyes tight. Shutting out Moses and Rebekah and sunlight and *him*.

"Do circles. Please." I force the words out through clenched teeth, because I don't want to encourage this — but I do. God help me, I just want something to feel good in this nightmare, and this feels good. He changes from the awkward up and down motion to circles, just as I asked, and I choke back the quiet cry of pleasure. I try to take a step, to spread my legs for him, and almost trip over the shorts tangled around my ankles.

"Does this feel good?" he asks, seeking confirmation like every one of my high school boyfriends, and I make myself nod again because I just need a little more. A little more and I can tell him — *ask* him to stop.

"Please," I whine, begging for more for what should be the first, and last, time ever. Not like I'm hiding any of this successfully. Pressed back against his hard chest, I know he can feel every lift of my hips, hear every stifled moan as it rolls up my throat, but I'm too far in to turn back now.

Little tendrils of bliss are snaking their way over my bones, winding up my spine like golden strands of ivy, and he's so goddamned strong that every swirl of his fingers feels like a pulse through every nerve ending. I'm panting, scattered, but somewhere in the haze of arching into his chest and feeling his hand sliding under my shirt, I manage to free one of my shoes so I can step out of my shorts — and I part my thighs for him. It's self-serving, desperate, but no less wrong.

I'm grinding against my monster's hand, half-supported by his arm angled across my torso where his other hand is working inside my bra. I wish I could hate the way his thumb rolls over my nipple, the way his fingers dig into the flesh of my breast for a moment before he cups it gently again... but I like it. I like all of this, and I'm going to pay for it.

"Faster, please," I plead, panting, and he kisses my neck, licks my sweat-soaked skin, and rolls his fingers faster. Every shining strand inside me starts to tighten, my muscles stretching as I lift on tiptoe, and he lets me, supports me, holds me as I arch against him and the world starts to fray at the edges. "God, yes!"

Ecstasy hits like a bomb going off, and I think I shout or scream or cry as the glittering shrapnel turns my veins to fire. I come so hard colors bounce behind my eyes, and for one perfect moment I only feel good. I feel incredible, even as somewhere outside the bright glow his thick fingers are slipping down and then inside. I can't help the moan as my body shivers, and then I'm lifted off my feet.

My eyes open to bright sunlight reflecting off shiny metal just before he bends me over it. I catch myself on my arms, my feet barely able to reach the dirt as he presses against my ass, his fingers still buried deep. A low groan rumbles in his chest as his other hand squeezes my hip before yanking my underwear down.

"You're so wet, Jasmine," he says in a voice I don't recognize. It's hungry, edged by a growling undertone that I've never heard from him. Then he forces his fingers deeper and I whine because it aches, but in a way that my damned body likes.

Then they're gone, ripped away, and I try to stand up, but he picks me up like a toy and pushes me farther forward onto the shiny metal box. Shoved down hard, I lose my breath for a second, but then he's behind me again. Fingers back inside, and my hips twitch on instinct at the forceful stretch.

"That was beautiful to watch. You are so beautiful." His words aren't soft, they're things with rough edges, punctuated with thrusts of his fingers until he takes them away, and his cock takes their place.

He takes his time with the first few inches, and I hate him for it because I'm still hazy, confused, and the sounds I make aren't meant for him. Not for *this*. I don't want this to feel good, I don't want to feel my body stretch blissfully for the first time around his impossibly thick shaft, but he makes me. One hand on my back, he holds me still even as I twist and try to push up from the warmth of the metal under me. Another inch, and my body shudders, pleasure sneaking in past all my damaged barricades… and I moan.

"Yes, Jasmine," he growls and slams into me so hard the fronts of my thighs bruise against the edge of the box, but I don't even care. I cry out, in pleasure not pain, and I hate myself as he starts to fuck me, and I *enjoy* it. Tears burn at the corners of my eyes, contradicted by the wet sounds I can hear between my thighs and the steady sighs and whines of my own hedonistic needs. I'm urging him on without words, but he doesn't need them. He's never needed my words to do what he wants, and for the first time my body is ready for his size, able to take him in with only the slightest twinge of pain when his hips meet my ass. But even that small pain just adds to the fire, brings back the flare of golden light in my veins until I'm drowning again.

I can't breathe, can't think. All I can do is feel. Each vicious thrust that stretches me to my limits, pushes them, and leaves me craving more with each withdrawal. The fire in my veins is too much, the heat all encompassing, and just when I think I can't handle another moment of it — everything snaps. I arch off the box, and he lets me, his hands moving to my hips as I cry out and let the light swallow me whole again.

Then the world flips and my head spins as I open my eyes to blue sky and bright sunlight. Daniel rips my other shoe off, along with my shorts and underwear, and then he's back between my thighs, cock driving in just as hard as before, only now I'm facing him.

No. Not this way.

I don't want to see him, I don't want to look, but when I try to drape my arm over my eyes, he grabs my wrist and slams it down beside me.

"Look at me," he growls, demanding, harsh.

I wince as pain shoots up my arm, but I force my eyes open, and he lets go, leaving my wrist pulsing as he shoves my shirt up, then my bra so he can lean down to capture my nipple in his mouth. The cloth bunches at my throat, held there by his hand as he moans around a mouthful of my breast. Each thrust rocks me on the box, but the pleasure is a distant thunder as reality descends again.

This isn't some boyfriend, or even some one-night stand... this is my monster. The man who has tortured me, brutalized me, imprisoned me — although Daniel doesn't look like himself as he leans up to stare down at me. There's a fierceness to his expression, something hard and intense and terrifying.

"Again," he commands, and I know without asking what he wants. He wants me to come again, but that's not going to happen. Not now. Not with him above me. His hips rock steadily, but he's not thrusting hard anymore, and I whine because I just want him to finish.

In a flash he grabs me by the back of the neck and lifts me up, crushing his lips to mine, delving his tongue into my mouth for the roughest kiss he's ever attempted, and then he pulls me back.

"Again."

"I can't," I whisper, and his fingers tighten painfully at the base of my skull. "Please! I-I can't!"

"Yes, Jasmine. You can." He releases me, nodding with a strange look in his eyes, and I can see exactly where his gaze is aimed. "I'll help you."

"Please, Daniel, I—" My words are cut off as he tries to twist his hand to use his fingers on my clit, but when that fails, he plants his thumb over the place *I* showed him and begins to rub.

My fault. My fault. My fault.

I whimper as I drop back to the box, fighting the weak signals my body is sending, because even though I'm oversensitive, friction is still friction. He's brutally patient, refusing to even move his hips as I writhe and whine. "Please," I beg, but there's no humanity in his eyes.

"Again." It's a simple command, and the problem is that I think my body is listening. While at first the rubbing had hurt more than it felt good, now it's changing, morphing back into teasing jerks that make me clench him deep inside. He groans, thrusts once, and then continues to torment me. Using his other hand to grope my breasts, squeezing, pinching my nipples before soothing them with a stroke of his thumb in the same tempo of the other on my clit.

I fucking hate you.

I try to get that through in my eyes, but it's hard to do that when my back arches, and all my body wants is another thrust. Daniel waits, holds back until I'm panting again, whimpering broken pleas that I won't really let past my teeth. He doesn't move until I'm moaning with every subtle shift of his massive cock inside me, until I've ripped my shirt and bra off to get rid of the constricting feeling at my throat.

"Yes, Jasmine, like that," he growls as he grabs onto my hips and pulls back to slam in hard and fast, over and over and over. I'm lost before I even have the chance to contemplate the ache between my thighs. Sparks flicker and then ignite, and I cry out as I come for him. Again. He thrusts once, twice, and then forces himself deep enough to hurt as he comes. Spilling his seed inside me with a shout while his hands glide up the backs of my thighs so he can bend my knees toward my shoulders and lean over me.

He's all I can see, taking over the sky above me, trapping me where I feel every twitch of his cock, and I'm forced to watch the way his massive chest expands and contracts inside his sweat-soaked shirt. He doesn't look like Daniel anymore, there's too much on his face, too much tone in his voice as he groans and presses me harder into the shining metal box.

This is a new low. A new depth to the hell he's created, and like all roads I'd paved this one with selfish good intentions. For this, just this, I have no one to blame but myself.

Daniel spreads my thighs wide enough to make them burn so he can lie on top of me, our faces close enough that I can feel his heavy breaths on my lips. There's something new in his gaze, something wild that makes me nervous as he strokes his thumb across my cheek. "I love you, Jasmine."

I swallow in a too-dry throat, fighting the shivering aftershocks making my muscles tremble, but when he smiles I'm not completely sure they're the only reason I'm trembling.

"I want you to say it."

Oh God, no.

"Jasmine..." There's more than a threat in his not-so-monotone voice, and with his cock still buried inside me I can't do anything. I can't be anything but who he wants me to be... and it's all my fault.

Just say it.

It's just a line. Just another line.

"I love you, too."

The kiss bruises my lips, the same lips that just damned me, the same lips I used to moan for him, to beg for him.

This is all my fault. Mine. Me.

FIFTEEN

Mason

The FBI flies coach.

I learned that years ago, after Quantico, and to this day I'm not sure why that was as much of a disappointment to me as it was. There was just a part of me that believed back then that being an FBI agent was something unique, and that being a part of the agency would come with certain perks regardless of budgets and all the other shit.

Heh. Yeah... I was an idiot.

LAX to Amarillo is a four-hour flight, and four hours in coach at the crack of dawn on a Wednesday morning commercial flight could have been worse, but today is my day. The flight is only half full, my row is empty except for me, and the flight attendants have already seen by the profile on their manifest that I'm an agent, so they leave me mostly alone. I spread out my paperwork to pretend I'm working, but I'm not. It's all a smokescreen to keep them away after they've given me my bag of pretzels and a can of Coke.

Jasmine

I could have asked for rum to go with it. But I didn't. I kept up the illusion that an agent really is a force for good, as much complete and utter bullshit as that is.

I sit in my seat and stare at the files, but my mind is elsewhere. I'm still thinking yet again about my interview with Ms. Tucker. I know I'm as jaded and fucking cynical as they come, a burnt cylinder in an engine that has wanted to give up the ghost a long time ago, but... damn her. She's pricked at something I've thought long dead and gone inside me. My conscience. And I can't figure out why. Nothing she said to me should have affected me to this degree. And yet here I am, headed to Texas just like she asked.

Except you're not doing it for her, Mason, are you? You're just doing it to flesh out your report and keep Sinclair happy. Nothing more than that, right?

Right?

I skim the papers in front of me out of sheer boredom. Sloane Finley had gassed up in Stockdale. Her little Civic had pulled up to the Shell station, debit card closing out a purchase for $32.45 for gas, followed by a $5.36 purchase from the store. Then the now dead girl had pulled out of town headed north on highway 385 toward Rita Blanca where her cell phone pinged off a tower another twenty-five miles further up the road. At some point she'd stopped and taken a picture of herself looking back at an old farm, the one that Trish Tucker had bleakly explained to me.

And then Sloane Finley and her little blue Honda Civic disappeared off the face of the earth.

I've been over this so many times it's beyond redundant, and the report is one that I can spout verbatim. No further cell phone pings, all calls straight to voicemail, and if my suspicions are correct, that Civic was parted out in a chop shop somewhere in Amarillo weeks ago. And Sloane Finley is buried in one of those gullies that weave around the pointillism patterned fields that make West Texas on Google Maps look like a Seurat wet dream.

Stop, Mason. Just... stop.

"Can I get you anything else, sir?" The flight attendant is looking down at me, all smiles, and I catch her scanning the paperwork spread in front of me. *Go on, honey.* There's nothing there but the remnants of a miniscule life cut short.

"Another Coke would be great, thank you."

She smiles, eyes giving one final dance over the pages before she leans back up to her cart. A moment later we shuffle empty cup for full. "If there's anything you need, please don't hesitate to ask."

I give her a tight, polite smile. "Of course."

I sit and ruminate for the remainder of the flight. What bothers me most is those goddamn figures that never leave my head. 68,000 women. Poof. Gone. Disappeared. And less than a quarter of them warrant a picture on the proverbial milk carton, or a poster on a Walmart bulletin board. Just another carbon copy on a conveyor belt that passed beyond an event horizon and blinked out of existence. Tens of thousands of Sloane Finleys lined up like ducks in a row, moving forward one step at a time, not knowing that their little blip in time was going to end a lot sooner than on a death bed in a hospital surrounded by a loving family.

Jasmine

I'm not even two hours out of LA and already I'm ready to head back.

Jesus fucking Christ, I'm old. And tired.

So damn tired of it all.

What little I see of Amarillo once I'm in the cab heading to the station does not inspire confidence, and the thirty-minute wait they put me through does little to improve my impression. I know I shouldn't complain, because it's really not that bad. I've certainly been through worse, but I never wanted to be here in the first place.

When I finally get called into the assistant director's office — Whitmann is his name according to the plaque on the wall — it's him and another agent. A woman only a few years younger than me.

"Agent Jones. Pleasure to meet you," Whitmann greets me.

No it isn't, but we have protocol to follow here, don't we?

"Sir. Thank you for your time." I shake his hand and glance toward the other agent, who stands by silently.

"Please, sit," he says, motioning me toward a chair. "How long have you worked for David?"

Hmm. First-name basis. Noted.

"Director Sinclair has been my supervisor for eight years now."

Director Whitmann smiles at me. "You enjoy working for Dave?"

Careful, Mason.

"I believe I enjoy working for Director Sinclair far more than he enjoys working with me."

He laughs.

"Yeah, I'm betting your lying, but I get it." Whitmann leans back in his chair, grinning. "I went through Quantico with Dave for our initial training, and I've done classes with him since. When he got assigned to the LA station I wasn't surprised in the least."

I keep my face blank as I answer. "I'm certain his qualifications were a leading factor in his being awarded the assignment, Mr. Whitmann."

"Oh, of course, of course. A very circumspect response, Mr. Jones." He glances over at the other agent, who during all this has sat silent, watching me. "Sorry, where are my manners. Agent Jones, this is Agent Rodriguez. Carmen, this is Agent Mason Jones out of the LA station."

The woman leans up from her chair, extending a hand toward me. "Agent Jones."

I return the firm handshake she offers. "Agent Rodriguez."

As we both sit back down the room goes quiet, and I take a moment to look at her. She is a tight, compact woman, with a no-nonsense look like any other agent. She catches my eye for a second and acknowledges my stare. All part of the shakedown process I figure we've both been through a hundred times.

"I read the report you forwarded. I'm sure you'll understand if I have questions." Whitmann's voice breaks me out of my reverie.

"I've little doubt, Director."

"So, you want to fill me in, or do you want to spend the next hour going through a Q&A session?"

I admire that. He's not like Sinclair. 'Dave.' He's giving every appearance he wants to cut through some of the normal back-and-forth bullshit that tends to go on every time an out-of-towner shows up at a station to investigate something outside their jurisdiction, which is definitely appreciated. I take a deep breath and rattle off the details I'm pretty sure he wants to know.

"Ms. Finley's father is an executive with Parson's Corporation. Not exactly a well-known name, but they handle the Newport Chemical facility for the US Army out in Indiana. Which just happens to be one of the largest concentrations of chemical weapons in the world. Now, as you might imagine, at the moment that makes him somewhat of a VIP, especially in certain political circles. Suffice to say he knows some people who know some people, and when his dear daughter turns up missing and the LAPD figures out her last known location was Stockdale, Texas, the case is punted directly to us." I stop there to see how well he can fill in the blank spaces himself.

Whitmann stares at me for a moment, then looks to the far wall. His lips push against each other in an almost grinding motion as he mulls what I've said over. "So, Dave's looking to use this to bolster his upcoming budget requisition, make nice-nice with... I'm guessing a California politician of some sort. Maybe a senator? And do a little empire building all at the same time."

Impressive.

"I'm certain all of that is way above my paygrade, Director."

"Oh..." He gives me a tight, knowing grin. "I've little doubt, Agent Jones."

He's throwing my own words back at me, but I'm still impressed. He's nailed this thing down almost to a T. I suppose it's not hard to understand the motivations behind this case, but I still have to give respect where respect is due. Sinclair would have dragged this damn thing out, if only to power play it for everything he could. Whitmann obviously values his time more than that.

"To be clear," I add, filling in the gap, "the U.S. Senator involved is Senator Harris. Who sits as a ranking member of the Senate Appropriations Committee."

"Ah." Whitmann nods, appraising me.

"Obviously we would react the same for any case involving a young woman gone missing, but the senator asked if we could take an especially close look into this."

For the first time in the meeting Agent Rodriguez makes a noise. It is a grunt of disdain, and I glance over to see her finishing a shake of her head and looking away.

"Of course," Whitmann says, ignoring Rodriguez entirely. "Well, I know you're aware that the local authorities did a thorough search for the young woman as requested by the LAPD, and they found no trace of her or her vehicle."

"Yes, sir."

"And while we are always willing to help out our brethren in need from LA, my resources here are stretched tight as it is."

"I'm sure they are, sir."

There is a pause while he stares at me. No doubt trying to gauge whether any part of me is being sincere, or completely flippant as I'm sure he suspects.

"How long were you planning on staying in Texas, Agent? Just long enough to fill in some checkboxes and file a halfway decent report?"

It's a goad, but I don't rise to the bait.

"As long as I need to, Director. Since so much investigation has already taken place, as you noted, my initial projection was no more than two to three days."

Whitmann nods, face impassive. I don't know if that's because I didn't take the bait as he'd hoped, or what.

"I'll allow for three days, Agent Jones. Three days. You can tell Dave no more than that. As I said, my resources are better utilized elsewhere than on a rehash just so he can give a reach around to a California senator." He emphasizes the word *'California,'* and the message is clear — he has no stake in this, so he's not going out of his way for me. "Otherwise, please let Dave know that we'll be happy to help him out. Just have him transfer the case here, and we'll take over."

He shoots me a slick smile, and I nod in return. Nothing I enjoy more than being the messenger boy between dueling egos.

"I'll pass that along to Director Sinclair, sir. Although I am certain I can wrap up whatever's needed here in the time you've so generously allowed."

"You do that." Whitmann's voice is all director-firm. "I'm going to have Agent Rodriguez birddog you while you're here. She knows the area you're going into, and I'm sure she'll be able to help out with the locals and anything else you may need assistance with."

I don't even try and argue against it. There's no point. He's not about to turn me loose in his playground all on my own, and on the off-chance I do turn something up, he is going to want to piss on it and lay claim as quick as he can.

"Of course, sir. I'm grateful for the assistance."

He glances over at Rodriguez, who is sitting with a stony face, looking beyond me to the back wall.

Not any happier about this than I am, are you?

"Three days, Agent Jones. Then you toodle off back to Dave and send him my regards."

"Yes, sir."

"Good. I'll let the two of you get acquainted and work out whatever details you need to for the balance of your time here with us."

"Thank you, sir." I start to rise.

"And let me be clear, Mr. Jones." His voice stops me.

"You get Agent Rodriguez and a car. That's it. Don't go asking for flyovers or any bullshit like that. Dave does *not* get to spend my money unless there's a quid pro quo. And the last time there was supposed to be that, I didn't get so much as a half-assed handjob. Clear?"

"Crystal, sir."

"Good. Enjoy your time in Texas, Agent."

"Thank you, sir."

A moment later, I'm out of the office, standing in the hallway waiting. I don't know what he's saying to Agent Rodriguez, but I can guess. One final conversation to emphasize keeping me on a short leash, and if I find anything, to plant a flag in it and lay claim immediately. *As if that's going to happen.* The door opens a few minutes later, and Agent Rodriguez steps through, stopping to give me an appraising stare.

"Let's go to my office." She jerks a thumb in the direction of the hallway, and I follow silently behind her.

This is a resident station, so they don't warrant their own government building. The offices are housed in a surprisingly modern bank building, all mirrored glass windows and cool tiled flooring. No cast concrete monolith dating back to the fifties for the folks here. The office Agent Rodriguez leads me to puts mine to shame. She moves and sits at her desk while I take a chair across from her.

"So who did you screw over to draw this short straw assignment?" she asks.

I chuckle. "This is as important a case as any other assignment, Agent Rodriguez."

"Uh huh." She gives me a pointed stare.

"As I said to Assistant Director Whitmann, I believe...

Dave," I emphasize his name with just enough disdain to make it clear. "Enjoys working with me far less than I do him."

"Wow." She shakes her head ruefully. "So you've seriously pissed your boss off that bad, huh?"

"For several years now."

Rodriguez snorts, and then begins tapping out a staccato pattern on her keyboard.

"Sooo," I draw the word out while she's typing. "Care to tell me what *you* did to get saddled with this babysitting job? Seems holding my hand could easily be foisted off on one of the juniors? Or maybe a janitor."

She glances up for a second, fingers pausing. Then her eyes flick back to the screen as she continues, finishing whatever it is she started. Once she's done, she reaches to a picture frame sitting on her desk, and turns it to face me. Behind the glass is a close-up of two women, both laughing, heads pressed together, one turned quarter profile as if beginning to kiss the other.

I don't recognize one, but the other is easy. It's Agent Rodriguez.

"My wife." She says nothing further, and I look from her to the picture and then back. Expression blank, she turns the photo around to face her as it was a moment ago.

We sit in silence until I clear my throat. "I see."

"Do you?"

"Well... no." I shake my head, because it's true, but I understand the essence of it. "Not entirely. But I've been around long enough that I can connect the dots." I purse my lips, and take in her sleek, fancy, glass-windowed office and realize it's as much a cell as mine back in LA is. Just prettier. "I suppose it's... difficult here."

"More so than in LA?" She gives me a look. "I would imagine, but you tell me."

I nod my head. "I'm sure it is."

"Well, then, there you go." She leans back in her chair and lets out a long sigh. "I didn't do myself any favors bucking command with the Davidians. After that, getting married just put the screws to my career even further."

I sit up a little straighter. *Davidians?* I'm pretty sure I know what that refers to.

"You were on the Waco operation?"

"Yep." She pulls the syllable out in a way that is defeat, bitterness, and sadness combined.

"What happened?" It's a question I shouldn't ask, but I can't help myself. In the ranks, the siege at Waco is something that people talk about in the same tones that first responders speak of the Twin Towers, or ship captains of the *Exxon Valdez*.

She sighs, and the story she tells is a familiar one. Egos colliding with reality and dead bodies in the wake. Carmen trying to advise a superior against an ill-thought-out plan, and paying the price in the end when it all went south.

"Anyways... we both know how this story ends, right? The guys in charge made sure my file got some serious black marks thrown in it before they took the long walk into the wilderness. And you know as well as I do that once you get a rep, you don't come clean of it easily. Especially a rep connected with something like Waco." She leans back in her chair. "You add all that together with certain non-work-related choices, and…"

I nod, and she gives me a grim smile.

"The agency doesn't have 'Don't Ask, Don't Tell' but…" She spreads her hands out in front of her, one pointed directly at the picture that now faces away from me, and she doesn't need to say another word.

"So," she adds, breaking the silence that had settled over us.

"So."

Rodriguez shifts in her chair, folding her hands to rest on the desk. "What's your game plan here, Mr. Jones? Are you just here to 'fill in some checkboxes and file a halfway decent report?' Or is there something more to your visit you want to accomplish?"

There's no point in lying. Agent Rodriguez is one of the good ones. I like her, and I don't even need to know the rest of her story. She's spelled out enough for me to draw my own conclusions.

"Nope. Your director pretty much nailed it. I just want to run up to Stockdale, talk to the sheriff there, maybe drive around a bit, make a nice clean report, and then get the hell out of your hair." I give her a tight, apologetic smile. "You and I both know I wouldn't even be here if it weren't for Senator Harris, and I'm just an errand boy sent running around until this whole thing blows over. Or the budget appropriations are approved for the next fiscal year. Whichever comes first."

Rodriguez nods solemnly. "Young girl?"

She's seen the file. She knows.

"Yep," I reply with a clipped pop of my lips.

"Always is." She stops and turns her head to stare out one of the mirrored glass windows that look out over the city center of Amarillo. "No way of knowing who it was. Meth heads. Drug runners. Shit. Maybe it was even some rando passing through. Who. Fucking. Knows." She turns to look at me with bleak eyes. "But she's dead, isn't she?"

"Yep. Number sixty-eight thousand, nine hundred and ninety-nine."

Her eyes narrow, and then she nods. "What do you give it?"

"Five years. Ten max."

"Out here? The dirt and grass of West Texas can hide a lot of secrets, Agent Jones. Don't let the appearance of wide-open spaces and nothingness fool you. Secrets can stay hidden here for a long, long time, and when they are revealed, you'll wonder how you could have ever missed it." She stretches, arms out, back curving away from her chair. "Call it twelve with some side money on eight, and you'll get some action."

"I'm not a betting man."

She grins. "Then you're in the right business."

SIXTEEN

Mason
———

The trip from Amarillo to Stockdale is two hours. Carmen — Rodriguez has me calling her that before we've left the city limits — lists off the towns, and it's like a slice of rural Americana. "Bushland to Vega and then we'll turn north to Tacosa, past Boys Ranch, up through Channing, Hartley, Dalhart, and then Stockdale."

The A/C whooshes softly, and we talk while she drives. The more she speaks, the more I realize what a wasted asset she is, which is so fucking typical of the agency, and the government in general.

"Where are you from, originally?" I ask, because the slight twang on some of her words has caught my ear.

She grins. "My voice doesn't give me away?"

"Well... you do have a certain lilt. But, hell, I'm from California. That could mean anything."

"Ha!" Her laughter is bright, genuine. "Well, now you've stumbled onto another reason why Whitmann sent me with you." She flashes me a grin. "I'm a native Texan. Born and raised."

"Really?" I cock my head, smiling inwardly because I was right.

"Yep. I was born in Dumas. Lived in Cactus for a time, and then up in Stratford when my daddy got hired on by the windfarm people." She glances out the window at the flat, tan country slipping by the gray ribbon we're on. "Where we're going is my country. *Mi gente*. My people." She shoots me another look. "*Pareces un gringo, pero eres de California. ¿Hablas la lengua materna?*"

I grin back at her. "Not a fucking clue. Umm... *uno cerveza, por favor. Alto!*"

She laughs again, and it is a joy to hear.

"Yeah, you're a gringo." Carmen gives me a shit-eating grin, and I can't help but return the same.

"So, you know this country?"

"I do."

"Anything worthwhile you want to fill me in about it?"

Her face goes serious, and for a moment she's lost in thought. "There are three things you need to keep in mind about people in West Texas. Folks here are very private, and they believe in two things: God and football. And on any given day, not necessarily in that order."

"Isn't that a bit of a cliché?" I ask, my mouth quirked into a half-smile.

She looks over at me soberly. "Not where we're going,

Mason." Her eyes turn back to the freeway, her expression never changing. "You'll see."

We continue, passing pick-up trucks and semis with tarp-topped trailers. I look over at Carmen, and she's lost in thought. "So, you grew up here."

"Yep."

"Must have been hard. You don't seem the football or God type."

She shoots me a quick glance, her mouth a slash of dismay. "While I'll agree with you about the God part, you disappoint me, Mason."

"Why's that?"

"Pretty sexist thing to say." She's got her eyes back on the road, lips thin. "Thinking I might not enjoy football."

I nod. She's right. I give a slight shrug. "Fair enough. Mea culpa."

"I never played, mind you, because girls don't play football in Texas. Least when I was growing up. But I loved the game. Loved watching it with my dad. Being in the stands on a Friday night, huddled up with him, screaming for whatever local team was ours at the time. Saturday college games, Texas Tech, A&M, UT. Sunday Dallas NFL games, or any other team if they weren't playing." She glances over at me. "Football is pageantry, Mason. People think every girl wants to be in a Miss America pageant, or a ballerina... for me, football is *both* those things. It is spectacle and cheering crowds watching highly skilled, well-trained men perform an intricate dance on a hundred yards of grass stage for four quarters."

"Okay." I chuckle, grinning at the imagery. "If you say so."

"I do. I love football. I love everything about it. I loved it then, and I love it now. And you'd be surprised how well that has served me out here."

"Fair enough," I agree, and we drive on, passing through several more towns that have 25mph speed limits through downtowns that are four blocks long, bracketed at each end by rows of neat little houses with tidy trimmed lawns. It's all so Norman Rockwell I begin to think it's a set-up. When we pass through Dalhart, I see the sign on the edge of town — 'Stockdale - 15.'

I point at the sign. "Almost there."

"Yep." The Suburban starts to pick up speed. "Sherriff's first?"

"I think so."

We slip into Stockdale just past one. It, like the other towns we've passed through before, looks as if it were punched from the same cookie-cutter pattern. There is a single blinking red light strung over the crossroads dead center of town, and Carmen makes a right and heads down the side street until she pulls up in front of a low-slung cinderblock building. The two white sheriff's vehicles outside of the building give away its purpose before the plain metal letters attached to the front. DALLAM CO. SHERIFF'S OFFICE. Carmen pulls the Suburban into one of the adjacent parking spaces, and we climb out, stretching after the drive.

"Let's get this over with," I grumble as my back pops, and we head up the short steps. Inside there is a lobby with some worn, utilitarian chairs lined along the inside of the front wall, facing a counter with a young woman seated behind it. Her mouth works as she eats her lunch, studying something on a computer screen facing her. When we enter she looks up, glancing back and forth between the two of us.

"Afternoon. How can I help you folks?" Her voice is pleasant, blandly professional, polite.

"Afternoon." I step to the counter, smiling. "I'm Agent Jones, Federal Bureau of Investigation. This is Agent Rodriguez." I motion to Carmen, who stands beside me. "We're here to see Sheriff Braddock."

"Ah, right. Sheriff mentioned you might be coming. Hold on a sec." She reaches down, picks up a handset, and a second later she smiles a bit. "Sheriff, you've got two FBI agents out here in the waiting area for you." There is a momentary pause, and then her head bobs. "Yes, sir. I'll send them back."

"Go on ahead through that door over there." She sets the phone back into its cradle, smiling. "Sheriff'll be inside. Can't miss him."

I shoot a glance at Carmen, and then we head through the doorway into a room with several desks and an office sectioned off at one end. There are two men inside, the younger of the two standing at one of the desks. The other is a man a few years older than me, standing in front of the office door, hands hanging loosely at his sides. I move toward him as Carmen follows, and when I get close enough I extend my hand.

"Sheriff Braddock? Agent Jones, FBI."

Jasmine

He reaches for my hand, a genial smile creasing a face that's seen more than its share of hundred-degree days. "Pleasure to meet you, Agent. Welcome to Dallam County."

I catch his eyes flicking toward Carmen, and when we release hands, I motion toward her. "This is my associate out of our Amarillo station. Agent Rodriguez."

She steps to my side, pushing her hand forward.

"Afternoon, ma'am." Braddock's voice is a laconic drawl as he sizes her up.

"Afternoon, Sheriff Braddock," she replies, shaking his hand firmly.

"Now where are my manners." Braddock motions to the younger officer. "Agent Jones, Agent Rodriguez, this is Deputy Nolan. Clint, this here's the FBI agent handling that case you've been poring over so diligently."

The young man steps away from the desk he's been standing in front of, approaching me solemnly.

"Nice to meet you, sir." He thrusts his hand out at me, and I shake it.

"Deputy."

"Ma'am," he pushes the hand toward Carmen, and she greets him with a gentle smile.

"Afternoon, Deputy."

Braddock turns to us with an affable grin. "Can I get either of you anything to drink? Coffee? Water?"

"Water would be nice." Carmen smiles as I shake my head,

declining. Braddock motions to the deputy, who turns and heads across the room. As he's getting the drink, Braddock moves to one of the desks, and leans against it, arms crossing his chest.

"So, Agent Jones, pretty sure you're here to quiz me on my handling of that missing girl case you sent the file on. The one I already went over with the other folks from LA. The one that I wrote my fifteen-page report on." His voice takes on a distinct edge as he continues, emphasizing the word 'fifteen' to make sure I fully understand the effort he's already put in.

Still, his tone doesn't stray more than two degrees from country polite as he finishes.

"Unless I'm mistaken." He pauses, head cocked. "Agent." He stares at me pointedly as the deputy returns from the refrigerator and hands Carmen a chilled plastic bottle.

I smile, and spread my hands in supplication. "No, sir. You are one hundred percent correct."

As the seconds tick past, I watch as the corner of Braddock's mouth rises a millimeter at one corner. He takes a deep breath, and then lets it out quietly. "Well, Agent, I'm sure your time is as valuable as mine, so why don't you do us both a courtesy and ask for what you need."

"Sheriff Braddock, I've no desire to make you review anything in your report." I give him my best 'we're-all-in-this-together' voice. "I've read it, and it's as thorough a report as one could ask for. I've been assigned to come out here by my supervisor to review certain aspects of this case, and that's simply what I'm doing."

Jasmine

He gives me a contemplative stare. "Huh. So the government sees fit to spend hard-earned taxpayer dollars sending two Federal agents out to Stockdale, Texas to look for one little lost girl from Hollywood, and when I had a missing persons case a couple years back I couldn't even get so much as a return call from your folks in Dallas, much less the locals in College Station." He shakes his head slowly, voice thick with faux confusion.

I don't buy it for a second, but the comment he's made makes me glance at Carmen, and I see by the look in her eye she's picked up on it too.

"Now, y'all will have to forgive me, because I'm just a simple county sheriff here. But it seems to me that two FBI agents sent to 'review certain aspects' concerning one missing persons case for a young woman who don't look all that important from where I'm standing might make me just a tad bit... curious." He stares at me with a gaze that's part challenge, and all pointed.

I say nothing, just give him a slight smile. If he wants answers, he'll have to work for them.

"Who is she?" Braddock's voice is flat, and now it might be just a degree or two south of polite.

"Her father is the CEO of a company that handles chemical weapons for the Army. Bad chemical weapons. Of the very nasty WMD kind."

He nods slowly. "Ah. I see." Running a hand across his face, he sighs. "So daddy has some political pull, and lo and behold now I got two FBI agents digging into me like chiggers."

"Sheriff, let me clear something up." I've had enough playing, and something he's said has piqued my interest. "I have about as much interest in being here as you have in having me here. This is all a bunch of political bullshit, and in the end, it's not going to amount to anything more than a bunch of words added to a report given to a grieving father to assure him that we really, truly did everything we could. For all the crap *that's* worth."

His eyes narrow as I talk, and I can see I'm getting through to him.

"All I want to do is the bare minimum I have to so I can add some more words to that report, tick off some checkboxes to keep my supervisor happy and off my ass, and then I swear I will dig my chigger head out of you and be on my way."

A moment of strained silence hangs in the room, and then he gives me a nod of recognition. "Well, I'd say that does clear things up a bit, Agent."

"Good."

"So..." He braces his hands back against the desk, lips pursed. "Just what *can* I do for you? You looking for a tour of Rita Blanca? Sample our finest cuisine? Watch the paint dry?"

I chuckle. "I'll get back to you on those." I glance around, find the desk behind me empty, and move back to sit on the edge of it. "A minute ago you said you'd had a missing persons case some time back. I don't remember any mention of that in your report."

"Wasn't no need. It was near two years ago now, and it had nothing to do with your missing girl."

Jasmine

"Humor me."

He shoves out a lungful of air. "Weren't really any need to call it a missing persons case, to be honest. But that's the way her parents filed it, and rules is rules." His tone hovers between annoyed and resigned. "Had a young woman who had notions of becoming a vet after she graduated from high school. Her parents had other ideas. She spent time working 'round town, mostly with Doc Atha over at the large animal clinic. Then, one day, she up and disappeared."

"Oh."

"Yep," he drawls out the word, letting the vowel tell a tale far longer than the single word does. "Momma and daddy had plans for a family. Grandbabies. Young lady had other ideas." Braddock arches his back, sighing. "Her parents shoved her in front of damn near every single male in the four counties area. Nothing ever took. My opinion... I think she got fed up with it. Decided to take matters into her own hands."

"I see."

"And Jasmine Turner was a smart young woman. Now, she wasn't what you'd call a social butterfly. She was strong-willed. Determined. She wasn't the kinda girl that just laid down and did what anyone told her to do, no matter who they were. She'd fight back, in her own way. Even if it was with her own parents, and she had plans for her life."

"Let me guess, that comment you made about not getting any response from the people in Dallas, and... College Station?"

Braddock nods. "College Station is Texas A&M, Agent. Home to one of the finest veterinary schools in the country."

"No doubt with thousands of young women coming through every year."

"A lot more than that I'd say."

I huff out a heavy sigh. He's right. This has nothing to do with Sloane Finley.

"If I was a betting man," Braddock continues, fingers splayed to brace himself against the edge of the desk he's leaning on. "I'd say she saved up all that money she was earning them four years after high school. Ain't like she had any expenses, living with her parents. And as I made mention, she weren't no social butterfly, so I don't expect she was spending money on them sorts of things. I'm betting when she saved enough, she took herself down there and got herself set up all on her own. Like I said, she was a damn smart young girl. And them folks in College Station already got enough on their hands trying to keep the peace every weekend, 'specially during football season. They got more important things to do than trying to find one headstrong girl who might have her own reasons for not wanting to be found. And who ain't broke any laws on top of that."

I glance over at Carmen, and she shoots me a knowing, sympathetic look. I've no doubt she can relate in some fashion.

"I've little doubt of that, Sheriff. And you're right."

Braddock raises an eyebrow slowly.

"This has nothing to do with Sloane Finley."

He gives me a slow, approving nod. "When we first got them files from the LA people I will admit my first thought was that this was just another repeat of Jasmine Turner, 'cept from some LA runaway. But more we looked into it, more I think your girl didn't so much as run away from something, but probably ran into it."

"My suspicions run along the same lines, Sheriff."

"Well, we tried, Agent Jones. That's the best I can offer you. We tried, and though I have been fortunate that circumstances of this nature have been few and far between"—he raps his knuckles against the wood top of the desk he's leaning against—"it's not an unheard of thing in these parts. And I don't think it'll be the last time I run into it."

Carmen clears her throat, and Braddock turns from me to look at her.

"Have you had other cases similar to the Finley one recently?"

Braddock shakes his head. "Nope. Not me. Duane Jenner over in Hartley County sent over an ATL a couple of days back on a pipeline company guy that hasn't reported in, so we're keeping our eyes out for that. Might be a similar situation to what I think we all suspect happened to your girl, or maybe the guy just got himself into something he couldn't get himself out of." He shrugs, and it becomes clear that Braddock has seen enough of these types of cases in his lifetime to be jaded in his own right. "Won't really know which it is until we find something." He pauses, pushing out his lower lip with his tongue. "*If* we find something. And who knows how long that will be."

The room goes quiet for a moment, the whirring of the air conditioner white noise to our individual thoughts.

"I have a question, Sheriff." I push back against the edge of the desk, shifting weight from one foot to the other. "The picture that Sloane Finley took. The last one that anyone ever received. Exactly where is that location?"

Braddock stares at me, brow knitting like tumbleweeds crashing together. He glances over at his deputy, and I follow the look. The corners of Deputy Nolan's mouth have turned downward, eyes narrowing as thoughts race behind them. I turn back to Braddock and now he's frowning too.

"I'm afraid I'm not exactly sure what you're referring to, Agent?"

"The last picture Sloane Finley took and posted to her Facebook page before she disappeared."

Bradoock looks at me, one eye narrowed, mouth twisted in confusion. It's clear from his demeanor he has no idea what I am talking about. "Her Facebook?"

"Yes. The Facebook page she created for her trip."

As Braddock continues staring at me as if I'm speaking gibberish, I glance over at Nolan, and he's watching the two of us, mouth half open in surprise.

"Where is the file I sent you?" I'm suddenly tense. Something isn't right here. Why are they both acting like they have no idea what I'm talking about? I shoot a look to Carmen, and now her face has gone serious too, and she's moving to where Deputy Nolan has sidled behind what must be his desk.

Jasmine

"Is that everything?" shes asks the question softly, and both Braddock and I move toward the desk.

"That's everything I have." The deputy glances up as I approach, and I come around and look at his screen. There is a folder with files, including the images I've been looking at for weeks now.

Except these aren't my files. These are the original ones from the LAPD.

"Those aren't all the files I sent you."

The deputy looks up, catching Braddock's eye. The man's frown has become a grim line as his eyes dart from the screen to Nolan to me. "I thought they were the same as what the other detectives already sent."

I take a deep breath. "Well, they should be. But you're both acting like you haven't seen the files from Facebook."

Nolan speaks up. "They sent us a link, but when I tried to go there it was dead, so it didn't seem important."

"Goddammit," I whisper the epitaph under my breath. *Fucking LAPD...*

"So, you never saw any of the images or videos she'd posted?"

"No, sir."

"Do you have the files..." Before I can finish the sentence, Braddock is moving across the room to his office.

"I'm sending them to you in a second, Clint," he calls back over his shoulder.

I turn back to Nolan's computer screen, looking at the file names to see what he does have. At first glance it looks like everything is there, except that there are none of the screenshots and images from the Facebook page Sloane Finley created for her cross-country roadtrip. The ones the LAPD amassed before Sloane's family had her account shut down.

Shit. Those fucking idiots.

A notification pops up on Nolan's screen, and he opens the email Braddock just sent him. There's a link to a location, and then he's moving the folder to his desktop as the sheriff returns to us from his office.

"I got it. Gimme a sec," Nolan says to everyone, and we watch the cursor spin as everything transfers over. Once it's done, the deputy opens it and looks expectantly at me. "Which one?"

He steps slightly back, and I take over the mouse, clicking through the nested folders until I find the one I'm looking for. The one that the idiot detectives from the LAPD sent to me, but not to them.

"Here. This one." I double-click on the last image Sloane Finley posted on Facebook, the last thing that anyone ever heard from her that day or since. It's the image that Trish Tucker and I discussed in our meeting. The one where she's lying in the grass, looking over her shoulder at the far-off buildings. "I take it neither of you has seen this image? Or any of the others from her site?"

There is silence from both men as they stare at Nolan's computer screen.

Braddock looks at his deputy, who's engrossed with the images on the screen, his face hard. He's scrolling through the thumbnails behind the picture of Sloane, and his look makes it clear that these are all new to him.

"Clint? You seen these before?"

"No," he snaps, voice tense. "I ain't seen none of these until just now."

I glance over at Braddock. Nolan's response is laced with a lot more than just annoyance at being questioned about these pictures. There's a decidedly intense undercurrent to his words, and certainly not anything expected. Braddock gives me a nearly imperceptible shake of his head, and I know there's a conversation for later waiting there.

"Okay, my friends at the LAPD's fuck-up aside, do you recognize where this is?" They both stare for a moment at the screen, Nolan drawing in his lower lip and chewing on it.

"Dammit... I know..." His voice dips. "I swear I've seen it before, but I just can't—"

Braddock clears his throat. "Clint here's our resident expert on this case. Ever since we got the files from the LAPD, Clint's taken an... interest in staying on top of it." Braddock shoots me another glance, and the tone speaks volumes. *Conversation for another time.* "He's been doing some investigating here and there to see if he might be able to dig up anything on your girl. Checking spots around the county."

"Do either of you recognize where this is?" Carmen asks, pushing them.

Neither of them says anything. Nolan's eyes are burning holes into the screen, and again I take note that he's far more intense about this than I'd expected.

"Wait," Nolan says it softly. He leans toward the screen, pointing at the two buildings in the background. "I think I remember these..." He pauses, squinting, and then he taps the screen with a finger. "It's out off County Road 143, 'bout four or five miles, I'm pretty sure."

"That's Harold Christiansen's property, ain't it?"

Deputy Nolan blinks, then stares at the screen even harder. "I think it is. Honestly, I ain't been out by *that* place in a long time..."

"Since the old man passed away?"

"Maybe even before that," Nolan murmurs. "But I know I've seen this place." His finger tinks against the screen once more.

"So... you recognize it?" Carmen's voice cuts through their discussion.

They both turn away from the screen, looking at her. Deputy Nolan is the first to speak. "Them buildings are kinda far off in her picture, but I'm pretty certain it was taken near an old abandoned house on..." He glances over to Braddock. "Harold Christiansen's property?"

Braddock nods in confirmation.

"I could be wrong..." Nolan's voice pauses for a moment before he continues. "There's a ton of these old places scattered around Dallam County." Both he and Braddock turn back to the screen.

Jasmine

"Okay." I stare back, waiting for either of them to speak. When they don't, I press on. "This Harold Christiansen... could we call him? Maybe ask if we could come out and show him the pictures? See if any of it rings any bells?"

Braddock shoots a quick glance at Nolan, and then turns back to me.

"Well, there's two problems with that." He pauses for a moment, thinking something through. "You need to understand people can be a little different out here, Agent Jones. Folks around here tend to be very... private."

I fix him with a stare, making it clear I'm not seeing how this is going to prevent us from doing what I've asked.

"Harold Christiansen was a God-fearing man. And he didn't have much use for technology and things of that nature. So... he didn't have a phone out at his place. They ran the line, but he cut it at the pole."

"Great." Wonderful. A Luddite. A freaking Godly Texan Luddite. Perfect. "So we'll drive out, look at this place"—I point to the computer screen—"and then we'll go to his place and talk to him."

Braddock's eyes snap to Nolan, and then back at me. "Well, that's issue number two." He looks down, scratching the side of his nose. A half second goes by before he looks back up. "Harold Christiansen's been dead for over three years."

I grunt. "Of course he is." I take a deep breath, let the air slide out on a '*wouldn't-you-fucking-know-it*' sigh. "Wife?"

Braddock shakes his head slowly. "Maureen died maybe half a year before he did."

Well fuck.

I guess I'm not hiding my thoughts well. Braddock gives me a grim smile. "Harold Christiansen was a big man. A strong man. But his heart wasn't that strong."

I nod. Wonderful, heartwarming story it may be, but it doesn't mean shit to me because now any chance that the Christiansens might have held for providing a clue about the last known location of Sloane Finley has just gone up in the Hallmark movie moment Braddock's laid out.

"So this place"—I point again to the picture Sloane took—"and the Christiansen place have been empty for years. Is there any chance that squatters have set up out there? Or, who knows, maybe a meth lab?" I'm being overly sarcastic, but I'm irritated at this point. So much of this shit could have been avoided if only the LAPD *had done their fucking job*!

"Christiansen place ain't been empty." Nolan's voice is quiet, but it cuts off my thoughts and has both Braddock and I turning towards him. "I'm pretty sure Daniel still lives out there."

My head flicks back and forth between Nolan and Braddock.

"That's right. Daniel does still live out there, don't he?" Braddock looks over at his deputy, nodding in recognition.

"Who's Daniel?" Carmen asks, the corners of her mouth pulling down.

Braddock's gaze shifts to her. "Daniel Christiansen. Harold and Maureen's son. Boy made quite a name for himself playing ball couple a years back. Think everybody thought he might play college, maybe even go pro. But I don't think his parents had much thought for that." His voice trails off, and he's thinking.

"Wait…" Carmen's voice is lilted with surprise. "Are you talking about that boy they called 'The Wall?'"

Both Braddock and Nolan's faces show astonishment.

"How 'n the hell do you know about 'The Wall?'"

"I know my football, Sheriff Braddock." Carmen's voice takes on a defensive tone.

"Is that right?"

"Yes. That's right."

For a moment he stares at her, and then he gives a short nod. "Well, you're right. That's Daniel. One 'n the same."

"Didn't he just kinda disappear after high school? I remember lots of talk about him being scouted," Nolan says.

"There was. Nothing came of it, though."

"People in Dallam County don't believe in higher education?" I ask, remembering that other girl whose parents hadn't wanted her to go off to become a vet, but to stay here in Stockdale and family up.

"Like I said before…" Braddock frowns, his voice taking on a slightly defensive tone. "People here have their own ways. And they can be set in them. I ain't one to tell people how to live their lives, nor how they deal with their children. 'Less it becomes a matter for the law to step in."

"Okay, I get it." I hold up my hand, hoping to stave off any further reaction. "So, this son of theirs, Daniel... he still lives out there?"

"Yep." Nolan speaks up once again. "I remember seeing him in town maybe... three or four days ago?" He looks over at Braddock. "I saw his truck outside of Mattie's Café, but I think he was over at Bower's Pharmacy. I saw Laurie Ann out front of Mattie's. I bet she seen him too."

"Yeah, well Laurie Ann got hawk eyes for every man that comes into town any given day, so I don't doubt it." Braddock's voice is bemused, and there's obviously an inside joke here where I can connect my own dots.

Deputy Nolan chuckles at the comment.

"Yeah, don't laugh, son. She's got her eyes on you too."

"I ain't interested in Laurie Ann Maddock!" Nolan's voice rises, and he catches Carmen as she grins. His cheeks flush, and then he looks away from all of us back to his computer screen. This time when I look at Braddock, I catch as his eyes slide deliberately from Nolan to the computer screen and then back to me. Once he's locked onto me, he raises one eyebrow that indicates there's something here I should understand. I trace back along the path his eyes have just come from. Nolan to the computer screen where he's once again staring at the picture of Sloane Finley looking up the hill to...

Wait. No. No way. I watch for a second.

Seriously?

"Well," I say, giving Braddock a slight rise of my own eyebrows. "I don't suppose this Daniel had the phone repaired out to his parents' old place."

Jasmine

Braddock saws his head back and forth. "Doubt it. I remember now a conversation I had with the Hernandez brothers a couple of months ago. They've gone out there a couple of times to help him with his cattle, and they say the place don't look like anything's been touched or changed since Harold passed. Daniel just lives out there by himself, all alone with the horses and cows."

"Seem strange to you?"

"Like I said, Agent Jones." Braddock's tone is chiding. "People 'round here tend to be... private. And we respect their privacy." He gives me a pointed smile. "Harold was a big man, but his boy Daniel is even bigger. And he ain't done nothing I have any reason to be suspicious of." Braddock moves and leans against the edge of one of the empty desks. "I'm betting he's taking care of himself just fine out there."

"Did anyone talk to him back when the Finley case first came through?"

Braddock glances over at Nolan, who looks up and gives a slight shake of his head.

"Wasn't no need to," Braddock answers, knowing the reasoning even without his deputy's confirmation. I know it too, even before he tells me. "Them fellas from the LAPD didn't send us those pictures, so we had no way of knowing she'd been out that direction." Braddock leans back, stares up at the ceiling. "The last ping from her cellphone was up there damn near to Rita Blanca. From there, there weren't no way to tell which way she went. She coulda headed to Hartley, Moore, or even Sherman county. Let me tell you, Agent Jones. That's a lot of territory to cover. No one's ever picked up a trace of that little blue car of hers. And we had no reason to look specifically out by that abandoned ranch, the Christiansen place, or anywhere in that direction."

"I understand. But now that we do know..." I give him my best FBI due diligence stare. "There's always a possibility he saw something. Maybe even found something."

"You looking for a big break here, Agent Jones?" Braddock's voice is polite, but it conveys all the skepticism it needs to.

"Nope," I shoot back, giving him my normal sardonic grin. "All I'm looking for is a couple of paragraphs for my report, and a chance to bust some detective's balls."

Braddock looks over to Carmen, and then back to me, grinning. "All right. I think we can help with that."

He pushes himself away from the desk.

"Clint," he calls out, and Nolan turns his face away from the picture of Sloane for the first time in several minutes. "These here FBI agents have a desire to do a little sightseeing. Why don't you take them out for a ride."

SEVENTEEN

Her

It's Wednesday. Three days since the last pill, and I need to take another one, but he hasn't left me alone for a single second. He fucked me as soon as he woke, his big hand shoving between my thighs yanked me out of sleep — and then his fingers on my clit woke me up the rest of the way.

My fault. I should have never made that mistake. He uses every single one against me, but at least this morning he was too impatient to make me come. To make me participate... enjoy it. But he did make me bathe him in the shower. Just another way for him to make this seem normal, to pretend I want to be here, that he didn't just rip me out of a field and kidnap me and force me to be his perfect little fuckdoll wife.

My anger is hard to keep down this morning, and I have to get it in check. Because my horrible decision-making yesterday had one positive side-effect... he's in a great mood. All smiles and weird little compliments that I hope mean he's leaning toward trusting me again.

I just need one more chance. One more.

I'm sweeping the floor in the living room, listening to him walking around the house, and I can't help but grit my teeth because he's been inside all damn morning. He even watched me dust in the sitting room, talking to me about how much he loves he. How perfect our family is going to be. What a 'good wife' I am.

Every word has felt like a splinter shoved under my skin, but I've kept smiling. Waiting. Playing the part because I just need him to leave the goddamn house.

"Jasmine." His voice makes me jump, and I spin around to find him in the doorway near the stairs. "I'm going to let Moses and Rebekah out and…"

Just the memory of yesterday makes my skin feel slimy, and I have to fight the churning of my stomach as I struggle to plant a smile on my face. "Okay, Daniel."

"Well…" He tucks his thumbs into his jeans, and then nods. "You're doing a good job."

"Thank you," I answer, staying completely still as he turns and walks toward the front door. Every muscle in me is tense as I listen to it open, the creaking of the old hinges, and then it shuts firmly.

I make myself count to ten before I walk to the edge of the entryway and lean my broom against the wall. Through the thin curtains on either side of the front door, I can see him walking toward the barn, and that's all I've been pleading for all morning. *Finally, a break.* I bolt up the stairs and into the bathroom. Ripping open the cabinet, I grab my bag and kneel down on the floor to take out my birth control. The

Jasmine

first case I grab is empty, and it makes me cringe as I shove it to the bottom and dig out the new pill case.

Fuck.

Only twenty-one chances before I'm ruined. That's all I have. Pushing the first one into my hand, my heart falls a little more. *Twenty now.*

Popping it into my mouth, I stand up and turn on the faucet, cupping water to swallow it.

"Jasmine? Do you want to come help me with Moses and Rebekah?" His voice echoes from inside the house and makes me stand up straight, swallowing hard. Panic turns my heartbeat into a race as I spin to find him entering the bedroom, approaching me with a smile. "What are you doing?"

"My medicine. I'm taking my medicine." Crouching down, I shove the pink case back into my bag as fast as I can, but then I feel his hand on my shoulder.

"What is it? Do I need to get you more?" he asks, showing his version of kindness as I push the bag inside the cabinet and shake my head.

"No, no. It's okay, Daniel. Thank you though." I twist to stand up, and he lets me, but when I reach to close the cabinet, he catches it.

"If you need to take medicine, Jasmine, that's important. You can't get sick, especially if you want to go riding with me." There's some twisted kind of concern in his voice, and I hate it. I hate *him*, but I force a smile and make myself touch his arm gently.

"I won't get sick, I promise. Let's go downstairs—"

"It's my job to take care of you, Jasmine. You don't need to feel ashamed." He reaches into the cabinet and lifts out my bag, setting it on the counter, and I fight the urge to lunge for it. To rip it out of his hands.

"Daniel, it's fine. I promise." Using his name just makes him smile at me again before he takes the little pink disk out. He's holding my life in his hands, and he doesn't even know it. "Can we go downstairs? Please? I need to finish my chores so I can see the horses."

He ignores me, opening the case, turning it over, and then he looks into the bag and pulls out the little paper insert, and my blood runs cold. I'm trapped because I can't get past him into the bedroom. I'm stuck by the door, watching as he reads and his face changes. For a moment there's confusion, his brows pulled together, and then there's only anger.

"Birth control," he says quietly, his voice razor sharp in the silence, and I see the paper shaking in his grip for a moment before his fingers tighten into a fist, crushing it as he turns to face me. "This is your medicine?"

I can't speak as I press my back to the wall, but there's not enough room. He towers over me, holding up the fist filled with paper like the accusation that it is.

"You... *you* took these?" His other hand shoots out fast, grabbing my arm in an iron grip that immediately has me whimpering.

"It's not—"

"DO NOT LIE TO ME!" he roars, shaking me hard, his

fingers bruising rings into my upper arm as fear takes over, and I start crying.

"Please, please..." Another hard shake that ends with him shoving me back into the wall.

"I'm not stupid, Jasmine. I can read. I know that only whores take birth control. Whores that want to open their legs to anyone and *not get pregnant*." His voice goes dangerously soft on the last words, and I can't look away from the wild glaze in his eyes. "This was you. It was all you. God has been trying to bless us with a child, and you've been *killing it* with these?"

"No, no!" I shake my head, trying to find the right words to explain that's not how it works, but he grabs me by the throat. The paper insert that damned me is crushed against my skin where he squeezes, making blood pound behind my eyes as I wrap my fingers around his wrist.

"Do. Not. Lie. To. Me." Every word is hard-edged as he tightens his grip until I can't draw any air. Desperate, I claw at his hand, shaking my head the little I can, but he won't let go. Black starts at the edges of my vision, slowly inching in as pins and needles pop up across my body.

He's going to kill me. Jesus Christ, he's going to kill me.

In a panic, I bring my leg up hard, right between his legs, and he shouts as he stumbles back, catching himself on the counter as I wheeze air in and throw myself out the bathroom door. My vision is coming back while I run for the bedroom door, coughing as my bruised throat tries to let air past — and then I lose all the air again.

It feels like a truck hits me, every bone in my body jarring violently as he tackles me to the floor, and I hit hard but I'm fueled by pure adrenaline now, and I barely register the pain. Flipping over, I twist to kick him off me. Somehow, I manage to catch his shoulder and shove myself away at the same time. Scrambling to my hands and knees, I make it another few feet closer to the door before he grabs my ankle, and I scream with my first full breath.

His fingers dig into clothes and skin as he drags me back under him, forcing me onto my back, but I'm not ready to die. *I'm not going to die.* That one thought slices through my mind, and I go for his eyes as he shifts over me, but my thumbs barely dig in before he jerks back.

I get one look at his grimace of rage before he backhands me, and white-hot pain explodes across my cheekbone, my teeth rattling as I taste copper on my tongue. A second later, my face is in his hand, fingers digging into my cheeks as he leans in close.

"YOU DID THIS! You killed our child! You defied God, His plans for us!" He's shouting, more emotion than I've ever heard in his voice, and of all the times I'd begged to see some kind of emotion in him... I'd never expected rage like this. He's terrifying as he seethes above me, and then a roar rips out of him, and his fist slams into the floor beside my head.

"I'm sorry, I'm sorry, I'm sorry," I babble through the grip he has on my face, but he just shouts again. A raw roar of rage and pain against which I clench my eyes tight, but I feel the spray of spit and hot air against my skin.

"ARE YOU A WHORE, JASMINE?" he screams into my

Jasmine

face, and I try to shake my head before I realize I can't move it at all.

"No!" I force the word out as I sob, terror freezing my limbs. Leaving me useless, limp.

"TELL ME WHY! Why did you do this!"

All I can do is cry, because I can't think. I can't think of an answer that will keep him from choking the life out of me.

"WHY, JASMINE!" Another roar, and then he lets go of my face, twisting away from me to push himself up. The second he's off me, my brain screams 'RUN!' and my body releases like a spring. I flip to my stomach and I'm off the floor before he's even halfway up. I reach the door frame and use it to launch me into the hall, running for the stairs, but it's the 180° turn that ruins me. That, and his long fucking legs.

He catches the back of my shirt, pulling me into him, and then he spins us, slamming me into the wall so hard my vision flickers.

"LET ME GO!" I scream, but what I'd meant to sound strong comes out desperate and full of panic. I try to hit him, I try to throw myself to the side, and then I try to knee him again. This time he avoids it easily and throws me to the floor instead. I manage to catch myself, sobbing as I try to crawl away from him, back down the hall, but he rips me upright by my hair.

"You said you loved me," he seethes, fist tightening until pinpricks of pain spread across my scalp. "You said you loved me while you were killing our child."

"You made me say that!" I shout back, my fingernails uselessly digging into his hand.

"You're a liar, Jasmine. A LIAR!"

"MY NAME ISN'T JASMINE!" I scream, my voice breaking on her name. Not mine. It's not mine, but it doesn't matter. Nothing matters as he fumes, his face red with rage, and then he turns away, dragging me toward the stairs.

I panic and kick, trying to grab hold of the bannister, but he just yanks me away from it, down the stairs where my legs and arms collect bruises on the wooden steps. By the time we're at the bottom I'm sobbing, because I know where we're going.

"Please, please don't—"

"QUIET!" he roars, dragging me toward the front door by my hair. I try to get to my feet, but I keep stumbling, back to my knees that scrape across the wood floor, and then the door jamb as he pulls me onto the front porch.

It's useless, like everything I've ever tried, and I feel every rock as I fall again and again on the walk to the barn because I can't keep up. He doesn't release me as we get to the door, doing it all one-handed until we're inside and he slams it shut behind us.

"Please, please just listen to me. For once just listen—"

Daniel rounds on me in an instant, face bent down to mine as he hisses, "In the end she is bitter as wormwood, sharp as a two-edged sword... You are a *liar*, Jasmine. Sinful. Tainted."

Jasmine

"Then let me go. Please, just let me go." I'm crying as I plead, begging on my knees, because I know I've finally pushed him too far.

"No. There is evil in you, Jasmine. The Devil is burrowed deep inside you, rotting you from the inside." He shakes me, his face a terrifying mix of determination and fury. "But I'm gonna fix you, purify you. Then... then God will forgive you for this."

"NO! No, Daniel—" My words stop as he drags me forward, my knees scraped raw on the concrete as I scramble after him. At the post, he finally lifts me to my feet and pushes me chest-first against the wood.

"Do. Not. Move." His voice is dangerous, and all I can do is watch as he walks away from me, toward the wall where so many things are stored.

I want to leave, to try and save myself. I want to have the answer, to be the kind of woman who survives something like this... only there's nothing to do. I just stand where he left me, shaking with fear and adrenaline as everything in me tells me to run, but as I look at either end of the barn, I know I wouldn't get anywhere. I wouldn't even get to the door before he was on me again. I hiccup on my next quiet sob as he walks back with rope, and I can't resist the urge to back away. "Please don't."

Running wouldn't have stopped this. I don't think anything would have, and this time when he grabs me, I don't resist at all. I'm going to need my energy, and I know it — *if* he doesn't kill me.

He thinks I killed our child. Oh God.

I'm shaking as he weaves the coarse rope around my wrists, cinching them tight with a knot before he ties a loop at the other end. Silently, he shoves me back to the post and forces me up onto tiptoe to slip the rope over a hook well above my head. I'm stuck like that, on the balls of my feet, because I can't get my heels down and every time I try, the rope digs painfully into my wrists. But I forget all about that when I feel him pull my shirt back and I hear the fabric tear. I try to twist and look, and he slams me back against the post with a firm hand between my shoulder blades.

"Don't move. I'm using my knife." The words keep me frozen, glued to the pillar as he rips through the shirt from top to bottom, slicing the short sleeves so he can toss it away. The blue of it seems unreal against the dull concrete, and as he cuts through my bra straps, I realize that it was one of *my* shirts. Not hers. And now it's gone... like her.

My bra lands a foot or so away from my shirt, and then his hands are on my shorts, undoing them before he rips them down along with my underwear. I step out of them because I don't know what else to do. I can't think straight. Aches and pains from a hundred places on my body are surfacing as the adrenaline fades, my throat hurts every time I swallow — and he hasn't even started yet.

That thought consumes me the most as I watch him stride back to the wall where he drags a box out from under the workbench. He digs through it for a minute, shoving things aside, before he finally removes something and sets it beside him. I can't tell what it is until he nudges the box back into place and picks it up... then I see it. It's a whip. A short one, not like the ones I've seen in movies, but I recognize it all the same as it hangs at his side.

Jasmine

"No, no, no, please! Please don't do this, please!" I beg, but he keeps walking toward me, that same look of intense determination and fury on his face, and I whine as I jerk against the rope. "I'm sorry, okay? I'm sorry!"

"Ask God for forgiveness." That's his only answer as he disappears behind me, and I clench my teeth a second before my back explodes with fire.

It steals all my breath. I can't even scream as I press into the wood of the post. Another blow lands just as I try to choke in air, and I let what little I gained out on a sob. It's excruciating, the worst pain I've ever felt, and instead of fading it just seems to concentrate into vicious stripes.

He whips me again, and I cry out as the agony swells, a brutal swath of fire running diagonal across the top of my back. Another, and I finally manage a scream, but it dissolves into a sob as I twist and pull at the rope until my fingers pulse and tingle.

"PLEASE!" I shout just before another lash lands, a keening whine escaping through clenched teeth as the pain builds. "Please stop..."

"Only God can wash you of your sins, Jasmine. Call out to Him. Pray and offer Him your penance." He doesn't strike me again, not yet, and I hiccup on my next sob as I nod fast.

"Please God help me. Forgive me. Please, please, help me —" I scream as the leather slices across my back, leaving torment in its wake. My anger spikes amid the pain, and I scream at him. "I'm fucking praying! I'm doing what you said to do!"

He grabs my face from behind, twisting my head to look at

him. "Don't curse or I'll fill your mouth with soap. Now, admit your sins, Jasmine, or your blood can't wash them clean in God's eyes."

"Please just stop," I whisper, pleading with my eyes, but he simply lets go of me. I try to prepare myself, except nothing can help when the whip cracks across my back again. It hurts more, if that's possible, and I start to babble, saying anything that might stop him. "I'm sorry, God. I'm sorry that I took the birth control, I'm sorry that I ruined Your plan. I'm sinful, I'm horrible, I want your forgiveness. Please!"

Daniel brings the whip down again and my knees buckle because it hurts too much. It's like a knife of fire splitting my back open, and if his God wants blood, I think he has it now. Another strike and all I can do is cry.

It's the burning ache in my wrists that forces me to plant one foot back on the ground and lift myself as I try to satisfy him. Echoing every insane thing he's said as I talk to the post. "God, forgive me for being evil, for killing the child you planned for us. Forgive me for— GOD!"

"Continue," he commands from behind me, as if he didn't just whip me, and for a moment I wonder if he'd just let me hang here. If I just let go, would he stop? Would he let me down? Does he ever plan on stopping?

My back is a spider web of agony, so intense I can't tell the individual strikes apart anymore, and as I stand there in silence, he adds another, but I don't have the energy to scream again. I barely cry out.

"Continue, Jasmine."

Sure, okay. "Forgive me for my sins. Forgive me for being a bad wife. Forgive me for failing you. Please, God—" Another strike, and I whine as I lean on the post, the pain swelling and then blending in with the rest of it as I switch feet to try staying upright a little longer. "I'm sorry, God. God, I'm so, so sorry..."

I'm so sorry I'm not stronger. Sorry I didn't keep running when I had the chance. I'm sorry I'm weak. I'm sorry I won't see my mom and dad again, and it's all my fault.

A vibrant strike of lightning strokes down my back, and my legs give out.

I'm sorry. I never should have been here. I should have gone home.

"Up," he commands. Harsh, unforgiving, and then I feel something pressed against the side of my foot. I lift it and stand up on something smooth and hard that moves to the side, and then I feel Daniel's hand on my other leg, lifting that foot onto the surface too. Pins and needles explode in my fingertips, and I glance up at them. They're a bad color. Purply-red.

"I can't do this." The words come out on a whisper, but I never meant for them to be out loud anyway. He's not listening. I rest my head on the post, soaking in the moments without new pain, trying to remember how to breathe correctly, because every breath hurts, and I know it shouldn't.

"An excellent wife is the crown of her husband, but she who brings shame is like rottenness in his bones. That's from Proverbs, Jasmine. Something you would know if your parents had raised you in a righteous household, if they had taught you how to remain pure." He grabs my chin, lifts my head, and I open my eyes to look into the blazing darkness of his. There's still rage there. Bottomless, and it shows in his voice that isn't monotone at all now. "You were penitent to God, now you will apologize to me. For tainting our union, our marriage bed, our home."

I stare at him, trying to memorize the words so I know what to say, but as soon as he lets go of me, I hear the buckle on his belt and I forget them. *He's not done. It's not over.*

"Apologize." The word is a growl punctuated by the snap of his belt across my ass. It's blunt fire in comparison to the whip, but it still hurts. It hurts more when he lands it again, and again, and again until the burn of it starts to tug me back from the blissful darkness I could almost reach. "APOLOGIZE!" he roars.

"I'm sorry."

He lands the belt anyway, another stroke of pain in the multi-colored haze in my head.

"I'm sorry I was bad. Rotten." I whimper when he lands a slash across my thighs, because I don't have the energy to scream anymore. "I tainted you with my evil. Tainted our bed."

"You lied, Jasmine! You killed the child we were meant to have!" he shouts at me, and then there's nothing but agony. I can't count the strikes, the snaps of the belt, and I lose track of the pain. It rises like a tidal wave, choking me before it drowns me completely and finally it seems someone heard my prayers because the black rises too and swallows me whole.

Him

Carrying her across the drive, toward the house, I can feel the blood on her back smearing my arm, but I don't look down at her again. Not yet. When I get to the front door, I shift her, draping her over my shoulder where she stays, completely limp, but she's okay.

Jasmine is okay.

She's breathing, I checked when I realized she wasn't standing on her own anymore, and as soon as I took her down, I tried to wake her. I talked to her. I said her name, but she didn't answer at all, and as my anger continues to calm, I can feel something else underneath it. It's like a stomach ache, and it grows as I carry her down to the basement.

It's for her own good. *All of this is for her own good.*

If I had taken her as a wife sooner, if I had protected her purity like a good man should, then Jasmine would have never been swayed to something like those pills she took. As I remember them, the little slip of paper she'd hid from me, my anger surges back, and I tighten my grip on the railing until I can push it back again.

Daddy always said to never give in to anger. He told me that Wrath was the deadliest of the sins for me, and I know it's true. What Jasmine did was wrong, sinful, but I gave in to Wrath.

As gently as possible, I lay her down on the table against the wall, and my stomach ache gets worse. More than a few of the whip marks on her back are bleeding, and her backside and thighs have large dark splotches amid the red. Yet, it's the marks on her back that I can't look away from. I wanted her to repent, I wanted God to forgive her, to cleanse her sins… but I never wanted to give her scars like mine.

This is what Wrath does. This is why it is the deadliest sin.

Moving to the edge of the table, I push the hair off her face and trace the red mark on her cheek. It's swollen, and I can hear Daddy's voice. *'You never strike a woman in anger. That's not what God asks of us.'* Another way I sinned today, and although my sins are less than Jasmine's, they are no less a stain on our house.

I take a deep breath and make myself walk away from her and back up the stairs. Locking the basement is necessary, because she is still misguided, and I have to tend to my own sins before I can lie with her. As soon as she's secure, I head back to the barn and clean up the rope, put the wooden storage box where it belongs, and then I return to the post and kneel.

"Lord, please forgive me for faltering in my own sins today as I tried to be your shepherd for Jasmine." I pray aloud, removing my shirt and folding it before I set it aside. "Forgive me, God, for the sin of Wrath. Please let Jasmine see that while I failed to control myself, I was only trying to bring her closer to your light. To purify her in your eyes, as I seek to be purified now."

Lifting the whip, I adjust the length and raise my arm high before bringing it down hard across my back. The sting makes my back twitch in remembrance, but it tells me I'm doing it right.

I do it again, harder, and keep my mouth closed until I'm able to say, "Forgive me, Lord, for striking my wife in anger."

I do it again and again, until the pain soaks in, until I'm sure there's not an inch of my back that I can reach that is unmarked. If I am bleeding, it is God's will, and I stay silent unless I am asking for His forgiveness.

Eventually my arm is not strong enough to lay the lash the way I was taught, so I stop and put it away. Before I leave the barn I let Moses and Rebekah out to pasture, and I allow myself just a few moments to soak in the sunshine and remember the time I shared with Jasmine here yesterday. Proof that, although she has been misguided, she can still be saved. God's light still resides within her, and she can still be a good wife if I keep her close. If I help her fight the temptation of Satan's darkness.

That is what I must do. I must keep watch over her and keep her safe from temptation when I cannot.

I head back into the barn where I grab one of the thick blankets from the storage box, pick up my shirt, and then return to the house. First, I go upstairs and ready our bed. Spreading the thick, dark blanket over the covers, putting my clothes in the laundry bin, and... finally, I go to the bathroom. The sight of the small pink container brings the anger again, but I stretch my back and let the sting abate it before I pick it up. I dig through her bag and find another one with only blue pills, no white ones, and I take that too along with the paper on the floor.

When I stand, I remember holding her against the wall, and I wonder if God knows I meant to repent for that as well. I can only hope He knows, as the Lord knows everything.

I bury her sinful pills in the garbage in the kitchen, wash my hands, then go back to the basement to get her. As far as I can tell, she hasn't moved, but when I lift her into my arms she makes a noise. I'm sure it's her back, but I can't tend to that down here. I have to get her upstairs before I can take care of her and show her I'm repentant.

Once she's secure on my shoulder again, I carry her up to our bed and lay her carefully on her stomach. It doesn't take long to wipe her back clean with a warm cloth, and with the blood wiped away it looks a bit better. If she is forgiven, maybe she won't have scars at all.

Maybe God will see our sorrow and give both of us that gift.

Before I join her, I kneel on my side of the bed and pray once more that God will forgive us both and that we can still be blessed with a child. Then, even though it's only the afternoon, I lie down next to her to watch over her and wait for her to wake.

EIGHTEEN

Mason
———

We're all bundled into another SUV. It's a pattern I've noticed this trip, not that it comes as any surprise. This is Texas, after all, not LA. And though the white Dallam County Ford Bronco Deputy Nolan directs us to is not as nice as the Amarillo FBI's SUV, it's decently clean, even if the vehicle is older.

Carmen takes the front seat, and once we're all settled, she turns to Nolan. "You know where we're going, Deputy? The abandoned ranch and the Christiansen home?"

"Yes ma'am. I haven't actually been to the Christiansen house; I was a sophomore when Daniel Christiansen played his senior year, and I never was friends with him. But I been out that way more'n a few times."

"Okay. And you think you can find this spot? Where Sloane Finley took this picture?" She points at the printout Braddock made before we left.

Nolan nods. "I'll find it," he says with determination.

"Good. Thank you, Deputy Nolan."

He glances over at her, and then twists his head back at me, his mouth working for a moment. "You... y'all can call me Clint. If you want. Just sounds kinda odd. Nobody calls me Deputy Nolan 'round here."

I nod as he starts up the truck. "All right. I'm Mason. Mason Jones."

"Carmen Rodriguez," she adds from the passenger seat.

"Pleasure to meet you, ma'am."

"Carmen," she chides him gently.

He gives her a short, quick nod, and then pulls onto the street. As we stop at the single blinking stop light, he glances in the rearview mirror toward me. "Mason is kinda an unusual name, if you don't mind me saying..."

"So's Clint."

He gives me a perturbed glance. "It's... I'm named after the actor."

"Actor?"

"Well... yeah. You're from Hollywood. You know, the famous actor."

"Famous actor?" I ask, feigning ignorance.

He gives me an almost bug-eyed stare. "Clint. Clint Eastwood!"

This is going to be fun.

I give a shrug. "Never heard of him."

Carmen turns her head to the side, away from Clint, doing everything she can to hide her expression because now he is flat out agape. He says nothing for a moment, staring in the rearview mirror at me while the truck idles. "You... ain't never heard of Clint Eastwood?"

I shake my head, pretending to think. "Does he do daytime soaps or something? I don't really watch those."

Nolan doesn't speak. He simply blinks in rapid succession before he responds in an even, measured monotone. "You're screwing with me. You have to be screwing with me. Ain't no other way..."

I allow him a tiny smile. "Maybe."

As we head out of town, Deputy Nolan — Clint, I remind myself — stays quiet, and at first I'm unsure as to why that is. Maybe it's because I busted his chops about his name, or maybe he's got that 'you're a foreigner' attitude I feel like I've been bucking, and my teasing has only reinforced that. Or maybe there's another reason entirely I haven't caught onto. I catch him shooting me glances, looking away the second I return his gaze, and I decide to break the monotony of the drive and needle him a little further.

"So, you're dating this... Laurie Ann from the café?"

He overcorrects, not tremendously, but enough that it's noticeable. I watch as his adam's apple bobs before he chokes out, "I ain't dating Laurie Ann Maddock!" He snaps a glare at me, and then faces forward, eyes fixed on the road, knuckles white around the steering wheel.

"Oh..." I draw out the word, nodding slowly. "I'm sorry. You seemed very focused back there when Sheriff

Braddock was talking about the girl. Maybe I misread your look."

I let the silence hang as the road noise bears us along.

"Maybe it wasn't her that had your focus at all." I make the comment offhand, but definitely loud enough that I know he's heard. He doesn't respond, but I can almost hear the steering wheel creaking under his grip. I glance into the front seat and catch the look of admonishment Carmen shoots at me.

"So, I take it you've studied the Sloane Finley case?" Carmen's voice is much milder, much less pointed than my own questioning.

Clint doesn't answer immediately. It looks like he's weighing his response before he does. He's young, but it's obvious he isn't stupid. "A little. Enough so I know what took place up until she showed up here in Texas."

"Ah," she responds simply.

I watch the fenceline alongside the truck stream by, an endless river of tick marks as we continue to dive deeper into this featureless land. I let another mile or two get eaten up before I take up the thread of the conversation. "I imagine you studied everything about her, hmm? Looked at all those pictures she had taken? The headshots? The ones she used for auditions?"

He says nothing, and I watch his jaw working as another mile slips by. Carmen is frowning, and I'm betting she's suspicious of what I'm about to do.

"Those ones of her in that white blouse were pretty nice, you know? Really showed off her assets—"

"I looked at some of them, yeah." His voice is a little louder than it needs to be as he cuts me off, strained and tinged with barely concealed anger. Or jealousy. Maybe both. I do my best to hide my grin.

"Some of them, huh?"

"Well, everything them detectives from LA sent. I didn't know about them other pictures from Facebook until today."

"She was a pretty girl, wasn't she?"

He doesn't answer for a moment. When he does, his voice is wary, evasive, but still strained and firm. "I... I suppose she is."

"You suppose."

He flicks a glance my way, teeth gritted, mouth curled down into a frown. "Okay, fine. She's a pretty girl."

"*Was* a pretty girl."

His gaze moves back to me. "What do you mean, was?"

"Well, she's dead. I haven't seen very many pretty dead girls in my time." I hold up my hand. "Now, not that I judge or anything, if that's what you're into..."

This time Carmen twists her head back to shoot me an outright glare.

Clint's gaze is now fixed on me in the mirror, and we are driving blind. I'm not too concerned, because there's little traffic, and I don't think this stretch of road could get any straighter.

"What the hell..." His voice is soft, incredulous.

"Hey." I tilt the hand I've been holding up into a sign of assent. "If necrophilia is your thing, who am I to pass judgment..."

"Jesus Christ!" Clint stares at me open-mouthed. "That's a helluva a thing to say!"

"I'm just saying. You seem pretty fixated on a dead girl..."

"I ain't fixated on her!" Clint yanks one hand off the wheel for emphasis, and then realizes that he isn't watching the road. He twists his head forward and brings his hand back down to grip the wheel.

For a moment the truck continues to chew up the miles and then he breaks the silence.

"And how do you know she's dead? I didn't see no notice they found a body."

I shrug. "Well, it's the truth." I wave my hand at the window, sweeping across the grassland. "There are two truths I know for certain in the Sloane Finley case. One: she's dead. And two: she's buried somewhere out there." I point outside the truck, tracing a wide arc that takes in everything across our horizon. "Somewhere in all that nothing."

Clint doesn't say anything, but the bleak look on his face speaks volumes.

Pining after a dead girl. God save me...

We sit in silence as we continue down the two-lane highway that bisects this land like a thin, gray artery. The further out of Stockdale we've gone the more the terrain has become

Jasmine

less flat, and more rolling. The gentle rise and fall, rise and fall is almost imperceptible at first, until you realize you're cresting tiny hills every two miles or so.

It's Carmen who breaks the silence, and soon her and Clint are engaged in an animated discussion of football. They're both talking about teams I can only assume are local to this area, and players thereof, both past and present. At one point I hear them talking about 'The Wall,' which I remember is the nickname of the young man we'll be visiting later.

"Did you ever actually see him play?" he asks Carmen.

"No. I've lived in Amarillo for too long now. And back then, whenever I was visiting family in Stratford, they were either playing Dumas, or Dalhart, or one of the Hartley county schools."

Clint nods. "Well, he was something to see, I'll tell you. He shoulda gone pro."

"So I heard. Wonder why he didn't?"

He shrugs. "You know what it's like 'round here. Some people just don't want their kids going off and getting corrupted in the big city. Having them put crazy notions in their heads, stuff like that..."

Carmen nods, and I glance over to catch the pensive gaze that comes over her face. "Yeah. I know what you mean."

I reflect on the subtext within that statement, and then tune their conversation out as they go on once again about football. I watch as the barren landscape rolls past us, remembering Carmen's words: *'Don't let the appearance of wide-open spaces and nothingness fool you. Secrets can stay hidden here for a long, long time...'* The truth to that statement is becoming more and more apparent as time goes on, and if I'd questioned earlier how one young woman could have been swallowed up and disappeared in all the vast nothing that is this land, I no longer do now.

I feel the truck slowing before I see the road that takes off to our right. There's been no indication of it coming up, but suddenly there's an oddly incongruous green street sign on a pole sticking up in the middle of nowhere. As Clint slows to make the turn, I catch the lettering: Co. Rd. 143. The road we take is still paved, but it's obvious that whatever maintenance Dallam County has for their infrastructure, this road does not rate highly on the list. The edges are worn and crumbling, and the cracks spiderweb the surface in endless patterns.

I can count the number of buildings I've seen since we left Stockdale on one hand, aside from tiny wood or concrete structures that are obviously service related. *How long could a body be hidden in one before someone found it?*

Clint and Carmen have stopped talking, and he's scanning both sides of the road intently. Despite the condition of the pavement, he's not driving as fast as he could, and I start to take note of the area we're passing through.

"Are we close?" Carmen asks, searching outside as we roll along.

"It's been a while since I came out this way." His head continues its back-and-forth pattern. "But I'm pretty sure we ain't too far."

Another five miles pass by, and the strain of looking at what seems endless repetition is greater than I'd expect. We're on the downside of a hill we've just crested when Clint slams on the brakes, bringing us to an abrupt halt. Before I can say anything he's craned his neck around over his shoulder, looking back while he reverses the truck. We head up the hill where we've just come from, and I stay silent, looking around for whatever has caught his attention. We pull over the top until just a short ways on the other side he brakes hard again, and we stop, the motor idling.

"There." He points out my side of the cab, and I follow his finger.

It takes a second, but I see what he's noticed. Off in the distance, nestled in the vee of two other slight rises, are the outlines of a pair of buildings in the afternoon sun. It's hard to see clearly, but it looks to be a house and a barn. From our vantage point it's hard to tell, but one thing is clear; this is not the location that Sloane Finley took her picture. I don't even need to glance at the print to know that.

"This isn't where she took the picture." I don't say it accusingly, simply a statement of fact. Clint nods, taking it as such.

"Yep. There should be a dirt road taking off a bit further..." He sighs and puts the truck in drive again. We continue on, moving over two more gentle rises, and this time I see the break in the fence line the same time Clint does. Before we get to it, he slows and brings the truck to a stop.

"There." He points to the buildings which are closer now, but still far enough away that the details are indistinct. We're at the base of a gentle rolling hill, and the buildings are off in the distance, plopped dead center of a flat plain that lies between the rolling land.

"Carmen, can I see the picture?"

She hands it back to me silently. I glance down at it, and then look back up.

"This is them, but she took it out there." I point beyond the fenceline into the field that stretches toward where the buildings are.

Clint nods. "She had to have parked her car, then hopped the fence and walked out there." He shakes his head, as if he can't quite believe what she'd done.

I look around us. The fence line is practically right by the pavement's edge, and it seems hard to believe Sloane Finley, no matter how dumb and naïve she may have been, would have simply parked her car in the middle of the road to run out and take her picture.

"There must be a spot where she pulled off. That break in the fence line up there?" I point toward it.

"I suppose." Clint presses his lips together tight, thinking. "Must have been, because there ain't any other road I can think of near here, and damn sure no turnouts." He glances over at me. "As you can see, this ain't exactly tourist country."

"Clearly." My response is as dry as the land around us.

Clint puts the truck in gear, and we slowly advance until we come to the opening in the fence. It is a gate, blocking a dirt road that takes off angling away from the county road. Clint pulls into the small open area between the pavement and the gate, straddling a cattle guard that is set into the ground, barely visible. What was once a ditch beneath it is now filled with dirt, tumbleweeds, and windblown detritus. No one has maintained this in quite some time. He shuts off the motor, and we climb out into the Texas October afternoon.

The sun is trending toward the horizon, but it's still warm enough outside that the air-conditioned interior of the truck is something I miss. Moving up to the gate, I notice it's a simple affair. A piece of rebar stuck into a worn hole dead center of a cement plug is all that keeps it closed. No locks. The top of the rebar is bent over at a ninety-degree angle to create a handle, and I watch as Clint moves to grab it. He pulls on it with one arm, and the way his muscles strain I can tell the tension on it is surprising, given its age. He gives it a firm tug, and then it pops free, letting him shove the ancient, rusted gate out of the way. Clint stares at it for a moment before he turns to look back at Carmen and me.

"She didn't do that. What you just did." I glance around me. "This is where she may have parked, but she didn't go through this gate.

"Probably not," Clint agrees. "Doesn't look like that gate's been moved in a long while."

"She stopped here, took her phone, and headed out..." I point further into the field beyond the fence. "There. Come on, I want to take a look."

We climb back into the Bronco, and Clint drives through, but throws the truck back into park on the other side. He slips out and puts the gate back into place before rejoining us in the cab. "Don't know if there's cattle out here or not," he explains.

I nod and look down the road that stretches in front of us. It's a simple path, two tracks worn into the dirt. The lines are still visible, but the grass has grown back into place trying to erase them. It's obvious that it isn't used often, only enough to keep the wind, weather, and grass from obliterating it entirely.

We drive maybe another thousand yards, SUV bouncing all the way, and Clint slowly brings the car to a halt. He points out the window to an area just beyond the soft dirt edge of the road. "I'd say probably just out there."

I look out, then back down at the picture. "Yep. She parked her car, hopped the fence, walked out there and took her picture." I gaze at the gently sloping ground that stretches toward the buildings ahead of us. "And then disappeared forever."

I glance into the rearview mirror at Clint, noticing how his eyes harden at my words. He says nothing, but turns to face forward, and the truck begins to move once more.

As we get closer to the buildings, it's easy to see that no one has lived here in a long time. A very long time. The house is a shell, the barn even more so. And while it is apparent that no one has lived here, it's also apparent that people have been here since it fell apart. As Clint pulls up into the overgrown area that was once a drive, I catch sight of markings that have been made on the house in spray paint. Black-and-white symbols that resemble the graffiti and gang signs that pepper LA like scars. And while they are similar, these do look different somehow. Clint stops the truck and shuts off the motor. Carmen climbs out first before either of the two of us, and she's moving with a purpose. Clint watches her for a moment, and then scrambles out himself.

"Ma'am... Carmen!" he calls out to her, moving to catch up before she makes it to the dilapidated porch of the building.

"Y'all need to be careful 'round this. Place is barely standing on its own, and there's—"

She spins to him, and the look on her face cuts him off as she points a finger behind her towards the house. "You know what those markings are?"

Clint's eyes narrow, and he nods. "I do."

I come up to them just as Carmen turns back around. "What is it, Carmen?"

She looks back at me, and then points to the white markings I noticed earlier. "It's a drug drop. Place to pick up and drop off on neutral ground."

I know what she means by the term, because we've got them around LA as well, but this shack of a house doesn't seem all that convenient.

"Have you been here?" She glances at Clint.

"Hadn't made it here yet. Didn't know I *needed* to come here, or..." He trails off with a bitter look on his face.

"You've been searching for her," I say, because I can read it on him plain as day.

"Well, ain't that what you wanted us to do?" he snaps.

Carmen takes a step toward the house, then stops and turns back to us. "Clint." Her voice is soft, calm, but intense. "How many abandoned places like this *are* there in Dallam County?"

Clint purses his lips, glancing between her and I before answering. "'Bout seventy-five. Maybe a hundred if you add in sheds and barns, stuff like that."

"Jesus." The word slips out before I can stop it.

Clint runs a hand through his sandy hair. "I made a list of every one we knew about or could find on the maps. I been checking 'em out whenever I have a chance. I ain't found nothing, but I still keep looking."

"How can there be that many?"

Clint shrugs. "Sheriff Braddock could tell you the whole story, but much as I know back after the war a lot of people came out here to live. Started up little ranches and stuff. Then things changed. Got to be being a little rancher was a lot of work for not a lot of money. Young folks decided not to take up ranching, and moved on. Places like this"—he motions to the house in front of us—"were abandoned either after the older folk moved on, or died, or the banks foreclosed on them. Bigger ranchers like the Hartleys, the Dalharts, XIT, the Christiansens... they came in and bought up the land and property from the banks. All they really wanted was the land, so they just left the buildings be. Costs too much to come in and tear 'em down when either a fire, a tornado, or time'll take care of it on its own."

We all stand in silence as that info sinks in. Carmen breaks our reverie, motioning to me. "Let's take a look inside."

She turns and begins marching up to the house, moving gingerly onto the porch, then toward the front doorway that gapes like an open wound. Clint and I follow, and as we step up onto the creaking floorboards, Carmen ducks inside.

"Just be careful, m— Carmen. Like I said, won't take nothing but a gust of wind to bring this whole place down."

We duck through the doorway and into the gutted interior

of the house. Inside are a few other markings and random bits and pieces of trash that confirm what Carmen and Clint have discussed. Crumpled, empty plastic water bottles, the discarded wrapper from a loaf of bread. In one corner of the room there's a pile of blankets that's been spread out in a crude imitation of a bed. I move to it, and when I look down, I see a discarded condom crumpled in the dust.

Well, at least they were being safe.

"God..." Carmen's voice has gone soft, almost a whisper, as if the sound itself could bring the roof down upon us. "There's no telling if she might have been in here, or one of the hundred other places you've been looking at. It's been far too long by now."

I can only nod, because she's right. Any chance that there might have been of this place giving up a clue whether Sloane Finley had been here has long since passed. But equally as disturbing is the idea that there are ninety-nine more places just like this out there. And during the weeks and months since Sloane's disappearance, a single deputy has been the only person doing anything to check them out, and he still hasn't been able to make his way through them all.

'Secrets can stay hidden here for a long, long time...'

"Come on. Let's get out of here." I turn and make my way towards the door, leaving the bleakness of this place behind. We gather by the truck, and stand in silence. Carmen glances toward the west, and I do too. It's grown late in the afternoon, and the sun is edging closer to the horizon.

"We're not going to make the Christiansen place today," she

says finally, blowing out a gust of air as she glances at her watch. "It's coming up on four-thirty. We've got a forty-five minutes to an hour drive back to Stockdale, and then another two hours to Amarillo. That gets us home, best case scenario... 7:30, more likely 8 o'clock or later." She looks over at me. "I'll do whatever you want, but I suggest we call it a day and come back out tomorrow."

I could be an ass and demand we head to the Christiansen place now, but Carmen has reason to want to get back to Amarillo, and though a part of me doesn't want to make the drive back out here, there's no point in making her suffer for my desire to be away from this place as quickly as I can. It's all a waste of time and resources anyways, as I've always known. Today has just hammered that fact home, as tomorrow will no doubt do too.

"Yeah." I glance over at her, nod, and then look at the sun dipping toward the horizon. "How could I pass up the chance to spend one more day in this wonderland?"

Carmen gives me a frown, eyes narrowed, while Clint turns away with a look that is both a touch offended and embarrassed.

"No offense, Clint."

"Sure," he grumbles.

I look to Carmen, catch the scolding in her gaze, and give a slight hitch of my shoulders. "Besides, it'll burn one more day of Whitmann's resources, and I'm sure that'll put me in Dave's good graces."

Carmen rolls her eyes, while Clint looks confused. I

chuckle and reach for the truck door. "Come on. Let's get the hell out of here."

On the way back to Stockdale, Carmen and Clint pick up with their football conversation, while I contemplate how I'm going to rip a certain Detective Ressner and the bulk of the LAPD Vice Division a new asshole when I get back home. We're on the main highway, within miles of Stockdale when I hear Carmen chuckle.

"Hold on, Clint. I'm betting this is my boss checking up on me." I glance up to see her pull her cellphone out, raising it to her ear.

"Agent Rodriguez here."

I look back down as she listens, thinking about how to phrase the term 'completely moronic group of nutsucking single-celled creatures' in polite words when the sound of Carmen's voice jerks my head upward.

"How? How did it happen?" Carmen's voice is tense, a bit louder than before, and I stare at the back of her head. She's got her cell glued to her ear, eyes boring holes into the dash of the Bronco. Whatever discussion she's having, it's obviously strained. I watch as Clint glances over at her, and then catch his eyes looking back at me in the rearview mirror.

"No. I'm just outside of Stockdale." Her voice is tight, very tight, and there is something definitely wrong.

"North. In Dallam County." There is a pause. "Two hours once I get going." I look at the fingers around her cell, and they're clenched white. We're just coming into the edge of town, and Clint doesn't slow down to match the speed limit.

"Yes. Yes, I will. Thank you." Carmen ends the call and shoves the phone back into her pocket. Her body is tense, coiled tight. Something bad has happened.

"Carmen, what is it? What's going on?"

She swivels to look back at me, and her mouth is a thin line, tension stretching the skin of her face. "When we get back to the station we need to leave immediately, Mason. Immediately." She turns her head, looking forward, scanning ahead of the vehicle as if she can find a portal to get us their quicker. Clint reaches over silently and turns the lights on, and the Ford picks up speed.

"Carmen. What the hell is going on?" I ask when she stays silent.

Her jaw is set, and while irritation rolls off her in waves, her voice remains even. "My wife's been in an accident. She's in the hospital." She turns to look back at me, and while everything else about her is coolly professional, tension notwithstanding, her eyes are bleak, and I see pain there. Pain that is raw, and real. The same pain I saw in Trish Tucker's face when she asked me to find Sloane Finley, except multiplied by a thousand. "And we are leaving. Now."

It only takes a few minutes for Clint to race through the streets of Stockdale, and we sit in silence until he pulls up to the station. The reflection of red, blue, red, blue off the cinderblock walls bathes everything nearby in carnival lighting, including us. Clint hits the switch, killing the lights, but Braddock has obviously seen them. He comes out of the front door, followed by another deputy I haven't seen before.

Jasmine

"What's going on?" Braddock's voice is concerned as he looks between the three of us while we pile out of the cab. I ignore him, instead reaching for Carmen as she turns to head for the white Suburban sitting where we'd parked it this morning.

"Carmen."

She turns around, staring at me, and her mouth is setting into a rigid line that I know says she's girding for a fight I do not want to have. She ranks me here, and if push comes to shove I'm going to do what she says. But I'm not ready to leave yet, and my window of opportunity is going to slam shut fast unless we can work this out.

"Mason. Now."

"Yes. Now." I make a gentle motion with my hand. "I want *you* to go. Right now. I'll stay here and figure this out. You just go."

"I can't do that." Her voice is strained as she snaps out the words. "Whitmann will have my fucking ass."

"No, he won't. And you know it."

"Dammit, Mason I don't have time for this. My wife is in the emergency room!" She gives me an irked twist of her head, body shifting toward the SUV she already wants to be in heading out of town.

"Listen, I just want to follow through on this one thing. You go. Take care of your wife. Come back and get me tomorrow, or, if you can't, I swear I'll find a way to get back to Amarillo." I shoot a quick glance towards Braddock, who along with Clint and the other deputy are all standing there watching this play out.

She shifts on her feet, her whole body leaning towards the truck, and I know I've made it.

"Whitmann is not going to do shit to you. At worse he'll try and 'manage' you and hit you with a personal intervention plan or some bullshit. You can weather that." I look at her, and she's taking a deep breath to counter my words, so I press on. "There's nothing going to happen here. I just want to take care of this one little thing that the LAPD jacked up. That's it."

She's wavering, because she knows as well as I that nothing I do here is going to be important or resolve anything. Just adding another paragraph to a report that's already nothing but crap.

"Go, Carmen," I press, because her wife is sitting in some hospital room in Amarillo, and that's where she needs to be. Not here worrying about her supervisor or arguing should-I-stay-or-should-I-go with me. "I'm just going to eat some fine country cuisine, watch paint dry, and then go pay a neighborly visit to Mr. Christiansen tomorrow. Nothing more. I promise." At those words her gaze shifts to Braddock.

"If there's anything we can do to help, ma'am..." His voice is soft, serious, and sincere.

"Keep him out of trouble." She jerks her thumb in my direction. "If he tries to get away and do anything stupid, shoot him."

Braddock laughs. "Yes ma'am. I'll make sure to get him back to Amarillo in one piece. Maybe a few extra holes, but one piece."

She looks from me to Braddock, and then back to me.

"I'm going to fucking regret this, aren't I?" Carmen's voice is soft but tinged with eagerness. She wants to be away from here, and she knows she's signed the deal on the dotted line, moments from being free and clear. She points a finger at me. "I swear to God, Mason. If *anything* comes up, you call me. Immediately." The finger stabs toward me for emphasis.

"Nothing is going to happen, Carmen. There's nothing here *to* happen." We stare at each other, and she's already twenty miles down the road in her head. "Go."

At that, she turns, striding down the sidewalk towards the Suburban in steps that eat up the distance measured in heartbeats.

"You call me! For anything!" Her voice bounces back as she rounds the hood of the truck and jumps inside. There is a roar of the V8 as she fires it up, and then with a squeal of tires she's gone.

I hear the truck make the corner at the light without stopping, and then the engine noise fades, leaving us in silence. None of us move for a moment, and I catch all three men staring at me. Braddock is appraising me, no doubt trying to make some sense of what just happened here, and Clint is giving me a stare that is equal parts wary and intrigued.

"Her wife, huh?" Braddock's voice slices the silence in two, and for a moment I feel my hackles rise. This is my worst-case scenario for this situation coming to life. Except his voice is not judgmental, condescending, or any of the things that my first gut reaction has sprung on me. It sounds genuine with concern, and when I look over at him it appears to be that and nothing more.

"Yeah. Her wife."

He nods, lips pursing. "She gonna be okay? You think you ought to have gone with her?"

I ponder that for a moment, then shake my head.

"No. She was just babysitting me anyways. For her boss. Seeing as I'm from *California*..." I emphasize the word, making sure it's clear I understand my foreigner status is not just limited to Whitmann back in Amarillo. "Last thing she needed was to have to figure out what to do with me while she's trying to take care of her wife too. I figure you gentlemen are more than capable of that."

Braddock looks over at his deputies, and the two of them frown a little as if on cue.

"Besides, I never got the chance to meet 'The Wall' that Deputy Nolan and Carmen spent so much time going on about today. Or partake of some of Texas's finest cuisine. Or watch paint dry." I give Braddock a bland smile.

"Hmph." Braddock rubs a hand across the bottom of his face, then pulls it away and points at me. "I suppose you expect me to just drop whatever I got going on to take over babysitting duties, huh?"

"To be honest, I don't expect you to do anything, Sheriff."

His eyes narrow, but after a second he gives me a short nod. "Yeah, well that may be the way you do things out there in *California*," he mimics the word back to me, and then his finger turns from me until it's pointing at his chest. "But here in Dallam County we show our guests real Texas hospitality. So I figure we can more than accommodate you in your... needs. Fix you up with some of the best food you're likely to wrap a lip around. That is, assuming you *California* folk do eat more than wheat germ and tofu?"

I push back a grin. Braddock's baiting me, and I'm okay with that because I know he knows I'm aware. I can play into this as much as he can.

"I dunno..." I press my lips tight, giving it my best consideration look. "Being as I'm so far from home, my chakra is just all out of whack. It's been twenty-four hours since I sat in my Prius, and it's been nothing but pick-up trucks and cowboy hats out here. On top of that, the energy from my crystals is really starting to fade. Who knows what kind of craziness I could get myself into?"

We all stand in silence on the sidewalk, staring at each other. When he finally speaks, Braddock's voice is quiet, assessing. "You really don't buy into much bullshit, do you Agent Jones?"

"As little as I possibly can, Sheriff Braddock."

He gives a short, sharp nod. "Then I imagine for the next twenty-four hours we're gonna get along just fine."

Whatever little challenge Braddock has run me through I seem to have passed, because the tension eases.

"C'mon inside, and let's get this sorted out." Braddock motions with his hand toward the door, and I follow as we all head into the station. Once we're in the main office we gather around the cluster of desks. The deputy I haven't met before approaches me.

"I'm Deputy Talbert." As he steps up to me, hand extended, I take the man in. He's young, a bit older than Clint, but maybe only by a few years. Where Clint is fair, and rangy, Deputy Talbert is stocky, dark, and swarthy. There's indication in everything about him that screams Tex-Mex.

"Agent Jones, FBI."

Deputy Talbert nods, shooting a glance toward Clint. "You're the Fed from LA that come out to quiz Deputy Dawg here 'bout his girlfriend, right?"

And there is yet another confirmation of my suspicions.

"Fuck off, Duane." Clint's voice cuts across the room, thick with annoyance. Deputy Talbert doesn't even glance back but gives me a shit-eating grin.

Before anyone else can say a word, Braddock sighs. "I swear to God, I thought I was done raising children when I sent my two off to college..." He shakes his head slowly, and Talbert gives a low chuckle. "Duane, do me a favor and give Nikki at The Ranch House a call and set up a room for Agent Jones. Tell her to bill it to the department."

I turn my head toward Braddock. "I can take care of the bill."

"Like I said, Agent, that's not the way we do guests 'round here." He gives me a pointed smile. Deputy Talbert moves to one of the desks, sits, picks up a phone, and begins dialing. Braddock shifts closer to Clint's desk, and I step in too.

"Y'all find anything out there today?"

Clint looks up at me, and I shake my head, looking at

Braddock. "Empty house being used as a crash spot for deals. Any chance of it having even a remote clue as to whether Sloane Finley was ever there... that's long gone."

"Well, you can blame your friends at the LAPD for that." Braddock's voice is laced with disgust.

"I know. Trust me."

"Nothing else?" he asks.

"Nope."

Braddock huffs out a sigh. "I take it from your earlier comment you didn't get out to the Christiansen place?"

"No." I shake my head. "It was getting late, and the intention was to head back to Amarillo and come back out in the morning."

"Well, ain't you the lucky one. Seems to me all this saved you a trip there 'n back."

"Maybe lucky for me. Not so much for Carmen's wife."

Braddock's mouth goes tight. "Fair enough." He glances at his feet before his eyes coming back up to mine. "I hope she'll be okay."

"Me too."

For a moment we stand in silence, then Braddock's voice cuts across the room. "Duane, you got that room squared away?"

"Yessir, Sheriff. All taken care of," Talbert calls back.

"Good man." Braddock looks over to Clint. "You think you can take care of getting Agent Jones here over to the Ranch?

And then take him out for a bite to eat. Hodie's or Mattie's, I'm thinking."

Clint nods. "Yeah. 'Course I can do that."

"I knew I could count on you." Braddock shoots me an apologetic smile. "Sorry, Agent Jones. I'd come with you, but unfortunately I have a prior engagement with my wife this evening."

I smile in return. "Well, I wouldn't want to interrupt that."

Braddock grins. "We're going to dinner at her parents' place." He reaches over and claps me on the shoulder. "I almost wished you would."

NINETEEN

Clint

I finish filling out my paperwork while Sheriff Braddock and Agent Jones talk. I want to go over and smack Duane upside his dumbass head for that 'girlfriend' comment, but it ain't the first time he's made that crack about me. Him and the Sheriff both think I'm dumb for what I've been doing, but everything they taught me in the academy says that part of being a good law enforcement officer is being persistent. I figure that if I keep at it, something will eventually turn up, and that'll be the break we need to find her.

Them detectives in LA oughta be fired. Why in the hell they didn't send us them files on Sloane's Facebook page just makes me see red. I've got copies of them now, and I'll go through them later on tonight to see just what I've missed.

Like that picture that sent us out to the abandoned ranch today.

I can understand why Agent Jones is pissed. She was right there, or damn close, but it's been months since that happened, and so much coulda taken place since then. Who'n the hell knows what mighta been left there by her. Not that it matters now. Whatever it might've been is long, long gone. *Dammit.*

I close out my time ticket for the day so Katie Lee can enter it tomorrow, and then wait until there's a break in the sheriff and Agent Jones' conversation to speak up. "Anytime you're ready, we can head on over to The Ranch House."

Agent Jones gives me a nod. "We can go now." He looks over to the sheriff. "Is there anything you need from me?"

"No, sir. I imagine you'll want to head out to the Christiansen place first thing tomorrow?"

"As soon as it would be appropriate to show up."

Braddock gives him a broad grin. "Daniel's from a ranch family. If you want to be out there at four AM, I'm betting he'll have breakfast waiting for you."

"I think nine or after will be just fine."

The sheriff chuckles. "Suit yourself, but you might have to track him down by then and that's a big property. Y'all stop by in the morning before you head out, just in case something's come up."

I nod in confirmation, and then the sheriff sticks out his hand to Agent Jones. "Well, you have a good evening, Agent. Enjoy your dinner."

"Thank you, Sheriff. You too."

We head out of the station, and I direct him to my pick-up rather than the Bronco. We pull out of the parking lot, and I

Jasmine

head over to The Ranch House motel where Duane's set up the room.

"You know, you don't have to take me out to dinner tonight, if you had other plans." Agent Jones darts his eyes toward me, and I catch the corner of his mouth pulling up. "With that girl... Laurie Ann I think her name was?"

I start to protest, but I know what this is. He's trying to bust my balls, like Duane was back there at the station. Well, I can be all cool 'n shit when it suits me. I clamp my mouth closed, and then play it like Clint Eastwood would. "I do what I want to on my own terms, Agent Jones. Don't no woman corral me."

He chokes, and I can see his lips pressed tight. Don't know what's so damn funny 'bout what I said, but he simply responds, "I see. And it's Mason, remember?"

"Sorry. Mason."

I pull up in front of The Ranch House, and we head into the little lobby they got there. Nikki is behind the counter, and she's got everything lined out. She hands Mason a key and directs us to the room she's assigned him. We move back to my truck, and I suddenly remember something.

"Did you have a bag? Did we forget it back at the station?"

Mason stops, and stands there for a moment, his eyes slowly closing.

"I did forget it." I start to turn to get back in the truck, but he continues, stopping me. "Except it's not back at the station. It's in Carmen's SUV."

Sonuvabitch...

"Damn. Are you... will you be okay for one night? I can get some things from my place for you? I'd take you over to Bower's Pharmacy, but he's done closed up for the day, I'm sure."

Mason pinches the bridge of his nose between two fingers, eyes shut tight. "It'll be fine," he says after a moment. "I'll be fine."

"You sure?"

"Yes." He lets go of his nose, looking up at me with a forced smile. "So... I think Sheriff Braddock mentioned something about dinner? Because right now I really need a drink."

I end up taking him to Mattie's. I figure if he's having a day like this one seems to be turning out to be, might as well give him the best Stockdale's got to offer. We get settled in at our table, and he's got the menu flipped over first thing, looking at the drinks.

"What do you recommend from these?" I look where his finger is pointing, and I can see it's at the beer list.

"Well, since you're in Texas, you at least gotta try a Texas beer." I point my finger at the Shiner Bock.

"Shiner Bock?" He pronounces the name slowly as he reads. After a second he looks up. "You aren't trying to get back at me for ribbing you earlier, right?"

"Maybe. Maybe not. Guess you'll have to try it and figure out for yourself."

His eyes narrow, and he gives me a shrewd look. "All right."

I order us some of the jalapeno quail appetizer, because it's just too damn good to pass up, even if he don't appreciate it.

Jasmine

He orders the Texas Rib-Eye, and I get The Big Daddy BBQ plate because I figure as long as the department is paying for it, I oughta get what I like most here.

While we wait for the food to show, he drinks the Shiner, quizzing me. "How long you been in law enforcement?"

"Since I graduated from high school. I went through the Law Enforcement Academy at Amarillo College, graduated, and came back here. Sheriff Braddock offered me the position that next summer."

"So you've always known this is where you wanted to be?"

"More or less. I kinda figured maybe someday I'll move on to a bigger city, bigger department. After I've gotten some experience here."

"Get your experience here, Clint. Skip the other part."

"Says the FBI agent from Hollywood..." I mutter.

He takes a long pull at his beer, and then lowers it. "Hollywood is bullshit, Clint. It isn't anything like what you've got built up in your mind."

I take a drink of my own beer, pressing my lips together. "Well, you ain't been 'round here long, so I don't suppose you got much experience to compare it to."

Mason snorts, tilting his bottle towards me. "I haven't skinny-dipped in a swimming pool either, but I know if I do I'll get my dick wet." He takes another swig, his eyes never leaving mine. "You're young, and you got ideas and ideals, and while that's real noble and everything, the longer you can hold onto them the better off you'll be in the long run." He swirls his bottle, watching the dark amber liquid inside spin. "You'll be able to do that a lot longer in a place like Stockdale than somewhere like Dallas or LA."

"Sloane Finley was from Indianapolis. And she went to Hollywood."

"Sloane Finley was a fucking idiot too."

I've never wanted to hit a man so bad, but I feel right now like I could climb across the table and cold-cock this sonuvabitch something fierce. All day he's been talking about her like she's a dead girl, and now he straight up calls her an idiot.

She ain't an idiot. She's... nice, and she deserves his respect.

"That's a pretty damn harsh thing to say 'bout someone, don't you think, Mason?"

"What it is, Clint, is the Goddamned truth." He tilts his bottle back and downs the remains of his beer. "Let me tell you a little something about Sloane Finley. She was a dumb little girl who came out to Hollywood thinking all she had to do was waltz into fucking town and show off those pretty little eyes and those tits of hers, and every fucking agent in town was going to start dropping scripts at her feet. Well, here's the thing: anyone with half a goddamn brain in their head and the ability to use the internet knows that's not the way it works. There are women in LA three times as beautiful as Sloane Finley ever was, and they spend their days flat on their backs in the Valley taking one dick in the ass while sucking on another and think themselves fucking blessed to be doing it at less than scale." His voice grows harsher as he speaks, and I'm 'bout one inch from getting up and walking the fuck outta here when he continues. "Sloane Finley was young and dumb, and she did a stupid thing that got herself killed. She is not someone to admire or emulate, Clint. She's someone to pity. And to learn from."

Our waitress comes by, drops off the appetizers, takes Mason's order for another Shiner, before moving off. Mason reaches over, takes one of the jalapeno quail bites and swallows it. I keep my eyes off his because I'm afraid if I do look I'm gonna say something I'll regret, and my momma taught me that sometimes you gotta know when to step away from someone filled with poison before they bite you like a snake.

After a long silence, Mason blows out a deep breath.

"Sorry." It's all he says, and I choose not to respond, 'cause ain't no reason for me to say what's on my mind.

The waitress comes by, drops off Mason's beer, and he takes a pull.

"Listen, Clint," he says, and his voice is quieter. "I've been dealing with this case since it got booted over to the agency from the LAPD because a California senator got involved. I've dealt with cases involving young women like Sloane Finley before. And, maybe calling her an 'idiot' was harsh. But she's nothing special, okay? She wasn't an 'actress.' She was a young woman filled with false hope who worked as a salesperson at Barnes and Noble while she tried to break into The Business along with about a million other young women just like her. She was naïve, and, I hate to say it, a bit dumb... but from everything I've discovered she was a decent, kind human being. Which makes what she did and what happened to her even more frustrating. If she'd just been smart and stayed home in Indiana, gone to school there, got a nice degree in teaching or something — hell, she could've even been a drama teacher! — you and I wouldn't be here enjoying this beer." He holds the bottle up. "And she would still be alive."

"You really are a jaded sonuvabitch, aren't you?" My voice is as bitter as I feel at the moment.

"Yep." He actually grins at me, happy. "And I think that's the nicest thing anyone's said to me in a long time."

Dinner could be worse than it ends up being, but there's still a tension there, at least from my side. We talk about the case a little more, he fills me in on some details about Sloane and some other folks he's had to deal with that I didn't know about. And though some of it lets me know he's got reason to be cynical, it still don't forgive him for talking about her that way. He didn't need to do that, and it ain't right. And it still grates a little even after I've dropped him off at The Ranch House and head home.

Problem is, the way I see it, a guy like Agent Jones has given up. Unlike I been taught and believe, he's signed off this case and it ain't even begun. Like my forensics instructor at the academy taught us, a murder case ain't a murder case until you got a body. And we don't got a body. Sloane Finley ain't turned up yet, nor has her Civic, and that means she's still out there. Maybe she ain't in Dallam County, or even Texas, but she's somewhere. And the clue that will lead to finding her is still sitting there, waiting to be discovered. Hopefully. We just need to keep looking. Not give up and put her into the dirt like Mason has already done.

When I'm back at home, I open up the files Mason had us look at earlier today. The ones from her Facebook page that got shutdown. A shudder of anger grates over my nerves like

40-grit sandpaper. If I'd had these, including that picture she took out there by the abandoned house, that woulda been the first place I went.

Just like the poster from the movie Giant!

That's what she wrote when she posted the picture. Her lying in the grass, looking back over her shoulder at the old house and barn in the distance. There was a breeze blowing that day. You can tell by the way it's caught her hair, lifting it a little, spreading it across one shoulder in little wisps while the rest drifts down her neck to her back.

Damn, she's so pretty.

I open an internet window and search, *movie poster Giant*. Nothing comes up that looks like what she's showed in her picture. All that I can find is some guy in a cowboy hat sitting in a car, gloves in one hand, feet up on the dash, an old house off in the distance. I frown, wondering if what she's written is some sort of insider movie joke I don't get. *Probably.* She was smart 'bout things like that, from everything I've read on her blog. She knew how all those things worked, about getting the attention of the agents, producers, whatever. Stuff like that. Since I ain't from Hollywood and don't know all that stuff about 'The Business' like Mason called it, it makes sense. Sloane knew, and this picture was her way of letting folks that were in on the secret know she knew.

She's smart, even if he doesn't see it.

I go through the other pictures. Her at various places along her way from LA to Stockdale. Lake Mead. Grand Canyon. Some forest near Flagstaff.

"Oh my God! Would you look at this!" Her voice in the video is so full of delight, filled with happiness and joy as she holds the little kachina doll up to her cheek. She's nothing but sunshine as she cuddles it for a moment before setting it back down and moving on.

I think that was what first struck me about her. Ain't seen someone so damn *happy* so much in a long time. It's like she ain't got a negative thing to say about nothing. Not the weather, the wind, the dust, the sun, family that don't want you to do anything but keep doing the same thing you did yesterday, and the day before that, and the day before that.

She's just a little slice of heaven set down here on earth.

There's a couple of shots she took out at Palos Verde. Her tanned arms and shoulders visible in the tank top she's wearing balanced against the red sandstone behind her. And then I'm back to that picture again. The last one she ever posted before she disappeared.

She was there. And so was I.

I've checked so many places, and I was close. So goddamn close. Just too late.

But we'll find her.

I'll find her.

She just needs to hold on.

TWENTY

Her

"Wake up." His voice is terse as he shakes my shoulder, and it snaps me out of sleep like a gunshot. My body jerks to sit up, but pain runs like lightning through my nerves, and I croak on a cry as I flatten back to the bed. He doesn't seem to notice as he climbs out, his weight shifting and then making the mattress bounce back up when he stands.

I lie still, focusing on breathing through the horrible feeling centered on my back as his footsteps bring him around to my side.

"Jasmine." There's no mercy in his voice, but I guess I should be grateful I'm alive. My mind scours the darkness, running back the time, but I can't remember anything but being tied to the fucking post in his barn while he whipped me. He grabs my arm and tugs a little, and I yelp.

"Please."

"Get up," he demands, and I try to shift my arm under me as he lets go. I try to push up from the bed, but I can feel the marks on my back stretching and cracking with each shift of bone and muscle.

"I can't," I whisper into the rough, dark blanket underneath me.

He lets out a huff of breath, and then I hear him walking into the bathroom. Turning my head, I catch sight of his back and I'm shocked to see dark whip marks. Several of them look bloody, and the confusion distracts me from what he's doing at the sink. I know the water is running, but all I can do is stare.

Did he do that to himself?

"Punishments aren't to be tended," he says in that new monotone. The one with a dangerous edge that feels like he's a breath from snapping again. "But I will help you this morning, Jasmine, because I love you, and I want you to remember that."

I close my eyes as he returns to me with a cloth, biting my tongue so I don't say anything. *Love?* The idea makes me angry, or like I want to cry, or scream, or jump out the fucking window. They all seem preferable to his love.

"Oh God!" Air hisses through my teeth as the rough cloth strokes over my back in a brutal starbust of pain.

"Only *He* can forgive you, Jasmine. I have done my part, and together we will see this through." Another stroke of the cloth sends water running down my waist in a warm trickle, and I fist the blanket underneath me. "Once you can stand, I'll take you to the basement so you can pray today."

Back to the basement. It's all ruined. No more 'good wife' lie... and no more pills to keep me safe.

Jasmine

I'm going to die here. One way or another, I'm going to die.

Mason

I've worn the same clothes two days in a row before, but for some reason this morning putting my suit back on feels like I've been wearing these much longer. I hung everything up in the tiny closet of this motel room that easily dates back to when Eisenhower was president, and when I got up this morning there was a fine sheen of dust on everything. Freshly showered, I came out of the bathroom, opened the closet, and just stood there, looking at them.

How in the hell?

I brushed them off as best I could, but I can still feel dust. Or at least my brain is convincing me I can, and that's all it needs to do for it to become reality.

Clint swings by right at seven, just like we discussed when he dropped me off last night. He seems taciturn, maybe a little less than when he left me, and I wonder if he's taken time to think about what I said.

Probably. But did any of it stick?

We get to the station, and head inside. Deputy Talbert is sitting at his desk, and the door to Sheriff Braddock's office is open, his voice drifting out.

"All right, Delvin, I sure do appreciate it. No, no, nothing more than that." There is a pause, and then a low chuckle. "Yeah, well, you let me know, and I'll make sure you're all taken care of." Another short pause follows, and I catch

Clint looking at the other deputy, motioning with his hands. Talbert gives him a shrug, and goes back to whatever paperwork he's doing.

"You do the same. I'll talk to you later," Braddock says and then I hear him hang up the phone.

None of us have spoken while he's talking, all surreptitiously listening in on his conversation. I can hear Braddock get up from his desk and come out into the main office.

"Morning, gentlemen." Cup in hand, he heads over to a counter near the refrigerator where an ancient-looking coffee pot on a burner sends up wisps of steam. "Enjoy your dinner last night?"

"It was wonderful, Sheriff." I look over to Clint, who avoids my eyes and simply nods.

"It was good," he half mumbles before turning to something on his computer.

If Braddock notices Clint's response, he chooses to ignore it. "Coffee, Agent Jones?"

"Please."

He makes the drink, then returns, handing me a stained white mug with a faded John Deere logo on it. I accept the cup from him and take a sip.

It ain't Starbucks. It's better.

"You talk with Agent Rodriguez yet this morning?" he asks.

I blink once. *Fuck.*

"It's on my list of things to take care of before we leave," I reply, mentally cursing myself for not doing it before now.

Braddock's eyes narrow, but he says nothing if he's caught my reaction. "I see. Well, I called my counterpart in the Potter County Sheriff's Department, and he checked up at Heart Hospital, where they got her. She's stabilized, but it don't look like they're gonna be releasing her today." He takes a sip of his coffee. "So, I don't think I'd be expecting your agent friend to be showing up anytime soon."

I nod, taking a drink of my own. "I'd expect not. Looks like I may be in your hair a little bit longer."

"Figured as much." Braddock nods, and gives a slight smile. "I had Delvin put together some flowers and one of them gift basket things. He's gonna have one of the folks run it over later this morning. Asked him to make sure your name got put on the card." He gives me an appraising stare. "Hope that weren't too forward?"

"No, sir. No, that wasn't too forward at all. Thank you."

He gives me a soft grin. "Just the way we do things 'round here, Agent Jones."

We both sip our coffee, and then Braddock looks past me. "Clint, you still plan on taking Agent Jones out to the Christiansen place, or do I need to have Duane do it?"

"Wha...?" Deputy Talbert's voice rises in concern behind me, and Clint looks towards him and then over to me.

"I suppose that's up to Agent Jones. Whether he'd rather have Duane's company or mine."

"I... I just pulled a twelve-hour shift!" Talbert's response is a plaintive whine.

I catch Braddock's barely suppressed grin, and I smile.

"Much as I'm sure I'd enjoy Deputy Talbert's company, I think the plan was for Clint and I to head out there a bit later this morning. I'm still fine with that if he is."

Braddock nods. "Looks like you're off the hook, Duane," he calls out without looking in his direction. The deputy huffs out an exasperated sigh.

"Sure as hell glad to hear it!"

I spend the next hour taking care of a few things I need to. The first of which is to call Carmen and check in with her. She fills me in on what happened to her wife. Driving from her office to the courthouse, a young kid texting and not watching where they were going went through a red light and right into the side of her car. The speed of the accident is not on the low end.

"From where her car ended up, they say the kid was doing at least thirty-five."

"Christ."

"Yeah. Pushed her right into a light pole, which is the only way I figure it didn't flip her."

"She doing okay?"

"She's out of ICU, so..." Carmen speaks slowly, and I can hear the weariness in her voice. She's been up all night, I have no doubt. "And her fancy-ass Beemer is totaled."

"Well, as long as she's okay, right?"

"Yeah. But she's been at me to let her buy a new and fancier one, and so now..."

I laugh, because it's all so comical, so typical of a couple, and Carmen chuckles too. It's hearing her make that sound that lets me know she's going to be okay.

"Whitmann?" I ask.

There's a pause, and then a sigh. "He's playing it all concern and sympathy right now, but I have a feeling he's got a rocket coming for my ass as soon as all the dust settles."

"I'm sorry, Carmen."

"Eh, fuck him. I've been dealing with his bullshit and others for years now. I'm sure I can weather this too."

We talk for a bit longer, and then I let her go. It's close to eight AM, and I have no idea exactly how long it's going to take us to get to the Christiansen place. My stomach rumbles, and I realize I'm hungry, even after the giant meal we ate last night.

I get up and go to Clint's desk. He's studying the files on Sloane I gave him yesterday, and as I approach he looks up at me stoically, making no attempt to hide them.

"There some place we could grab breakfast before we head out?"

He looks at me for a moment before nodding. "Sure." He stands up, and calls out to Braddock. "Agent Jones wants to get some breakfast. I'm going to take him over to Mattie's. You want me to bring you back anything?"

"Naw," Braddock's voice floats out of his office. "I'm good. Thanks!"

Clint nods. "All right. We're going to take off out to Daniel's place from there, then, once we're done."

"Sounds good." Braddock's voice drift's back. "I'll see you folks when you get back this afternoon."

Clint takes me over to Mattie's, where we sit down at a table. The waitress greets him by name, all daisy-fresh warmth that seems more cloying that sincere. When Clint says her name — Laurie Ann — it all becomes clear.

He shoots me a look as she leaves with our order, and I keep my face blank. He waits a minute, and then gives me a challenging stare. "Nothing to say? No jab at me and my 'girlfriend?'"

I give him a bright smile. "Wouldn't dream of it."

"Uh huh." He blows into his cup, then takes a sip of his coffee.

"Listen," I say as I do the same with my coffee, and then lean forward. "Are you going to sulk like a child all day, or can we forget last night and just do a reset?"

Clint stares at me, his mouth cracking open, and then he leans back, suddenly chuckling. "Damn. It's true what they say 'bout you LA people. You all just move right from one thing to the next and never look back, don't you?"

I give him a shrug. "Maybe. I don't know, and I don't really care. What I do know is that we've got a job to do, and it's clear that we both have a different approach to this case. So here's the thing." I lean back to match him and take a drink. "All I want to do is go out and meet this kid Daniel, see if he saw anything the day that Sloane disappeared, or anything unusual afterward. After that, we both come back here, have another nice dinner, and then I make my way back to Amarillo and out of your life forever." I give him as warm a smile as I can muster. "And what would make that a whole lot easier on the both of us is if we could just be as pleasant to each other as possible, rather than bickering like an old couple."

He stares at me for a moment, and then slowly shakes his head, mouth pulled into a sardonic grin. I like it. It looks good on him. "I swear..."

"How long is it going to take for us to get to the Christiansen place?" I ask.

"I ain't actually ever been there."

"Guess."

"An hour, maybe a bit more depending on the road up to his place."

I beam. "See? Couple of hours out, ask a few questions, couple of hours back." I motion with my hands while I say it, explaining how simple it can be. "All we have to do is make nice-nice just that long, and then it'll all be over." I spread my hands wide. "I'll even do you a favor and let you skip the dinner."

Clint chuckles, pointing a finger at me. "And there's another thing you LA people are always doing."

"What's that."

"Selling something."

"Touché," I reply with a grin.

We have our breakfast, fend off Laurie Ann's flirtations, and it's 8:45 when we walk back to the station and climb into the Bronco. The drive out is the same one we took yesterday, right up to where we pass the dirt road leading out to the abandoned ranch. As we drive past it, Clint doesn't even slow. Our conversation has been sporadic, banal, nothing really to do with the case, or anything that relates to Sloane Finley. I almost want to bait him about his obvious fascination with her, but I don't. I was the one to offer the truce, and I'd really be showing my asshole colors if I was the one to break it.

We drive on for another few miles and I notice Clint is leaning forward now, hunched over the steering wheel, scanning the area to either side of the road. We're cresting another slight rise when I finally ask, "Any idea how much further?"

"Like I said, I ain't never actually been to the Christiansen place…" His voice trails off for a moment. "But I know it's out this way." His head continues its back-and-forth pattern. "And I'm pretty sure we ain't too far."

We've gone silent again when I finally spot a break in the fence line at the same time I feel Clint slowing the truck. He eases to the side of the road as we come up to a much more modern-looking gate than the one we came to at the abandoned property. Clint brings the truck off the pavement, and comes to a stop.

"This the road to the Christiansen place?" I ask.

"Yep. Has to be."

He shuts off the truck, and climbs out of the cab. I follow, looking the gate over. "It's locked."

"Yep."

"Cut it." I don't ask if he's carrying bolt cutters in the vehicle, I just assume it.

He frowns at me as if I've asked him to steal a man's lunch. "Ain't no need for that..." He moves past me to the gate post, inching up his lanky frame until he can look at the top of it.

"Five R minus two." I hear him say the words softly as he comes back down off his toes, and then he's turning to his right, walking down the fence line. I watch him as he moves off a short distance and comes to a halt by one of the steel stake fence posts. I watch as he kneels, rooting around at the base. A moment goes by then I see him nod, rising with something in his hand. He walks back to where I'm standing, and with a tight smile he takes the key and opens the lock.

"Interesting."

"You didn't see nothing," he says with a grin, swinging the gate open. "Come on." We return to the truck, and he pulls through to the other side and stops, leaving the truck idling. I turn and watch out the back window as he swings the gate closed, locks it, and then returns back down the fence line to hide the key at the third post where he'd found it. Once everything is in place, he jumps back in, and we begin moving once more.

"Never seen that before."

"Rancher's trick. That way your neighbors can get up your road if you need help, but people who ain't from around here can't."

"Duly noted."

Clint chuckles. "Like I said, you didn't see nothing."

We drive up the dirt road, kicking up a rooster tail of dust behind us. Mr. Christiansen, if he's here, or anyone else who may be ahead of us, is going to know we're coming. It's not exactly the approach I'd like to take, but Clint seems unperturbed, and I realize that for him this is just natural. An exclamation point of dust rising into the air must be the West Texas way of ringing the doorbell.

The road goes on for miles from the county road before we crest a small rise and I see a group of buildings ahead of us. As we get closer, they resolve themselves into a ranch with a house, a barn, two silver metal feed silos, and the ubiquitous windmill. It's an older place. A white clapboard house that is something straight out of Norman Rockwell, and though the barn is maintained and neatly kept, the weathered boards belie any notion that it's of newer construction. I'm taking all this in when I notice another thing.

A man is standing in the large dirt area between the buildings. A very, very large man.

Clint slows the truck as we get closer, letting the trail of dust we've been dragging behind us settle. I don't look over at him, but keep my eyes on the man, sweeping the area to either side of him for signs of anyone else. As we pull to the edge of the larger area I say to Clint in a low voice, "Daniel Christiansen?"

"Yep."

"Big boy."

"Now you see why they called him 'The Wall' back in high school. Best damn lineman Stockdale ever had."

Jasmine

"Well, I guess it's true what they say. You do grow'em bigger here in Texas."

Clint doesn't even chuckle at the joke as he pulls the truck to the side of where the young man is standing and shuts off the motor. We both get out and move to position ourselves opposite Mr. Christiansen. He stands motionless, eyes moving back and forth between us as we take our places. His hands are at his sides, fingers spread wide, not clenched. He doesn't seem tense, even though he's standing rigidly. For whatever reason the posture seems natural on him. As if this is the way he's always stood before smaller creatures below him.

Finally, when we're all arrayed under the heat of the late-morning sun, Mr. Christiansen breaks the ice. "How'd you get onto my property?"

I might have expected outright hostility, especially given the abruptness of his question, but the voice, though deep, is surprisingly quiet. Flat.

"Afternoon, Daniel." Clint keeps his own voice blandly pleasant, neutral.

"My gate was locked."

"I know that, but we needed to come talk to you." Clint motions toward me. "This here's Agent Jones of the FBI. He's come out from California, looking into a case that took place 'round here awhile back. He has a few questions he'd like to ask you."

"Questions about what?"

I take a few steps toward him and stop. I've never thought myself small, but I have to bend my neck back to look up into his face. 'The Wall' is a completely apt description for him. He is solid, muscular, a wall of flesh carved into a young man. I stick out my hand. "Afternoon, sir."

He looks at my hand stoically, then stares into my face. He looks neither unfriendly, nor angry. Just a blank slate with a monotone voice that reveals nothing about what's going on in that head, or behind those dark eyes that stare back into mine. At worst, he appears mildly perturbed that his privacy has been invaded unannounced, and that is discernible mostly in his words. It's just as Braddock had warned about people out here. They value their privacy.

"Afternoon." He takes my hand, engulfing it until it disappears completely within his. Now that I'm close, and in physical contact with him, it seems almost unnatural how big he is.

"Do you have a moment to talk?" I follow Clint's lead, keeping my voice politely professional and neutral as I pull my hand back from his.

He looks down at me, then over to Clint, his expression never changing. "What do you want?"

I pull the image I grabbed from the truck out of my pocket and offer it toward him. "Do you recognize this picture?"

He looks down at the picture for a moment, his head slightly cocked. I watch, but his expression doesn't falter for an instant. When he's done, he turns his face back to mine. "Never seen it before."

"Okay." I nod understandingly. "Do you recognize the young woman in the picture? Where it was taken?"

"That's my property."

"That's what we thought. Do you recognize the woman?" I repeat the question, keeping my voice even.

"No." Mr. Christiansen says it firmly, without inflection. He turns to look at Clint. "Is she from town?"

Clint shakes his head. "No, Daniel. She ain't from Stockdale. She's an actress. From out there in California."

"An actress?" For the first time I hear inflection in his voice. It sounds like confusion. That term — Clint calling her an actress — seems to baffle Daniel. "What was she doing on my property?"

"She was taking a picture," I answer the question, indicating the piece of paper in my hand. "This picture."

"A... picture? Why'd she want a picture?"

"Well, as Deputy Nolan said, she was an aspiring actress." I watch as his eyes come up to mine, and the confusion hasn't faded. "She was on a cross-country trip. To promote herself. She stopped here, where this picture was taken on your property, and after she took it, she posted it to her Facebook page."

His eyes narrow as I go on, the confusion growing even more pronounced. What Braddock explained at the station yesterday flashes back to me. The entire reason we are out here right now. No phone. No technology. This young man doesn't know what Facebook is. He has absolutely no idea what I'm talking about. I might as well be the man in the moon for all the nonsense I'm spewing.

He doesn't look back at the picture at all, keeping his gaze firmly on me as he says, "She was trespassing."

Her

At first I'm not sure that the murmur of voices I hear is real. It's like a television on in another room, a rumble of different tones that leaks into my ears slowly as I lie on the table, but then it clicks.

There's no TV here.

I whimper as I push myself up from the wooden surface, standing slowly, and even though the sight of the basement windows makes my stomach twist, I still reach for it to pull it open. As soon as I do, I can hear men talking. But Daniel's voice is there too. Low, monotonous, but there.

With people. Real people.

He'll just kill them if you make a sound. The thought invades as I try to build up the energy to scream, but then I hear the words 'Deputy Nolan' and my heart skips a beat. *The police.* This is it. This is my chance. My only fucking chance.

Shoving the window open as far as it will go, I look at the narrow space and then down at my body. I'm in a thin shirt that I can feel sticking to my back, but I know I've lost weight here.

I just don't know if I've lost enough to make it through the window.

Putting my arms on the ground outside, I kick up off the table and have to bite down the scream as my back hits the window. The voices continue, and even as fresh pain rakes down my back, I drag myself forward. Squeezing, digging my fingers into the dust and the thin grass.

Breathe out and do it, Sloane. Do it or you're dead.

Mason

'Trespassing.' That's all this wall of a kid has to say about Sloane Finley, and I knew it.

I realize with a crystalline clarity it's the full extent of what he knows and will ever know about Sloane Finley. *'She was trespassing.'* That's all it will ever be. Probably the last note I'll have to make in any report on her. Daniel Christiansen never saw Sloane Finley. She came, took her picture, and was gone without him ever being the wiser. And whoever did take her, wherever that may have been, the only thing he would know of her now is that she was the girl who trespassed on his property.

What a fucking waste of time.

"So you don't recognize her. Never saw her here on your property at any time?" I ask, even though I know it's pointless.

"No, sir. I don't recognize her. I know I never seen her, that I'm sure of. Don't really get many visitors out here."

"And her car, maybe? A blue Honda Civic. Ever see that around here or on your property?" Clint pushes, but I'm done. We're both done here.

"Nope. Blue car woulda stood out. Most folks out here drive trucks."

We stand in silence as the wind whispers around us, kicking up a small eddy of dust that swirls past us toward the barn. Clint scuffs the toe of his boot into the ground, then looks up at Daniel.

"You remember what was going on around here about two and a half months ago? You out here all by yourself, or was anyone else around?" Clint scratches his cheek, staring at the man with interest.

"Two and a half months ago we was finishing bringing in the head to pasture up." He glances over toward the fenced-in pasture area that we can see just beyond the barn. "I hired the Hernandez brothers to help out. You could ask them if they saw anything, but we was all together most of the time, so I doubt it."

Clint stares at Daniel, nodding slowly. "And after that?"

Daniel gazes back, face blank, devoid of any emotion. "Just fattenin' 'em up."

For a moment it almost appears like some sort of bizarre imitation of a showdown Clint is engaging in with Daniel Christiansen, except it's completely one-sided. The young man has no idea what we're here about, or why he's being questioned in regard to the disappearance of a young woman he knows nothing about. That much is perfectly clear to me. At best I had hoped he might have a tiny scrap of information about Sloane Finley's whereabouts on the day she disappeared. Maybe an 'I saw this blue car heading over the hill as I was coming back in from town,' or something of that nature. Instead, we've gotten exactly what I'd expected.

Nothing.

"Deputy Nolan, I think I have everything I need."

Clint's face snaps toward me, his mouth coming open for a moment before he speaks. "That's it? You... you sure you got all your questions answered?"

"As I said, I have everything I need." I give him a pointed look. "We can go now."

Clint's hand comes up, and for a second I think he's going to argue with me. But he drops it, mouth becoming a tight line of frustration. I face Daniel and give him a nod.

"Thank you for your time, Mr. Christiansen. Sorry to have disturbed you."

The boy says nothing in return, just gives me another of his emotionless stares. I turn and walk back toward the truck, leaving Clint standing there, still facing Daniel, unmoving. Looking into the window of the truck as I approach, I can see in the reflection that Clint is still in place, rocking on the balls of his feet as if he can't quite decide what to do next.

"I'll... I'll see you 'round, Daniel."

I stop at the door of the truck, watch as Daniel says nothing, does nothing but stare back at Clint in return. I put my hand on the door handle, waiting until I see Clint spin around and begin moving in this direction. Once he is, I climb inside, closing the door behind me. Clint comes around the vehicle, his face grim as he opens the door and climbs in, slamming it behind him. For a moment he just sits there, gazing out the window at Daniel, who remains immobile, staring back at us.

"That's it?" Clint's voice is strained and he doesn't look at me.

"What do you mean, 'that's it?'"

"That's all we're gonna do? That's all the questioning you got for him?"

"Clint, there's nothing here. That kid doesn't know shit about Sloane Finley. Goddammit, he doesn't even know what Facebook is, much less anything else that might pertain to her."

His jaw is working. I'm waiting for him to pull out the keys and start the truck. Turn us around and head us out of here. Instead, he's just sitting there, fuming.

Jesus. Christ.

"Did you really think we were going to discover something out here?"

He doesn't respond, so I press on.

"This is exactly what I expected. He doesn't know anything about Sloane Finley. He didn't see anything, because there was nothing for him to see. At best she was out there on his property for fifteen minutes, and after she took that picture, she climbed back in her little car and drove off. She was miles away from here and long gone when it broke down or whatever happened, and then whoever it was came along and found her and then killed her."

His head whips around as I say that.

Jasmine

"That is the truth, Deputy. That is the reality of what happened to Sloane Finley. And you need to stop fantasizing about this fucking dead girl"—I wave the paper photo in his face—"and come to terms with it."

His eyes blaze at me, and I know I've jabbed a coal into the nest of nerves I laid open last night.

"I didn't come out here to find Sloane Finley. And damn sure not to save her. I came out here to flesh out a few paragraphs on a fucking report to give to the grieving father of a corpse." I slap the paper down on the center console, and then jab my finger into it. "And I've got what I needed to do that. Now start the truck and let's get the hell out of here."

He's angry. Maybe furious. But he doesn't say another word. He fishes the keys out of his pocket, jams them into the ignition, and turns the motor over. He shoves the shifter into drive, and then wheels the SUV around in a tight turn, pointing us back the way we came. I look back in my mirror and see Daniel standing there, dust slowly shrouding him as we drive off. Soon the cloud becomes denser, then opaque until he disappears completely.

For his part, Clint does nothing but grip the wheel and point the truck forward, but I can see his eyes vacillating between staring down the road and glancing back in the rearview mirror to the fading form of Daniel Christiansen. I'm biting my tongue from saying anything more, even though a part of me says he needs it, when suddenly he slams on the brakes.

"Jesus Christ, Clint!" I shout, catching myself on the dash. "What the hell are you doing? Why are you stopping?"

"I..."

"What? You... *what?*"

"I thought I saw something."

"How the hell could you see anything through all that?" I motion towards the rearview mirror, and the cloud of dust behind us.

"I just thought I saw something," he snaps back at me. We sit there, the truck idling while the wind catches our own dust plume up to us, surrounding the truck in a filthy cloud.

"We should go back."

"What? Go back?" I look over at him. I wasn't going to push him any further this afternoon, but now he's got me irritated. "Look behind you. Do you see anything? Do you?"

"It's just a... feeling I got. There's something odd back there."

"Odd? God save me..." I run my hand over my chin and mouth. "Okay, you know what? You're right. There is something odd back there. *He* is fucking odd. And while I'll grant you that, let me tell you something. I'm from LA. Hollywood. I *know* fucking odd. I *live* fucking odd. If you think Daniel Christiansen is the oddest person I've ever had to interview, you are sadly mistaken, Deputy. Hell, compared to some people I've had to question, he's goddamn Stephen Hawking."

Clint doesn't say anything in response at first as we continue to sit, unmoving.

"I saw something. We should go back and look."

Jasmine

"There is nothing to go back and look at."

"I'm telling you, I saw something. What could it hurt to just go back and take another look?"

Now I'm starting to get more than irritated. Deputy Nolan is a nice-enough kid, and I'm sure he's a fine law enforcement officer and an all-around helluva guy, but I am over this. All of it. This case, this place, the dust, the never-ending grass, Andre-the-fucking-Giant back there. I am over every bit of it, including a young man who has the bit between his teeth for a fantasy revolving around a young woman who has been dead for months, but one he somehow believes is out there in a tower somewhere, waiting to be rescued. At this point I want only one thing: to get back to LA as quickly as I can get my ass on a flight headed west.

We are not going back there. Ever.

"Hey, Clint. Listen to me, and listen carefully. You're shadowboxing at something that doesn't exist, okay? There's nothing back there to discover. There's nothing around here anywhere." I slash my hand in an arc across the breadth of the cab. "Nothing that is going to change the fact that Sloane Finley is dead. Nothing back there is suddenly going to magick her up. Now, I. Am. Done. Here. And we're going. So do me and yourself a favor. Just put the goddamn truck in gear and let's get back to Stockdale."

He stares at me, his jaw cracking tight, mouth a slash that shows as much as his eyes just how upset he is about this. He's standing at the water's edge, watching his fantasy version of Sloane Finley sail off into the distance, borne on the words of a jaded FBI agent who just wants to get the hell away from here as quickly as possible.

"Fine," he grits the word out as he yanks the shifter back, and with a jerk we begin rattling our way down the road. Away from the ranch, the barn, the silos, Daniel 'The Wall' Christiansen. All of it.

Which makes what I do next even more exasperating.

Because I can't for the fucking life of me understand why I find myself staring into the side mirror and watching as the place fades behind us.

We make it two-thirds of the way back to Stockdale before Clint opens his mouth. "You gonna report me to Sheriff Braddock?"

I look over at him, and then back to the highway that slips by. "For what?"

"Mouthing off. Not obeying orders."

I snort. "I'm not your supervisor. I'm just a visitor here."

"You're a federal agent. I ain't stupid. You outrank me."

I start to respond with the first thing that comes to mind, but then stop myself, thinking better of it. He's right. He isn't stupid. He's young, and idealistic, and a good, decent kid, which he needs to have driven out of him at the earliest possible moment if he's going to survive in this field.

"No, Deputy Nolan. I am not going to report you." I put my hands behind my head, fingers lacing, and then I lean back, eyes closing. "I am, however, going to offer you some advice."

"What's that?"

"Stop believing you can make a difference. Stop believing you can solve anything. Just accept. Just accept that the world around you is an unstoppable force of shit, and that you are not going to be able to turn it into anything worthwhile."

He says nothing, and I open one eye and glance over. As I suspected, his jaw is set again, lips pressed together so tight they've turned almost white.

"I know you don't want to hear that, but if you want to stay in law enforcement, you need to wrap your head around the concept." I crack my neck, and then look over at him again. "You are not here to serve, and protect. You are here to observe and clean up. You are a glorified janitor for the worst parts of humanity. And at the very end, when you've swept all the body parts into a bag, you get to write a report describing everything you've observed and discovered, so it can either be filed away, never to be seen again, or used against you in a court of law."

I take a deep breath. "You think in terms of helping people. Saving them. Rescuing them from the evils of this world." He starts to open his mouth, but I continue without stopping. "And don't even try and tell me different, Deputy. I saw it last night and you wear it on your sleeve like a badge of honor." His mouth snaps closed, and he avoids my gaze. "Someday you are going to take a call. It's going to be somebody phoning from the side of a highway. There's been an accident. And you're going to get there, and there'll be a body lying on the ground. '*I didn't see her! She came outta nowhere!*' And you'll go, and you'll see she's just some kid trying to make her way north. And you'll roll her over to check for a pulse even though you already know it won't be there. And that's when you'll find it. The child she was carrying in her arms, trying to protect. And it's still alive, but only for another minute or so. And you'll stand there and watch it happen because there's not going to be a goddamn thing you can do, no matter how much you want to be the hero. Because that's how life works. Life doesn't need heroes or want heroes. It wants cleaning people to tidy up the messes, and you just signed up for the worst shift of all."

Clint keeps his face forward, lockjaw rigid, adamant in his refusal to acknowledge what I've just said. Not that I expected any different. He's young, and it's going to take far more than me being an asshole to change his way of thinking. Especially because I've little doubt that's what made him become a deputy in the first place.

The tires make a sibilant hiss as we drive on, and my mind is starting to drift from what I've just said when his voice cuts through the cab, stiff.

"What makes you think I ain't already seen something like that?" He looks over at me, his face a mask of challenge. I stare at him until he can't hold my gaze any longer. And then I continue staring until he shifts in his seat, relenting. "Fine. I ain't. But that don't mean I don't understand what you're talking about."

"Yes it does. Because until you've seen something like that, until you've held that child in your arms until it sucks down its last breath and goes still, you're going to keep thinking you can save people. Change things. Make a difference in the natural order. And believe me, Clint. There is a natural order to how things work in this field.

Bad things happen to good people. In fact, bad things happen to good people more often than they happen to bad people. And you are going to see it happen. And there's not going to be a goddamn thing you can do about it.

"That's a shitty fucking way to live your life."

"It's a realistic way to live your life. And trust me, the sooner you accept it, the easier you'll be able to get through one day to the next without wanting to eat your gun, and instead, survive."

For a moment he sits in silence, driving, and then he talks to the windshield. "Let me ask you something"

"What."

"You ever been wrong, Agent Jones? Huh? Has there ever been one time in your career you've just been flat-out wrong? That your intuition just didn't get it right?"

"That's not relaven—"

"That ain't answering my question, Agent Jones. I asked you if you've ever been wrong. And more important, if you *have* ever been wrong, was there somebody who paid the price for your mistake?"

And it's my turn now to grit my teeth.

I unlace my hands from behind my head, turn, and gaze out the window of the Bronco. Watch as the sun burns high in the sky, bleaching everything from the world in its brilliance.

"Yeah. I've been wrong before. More than once."

I pick up the crumpled picture from the seat and look at it. Stare at it. Remember voices from the past.

'You think I'm ready for this, Mason?'

'You'll never know until you try, right?'

'Can you see her? I can't get a visual!'

'Man down! Man down!'

I feel my hand clenching the paper, beginning to crumple it. I force myself to stop, my eyes bringing the image into focus once again. And the voices continue. Newer. More recent.

'Pretty girl. Dead girl.'

'You don't know that.'

'Are you going to find her, Mr. Jones?'

'You aren't, are you? No one is.'

But those voices shouldn't be here. Because I'm not wrong this time. I'm right. I know I am.

I know it.

"Yeah, I've been wrong before, Clint. But this time I'm not. This time I *am* right." I hear the defensiveness in my voice, and I shove that emotion back. I don't need to be defensive. There is nothing for me to feel defensive over.

I am right.

This time.

"Yeah?" Clint looks over at me, and his gaze is reproach and sympathy wrapped together, each one fighting for dominance over the other. "Well you'll excuse me if I find that notion kinda funny, Agent Jones. Seems to me if you were so goddamn convinced of that, there shouldn't have been a problem going back to take another look, should there?"

He gives me a pointed glare, and I can't believe I have to keep myself from looking away.

Fucking kid.

And then he gives me one final parting shot.

"But maybe you just didn't want to find out you might be wrong, did you?"

TWENTY-ONE

Him
———

I keep my boot on Jasmine's back, holding her on the ground as she makes quiet sounds, but I don't look at her. No, my eyes are on the drive where the dust has stopped kicking up because those policemen are stopped somewhere over the first dip of the driveway.

When she squirms, I dig my heel in harder until she stops, and I can feel the anger rising in me. Wrath has always been my weakness. It was my weakness on the football field, and the Devil has made her test me with it again and again.

But this... this I can't ignore.

The dust starts rising again, a new plume flowing up like a miniature sandstorm as their SUV heads out toward the gate. I watch it for another minute before I look down at her. There's blood on the back on her shirt, a hole that wasn't there this morning, and I know she got it climbing out one of the windows.

Should have boarded them up.

Jasmine

Shoulda, woulda, coulda.

She's crying and it should make me want to give her mercy, but I gave her that last night. I gave her mercy this morning when she couldn't get out of bed... and what did she give me in return?

Betrayal.

"You just don't learn." I lift my foot off her back and try to breathe, try to unclench my fists as I stand beside her. "Get up."

Jasmine just cries, her face in the dust, and I'm disgusted by her as I grab her arm and pull her off the ground. One glance at her clothes and I can tell they're ruined.

She's ruined.

"You are dirty. Filthy." The words slip out as I start pulling her toward the barn. She fights, trips, falls, and I drag her the rest of the way because she doesn't deserve to be carried. She doesn't deserve my mercy, my love, my care.

I have given her all that and more over and over and over.

And she kills our child. Tries to leave me. Tries to destroy our family.

Ripping the door to the barn open, I toss her inside and then lock it up. Just in case they come back.

They won't come back. They're looking for someone else, not Jasmine.

Jasmine is mine.

Her

He walks away from me, and I want to run. I want to run more than anything in the world, because the police are out there. In that cloud of dust that choked my lungs. But it takes everything I have just to sit up.

My voice breaks on a sob as I stare at the cement under my hands.

If I'd just been faster. If I'd pushed harder.

So many mistakes. So many many mistakes and now I'm going to die for them. I know it, and a large part of me just wants to accept it. It wants me to lie down and just let it happen, however he wants to do it, but there's still a tiny voice begging me to fight. To run.

I hate that voice.

I hate myself.

"You're filthy. Take your clothes off." He's back, standing over me, but I can't move. All I can do is stare at the dust coating my arms, turning them pale and chalky. Daniel isn't patient today though, he grabs my shirt and rips it upward, peeling it off my butchered back as he forces my arms up to yank it over my head.

I definitely hurt it worse squeezing through the window. I felt the wood scratching me through the shirt, and every single inch was torture until my ribs were free.

And it was all for nothing.

"NOW, JASMINE!" he shouts, and I flinch. No bra because I couldn't stand one against my back, but I'm in shorts. Underwear. I bring my shaking hands to the button on my shorts, only fumbling with it for a second before he grabs me off the ground. I'm nothing but a doll in his hands, barely able to get my feet under me as he shakes me. "NOW!"

"Okay, okay," I whisper, nodding over and over as I pop the button and shove them towards my hips. Bending hurts so much, but his impatience wins out and he rips them down, and then my underwear. As I stumble out of my clothing, he grabs me again and shoves me ahead of him toward the wall by Moses's stall. I wonder if the horses are in there, or if they're roaming happily in the pasture.

I hope they're not in here. *I don't want them to hear this.*

Cold water hits me like a thousand tiny needles and I squeak out a scream as I try to turn away from it, but the pressure of it on my back is torture. I end up turning in circles, trying to shield myself as he sprays me with a hose. When I try to speak, to beg, he aims the water at my face, and I spin away, sobbing as I hide against the wall, sliding down it as he continues.

"Filthy. Disgusting." There's only rage in his voice as he stomps closer, tossing me to the side easily so he can spray where he wants. "Wash yourselves; make yourselves clean; remove the evil of your deeds from before my eyes," he mumbles, half under his breath as he grabs my hand and scrubs at it with his.

The water puddles under me, and I'm shivering from the icy temperature of it as he shoves me again and sprays my back. I cry out, trying to crawl away, but he pushes me down again with the toe of his boot.

"Cease to do evil, Jasmine. CEASE TO DO EVIL!" he roars, his voice completely different as he rants. "That is Isaiah, Jasmine. From the Bible. God tells you the truth in His Word, and you ignore it! Deny it! You deny me!"

"No, no, no, please..." I'm babbling, and it's useless, all of it, but my brain isn't working right anymore. It's on autopilot. It wants to live. It wants to survive another day... stupid, stupid, stupid. There's no hope here. None.

"You deny God when you defy me, Jasmine!" His fist finds my wet hair, wrenching me upright, and I can barely see through my tears as he drags me across the barn to the workbench, shoving me down onto it.

"Please, please, don't—" My head cracks against the smooth wood, a strange pop of sound from the force of it, and it's like my ears are ringing. Before it stops, he rips my head up again, and I taste leather as he pushes it past my lips and teeth.

"No more talking. Be silent," he growls from above me as the leather yanks at my mouth. He's tying it behind my head, and I try to plead through it for him to stop. "BE SILENT!" he shouts, tightening it before he shoves me back down. "God bids you to be silent, Jasmine. You cannot continue to defy me, because God bids you to obey. God demands of you to listen to your husband, to obey, to offer me your body freely."

I scream an unintelligible version of 'no' just before light flashes behind my eyes, followed by a disorienting pain. It takes me more than a few seconds to realize he slammed my head into the table again, but I think it was harder this time.

Everything is swimming, and I feel nauseous even before I feel his cock prodding between my thighs.

"Accept me," he snarls, one hand on my ass as he shoves me forward until my head bumps into the wall. He tries to thrust, but it won't go in at first, and then I hear him spit. His fingers take his dick's place for a moment, and those he gets in on the first try. There's nothing gentle, and I don't expect it as he shoves them in and out, mumbling his insanity aloud. "The wife is meant for the husband, meant to be one flesh. Meant to carry his child."

No. I'll die, the first chance I get. You'll never use me like that.

His cock drives into me, still nowhere near wet, and I groan against the leather in my teeth as he forces himself in. I think it hurts, I'm pretty sure it does, somewhere in the wasteland of my body, and all I can think about is how much easier this would be if I hadn't made him angry. If he'd never found the birth control. If I'd never betrayed the weak trust I'd started to build.

I was so close. So close.

"One flesh, Jasmine. This is what we are meant for. It is God's plan." He grunts as he works himself inside me, trying to get all the way in, but my body is slow to respond today. Not that he understands why. He doesn't understand anything.

Suddenly, he pulls out of me, dragging me off the table. The world spins, and then I'm on the concrete, on my back, a million flares of agony turning me rigid as my back scrapes against it.

"You will accept me, Jasmine. It is what you are meant for." There's no sanity left in him, and I should be quiet, but the scream is impossible to hold back as he climbs on top of me, bending my knees up and out so he can fit between my thighs. He lines up, staring between us before he shoves forward, driving me into the concrete as I try to be anywhere else.

I want to black out. I want to die.

But his God doesn't grant me that.

In this position, my body starts to respond, to ease the path for him, but that's the only easy thing about it. Every thrust is grating pain across my back, my head is throbbing, and every time I open my eyes, I find his closed. Intent on what he wants from me, the only thing he wants from me. No prayers this time, no apologies, he's gagged me so I couldn't even if he demanded it.

All I can do is make sounds, whimpering, crying as he finally gets all the way in, and I feel the pinch of pain that always accompanies his size. It's like a different note in the maelstrom of torment he's inflicted on me during the past few days, a higher pitch. I focus on that as I let my eyes close. The low thrum of pain all over, the screeching strings of my back against the floor, and then the steady sharp note with every deep thrust. Over and over and over.

The nausea gets worse when I try to lift my head, and I drop back to the floor limp. *This* is what he's always wanted. An empty vessel he can do what he wants with. Fill with his seed until I can make him the child he wants so much.

He's going to get it. One of these days, it'll happen.

That thought weighs on me like an anchor in the ocean. It drags me down, tethers me to the bottom, in the dark, and I let it.

I don't want to be here anymore. I don't want to be awake.

He groans loudly, hands braced on the floor above my shoulders, and I know he's coming. I can feel it. All I can do is bite down on the leather between my teeth, silent as he rocks inside me.

There are no nice words this time. No *'I love you.'* Nothing except the sudden absence as he pulls out and pushes himself up from the floor. It takes him a minute to put his dick away and rebutton his jeans, but I don't move. My feet find the cement, but I leave my thighs parted and that's where his gaze stays. Right where he's hurt me so many times.

"You will learn to be obedient. You will learn to follow God's word, Jasmine."

I'm not sure if he expects me to respond while gagged, but he keeps staring at me, alternating between my face and between my legs.

"You deserve another punishment, Jasmine. You know that, don't you?"

I shake my head from side to side, fighting against the rising nausea as I do it, but he just huffs as I whimper.

"You did this to yourself, Jasmine. Your choices. Your disobedience. Your betrayals to God, to me." When he grabs me, I don't fight, but I don't help either. I let him lift my dead weight, and he only pauses for a moment before he adjusts his grip and picks me up. A second later I'm bent over the workbench again, head swimming, and I hear his belt swish free of his pants.

Why.

"Think of your failings, Jasmine. Think of how you can push the devil away so you can be closer to God."

Pain spikes as the leather snaps against my skin, but I can't cry anymore.

"You can be better, Jasmine. You will be." Another crack of the leather, but my head hurts so much I can't focus on it.

"You will be a good wife, Jasmine. In time. It will just take more time."

More pain, but it doesn't matter.

You will be better Jasmine.

You will be Jasmine.

You will.

A part of my brain tries to fight, flickers. That voice is so weak. The one that used to shout, 'Don't give up.' It's been getting quieter for a while now, whispering, pleading, begging. But I can't hear it through the pain. Not as another strike lands in an endless stream.

I don't want to fight anymore.

I don't want to be Sloane anymore.

I'll be whoever he wants as long as this stops.

TWENTY-TWO

Mason

'But maybe you just didn't want to find out you might be wrong, did you?'

Clint is just a kid, but those words burrow in as we finish the drive back to the station in silence. Neither of us tries to fill the empty space with words that'll probably only make things worse, not better.

He doesn't stick around long once we're back. He's angry, and Braddock keys in on the tension the minute we're both in the station. Once he's gone, the Sheriff and I have a conversation I've been waiting for, and it's just as I suspected. The deputy has taken the case of the missing girl a little closer to heart than he should.

"You know, Clint's a good kid. He's just young. Got all them young man notions about duty, honor—"

"Saving the world," I cut in.

Braddock nods. "And maybe a damsel-in-distress or two." He stretches, then points to the picture I've set on Clint's desk. "Young girl like that... pretty... actress from Hollywood gone missing." He gives me a world-weary grin. "Plays right into the fantasies of a country boy like Clint."

I spend a while checking email, catching up on things before I leave the station. I eat my dinner at Mattie's Café, and then walk back to the motel. Sitting in the chair outside of my room, I watch as the sun inches toward the horizon, heralding the end of the day. A brilliant ball of orange that tinges everything in the world with brightness, offset only by the deepening shadows that indicate the darkness of night approaching. Shadow and light, harsh lines delineating the edges of all things.

It's beautiful, but my mind keeps going back to the kid.

'The fantasies of a country boy like Clint.' That's what the sheriff said, and that's what it is. A fantasy. I keep telling myself that as I drink my Shiner Bock beer, watching as the moths flit around the light bulb on the wall just outside my door. I keep repeating it as I sit and listen to the deafening silence of a small, West Texas town at night. An occasional car or truck drifts by on Main at a sedate 25mph, and by Hollywood standards it might as well be the aftermath of the apocalypse for as much noise as there is. Which should be comforting, except that it allows me time to think.

And I do not like the thoughts that intrude.

'You ever been wrong?'

'Seems to me if you were so convinced...'

Damn kid.

Clint

I stare at her face on the screen.

In it she's laughing, pointing to the roadside billboard that says 'Mystery Hole!' as if it is the funniest thing in the world. I tip the bottle back, let the now slightly lukewarm liquid slip down my throat as I finish off my third beer of the night. It's her laughter that jabs into me like the spines off a cactus. Barbs that get under my skin and itch and irritate and just won't let go. I point my cursor over the two little white double bars, pausing the video. Her face freezes with her head tilted back, mouth open in a moment of pure joy, eyes almost closed as she looks upwards. I lift the bottle to my lips, tilting, waiting for it, then remember it's empty. For some reason I feel an irrational rush of anger push through me, and I slam the empty down.

Goddamn him.

I sit and stare at the screen. At the picture of her face, caught frozen in a moment of sheer beauty. He'd given up on her before he even came out here. I'd wanted to believe he was here to make an effort, but he made damn sure I knew that was a lie. *'I came out here to flesh out a few paragraphs on a fucking report to give to the grieving father of a corpse.'* He made sure I knew just what he thought of me, of what I've been trying to do, and confirming all them things I know Sheriff Braddock and Duane been saying about me behind my back.

Chasing a ghost.

Clint's girlfriend.

Agent Mason fucking Jones didn't say those things behind

my back, though. He said them straight to my face, and he made damn sure I heard and felt every fucking word.

And tonight. Tonight, for a brief moment, I started to believe him.

Because maybe he is right. Maybe they're all right. Maybe Sloane Finley is dead. Maybe she's been dead for weeks, months, all this time, and I *am* just a dumb hick kid chasing after a dead girl's ghost. Maybe it's time to wise up, grow up, recognize that bad things happen all the time to good people in the world around us, and that thinking that you can do some good by believing you can make a difference is dumb. Childish. Better to grow that thick, callused skin the way a calf roper builds them up on their hands. So you can stop feeling. Feeling compassion. Or pain. Or anything. Like he said, don't feel. Just react.

I started to think about that, and then I started to believe… until I saw her face on that screen and she tore it all back down.

Because I ain't ready to become a Mason Jones yet. I ain't ready to let pain take away my belief. My humanity. 'Cause I can tell that's what life has done to him. I don't have a fucking clue what he's been through, but I damn sure know one thing. He's got calluses built up on his soul thicker'n any roper I've ever known, and he can't even feel the strands he's tied himself up in anymore.

I really can't say what I saw out there at Daniel's place. Or why I felt what I did. But something's going on out there. I been sitting here since dinner playing out scenarios in my head. Maybe he's gotten in with them drug dealers to hole up on his property as they pass through. Maybe even stores

Jasmine

kilos out there, somewhere we don't know about. There're a hundred other things I think about that could be going on out there that I ain't gonna take to Jones or Braddock or anyone else. 'Cause why in the hell would they believe any of it? I ain't seen a damn thing. No one has. Daniel Christiansen's been living out there mostly alone for years now, and ain't nobody said boo about him. Just a big giant who was once the star of Stockdale now out on a ranch all by himself, alone. That ain't nobody's business 'round here, and that's just the way it is. That's the way people want it. But I know I saw something. I know what I felt. And I can't help remembering what one of my instructors at the academy said.

Never second guess yourself. Always go with your gut.

I pick up the empty from my table, and head to the kitchen. I throw it in the trash and open the fridge where a fresh six-pack is sitting, the brown bottles and yellow labels staring back at me. It's dumb, what I'm thinking. It's dumb, and stupid, but then... that's what Sloane Finley and I are, right? Just a pair of dumb, stupid kids.

I grab the six-pack off the shelf and head for the door.

I know I'm going to regret this.

But I just don't care.

I find Mason sitting in a chair just outside the door of his motel room. He's got it propped open, and he seems to just be sitting there, looking off into the distance. I ain't even sure he recognizes who I am until I'm out of my truck and halfway to him. Then I see his eyes focus on me, and his feet come down off the post where he's braced them.

He leans forward, hands folding into his lap. Mason doesn't say a word and neither do I for the moment. I find a chair from the next room over, pull it up close, set the six-pack on the ground. I pull the first one out and pop the cap off, handing it over to him wordlessly. He stares at me, then takes it out of my hand, saying nothing. I pull out the second, yank the cap off, and take a long pull. We both just sit there, and for a spell I just let my nerves calm before I start saying what I got to say.

He beats me to it.

"It won't change a thing, Clint." His voice is low and weary. I've heard Sheriff Braddock's voice sound something like that, but Mason's right now... it's different. There's a depth to it I can't quite put a finger on.

"What won't?"

"Going back out there."

I don't say a word. I just drink for a minute before I rest the bottle on my leg. "How'd you know?"

He looks down at his bottle, lifts it to his lips, and I watch as he swallows. When he's done, he lets out a sigh that comes from a place far off and deep down. "Because there was a time..." His voice drifts, and then there's nothing more.

I sit and watch as a moth flies past, heading like a comet for the sun that is the light behind him. "Why'd you give up on that, Mason? What happened that made you stop believing in yourself?"

Jasmine

He looks over at me, and then through me. Beyond me. And for a minute he's not here. He's not in Stockdale, Dallam County, or even Texas. I don't know where he is, but it's a place that turns his jaw slack, and his eyes dull. And then he stiffens, his eyes coming back to focus on me. He lifts his beer, drinks, and then points the neck at me. "I got experienced."

I tilt my head, because that word he's used — *experienced* — is starting to sound a lot like beaten.

"Well," I say, taking another pull at my beer. "I ain't there yet."

"You will be. Someday."

"Maybe."

"No maybe about it, kid. It happens to everyone. Sometimes you can see it, feel it. And other times it just sneaks up on you until one day you realize that even though you thought you were fighting against it, you weren't. You'd accepted it all along, and you just didn't know it." He takes another drink, and I look down at my beer.

"Maybe so, Mason. Maybe so. But you just used a word I did earlier today, and it was you who called me out on it. Told me how wrong it was."

He gives me that look. The one he seems to draw on a whole lot when he thinks he's got the world pegged for all the fucked-up shit it is. "And what word's that?"

"Feel."

His eyes narrow. He starts to lift his beer to his lips, stops.

"I never said..." And stops again.

I lean forward until my elbows rest on my knees, bottle dangling between my legs. "See, that's the thing I'm starting to notice, Mason. You cherrypick. When it suits your way of thinking, then you'll allow that a person *can* feel. But when it goes against your... experience..." I lift the bottle, take a swig. "Well, then it's just wrong."

He stares at me hard. His eyes are black, intense, and for a single moment I realize there's something there. That I've pricked him, and he don't like it. No, he don't like it one. Damn. Bit.

The stare goes on for a while, and then it morphs into a grin.

"Well, I'll give you credit, kid. You aren't half bad." He lifts his own beer, finishing it off before he sets the empty down next to his chair. "What is it they say? 'Even a blind squirrel finds a nut?'" He brings his hands together in a slow clap. "Congratulations."

I could be angry. Should be angry. His tone... it's patronizing. He's trying to make me feel exactly the way he thinks of me. Just a dumb kid. But I'm not angry. No, right now I just feel tired. And sad.

"Tell you what, kid. You got a feeling? Fine. We'll head back out there tomorrow."

"I don't need your pity, Mason."

Suddenly he's leaning forward, and when he speaks his voice is almost a snarl. "It isn't pity, you dumb sonuvabitch. It's a goddamn lesson. And one you need to learn. Quick."

I shake my head, standing slowly while he watches me. I

Jasmine

turn slightly to stare down at him, and he stares back. Defiant.

"I'll see you in the morning, Agent Jones," I reply, my voice even and calm before I turn and walk toward my truck.

"Hey, kid!" he calls out to me. "You forgot your beer!"

I don't stop, or even turn around. "Keep it."

You need it more than I do.

TWENTY-THREE

Mason
———

"Mason?"

I set the phone down, balanced on the edge of the tiny sink in the tiny bathroom of my tiny motel room. "I'm still here, Carmen."

"Okay. Anyways, they say they want to run one more test, just to be safe, and then they'll release her."

"All right." I nod to myself, staring into the mirror. I look more tired than I feel, even though I'm aware how fitfully I slept last night.

Goddamn kid.

"I'm glad she's okay. Well, as okay as someone can be after getting T-boned."

Carmen chuckles. "Yeah. She's got a helluva bruise across her shoulder. It's gonna be all manner of pretty colors here in a few days."

I grin at myself in the mirror. "Ha! Her own personal Pride flag."

For a moment there's silence, and then Carmen's bright laughter filters over the phone. "Damn, Mason. I wish I'd thought of that."

"Feel free to steal," I answer back, smiling. It's good to hear cheerfulness in her voice after the pain of the other day.

"Anyways, I figure it'll be two, three o'clock before I'm able to get up there."

"That's fine. Deputy Nolan and I are headed back out to the Christiansen place this morning."

"Why?" Her voice is mildly apprehensive.

"Well..." I rub my hand over my face. Admitting what has kept me restless since last night is not something I want to do with Carmen right now. Instead, I choose to set the blame squarely on Clint. Not that he doesn't deserve it. "Deputy Nolan had a... feeling."

"A... feeling."

"Yep."

The line is silent for a long moment. "You going soft, Mason?"

I chuckle, looking in the mirror. "Three days and you already know me too well." I should shave. I open the tap, run water into the sink, then realize I have nothing to shave with. Everything is still in Carmen's FBI Suburban.

I sigh. "I've been trying to school our young deputy, and I figure this'll be yet another opportunity."

"Okay." There's a pause, and then her voice comes back, serious. "There's nothing out there is there, Mason?"

For a brief second I contemplate telling her about that feeling. But it passes just as quickly.

"No. Of course not. Just a really big, really odd young man living by himself, alone in the middle of fucking nowhere." I grin, thinking of my next line. "You know, like you told me when we first came out here. Your people."

She chokes back laughter. "Fuck you."

It's good to hear her happy. "So, see you around three?"

"Yeah. Maybe earlier if I can. Just make sure you're at the station and ready to go."

"Count on it." I grab the phone and switch it off speaker. "Drive careful, Carmen."

"Will do. Bye."

The call ends, and I go to take a shower, which feels pointless when I put on the clothes I've been wearing for the past three days. Two days in Texas was what I'd hoped for, max. I'd packed for three, but that had all flown out the window when Carmen had driven off with my bag. I've spent the last few days in Stockdale wearing this same suit, and if there's anything that makes me want to get back to Amarillo, it's to rescue my bag. One night in a decent hotel, my bag with fresh clothing, and tomorrow morning I'll be on a plane headed back to LA with information in hand for the final report, and enough ammunition to bust some LAPD balls too.

Not a bad trip, all in all.

The only thing I need to do now is show Clint that good law enforcement work isn't based on feelings. It's based on reacting. Assessing a situation and accepting it for what it is, and then reacting to how it unfolds accordingly. Feelings have no place in it.

Even my own.

I'm dressed and standing outside the door of the motel office when Clint pulls up in the Bronco. He gives me a curt nod as I pile in, and then he pulls out onto the main drag.

"Are we going back out to the Christiansen place?"

Clint turns his head towards me. "We ain't gotta do that. Like I said last night I don't need to be pitied."

"You still think I'm pitying you?"

"You are."

We're sitting at the stoplight, unmoving. In LA horns would've already been blaring for ten seconds, and I'd probably be dealing with a road rage incident. Here, there is nothing.

"I told you last night we could go back out."

"Yeah, you did." Clint gives me a tight nod, mouth pulled taut. "But I ain't an idiot. You're just doing it to show the dumb hick kid how wrong he is."

"Maybe. But weren't you the one yesterday that rubbed my nose in the fact that I've been wrong before?" I stare at him patiently. "You going to pass up your one chance to show me that I'm wrong this time too?"

He twists his head, giving me a hard look.

"Like I said. You're doing this out of pity."

"Then prove me wrong on that too."

He jerks the steering wheel hard to the left, tires barking slightly as he turns down the street towards the sheriff's office. He pulls us up out front, and then yanks the door open and heads inside. I follow behind, moving past the clerk and into the back offices.

Clint is standing at his desk, leaning over it and studying something on his screen. Braddock sees me, and comes out from his office.

"Morning, Agent Jones." He glances over to Clint, and then back to me, one eyebrow arching upward.

"Morning, Sheriff Braddock." I give him a polite smile, and the briefest narrowing of my eyes.

"Coffee again?"

"That would be great, thank you."

Braddock heads over to counter, and brings me back the same white mug with faded John Deere logo from yesterday.

"I didn't figure on seeing you gentlemen this morning." Braddock moves past, shooting me a look as he does. He goes to one of the desks, propping himself up on the edge of it. "Thought you'd decided to go back out and pay Daniel 'nother visit."

"We ain't gotta—"

"That's just what we were—" Clint and I talk over one

Jasmine

another, and then we both stop. He stares at me, and I stare back.

Ball's in your court, kid.

"We... we just came back so I could look something over real quick. Then we'll be heading out." Clint's voice is firm, and his eyes never leave mine. Yet again there's challenge in them, and I can't help but give him a grin of recognition.

Wasn't sure you had it in you.

I lift my cup, taking a long pull. Braddock is watching Clint closely, and then he looks to me.

"I just came for the coffee." I raise the mug up in a mock salute.

"All right then." Braddock gives a slow nod, and then pushes his chin toward me. "You heard from Agent Rodriguez yet this morning?"

"Spoke with her a little bit ago. Her wife is being discharged sometime today, hopefully before lunch. As soon as she is, she'll be heading up here. She thinks she should be here sometime around three, maybe sooner."

"Sounds good. I'll take that to mean I don't need to have Clint here drive you to Amarillo?"

"I don't think that'll be necessary." I take another sip of my coffee. "Besides, I think once we're done out at the Christiansen place, Deputy Nolan will have had his fill of me for the day. Or for a lifetime." I give Clint a bright smile, as fake as I can muster it. He shoots me one back no less so.

"And I'm sure Agent Jones will be relieved not to have to listen to me crow all the way to Amarillo either."

It's dueling toothy smiles, and Braddock's voice is thick with amusement as the two of us stare each other down. "Well, I'll let the two of you sort things out." He lifts himself off the desk. "Clint, you just make sure Agent Jones is back here in time to meet up with Agent Rodriguez. Or you *will* be taking him into Amarillo, no matter *what* either of you wants."

Twenty minutes later Clint has gotten whatever information he was looking for, assuming there was anything to begin with. We pile into the Bronco and retrace our steps, heading back out to the Christiansen ranch for a second time. At first Clint says nothing, keeping silent and to himself, but once we're tooling along the highway, he finally clears his throat.

"You know... I know you think I'm just a dumb kid—"

I hit the seat of the truck with a *smack*, cutting him off. "I'm not listening to that shit, deputy."

He swallows whatever he was about to say, and I continue.

"I think you are young, determined, chivalrous, and naïve as hell. But I do *not* think you are dumb." His eyes shoot back and forth between me and the road, and I can see from his expression what I've said has mollified him a little. "In fact, I'd say you're probably just a bit too smart. You still believe in all those things I talked to you about last night. And part of that is because you're young and haven't had experience yet."

"Like you have?"

"Yes."

"So, I'll be a better officer once I see some dead people, huh?

Picking up some bodies is all I need to turn me into a good, experienced, cynical law enforcement officer like yourself, right?"

I know what he's doing. I can see he's trying to bait me. It won't work, because I am all those things, and if Clint Nolan decides to continue wearing that uniform and pinning that badge on his shirt every morning, he will be too.

But I'm not going to rise to the challenge. He's misjudged me if he thought that.

"Yes, Clint. That's exactly it. That's all you need." I don't even try to hide my derision, and I know Clint hears it. He snorts, and we continue in silence until we come to the gate blocking the road to Daniel's ranch.

Clint puts the Bronco into park, starts to unbuckle his seatbelt, but I stop him. "I've got it."

I climb out, remembering the secret place the key is hidden, and it only takes a few minutes to get the gate out of his way so he can drive through. Once it's secured again, I get back in the SUV so we can get this over with.

As we draw closer, I speak up. "Clint..."

"Yeah?"

"This is not going to turn into a full-blown interrogation, okay? I want to be clear on that. You ask him whatever questions you want, but you make it quick. And unless something happens, we are in and out of here. I am not going to have this kid get a wild hair across his ass and make trouble for me later. You want to come back out here on your own, you clear it with the sheriff, and you do it on your time. After I'm long gone." I look over at him. "Clear?"

"Sure. Perfectly," he replies with no tone at all. It's short, clipped, but I've made my message crystal, and even if he doesn't like it, I know he'll comply.

As we pull into the large, open dirt area that sits between the house and the barn, I can see Daniel standing on the porch. He watches us, face masked in shadow from under the eaves of the overhang, body stiff as it was yesterday, and again I'm struck by how big he is. He's got to be over six and a half feet tall, and I've no doubt the NFL would have grabbed him in a second. If Clint pisses him off, I'm not taking a right hook for the kid. He'll have to pick up his teeth and his dignity on his own.

Clint parks the truck, and we both climb out. Daniel doesn't move from the porch, but tracks both of us as we approach.

"Morning, Daniel." Clint addresses him first, voice low, personable.

"Morning, Mr. Christiansen." I follow him up, giving Daniel a slight nod.

Daniel's face swivels back and forth between us, still showing no emotion as he takes us in. "Why are you back?"

Clint takes the lead, and I have to put effort into not reacting to the first thing that comes out of his mouth. "Well, we was out again this morning at that old place where the young woman took that picture—"

What?

Jasmine

"She was trespassing," Daniel interjects in a monotone, as if that needs to be clarified. Again.

Clint pauses for a breath, then continues. "Yep, that's true. Like I was saying, we went out to check the old place out again, doing some further investigating, and figured as long as we was in the neighborhood..." He gives Daniel a personable grin. "Thought you might have remembered something since we spoke yesterday. Maybe jogged your memory?"

Daniel stares at Clint for a moment, and then slowly shakes his head. "I don't know her. Never seen her." And then, as if it's the only thing that *does* register with him, "She was trespassing."

"Yeah, that's right, Daniel. She sure was." Clint's voice is faux patient, but if Daniel picks up on it, he shows no sign. Clint watches him for a moment, eyes searching for any reaction that Daniel might have, which despite the potential jab appears to be nothing. Seconds go by in silence, and then Clint looks skyward, reaching up and wiping an arm across his brow.

"Sure looks like it's gonna be warm today, huh?" He looks back at Daniel, smiling. "Got pretty hot out there while we was tramping around, and here I forgot to bring anything to drink in the truck. Don't suppose we could trouble you and come in for a couple of glasses of cold water?"

Daniel's face remains impassive, but now there *is* a reaction. I catch as his hands begin to close, clenching into fists. All three of us stand there, Daniel watching Clint, Clint watching Daniel, and myself taking it all in. His fingers have nearly curled in upon themselves when they stop, and they slowly relax, flattening back out.

"Okay." There's nothing welcoming in the statement. None of the 'Texan hospitality' that Braddock spoke of on my first day here. It isn't begrudging, but it barely registers as an invitation. However, he does move to the door and opens it, turning to look back at us.

Clint glances over at me, and then he moves off, taking the steps two at a time. I follow, watching as Clint disappears into the dark interior of the house. I step past Daniel and slip into the entryway where Clint has stopped. Daniel closes the door behind us, and then motions towards an opening to the left of the stairs.

"You can sit in the family room. I'll get you your water."

Clint gives him a polite nod. "Thank you, Daniel."

He steps through into the room, and I follow suit. There are four bookcases along one wall of the room, carefully tended, obviously dusted recently. The rest of the furniture consists of two chairs, a coffee table that looks as if the top has been hand-hewn from a solid slab of wood, a pair of end tables, and a couch with pillows and a blanket over the back. The room is simple, austere, and yet it looks as if it's been kept up for use. I glance at the bookcases as I pass by to take my seat, and they're all full, the spines neatly arranged, facing outward. There is a larger Bible placed on the table, and another smaller one on one of the end tables. It's homey in a weirdo Luddite kind of way.

I sit down, while Clint remains standing, perusing the bookshelves. Daniel looks at both of us for a long second, then turns. "I'll be right back."

Jasmine

I listen to him stride through the doorway, boots echoing in loud *clump, clump, clumps,* and then the noise fades as he disappears into the kitchen. No sooner has the sound gone distant than Clint is moving, heading out into the hall near the front door.

"Hey," I hiss at him, keeping my voice down. "Where are you..." Before I can finish, he's out of the room and gone. I get up, start to follow, but then stop. When Daniel comes back, one of us needs to be here. If he catches us both snooping around in his house, I don't want to think about the kind of hell there could be to pay. We have no warrant, and absolutely no legal reason to be prying through his home. I may think the young man dense, but I'm not willing to risk that he's not savvy enough to lawyer up if he feels he's been wronged.

Instead of going after Clint, I stop and listen. I can hear the faint sounds of Daniel in the kitchen. A cupboard door opening, then closing. A tinkling noise; cups on a counter, or ice in a glass? It goes quiet, and I take a quick peek through the doorway, where I can see a kitchen table. Daniel isn't in sight, but Clint hasn't reappeared at the entryway. I move back toward my seat as tension builds inside me.

Clenching my hand open and closed, I stop at the bookcases, checking the titles. They're mostly religious tomes and books on ranching. There's nothing here that is not either practical to the business of raising livestock, or to the saving of one's soul.

What the fuck are you doing, kid?

I can't hear any sign of him, but Clint needs to finish up

whatever the hell he's got going on and get back in here because the last thing I want to deal with is Daniel stumbling into him sneaking around out there. The giant has been passive throughout everything so far, but I sense a level of suppressed anger there. An undercurrent just beneath the surface that I have no desire to butt heads with.

Come on, Clint. Get the fuck back in here.

I hear the heavy sound of boots returning, and Clint still isn't back. I turn from the bookcase just as Daniel enters, a white stoneware cup held in each hand. He sees me, stops, and then looks around the room slowly.

"Where is he? The other one?"

Think fast, Mason.

"He had to use the bathroom."

Daniel stands for a moment, and then he turns back towards the kitchen without a word.

"He should be back in a second," I call out after him, but he doesn't stop at my voice. I hear his boots in the narrow hallway off the kitchen just as Clint darts out of a smaller side room near the front of the house. He moves swiftly toward me, and his face brings me up short. His eyes are bright, intense, pupils wide as he approaches.

"*Lud,*" he whispers in a rush as he moves past me and to the bookshelves.

Lud? What the hell is that? Someone's name? Am I supposed to recognize it?

I turn to look at him just as the sound of Daniel's boots come back in this direction.

Jasmine

Daniel appears in the doorway, blocking it as he sweeps his gaze between the two of us. He takes two steps into the room and then comes to a halt, brow furrowed.

"Hey, Daniel. Sorry, I was trying to find your bathroom." Clint gives Daniel a tight smile, and then moves up to him, reaching for one of the cups of water Daniel is still carrying.

Suddenly I'm tense. Because as he moves beside Daniel, Clint catches my eye, and the look I see tells me there's something wrong.

Very wrong.

Daniel silently pushes one of the cups into Clint's waiting hand, and then steps forward to offer the other over to me.

"Thank you," I reply in the most polite voice I can muster before I take the cup.

Daniel says nothing in return as we all stand, and I take a long pull of my water. *Lud.* I'm still not sure what that means.

Clint is tense, although he's doing his best not to let it show. He's seen something, and while I have no idea what it is, it's clear he's only suspicious at this point, because he's not making a direct move toward Daniel. And that suggests he needs more time to suss it out.

Lud? Shit. Clint was trying to tell me something, maybe a warning, but I'll be damned if I can figure it out. Maybe he's freaked out that he's a Luddite? No, he knew that, so it's not 'Lud'. I could have misheard him. Maybe it's another word. Ffff..lud. Flood? No. What the hell would that have to do with anything? Lud. Crud. Mud. Dud.

Blood.

Fuck.

I finish the last of my water, and then move closer to Daniel, keeping his attention on me.

Let's see if you still got it in you, Mason.

"Mr. Christiansen, I do appreciate the water." I hand him the empty cup, and then ease my way past him and Clint until I'm standing near the doorway. "Now, there's really only one more thing I'd like to ask of you today, and then I promise we'll be out of your hair." I take a few steps further until I'm out in the hallway.

Daniel glances back and forth between Clint and me before taking a step in my direction.

"When we got back to Stockdale yesterday, after talking to you, we went and spoke to the Hernandez brothers as you suggested. They said when they were working for you, they remembered seeing a blue car out in your barn. Mind if we see it?"

Daniel suddenly stops short. For the first time since I've met the man, real emotion flickers across his face.

It looks like confusion.

And fear.

"What?" He says the word as if the comment I've made is incomprehensible.

I move a bit further into the entryway, backing toward the front door. Daniel is following me, and his expression is a mixture of alarm and concern. His eyes dart from me to the

Jasmine

side, as if he's trying to keep track of both Clint and me at the same time, which is exactly what I intend to prevent.

"I'd like to see this blue car out in your barn they were telling us about. It won't take more than a minute, I'm sure."

"There is no car in the barn."

I've almost made the door. Behind him I can see Clint staying back, and Daniel's head is swiveling back and forth as he tries to track us both.

"Well, then there won't be any issue if I just take a quick look to confirm. Just to see whether the Hernandez brothers were mistaken or not."

By now I've made it to the door, hand on the doorknob, and Daniel's step quickens. Without hesitating, I turn, pushing my way through and striding as fast as I can without breaking into a run. I step off the porch and head across the broad dirt lot toward the barn, listening to the sound of Daniel's boots thump onto the porch, as his voice rises behind me.

"There is no car in the barn." He's not shouting, but it's clear that what I'm doing is something that he doesn't approve of.

Shit. Shit, was the kid actually right?

I continue to eat up the distance across the open area separating the house from the barn, and now I can hear Daniel's feet growing closer behind me. What happens next, I don't expect. There's suddenly a massive pressure on my shoulder, and I'm spun around mid-stride.

Jesus Christ he's strong.

Daniel has me in his grip, halting me from going any further. I crane my neck up to look at him and find him staring down at me, eyes wide, breathing elevated. His fingers dig into my flesh and though it fucking hurts, I don't let on.

"Whoa! What's going on here?"

His chest rises and falls rapidly. "There's no car in the barn."

I look to his hand, and then slowly back to his face. Things are either going to get very interesting here in a second unless he decides to be smart and let go. I catch Clint coming down off the porch, moving in light, quick steps toward the Bronco. He ducks around to the side opposite of us, disappearing.

"You mind letting go of me, Mr. Christiansen?"

For a moment he doesn't, continuing to hold me in place. I can see his mind working, and I realize that something *is* going on here. Clint's right. There's something out here.

And Daniel Christiansen is hiding it.

"I'll ask again politely, Mr. Christiansen." I keep my voice low, as non-threatening as I can muster when my shoulder feels like it's clamped in a vise. But I can feel myself tensing, because right now I have no fucking idea what this kid is going to do, and I need to be ready to pull my gun if I have to. Several seconds pass before I feel the fingers slowly relax, and then he takes his hand away.

His face has gone flat again, and I take two steps back to put a little distance between us. As I do, Clint dashes from the truck, something in his hand. He takes the porch steps as silently as possible, disappearing back into the house.

Are you fucking kidding me?

"There is no car in the barn."

I bring my focus back to Daniel. Whatever the fuck Clint is doing, I need to buy him time. Keep Daniel's focus on me. Without letting him get a hand back on me, though, because I'm not letting that happen again.

"No car," I echo him as I take another step back toward the barn, feeling the reassuring weight of my gun under my suit jacket. "You keep saying that, Mr. Christiansen. But if there's no car in that barn, then I really do have to wonder if you haven't got something else to hide…"

Clint

I wasn't sure if Agent Jones understood me, but he got Daniel outside, so he must have got the gist of it in some way. And he's kept Daniel's focus tied down long enough that I've gotten back inside unnoticed, at least for now. When I saw the blood on the door jamb, and then the spots on the floor, I knew something wasn't right. Plenty of ways for a person to get hurt on a ranch and bleed, but Daniel ain't wearing no bandages, and it don't make any sense that there'd be smears and drops of blood just left like this. Something bled here recently. Recent enough that Daniel ain't had the time to clean it up. And I'm betting it's on the other side of this locked door.

I'd tried it earlier, but the thick padlock hadn't budged, and just its presence makes it even more suspicious, 'cause why in the hell would Daniel keep a door locked in his own house? He's the only one here.

I take the crowbar I pulled out of the truck and wedge it under the little bar of steel keeping the door shut tight. I push against it and the wood creaks. The timbering in this house is thick, and heavy, but it's also old, worn, dried out from over the years. As I increase pressure on it, I watch as the wood cracks, begins to splinter. I'm trying to go slow, easy, so I don't create a loud noise that'll draw Daniel's attention away from Mason. Inside here, I can't hear either of them, but I keep one ear cocked for the sound of Daniel's boots on the porch. Big as the sonuvabitch is, them boots of his give off a noise you can hear a mile away.

I lean into the crowbar a bit harder, and the semi-circle buried in the doorjamb starts to give. The wood creaks, cracks again, and suddenly it pops free. I almost drop the crowbar as it slips forward, but I catch it as I stumble into the jamb. Shoving the bar behind my belt, I hook it in place and push the door open.

Stairs. Stairs that lead down into the basement.

The stairway is dark, but there's muted light at the bottom where the steps end, and then the basement takes off to the right. I can't see much of the actual room and I glance over to find a light switch, but I figure I better not. If there's something down there, I don't want to be giving them a better chance to spot me before I spot them. Plus, if Daniel sees the light coming on from outside, he'll come charging in here like he took down Henry Carter in that Dalhart game. Damn near broke his neck when he hit him, and I don't

Jasmine

want to be tussling with Daniel like that inside this confined space.

I move onto the first step, pause for a moment, and then do something I ain't ever had to do before. I pull out my gun, and hold it in front of me, at the ready. Sheriff Braddock sent me to all that training down in Amarillo, and I remember the courses, but I've never had to draw on them. Until now. My hands are jittering a little, and I force them to stop. I ain't got time for that. I need to get down here, find out what clues I can about that blood up there, and then get back outside before Daniel notices I ain't there.

I start cautiously down the stairs, doing just like they taught, keeping the gun sweeping in front of me. Looking down, I can see little splatters every few steps. Even in the dim light I'm pretty certain they're blood too. I don't stop or focus on them. I need to keep moving. As I get closer to the bottom, I can see that the light I saw earlier is coming from the basement windows built into the foundation of the house. They're dusty, and the light filtering through is diffused, but there is enough to see by and catch the details of the room.

At the bottom I pause, listening, but I don't hear anything. I dart a quick look around the corner of the stairs, then pull back. This is where Daniel does his laundry, obviously. I saw a washing machine, a dryer, but not much else. I wait, straining my ears, but there's no reaction from anyone or anything from my glance past the stairs, so I step off of them.

I sweep my gun ahead of me. Past the washing machine, the dryer next to it, and the cabinets at the far end. On the other side of the room is a table under the windows, two empty laundry baskets stacked neatly on top. In the dim space beyond the stairs there are old shelves, mostly empty, and I let my gun angle toward the floor as I turn in a circle.

Shit. There ain't no one in this room. It's empty. I turn back to the stairs and follow the trail of blood drops. They're sparse, but they trickle past where I'm standing, into the dim space beside the shelves where there's a pile of cloth someone's dumped at the far end of the room.

Except it's not cloth.

I blink, and then take a step forward. The body is lying with its back to me, on top of a dark blanket, and as I take one more step the lines I thought were just folds in fabric resolve themselves into cuts in flesh. Long slashes that have been opened on the back of this person. The edges are dark, raised, and there's liquid, blood, or whatever it is weeping out, staining the skin so that it glistens. I take another step, and I'm almost on the body when I can see dark hair matted against the neck and back, held in place by the blood.

Jesus Christ, Daniel. What have you done?

I run my eyes the length of the body, and it's then that I realize it's a woman. A young girl. For the first time it dawns on me she's naked. I ain't seen a lot of nude girls before, but I've seen enough I can definitely tell the body is distinctly not male, especially down around her hips and such. I swallow, 'cause my throat's gone dry, and I might be freaking out a bit 'cause this is my first corpse. And Agent Jones was right. It ain't nothing like what I expected.

"What the fuck have you done here, Daniel?" I whisper hoarsely, and the body moves.

I almost stumble back, a hundred horror movies flickering

Jasmine

through my mind. I start to lift my gun but I catch myself because in that same instant, I realize this ain't a body. It ain't a corpse. She's alive, whoever this is, and I only have one thought; I need to help them. I regain my balance, holstering my weapon as I start to kneel. The body is twisting, trying to turn back to see who is behind her, and I open my mouth to tell her who I am. To tell her to stay still, that it's gonna be okay, that I'm here to rescue her, but the words die on my tongue as the world seems to tilt for a second.

Her face comes into view, and I know it immediately. There ain't no way I wouldn't recognize it.

I've stared at it a million times.

Memorized it.

It's Sloane.

Mason

"I am not lying to you," he says, flat but somehow still intimidating.

I take one more step back, and Daniel matches me. He's been doing that as I've crept slowly back toward the barn doors, because I'm trying to maintain enough distance in case he decides he's going to charge me, which is definitely a possibility. I have no idea what Clint saw inside, but I know without any doubt that there's something going on here, and he was right, and I was wrong, and there'll be time enough later to admit that — but right now I need to keep Daniel occupied. Close, but not close enough that he can get his hands on me before I can draw my gun.

Because this sonuvabitch is big. Big, strong, and powerful, and if he gets a hold of me, I've no doubt he'll fucking break me.

Talk, Mason.

"Well, here's the thing, Mr. Christiansen. You keep telling me that, but you keep trying to stop me from getting into the barn. Now, I'm sure you can understand how that might leave me with the impression that you are lying."

"I am not lying!" His voice now matches some of the emotion he's been letting creep across his face the past few minutes. His agitation is growing, and that means that one of two things needs to happen: either I diffuse this situation, or I take him down. As big as he is, I'd rather have Clint here to help with the latter, but he's still inside the house. So at this point the best I can do is keep up this dance with Daniel, although how much longer I can do so is debatable.

"I am a Godly man. An honorable man. I do not lie. I follow the tenets as laid down in the Bible by our Lord and Savior, and as paid for by the blood of His Son on the cross at Calvary."

Oh great.

"Well, that's all well and good, and sounds fantastic, but it still doesn't explain why you seem bound and determined to stop me from just taking a look at what's in your barn."

"Because I am not lying! Why are you questioning my word?"

Jasmine

I skip back one more step. "Sorry..." I give him a shrug. "That's just the way I am. A real goddamn asshole, as most would tell you."

His brow furrows. "You used the Lord's name in vain."

"Yeah, like I said. A real fucking asshole."

The curse draws his eyebrows together even tighter. He advances a step, and this time he skirts to my right side.

Oh. Nice move. Trying to flank me.

I step back, and he skirts once more that direction, and I'm going to have to change tactics or he'll put himself between me and the barn. And while that might be fine in the end — because I honestly don't give a shit what's inside there — it's going to put him into a position to see Clint when he finally comes out.

"Oh, shit, sorry." I raise my right hand as if in supplication, bringing it closer into position where I can reach my shoulder holster quickly if needed. "Where are my fucking manners? That sure as fuck wasn't the right thing to say to a Godly, righteous man such as yourself, was it?"

His eyes narrow. "Why do you mock me?"

"I don't, Mr. Christiansen. I simply want you to let me look in that barn."

"I did not take that car."

I hesitate for a moment. *What did he just say?* He didn't say 'there is no car.' That's what he's been saying all along, since I made up my lie. No, no, this time he said, 'I didn't take *that* car.'

Fuck.

While I'm absorbing that information, he's the one to take the next step first, and it lets him get in closer to me. I feint backward and try to angle my way back into my original position, but he follows, and now he's getting too close for comfort. I start to step back again, and as I do so, I see movement from the house. The front door opens, and I watch as Clint steps out into the shadow of the porch eave. He's carrying something in his arms. It's fairly large, whatever it is, and when he steps down the first step and out into the sunlight for a moment all I can see is a dirty, red thing. Except that it isn't a thing. In that split second it resolves itself into what it actually is, and I freeze, stunned for the first time in years.

He was right. The kid was fucking right.

Clint is carrying a body, and I'm pretty sure it's a young woman. Her back is flayed to ribbons, and she's been bleeding and still is. Clint is cradling her, his shirt and arms smeared with blood. He ignores us, walking in a daze toward the Bronco. Daniel must see the look on my face, because he stops and before I can react, I watch as his gaze turns toward where I've been staring.

"Jasmine." The name comes off his lips, a hoarse utterance of disbelief mixed with barely contained anger. Then things happen in that slow-motion way they do when everything goes to hell and your body is trying to react to keep up with what your mind is screaming at you.

"JASMINE!" This time it's a roar, and there is no disbelief. There's only rage.

I'm reaching for my gun. My mind is trying to tell my

mouth to form the words. The words I know I should be saying. '*Stop! Agent Jones, FBI! You are under arrest...*' Except that they won't come. The words remain stuck in transit from my brain to my lips. Daniel, however, does not remain stuck. In the same instant those thoughts careen through my head, he surges forward.

And hits me like a fucking cement truck.

He literally knocks me off my feet. The air is shoved out of my lungs as I sail backward, and I've got nothing as I hit the ground on my back. For a millisecond I think he's going to land on me, but he doesn't. He passes me, and then he's gone. I hear the buffeting of his boots against the dirt, can feel it coming up through the ground, and then I hear a yell.

Move, Mason. Get the fuck up.

I'm trying to suck in oxygen through lungs that tell me to fuck off. I roll, and the effort makes blackness ring the edges of my vision. I can see now what the yell was about. Daniel has hit Clint the same way he hit me. Knocked him to the ground, and the girl he was carrying with him.

The one Daniel called Jasmine. A thought flashes through my head. *That name... that name should mean something...*

I push myself to my knees, and my diaphragm gives me one — one — intake of air before it seizes up again. It's enough to let me push up, to stagger into an upright position. Daniel has picked up the young woman and is carrying her in his arms away from Clint. He's moving back toward the barn, toward me, and I reach for my gun.

But what am I going to do? Because all that Hollywood shoot from the hip, headshot on the fly bullshit aside, there is no fucking way I'm taking a shot at this man while he's carrying that girl. I don't have a fucking clue what is going on here, but this 'Jasmine' is clearly a victim in some fashion or another, and I'm not going to let her take a bullet while I try to be some sort of action hero.

I track Daniel as he strides across the dirt lot, heading toward the big double doors. I get one more lungful of air, and I'm about to try and force something out of my mouth when I see Clint pushing himself up. He's reaching for his gun, and suddenly telling Clint not to shoot shoves any words toward Daniel out of my head. But before I can speak, Clint falters. His hand pulls away from his holster, and then reaches behind him. At the same time he's reaching behind him I can see his legs push off against the ground, and he's running. As he sprints toward Daniel, bent almost double, his arm curves from behind his back, a crowbar in his hand.

I choke on the words I was going to say. Instead, I bring my hands up, gripping my gun, aiming at Daniel.

He's covered a little over half the distance to me when Clint hits him. Rangy as the kid is, he's got momentum behind him, and he aims low. He swings with every bit of force he can put into it and catches Daniel right behind the knee.

It's enough.

Daniel bellows a cry that is pain and rage in equal measure. He staggers and goes down on his good knee. Clint skids past in the dirt, scrambles up as Daniel goes down, and then Clint flings himself in a half arc, swinging the crowbar downward as he does.

He doesn't have the force he had on his running pass, but

the crowbar hits Daniel in the shoulder with a thudding noise that sounds like a punching bag being struck. Daniel roars again, and this time he loses his grip on the girl, and she tumbles into the dirt. I keep my gun on Daniel, waiting for my moment, any chance when he is in the clear from Clint and the woman, and I can take my shot. Because I *am* shooting this sonuvabitch. There's no way I'm going to try and talk him down.

Clint sees the girl fall, and I watch him drop the crowbar, diving for her. I'm not taking my eyes off Daniel, who appears to be trying to track what is going on through the pain Clint has inflicted. Clint scoops up the young woman, stumbles,and begins running. He darts out of my vision, even as Daniel is rising from the ground, and that's all I need.

"MY WIFE! LET GO OF MY WIFE!" Daniel roars as he bursts forward.

Fuck the warning, fuck Miranda rights, fuck it all. It's been a while, but I know what to do here. This is not my first rodeo. I take in a breath, hold it, gauging the closing distance as Daniel surges toward Clint. I let the breath out slowly, easing my finger against the trigger until the weight...

The first shot rings out. The Glock kicks, pulls upward slightly to my left. I settle it back in place and *Jesus fucking Christ* he hasn't even broken stride.

The gun kicks again. Daniel twists slightly, and I see the spray of blood. It's a solid fucking hit and yet...

He's slowed, but he doesn't stop.

God fucking damn. He can't be human.

I take another breath, and the bulk of his body fills my sights. This will be the third round, and if he doesn't go down I'm going to be fighting to try and keep Clint and the girl out of the line of fire, and I don't fucking have time for this, and *why the fuck won't you just go down you enormous motherfucker...*

The gun jerks a third time, the empty casing spinning away as it ejects out of the chamber, the fourth round seating in its place, and he staggers.

He staggers, wrenching to his right, and he's going to go down. He has to go down. He's got three goddamn bullets in him, nine millimeters, 147 grains each and every one, and not even those crackheads on Normandie can take that many rounds...

He wrenches back. Lurches forward.

Fuck it.

I squeeze the trigger again. The bullet hits, a *thunk* that I can hear clearly, and a small fount of crimson bursts from a hole that appears on his chest, near his shoulder.

He twists the opposite direction, and everything he does now is as if it's in slow motion. He sinks to his knees, then leans forward until he's braced on his hands. I keep my weapon trained on him as I close the gap between us, watching as his fingers clench into the dry earth.

"Jasmine." He chokes the name out, and it's followed by a spew of gore that pushes up behind the word, past his lips.

He looks up. Still keeping my gun trained on him, I glance in the direction of his gaze. Just beyond me, Clint has the young woman encased in his arms, his back to Daniel, shielding her from his advance.

I turn back to Daniel as he chokes up another sound, voice almost unrecognizable. Blood foams at his mouth, his heart pumping blood to lungs that force his life out on every exhale. He looks up at her, one hand coming up from the ground toward her, fingers dripping dust and earth in a fine sheen. Like sand in an hourglass.

"As'muun!" The sound is a burble of liquid, an inhuman noise that is carried forth on a choke of crimson.

I hear a noise. A cry that is a whimper, and I turn back to see the woman struggling in Clint's arms. She's fighting, wrenching to be free of him. Finally, he relents, letting her go but keeping one protective arm in front of her as she stumbles to the side stark naked. The woman turns her head to look at Daniel, and when she does, it feels like a blow to my chest.

I watch as Sloane Finley shoves against Clint's arm, stepping past it. I can't speak. I can only watch in stunned silence as she moves one foot closer to the man dying in the dirt under the West Texas sun. She stops, and I expect her to be scared, horrified, but she's not. She looks... dangerous. Angry.

Cold-blooded.

"Asmuun." The word is barely discernible as he gazes up at her, beseeching.

"I am *not* Jasmine." Her voice is a sibilant hiss, filled with a rage that does not seem possible from one who looks so young. So innocent. She stares down at him with eyes that are as filled with anger and hatred as his are with madness.

"*My. Name. Is. Sloane.*"

There is a tension of violence within her that seems as if it might snap at any moment, but in the end she does nothing. She simply stands and watches as he stares up at her with an uncomprehending blank face. His mouth opens again, breath blowing a red bubble that wavers for a second in the warm air, then pops. Daniel's elbow gives way as he slowly collapses, crumpling into the sunbaked dirt that stretches out around us.

Dead.

For a moment there is only silence. No movement, not even a breeze, the only thing the soundless scream of the sun a billion miles away. Clint moves closer to Sloane, gently touching her arm. She flinches, jerking back, and he raises his hands up as she turns to look at him.

"We're the police," he says softly, and she crosses her arms over her chest, wavering on her feet as she appraises him with quick jerks of her eyes. When he spreads his arms, she steps wordlessly forward, and it's like they're having some kind of conversation I'm not privy to. Whatever it is, it ends with Sloane moving slowly forward until she presses against him. I hear her sob, and then her legs give out, but Clint catches her.

"Sloane Finley?" I ask, but my voice is hoarse. Quiet.

Her head turns, and she just stares at me, tears streaking her cheeks, rivulets that cut paths through the dirt that stains her face as she gives a single short nod.

Jasmine

"I'm Agent Jones. FBI." Forcing a breath, I do everything to calm nerves that are askew in ways that they haven't been for a long time. I start to reach out my hand to her, realize the stupidity of the gesture, and pull it back. I blurt the only thing that crosses my mind in this moment, "Are you okay?"

She stares at me as if the words have no meaning, and then answers with a voice that cuts through me like a shard of glass. "No."

I stand mutely as she turns back into Clint's chest, her hands fisted in his uniform as he curls her in tight. He doesn't look at me, only at the top of her head that shakes as she cries quietly. I turn away and walk to where Daniel's body lies in the dirt. Blood has soaked into the dry ground beneath him, creating a darker halo around his chest. A wave of irrational anger pushes through me, and I bring up my gun and point it at him. For a moment that's all I do, point the weapon at his body, finger on the trigger, and I know what I want to do... but the feeling passes, and I holster my weapon, turning and walking away.

I open the door to the Bronco, slide up into the seat, and pull the mic from the radio set.

"Sheriff Braddock?"

There is a slight hiss as I let go of the button, and then a long pause. Finally, a voice comes back over the speaker.

"This is Sheriff Braddock. Who's this?"

"Agent Jones. You might want to head out here to the Christiansen ranch." I pause, looking out the window to where Clint still stands, holding Sloane. It looks like he's saying something to her, probably whisperings words of comfort into her hair.

I swallow.

"We found Sloane Finley."

There's another pause, and I put the mic back into its holder. A second later the radio bursts into sound, Braddock's voice, but I'm not listening. I slip out of the cab, close the door to cut off the noise, and stand in the sun. I see movement out of the corner of my eye, up in the sky. It's a bird, large, black, riding a thermal that rises from the endless grasslands that surround us. I watch as it circles, a tight spiral that goes on and on, until it becomes a tiny dot in the infinite blue.

And then it's gone. Forever.

I'm not sure how long I stand there before I hear the sirens. Long enough that Clint has Sloane Finley wrapped in a blanket, sitting in the A/C in the backseat with him right beside her.

Alive. She's alive.

That thought keeps pinging around inside my head, and I keep glancing back at her just to remind myself it's real. The kid was fucking right, and if I'd been the kind of asshole I am ninety percent of the time... she'd be dead. Or wishing she was.

Jesus Christ, what did he do to her?

It's not like I don't have a pretty good idea. I went inside the

Jasmine

barn after Clint had to carry her to the truck because she couldn't stand on her own two feet, and based on the dark smears on the concrete, the blood splatter near the post, and the whip I found on the workbench... I've got a damn good idea why the girl can't stand.

He beat her, tortured her, and I don't have any doubts that he touched her. *Wife.* The maniac called her his wife, called her 'Jasmine,' and it's not until I see Sherriff Braddock getting out of his truck that I remember where the hell I'd heard that name before. His missing person, the girl that the FBI didn't bother to send some asshole like me out to investigate.

Another girl who probably looked just like Sloane Finley before she got buried in the dirt.

Another body that they *might* find in all this grassland. If they're lucky.

Sixty-eight thousand, nine-hundred and something of the stats for whichever year he took her. Fucking Daniel Christiansen. The Wall.

Neither of these girls stood a chance.

I shake my head as Braddock approaches me, red-faced and stunned as he looks between the corpse on the ground and the half-alive girl in the back of Clint's Bronco.

"What the hell happened?" Braddock asks, mouth hanging open as he watches Clint climb out.

"The kid's instincts were right. Bastard had her all this time." My gaze lands on the corpse again, the dust the vehicles kicked up is settling on the blood, leaving the big motherfucker as streaked and dirty as his victim.

Unfortunately, he didn't suffer like she did. He got to go out quickly by comparison, and I hate him more than a little for that.

But I hate myself more.

Why didn't you just go back, Mason? You were right here yesterday. Right fucking here.

"Agent Jones."

I can tell by the tone in Braddock's voice it isn't the first time he's said my name while I zoned out, but I try to play it off as I walk closer and join the conversation. I manage to say all the right things, explain why I discharged my weapon, all of it. Clint backs me up, says some shit about me saving their lives, but I ignore it.

If it weren't for him, no one's life would have been saved today, and we both know it.

"Well, Doc Hendricks shouldn't be too far behind us. Talbert called him before we left the station and told him how to get out here." Braddock lets out a sigh and looks over Clint's shoulder at Sloane. "She looks to be in real bad shape," he says in almost a whisper, and Clint's jaw goes rigid.

"Yeah." The word is clipped coming out of the kid, and I don't miss how he shifts his body to block Braddock's view. Still trying to protect her, but I don't say anything. I don't have the right to.

"I can't believe he'd do this. He was always a bit weird, but… shit." Deputy Talbert has been silent since he showed up, but his assessment sums it up.

Jasmine

It's shit.

The whole damn situation.

Braddock takes charge, and I don't say a word. I'm not interested in pulling rank here, and the body is on his turf. If I had my way, I'd walk away right now, but I'm too deep in this shit, and it's going to be one hell of a report by the time I sit down in Amarillo.

Carmen. Fuck.

I step away from them so I can call her, watching as Talbert covers Daniel's body in a sheet. I can hear the road noise when she answers. "Hey Mason, I'm on the way home with her right now. Should be on the road in a matter of—"

"We found her."

Silence fills the line for a second, and then I hear Carmen sputtering over her words. "Wh— Where— *How* did you find her?"

"Clint did, actually. Out here at the Christiansen place. Psycho's had her locked up all this fucking time, and—"

"She's ALIVE?" Carmen shouts the last word, her shock almost making me smile as I press on my ribs and wince.

Bastard might have cracked a few.

"Yeah. Not in great shape, but she's alive."

"Whittman is going to fucking kill me." She groans, and I hear her explaining to her wife before she comes back to the phone. "I'll be there as soon as I can, okay?"

"No rush. Had to shoot him so there's no suspect to deal

with." I take a deep breath and look back at the sound of a car pulling over the dirt and gravel. "Just bring me my bag, will you? I need a change of clothes."

"Sure, Mason. I'll head out soon."

"Thanks, Carmen." I hang up and tuck away my cell phone, watching as Clint carries Sloane Finley to the doctor's car. When he sets her down in the backseat, the doctor nudges him out of the way, and I catch his eye, beckoning him over with a tilt of my head.

I can tell he doesn't want to leave her side, but he does. His uniform is a wreck. Smeared in dark smudges of blood, and it's dried on his bare arms as well. He looks like he's been through hell, and it's in his eyes too. No shiny glint of hope, no puppy-like eagerness.

He kind of looks like me.

"Listen, Mason—" The kid starts to talk but I wave him off.

"You did good today. You saved her, and I'm man enough to admit that you were right yesterday. We should have come back here; we should have pressed. I'm sorry I didn't listen." I'd expected that there would be some lifting of the heavy feeling in my chest after I said the words, but it doesn't abate. It just squats there, beside the ache in my ribs every time I breathe too deeply. *Fucking hell.* My eyes wander past him to the car I know she's in. I can't see her with the glare off the windshield, but I can see the doctor crouched beside the open door. "She wouldn't be alive if it weren't for you, kid."

Clint's quiet for a minute, eyes focused near our feet, and then I hear him speak softly. "I thought she was dead."

Jasmine

"What?"

"When I found her in the basement. Couldn't even tell it was a person at first with the blood and the dirt. Then I thought she was already dead." He twists at the waist, looking back toward the doc's car. "Still can't believe she's alive. She looks..."

Clint trails off and I let him. I don't need to fill in the gaps there, because the image of Sloane Finley isn't going anywhere for a long while. I'm sure we'll both still remember her when we go into the dirt ourselves. Some things just stick with you, and I already know she's one of those. The girl I'd already written off as dead, the girl I made Clint drive away from yesterday, the girl who would have been a corpse if he hadn't dragged me back here today.

"She asked me not to leave her," he says, and his shoulders straighten out as his head comes up. "I'm going to ride with her to the doc's. Can you take care of getting the Bronco back to the station when everything's done here?"

"Yeah, I can do that."

"Thanks," he says, hurrying back to her, and I wander back to the sheriff as the doctor gets in the car and turns around to head up the drive.

"Guess you've got more'n a few paragraphs to add to that report of yours," Braddock says out of the corner of his mouth, and I let out a huff that makes my ribs throb.

"Definitely more than a few," I answer, watching the plume of dust rising as Sloane Finley gets carried away from the hell that was her prison for more than two months.

I know we've got to process the scene, take photos, somehow

load the fucker's corpse into one of these vehicles before we put him wherever they put their dead in Stockdale, Texas... but I can't help turning to stare at the house and the barn. All Norman Rockwell on the outside, picturesque and pretty. A lie.

Can't judge a book, or a case, by it's cover, Mason. Never again.

I know I won't. Not without doing my job, not without trying at least a little, because the next time my head tells me it's just another dead girl, I know I'm going to think her name. And, hell, maybe I'll find another one. Reduce that sixty-eight thousand by a digit or two before I kick the bucket myself.

It's probably bullshit, but it's possible. Anything is.

Because Sloane Finley is alive.

Epilogue

MASON

One Year Later

"You're getting the same calls I am, aren't you?" Carmen's voice coming through my phone's speaker is laced with mirth, and I chuckle.

"Of course I am. Sinclair is over the fucking moon. When things died down after the initial Sloane hysteria, you'd have thought he was going through smack withdrawals."

"Same with Whitmann. I'm his favorite person on the planet right now because the interview requests are pouring in, and he's angling to get back on camera." I can practically hear Carmen rolling her eyes as she huffs. "Our little media whores."

"And, yet, you and I are the ones getting all the screen time," I add. I can't help but smile because I know just how much it grates Dave Sinclair that it's not him.

"True." Carmen laughs before she says, "And speaking of which... I'm not turning down that invite from *The Ellen*

Show, so I better see your goddamn signature on the agreement soon. I want another trip out to Hollywood."

I grin, thinking about the last time they were out. The studio put them up at the Beverly Wilshire and Carmen had gone on about it for a month afterwards. "I told them yes! I just wanted it in writing that both you *and* Marianne would be coming. Then I'd sign."

"Such a gentleman."

"Hardly," I reply, and we both laugh. The conversation fades into a comfortable silence as I remember the months after we found Sloane Finley. Well, after *Clint* found her.

I'm still not sure, even after all this time, what exactly made her story go viral. It could have been Senator Harris's tweet about it, or the tearjerker story that WTHR Indianapolis did when she came back home to her parents. Or, maybe, it was just her, because that's another thing Clint was right about — it's hard not to like Sloane Finley if you spend even five minutes with her.

Whatever it was, the world fell in love with Sloane overnight. Her blog crashed from the views, her Facebook page exploded as soon as it went live again, and every talk show and morning news show wanted to cover it: the sweet, beautiful midwestern girl who went to Hollywood to become an actress, and experienced a horrifying tragedy on her journey home.

Fucking media gold.

It was public safety, and tragedy, and inspiration all rolled into one, and Sloane was everything the world wanted her to be. Strong, humble, positive, and smiling. Always smiling.

Jasmine

They couldn't get enough, and now a year later the press is back for more.

I'm still lost in thought as someone passes behind me with a speaker at top-volume, deep bass thumping loud enough that I can feel it like a hand smacking against my back. As soon as it fades, Carmen's voice comes through, thick with faux disapproval. "You're out at that bar again, aren't you?"

"I am."

In the pause that follows I can almost picture her looking at her watch. "Jesus Christ, Mason. It's only three thirty there."

"It's five o'clock some—"

"Oh my God, shut up." Carmen laughs, but a moment later it turns into a heavy sigh. "Tell me the truth, Mason. You sure you're up for the whole media circus again? Much as I'm looking forward to seeing you, we don't have to do this. We can just say no. From what I've heard, Sloane and Clint are declining requests this year."

"Yeah, I heard that too." I shrug, taking a sip from my beer. I've already had this debate with myself. Whether I really want to go sit on Ellen's couch and smile and laugh and pretend I'm a decent person so that the world can go on believing there are good people looking for all the little lost girls out there.

"If we don't go, who will?"

"Our bosses," Carmen replies, deadpan, and I can't help but chuckle.

"Then it sounds like we don't have any fucking choice, do we?"

"Agreed." She laughs. There's a moment's pause, and then her voice, serious. "It'll really be good to see you again, Mason."

"Same. Just let me know when all the arrangements are made, okay? When you'll be in town, excetera..."

"I will," she answers, and I can hear the smile in her voice.

"All right. I should let you get going."

"Yeah. I'm sure you'll hear from me soon. I'll no doubt need one more bitch session about Whitmann before I come out." Another bright laugh bursts across the line.

"Take care, Mason."

"Bye, Carmen," I reply and the call ends. The first few months after recovering Sloane had been a whirlwind of back-to-back interview trips for us both. During all of it we'd become friends, and as weird as it feels to admit it... I miss her company. I never have to pretend I'm not an asshole around her, and lately that's become a rare fucking thing.

Yeah, it will *be good to see her again.*

Holding my phone on the bar in front of me, I flip back to the YouTube video I was watching before Carmen called. It's a channel I've been following for some time now, and although I've fallen behind on episodes, I'm slowly catching up. I hit the play button and watch as it picks up where I left off. I'm still amazed at how popular it is. 2.35 million subscribers, and this video alone has 685,000 views and it's pretty new.

I shake my head, grinning at the video's corny title. *I Shot the Sheriff (But I Fell In Love With the Deputy!).*

I pick up my beer, taking a drink as I watch. I don't have the volume up high enough to hear what's being said, but that doesn't matter. I'm not really watching it to hear the dialogue. I'm watching it to see them.

"They make a cute couple, don't they?"

It takes effort not to be startled by the sudden sound of a voice directly behind me, but I play it cool as I turn my head, watching her come around my side.

"How're you doing, Agent Jones?" Trish Tucker pushes her sunglasses on top of her head, giving me a warm smile as she sits on the stool next to mine. After a moment she glances down at my phone, and I do too.

"I'm fine, and you're right. They do." I reach with my thumb to pause the video, turning my attention to her. "So, how did you find me, Ms. Tucker?"

"Oh, you know…" She raises her hand above her head, finger pointing downwards.

"Journalism major," I say before she can, repeating her line from a lifetime ago.

"Well, actually… journalist now."

I dip my head in recognition. "I see. Congratulations."

"I graduated last semester, got an offer from the *Times* a

month later. I mean, I'm just a stringer, but..." Her voice trails off, but I don't miss the pride in it.

"I've no doubt that's only temporary."

"Thank you." She smiles brightly, and orders a beer when the bartender approaches. "And another for him," she adds, gauging what's remaining in my bottle.

For a second she stares at my phone screen, and I follow her eyes to take in the image once again.

"The anniversary's coming up," she says, looking at me. "I imagine you're getting inundated with interview requests."

"I am," I answer stiffly, and I wait for it. Wait for her to make one of her own. But... she doesn't. Instead, she changes the subject.

"Have you spoken to them recently?"

I shake my head slowly. "I think it was... three months ago? Maybe longer." I continue to gaze at my phone, looking at the picture of them frozen in tableau. Clint behind the kitchen counter, head bent as if he's shaking it in disbelief at something she's said. Sloane on the other side, head tilted back, face bright with laughter.

I don't miss that his hand is reaching across, holding hers.

"I try to stay out of their lives," I finish, setting the phone on the bar.

"Why?"

"Because."

Trish purses her lips, staring at me. She reaches for her beer, taking a long sip, and when she puts it down her face grows serious. "She owes her life to—"

"No." I cut her off, and I hate how harsh my voice sounds. She doesn't deserve to be on the receiving end of that. "No," I repeat, this time tempering my tone as I tap my finger against my phone screen on the body of the young man holding Sloane Finley's hand. "That's who she owes her life to. Not me."

"The articles I've read tell a—"

"It's bullshit. All of it." I cut her off again. I hate doing it, but I don't think I could stand to listen to a recitation of what's been written about me.

She clamps her jaw closed, and I watch as her lips mash against each other as she bites back whatever response is going on in her head.

"You went out there, Mason," she finally says, softly, no doubt expecting more backlash but willing to accept it. "You found her."

I yank my beer up to my lips, taking a long pull, and when I set it down, it's with force enough to bring foam bubbles to the top.

"But that's the thing, Ms. Tucker. I *didn't*. They've all got it wrong. I didn't go out there looking for her. I went out there to finish off a report. A trip to write a dozen lines to send to her father. 'Did the best we could; sorry we didn't discover anything.' I didn't even expect to find a fucking body. Much less her. Living. Breathing."

I place my hands on the countertop, and the same anger,

frustration, and guilt that's stewed inside me since that day comes bubbling back to the surface.

"No, Ms. Tucker, I didn't have any intention of looking for Sloane Finley. But *he* did." I look to the screen. I look at the kid who's a better man than me in his worst moments than I am at my best. "He found her. He saved her. Not me."

"But you went."

I look at her, and I can't help the incredulous way my voice comes out. "So. What. That doesn't mean anything."

For a moment she says nothing. She lifts her beer, swallows more of the amber liquid before setting it down slowly, gently. "Did you ever see the interview he did on *Good Morning America*?"

I shake my head, thrown by the question. "I... I might have? I honestly don't remember."

She gives me a gentle smile. "Clint said that while you and he had differences in how you handled the case, that without you it wouldn't have ended the way it did. He said you pushed him. Challenged him. Taught him things about the realities of what it means to pin on a badge. Things that he had not been willing to believe until he had to face them head on." She laces her fingers together on the bartop, staring down at them for a moment before she looks back up to me. "He said you taught him the value of experience. And the importance of standing firm for what you believe."

Fuck. Damn kid is still getting under my skin, even after all this time.

"Yeah? Well, he's an..." I stop myself from saying it. Stop the word that should so easily slip off my tongue.

Jasmine

Idiot.

Go on, Mason. Say it. It won't be the first time you've called him that.

But I don't. Because as much as Officer Clint Nolan frustrates me, irritates me, makes me recognize things about myself I don't really fucking want to, there is one thing I know for certain.

He is a good man.

"Yeah," I say, picking up where I left off. "Well, he's a smart kid, and an incredible actor to boot if he's peddling *that* story. Sloane has really rubbed off on him." I point to my phone screen. "And this stuff probably hasn't hurt either."

Trish chuckles, and then shakes her head slowly, giving me a look that tells me she's not buying it. She's looking beyond my self-deprecating and self-loathing, and finding something that she thinks is good about me.

Dammit.

"You didn't ask for it, but here's an exclusive for you," I say, stabbing my finger at the screen. "Clint Nolan is the sole reason Sloane Finley is alive today. The *sole* reason. Carmen Rodriguez did as much as she could, as did Sheriff Braddock. Me?" I shake my head. "I didn't do a fucking thing."

"Thanks for the story, Mason." Trish smiles and tips back the last of her beer. "Too bad I can't use it. Nobody would believe it." She sets the bottle down, and then leans in closer to me. "And neither do I."

"Really?" I shake my head in chagrin. People keep on

believing what they want... "Well, they say ignorance is bliss."

Trish gives me a laugh. It is pure, and heartfelt, and sincere, and as frustrated as I am right now it cuts through my angst like a blade. Despite my best efforts, my mouth twitches upward toward a grin.

"I always did say you wore your cynicism like a suit of armor." Her eyes narrow, mouth slipping upwards in a sly curve. "But I see the chinks that are there."

My grin turns into a full-blown laugh as Trish slides off her stool.

She throws a pair of bills on the counter, motioning to the bartender. "Another for my friend." She looks over at me, smiling. "I'll see you around, Mason."

"See you around, Ms. Tucker."

She dips her head, turns, and I watch as she walks away into the beach crowd that flows down the sidewalk around her. A moment later the bartender comes over, sets another Artifex in front of me. I nod, picking up the one I still haven't finished, and turn to stare out at the ocean. The sun glitters off it, the surface a million shards of diamond. I tilt back the beer, and feel the sharp bitterness slip down my throat.

Maybe I *should* call them.

Add it to the list of things I have to do. Like those interview requests piling up for approval by the FBI. Because even a year later the obsession with Sloane and Clint's story isn't fading. Theirs is the kind of storybook romance that a million Hollywood producers would love to dig their claws into, but Sloane has spurned them all — and I have to admit I love her a little more for it.

I try to imagine for a moment what I might say to the two lovebirds if I did call them. More empty bullshit, undoubtedly. Just like what I'll say on every couch I sit on in the next few weeks.

I finish my beer, start the new one. I watch the gulls swerve toward the water, and smile. It's all just bullshit, and I probably won't call. But who knows? Like Ms. Tucker said, I've got chinks in my cynical armor, and Sloane is the biggest one of all.

And it's a beautiful day, filled with opportunity.

So, this time, maybe I will.

Sloane

The music changes and Billie Eilish starts to sing about wearing a warning sign, and I'm bobbing my head to the beat as I read through a sixth way to make slime. Making notes, I can't help but smile as I imagine Clint doing this blindfolded.

People will love it, but... everyone loves him. It's hard not to.

"Sloane!" he calls out from the living room, and I groan as I check the time in the corner of my laptop. "It's nine o'clock, babe. You—"

"I know, I know, I promised we'd watch Dark Phoenix

tonight. Two more minutes?" I ask, and he walks into the kitchen with an indulgent smile on his face.

"Two minutes?" he asks, slipping behind me to look at my screen. One of his hands lands beside my notepad, and the other starts rubbing my neck as he leans forward to read. "Slime, really?"

I hum an acknowledgement as his thumb finds the exact spot on my spine that's tense. Just as I start to lean back into it, he stands up and I turn my head to look at him.

"You want more of that, you're gonna have to join me on the couch." He sidles backward, swaying his hips in his cheesy sexy dance, and I can't help but laugh.

"Two minutes."

Clint sighs and shakes his head at me. "They're going to love whatever you come up with, babe, because you're a genius."

"Genius takes work!" I shout after him as he disappears through the doorway of the living room, and I hear him laughing.

"I'm starting a timer!" he calls back, and I roll my eyes as I go back to my notes. I finish as fast as I can, check the time, and then return to skimming the comments on our last video.

You two are amazeballs!

OMG, I want to be just like you guys.

Sloane and Clint are the best couple ever!

There are days, like today, when my life doesn't feel real,

Jasmine

and scrolling through three thousand comments doesn't help at all. Hundreds of people saying they love me, love us, that they want 'to be just like us,' but I know that's not really true.

They want the bad karaoke date nights, the no-hands cooking challenges, the trips to the mountains... they want to be in love like this. But they don't want the stuff that I never put on our YouTube channel. No one really wants to go through what I did to get here. No one wants to watch a video about my night terrors, about the nights when I end up throwing up and Clint sits on the floor beside the toilet rubbing my back even though he has to be up at four AM.

If anything, they want Clint. They want the kind of man who refuses to leave your bedside at the hospital, who uses all of his vacation time to sleep on a tiny hospital couch in Amarillo because he insists on giving your mom the recliner.

They want the kind of man who uproots his entire life to move to Indianapolis because he promised not to leave your side, and he meant it.

They want him, but you have him.

That thought is what finally pulls me away from the laptop, and I go straight to the living room couch to curl up against him. He laughs softly as he wraps his arm around me. "That was more than two minutes."

"I know, I got distracted."

"Found another slime recipe?" he asks, and I can hear the grin in his voice.

"Nah, just thinking about how lucky I am."

Clint leans down to press a kiss to my hair as I snuggle in closer, and then he says what he always does, "I'm the lucky one, babe."

I don't bother arguing, we never get anywhere with it, but it does make me smile. He always makes me smile, and that's how I know I'm the lucky one. He makes me happy, makes me feel loved, makes me feel alive.

Without him, I wouldn't even *be* alive, and that means I win — even if he'll never admit it aloud.

"Ready to watch Jean Grey be an epic badass?" he asks, reaching for the remote, and I sit up so I can grab a pillow.

"I am totally ready," I answer, planting the pillow in his lap so I can lay down, but then I groan. "Wait, did you answer that voicemail from *The Today Show*?"

"I did. I told them no," he answers, but I catch the look of concern on his face. "Did you want to—"

"No, no, I just had it on my mental to-do list. I really don't want to do any more of those, but..." I shrug, reaching for his hand to interlace our fingers. "You know, if you want to, you can totally do them."

"I think we've had enough of *that* kind of press to last a lifetime, babe." Clint kisses my hand, squeezing it as his blue eyes flick back and forth over my face. "You okay?"

"As long as I have you, I'm always okay." I smile and lean forward to sneak a quick kiss, but he catches the side of my face and pulls me into a real one. Butterflies take off in my stomach just like they did the first time we kissed. Months after he pulled me out of hell, after we'd been dragged in front of a hundred TV cameras side by side, after I'd already fallen in love with him. I'd had to make the first move, a clumsy, anxiety-ridden kiss outside a coffee shop that had left him looking stunned and me fearing I'd made the worst mistake of my life — until he yanked me against him and kissed me for real.

It wasn't love at first sight. Nothing as magical as that.

No, it was better. It was the kind of love that sneaks up on you in a million kind gestures, a billion moments of feeling safe and comfortable and cared for. Falling in love with Clint Nolan was incredible, but it wasn't magic. We'd worked for it. Thousands of hours of therapy, and too many late-night phone calls to count where I fell asleep listening to him breathing or telling me about his day.

When my whole world fell apart, Clint felt like home, and he still does.

He's my hero.

He nips my lip as he ends the kiss, and that infectious grin takes over his face again as he leans back to waggle the remote in the air. "Superpowers and explosions?"

"Superpowers and explosions," I confirm, and he hits play as I lay my head in his lap. His arm instantly drapes over my side, his other hand finding a strand of my hair to play with, and I smile as that warm, happy feeling suffuses me from head to toe. "I love you, Clint."

"I love you too, babe," he answers, squeezing me a bit before he adds, "But if you talk over Jean Grey blowing stuff up, I'm gonna cry."

I laugh, rolling my eyes. "My lips are zipped, I promise."

"Good, 'cause I've been waiting weeks to watch this, and I had to threaten to shoot Tommy to keep him from ruining it for me." The movie starts, and I'm still grinning as he talks about his partner. Transferring to the Indianapolis Police Department was just another sacrifice he made for me, but he'd done it without a thought, because he loves me, *really* loves me.

Just as the opening scene starts to play, I feel another laugh threatening to break free, but I stifle it so that it comes out as a sputter of air. With a heavy sigh, Clint pauses the movie and looks down at me.

"Out with it," he says in a faux stern voice, but he can't keep the smile off his lips as I start laughing for real. "Come on, Sloane, just spit it out."

"Popcorn?" I ask, and he sighs dramatically.

"God help me, yes. Fine. Popcorn." He helps me off his lap and shoves me gently toward the kitchen. "Hurry up! You're keeping me from superpowers."

"And explosions," I add, and he jumps up from the couch, chasing me into the kitchen where he corners me beside the pantry, my back against the door as my laugh winds down. "Sorry?" I offer, and he shakes his head with a chuckle of his own.

"No, you're not. I know you only watch these movies for me," he says, sidling closer, and his hands find my hips as he closes the gap between us. Leaning down, he kisses just below my ear, and then trails more down my neck to my shoulder. "But, I promise, if you watch it with me, I'll do whatever you want."

Jasmine

I grin. "Like make slime blindfolded?"

Clint's head pops up. "Seriously?"

"Please?" I ask, and he sighs indulgently before he presses another kiss to my lips.

"You know I'd do anything for you, babe. Including make slime blindfolded, whatever the hell that is." A grin spreads over his lips again, and he lifts me onto the counter beside the pantry. "But right now, we're doing popcorn and explosions."

"And watching Jean Grey turn into Dark Phoenix as she gets taken over by a mysterious cosmic force?"

Clint's eyebrows lift high as he stares at me. "You—"

"I googled it," I answer before he can ask how I know, and he yanks me into another burning kiss that makes all the darkness of our past mean nothing in the brightness of the future we have together.

"I love you so damn much," he says, and I smile at him as I nudge him out of the way to get the popcorn.

"And I love you more. Enough to watch two hours of superpowers."

"Which is why I'm the lucky one," he replies, grinning victoriously at me as I shove the bag in the microwave.

"We're both lucky."

"Damn straight," he says, pulling me into his chest to hold me tight, and with every beat of his heart against my ear I know that I'm exactly where I was always meant to be, and I know why I didn't give up.

For this. For every minute we've had together, and for every brilliant moment we will because he never gave up on me, and because I survived.

It wasn't magic, but it's still our happily ever after.

And I wouldn't have it any other way.

THE END

About Jennifer Bene

Jennifer Bene is a *USA Today* bestselling author of dangerously sexy and deviously dark romance. From BDSM, to Suspense, Dark Romance, and Thrillers—she writes it all. Always delivering a twisty, spine-tingling journey with the promise of a happily-ever-after.

Don't miss a release! Sign up for the newsletter to get new book alerts (and a free welcome book) at: http://jenniferbene.com/newsletter

You can find her online throughout social media with username @jbeneauthor and on her website: www.jenniferbene.com

About Shane Starrett

Shane Starrett has spent twenty-five years writing steamy, erotic technical documents (okay, the erotic part is probably a bit of a stretch) for major companies in the live events industry. His first novel, Submissive Lies, was long in coming, but with guidance from his long-time beta reader of 30 years (Ms. Starrett), it is now complete and available. When he isn't writing, which isn't often, he can be found hiking trails up and down the Sierra Nevada's, and the coastal range in Southern California.

Sign up for his newsletter and never miss a new release at: http://shanestarrett.com/

Also by Jennifer Bene

The Thalia Series (Dark Romance)

Security Binds Her (*Thalia Book 1*)

Striking a Balance (*Thalia Book 2*)

Salvaged by Love (*Thalia Book 3*)

Tying the Knot (*Thalia Book 4*)

The Thalia Series: The Complete Collection

The Beth Series (Dark Romance)

Breaking Beth (*Beth Book 1*)

Fragile Ties Series (Dark Romance)

Destruction (*Fragile Ties Book 1*)

Inheritance (*Fragile Ties Book 2*)

Redemption (*Fragile Ties Book 3*) – *coming soon*

Dangerous Games Series (Dark Mafia Romance)

Early Sins (*A Dangerous Games Prequel*)

Lethal Sin (*Dangerous Games Book 1*)

Standalone Dark Romance

Imperfect Monster

Corrupt Desires

The Rite

Deviant Attraction: A Dark and Dirty Collection

Reign of Ruin

Mesmer

Jasmine

Crazy Broken Love

Standalone BDSM Ménage Romance

The Invitation

Reunited

Standalone Suspense / Horror

Burned: An Inferno World Novella

Appearances in the Black Light Series (BDSM Romance)

Black Light: Exposed (*Black Light Series Book 2*)

Black Light: Valentine Roulette (*Black Light Series Book 3*)

Black Light: Roulette Redux (*Black Light Series Book 7*)

Black Light: Celebrity Roulette (*Black Light Series Book 12*)

Books Released As Cassandra Faye

Daughters of Eltera Series (Dark Fantasy Romance)

Fae (*Daughters of Eltera Book 1*)

Tara (*Daughters of Eltera Book 2*)

Anthologies

Bite Me: A Vampire Anthology

Also by Shane Starrett

BDSM Romance

Submissive Lies

Dark Romance / Thriller-Suspense

Jasmine